1

The Witches Of Stourton Hall

The Little Yew Tree Witch
&
Stolen Winter

Victoria J Hunt

Illustrations: Victoria J Hunt

01/03/2021

©

The little robin follows me wherever I may go.

For Dad & Grandad

2

The Unfortunate Event of a Wild Cat Who Called Herself Hestia: 1204

~~ * ~~

The gentle valleys were covered in ancient woodland where wild animals roamed and foraged the endless countryside, hidden deep from the eyes of man - the wild living only in fear of their natural hunter. A large and proud wild cat, who called herself Hestia, prowled and hunted freely in her domain. One day, Hestia fell in with very bad company. In the darkest part of the forest a coven of witches lived, and one fateful day they adopted her as their pet. Hestia at first enjoyed the mischief and the tours - the young witches loved to explore - but as their magical powers grew, so did their trickery and power. Hestia was so impressed that she forgot her freedom and life of ease and was soon a slave to their spells and plots. As Hestia grew older, she asked for a potion to make her stronger and perhaps to live longer, as she could see the witches did not age. And so, with cackles and prods they gleefully agreed and poor Hestia was tricked and set in stone. A statue she stood for hundreds of years until one day she was found, and placed gently upon a fine mantelpiece in a stately hall.

4

Stourton Hall: 1809

~~ * ~~

Octavia was the youngest of three; she had two elder sisters, Cecelia and Olivia. Octavia thought she had the worst possible name in the world; her father had just named her the month she was born, October, and from a very young age, Octavia felt no more than an afterthought. Her mother, Beatrice, had tragically died only hours after giving birth to her and her father, saddened beyond belief, would, she thought, have preferred a boy - an heir to his banking empire and vast inheritance. From a young age, Octavia called herself Avia and sought ways to entertain herself away from her father's disapproving eye. He was rarely in residence since their mother's death, so the girls knew little of their father, other than he had a passion for antiquity. Their grandfather had been a keen collector of Italian art and bought his ideas back to England, so Italian renaissance from the grand tour transformed Stourton hall and gardens. He had travelled through Europe, China, Japan, India and the America's, each time bringing back ideas in styles, cultures and cuisines. The huge stately home and stunning gardens became the envy of many wealthy landowners - who would seek invitations to lavish dinner parties, attended only by aristocracy and the very wealthy. Avia's father had been left all of this empire, but he had no appetite for it. Since the loss of his dear wife

Beatrice, he would leave the banking to others and pursue his love of archaeology and art.

Sadly, poor Avia had not felt her father's love - he could hardly look at her, and as she grew, he avoided home more and more. The children were left with their adoring Nanny Maud and a host of governesses and servants. They did experience more freedom than most girls of that era; however, they felt as if they were orphans at times, in a huge stately home with empty rooms and endless corridors. Avia and her sister Olivia were still too young for the social scene and were kept supposedly hidden in the wing of the nursery. Cecelia, being the eldest, would be the first to be found a suitable husband. He would have to be from a wealthy family with a very good standing in society to attain her father's satisfaction. Olivia, her middle sister, had already 'in secret' given her heart to a wealthy boy who lived not far away in a very impressive stately home just outside Bath; they had a huge deer park and although their gardens were nowhere near as impressive as Stourton Hall, the grandeur was still very imposing. The impressive young lord was called Thomas Blaywayt, but Avia doubted he would stick around forever as he was so young, although Olivia was the cleverest girl he would probably ever meet.

The three girls were incredibly different in both looks and personalities. Cecelia was fair with the greenest of eyes and small with a tiny frame. Olivia was taller and slim with light brown hair and greenish grey eyes, and Avia was tall and skinny with the darkest of hair and eyes; they were all exquisitely striking in . Cecelia loved books and spent hours in the library and would talk about her favourite books and the characters as if they were real - often, she would discuss them with her governess as though they were sitting right there in the same room. Avia loved it most when Cecelia read to her. Her favourite story was about a little princess who went to live in an orphanage and got rescued by her adoring father who had been away in India. Avia thought she would like to go to India - it sounded amazing with all the colours, spices, elephants and tigers.

Avia's other sister, Olivia, was different. She spent her life learning, she could speak French perfectly. She would often strut around talking of how she would love to go and be a scholar in London. Her friend Thomas was going to go to London to become a lawyer like his father; they were unbearably clever together.

Avia, by far the wildest of the three, loved the gardens and would spend hours roaming and learning all about the trees and plants and knew the names for nearly all of them on the estate. She was learning all about the flowers and how they like to be positioned. It seemed some were very fussy about full sun, shade or their soil and some preferred more water than others; some needed pruning and dead heading and to be given all sorts of attention; and there were bulbs and seeds that required different steps, and topiary, hedging, climbers and creepers - the list was endless. What she really wanted to learn though was how to take a cutting from a plant to grow another; this to Avia was the most fascinating of things it was like magic. She loved the gardeners and thought them her friends. They were always happy to chat to her and showed her how to weed and plant. Sometimes she got to go back to Tomsk the head gardener's cottage on the estate. His daughter was her age and called Lottie, and they would play in their little garden. Avia loved Lottie's cottage in the winter; it was wonderfully cosy, with a roaring fire in the one room that they all lived in, and you could smell the delicious bread cooking in the smoky range. In the summer, she loved the washing on the line and the way Lottie was allowed to take her doll outside and leave things lying around. Miss Bonneville the house keeper was very strict about leaving things lying around. Lottie's ma and pa were warm and friendly and were always hugging Lottie, and they played with her and listened to her. Lottie knew everything about her ma and pa, and it seemed her ma and pa knew everything about everyone in the village and on the estate.

Lottie's sister, Lucy, worked up at the hall as a scullery maid. She was always kind and cheerful, with lovely, long blond hair and blue eyes like her ma and Lottie. Avia thought it was funny how everyone came into the world a different shade. Her sister Olivia had explained it was to do with your genes, something like if a bay horse and a bay horse have a foal it would most definitely be a bay, with a slim chance it could be chestnut or a grey should one of its grandparents have been one of those colours. It was all a little complicated and Avia had just pretended to understand, although she had put the theory to her thoughts and wondered if you could mix up the colours of flowers. When she asked Tomsk, he had said that it was possible with something called cross pollination, but he had no time to show her. This was very disappointing to Avia and she was not certain he knew how. However, it was this topic of interest that forced her to the library on one cold and rainy day, imprisoned by the bad weather. Nanny Maud had forbidden her to step a foot outside in case she caught a cold and died. This seemed a little dramatic, but Avia did love her Nanny so didn't wish to upset her by dying and so stayed indoors.

The library was always a little stuffy and was kept warm with a fire and huge drapes that kept out the draft and candles lit the room for reading. Avia would select a book with difficulty. Flower and garden design books always won in the end, and she would then go and sit on the floor in-between the drapes and the enormous windows that stretched from the ceiling to the floor; this way, she could see the pictures and read some of the words and it was like she was almost outside but not, so she would not catch her death. Avia would often, though, end up just staring out of the window and daydreaming about being outside in the gardens, traveling the world or being a designer of the most spectacular gardens.

Nanny Maud would be, as always quietly watching and smiling; she would check on each of the girls - then scuttled back to her duties. Avia often thought Nanny Maud was like a little mouse, as when you entered a room, she was not really visible - so timid and small with dowdy colouring. Avia would watch her sniff the air twitching, and sometimes she would raise her little hands up together and rest them perched under her chin. She was never loud or bossy but gentle and kind, and instead of chastising the girls, she would invent a way to solve a problem: smocks and old boots for Avia with a bowl of hot water and a scrubbing brush on standby; for Cecilia, a piece of slate and chalk was put on her mantle with the things she had to do. For Olivia, it was simple, she trained her to count to ten and look around a room before she spoke, avoiding unnecessary arguments and hurtful remarks that she could not easily withdraw. Nanny Maud was totally trustworthy and they could tell her anything, she would always find them the best solution to resolve their quandary, or she would find a way for them to do what they wanted in a correct and more timely manner. Nanny Maud noticed everything and said very little herself; her mission was in no doubt that the Stourton girls would be content and well cared for in their extraordinarily affluent yet abandoned circumstances.

Agnes of Stourton Castle: 1809

~~ * ~~

Avia was in the garden, reflecting on how content she felt at this moment in time. Her sisters were being kind, her father away, and the house had an easy feel to it; the butlers whistled and the maids sang. The dawn had brought a crisp morning with sunshine and mild air, and Avia munched on a delicious, sticky Bath bun that she had pinched while running through the kitchen - Cook Anna had waved a finger at her with a huge grin. In the garden she saw Tomsk and the new assistant Jack. Tomsk was showing him how to mulch the flower beds up near the house to protect them from the winter, stop the weeds and keep the moisture in. Jack happily whistled away while working and seemed very enthusiastic. He had a broad open smile and thick curly blond hair and blue eyes, and it turned out he was one of Lottie's cousins. Avia instantly liked Jack although she did not introduce herself and just acknowledged him with a faint, polite smile. Jack returned the gesture and politely said 'Morning, Miss Octavia'. A little too sharply Avia bit his tongue off, insisting she was called Avia. Jack looked hurt and mumbled an apology and carried on with his mulching, and Avia stomped off feeling bad for being so snappy.

She took the path down by the lake and wound her way up and down through the trees, patting their trunks as though they were horses being praised. Some of the trees were huge with species from far and wide. She loved the ancient big red cedar and stood staring up into the its never-ending branches, wondering if they reached to another world. Avia ran along the path and ran up and down the steps to the Temple of Flora where she swung around the pillars, she had a small polite chat with a statue and then carried on passing over the stone bridge Avia paused to throw some crumbs to the ducks, she hung dangerously over the stone balustrades looking intently into the shallow water to see if she could spot a fish, and on cue for their performance of the day a little shoal of silver dace danced past, then darted quickly below into the weeds. Avia doubled back on herself walking around the stunning lake and soon reached the gothic cottage. The cottage had only recently been added to the garden and had once been hidden in the trees; with past tales of witches using it as their hovel locals said it belonged to a coven who ran wild in the valley stealing children and whatever else they could. Avia wasn't afraid though, and she was rather more drawn to its history, fascinated by folk tales. The wide path now swept passed it, and the surrounding trees had been felled, making it less spooky. The cottage had had a gothic style window added with a carved stone bench, and the roof was all re-thatched. Avia loved the cottage and was thrilled that Tomsk had allocated Avia a piece of land near to it. Tomsk had pegged out her area with string where she would be able to design her garden. She already kept her tools and baskets in the cottage and set to work. Her basket was full of pegs which she started to place in areas of the ground. She had a picture in her head, and on the next rainy day she would spend her time planning, sketching and painting her design.

Avia's attention was drawn to the huge yew tree that stood so proudly, and she wondered how many years it had lived and how many wonders it had seen - Avia wished a tree could talk. The bright, red berries on the tree were out; they were very poisonous and messy when they fell to the floor, but the birds did a good job of eating them. The yew tree roots were a problem as nothing would grow. Avia had an idea though. A stream flowed from a little milky spring not far away at the back of the cottage, and she intended to make a pond that would add charm to the little cottage. As she looked at the roots, she noticed something shiny in the earth, just poking out. She scraped away the soil and beneath was a little pendant on a chain; charmed by it, she put it in her pocket to study later. Avia turned her attention back to her job. She would need help; however, she started to dig a small trench from the tree towards the stream. It was hard going so she moved her spade and started to try from a different starting point. Avia sang an old Indian poem she had learnt from a book while she busily dug. She made some progress, and as she dug harder the earth surprisingly gave way, revealing a cavern that lay beneath the shallow surface. There were the remnants of what looked like hinges and a wooden box painted with strange markings. The box had what looked like a leather-bound books inside it and little clay pots lay strewn about the rocks. Something shiny caught Avia's eye in the gentle October sun-it glistened. Avia lay on the floor afraid to tread in the cavern should it disappear from beneath her feet. She could not reach it, so with a stick she carefully prodded around and tried to flick the item towards her; eventually she hooked the small chain onto her stick where it dangled precariously. Skilfully, Avia managed to balance it to the edge and then firmly into her grasp. As she clutched her second find of treasure, Avia heard a voice of concern from behind her - hesitantly asking if she was in need of assistance. Avia turned to see Jack, and she laughed as she tried to explain herself, while quickly popping the shiny jewellery into her pocket. Jack helped her up and said he would be happy to help with her garden on his day off. Avia said he would do no such thing and that she would instead ask Tomsk to lend his apprentice for her garden once or twice a week.

Jack and Avia walked back towards the house busily chatting about the plants and trees around them. Jack was impressed by her knowledge and Avia suitably impressed by Jack's own information of the gardens and birds and how he was able to recognise each songbird. They lingered by the Hall still chatting and giggling when Miss Bonneville's stern presence by the door prompted Avia to say goodbye. Avia ran up to the nursery wing and into her bedroom, where she quickly washed herself in the warm soapy water in the bowl left by the maid and removed her overdress. Avia carefully hid the necklace and bracelet in her box under the bed and ran down to dinner, where she joined her sisters as though nothing had happened, her rosy cheeks and glistening eyes gave no doubt that she was up to something and her sisters eyed her suspiciously. Luckily, the conversation concentrated on Olivia who had been favoured with an invitation. She was invited to Thomas's house by his sister Edwina for a game of lawn tennis, followed by afternoon tea and an evening dinner party, so she would stay overnight. They were sending their own carriage to collect her the next day with Thomas, as the journey was long. Lucy, the maid, would go with her, and everyone seemed very excited by this event, it was as though she had been proposed too. Avia stilled her sharp tongue to herself unlike her sister would have. She would often keep her bad thoughts to herself, and she was still gloating from her wonderful and curious day. She could hardly wait to be excused from the table and ran straight to her room saying she felt exhausted and feared a mild head-ache.

Avia closed her room door and ran to the box under her bed. She ran the chain through her hands and studied the pendent. It was so shiny, but Avia knew it was not a precious stone. Even in her short life she had seen diamonds, emer-alds, sapphires and rubies in her late mother's jewellery col-lection that had been carefully hidden by her sisters, as their father seemed to have lost all sense of value. This stone was cloudy, and it had a strange pink glow when you held it up to the light and its chain was small, so most probably a child's. The other chain was a bracelet with little metal charms at-tached, but she could hardly make out what they were. Avia slept heavily that night and had strange dreams. She was by the yew tree, but everything was different, and weird-look-ing people gathered; they wore strange clothes and chanted in words she didn't recognise. She could see fire and dancing and then she woke in a cold sweat with her bedroom win-dow open, banging in the wind. Avia cried out scared and Nanny Maud was soon there. She closed the window and sang a soothing little song while stroking Avia's forehead, lulling her back to sleep.

When Avia woke the next morning feeling tired, the pendent and bracelet were still clutched in her hand. She quickly hid them in her box and washed and dressed into the clothes laid out for her. Nanny Maud had had the local seamstress make several long smocks for her to put over her pretty dresses so she would not constantly ruin them with her love of gardening. Avia ran down the long corridor and the huge wide staircase that turned in different directions and that finally swept into the hall, portraits and stunning landscapes filled the walls. Side and centre tables in solid marble were positioned in the hall with huge, patterned vases filled with fresh flowers from the gardens' greenhouses. The marble floor stretched endlessly through adjoining rooms for enter-taining, with chandeliers that glistened in the morning sun that streamed through the grand windows. Avia's feet pattered on the shiny cold marble as she ran into the break-fast room, where a huge comfortable rug covered nearly all of the waxy floorboards. Avia, as always late, sat with her sisters who sipped coffee and looked at the newspaper ordered daily for their absent father.

The girls had become accustomed to reading about the wider world. Ladies were not really supposed to worry themselves about or read such things, but it seemed silly to let the papers go straight to the servants and the fire, so Ce-celia and particularly Olivia enjoyed discussing all sorts of topics. Avia still struggled with her reading, she did, however, enjoy the pictures that Cecelia passed to her explaining in brief the story to the picture, missing out any harsh facts. Cecelia felt it her duty to mother her little sister. Being five years older she had had her Mama, so remembered her gentle ways, pretty face and sweet smell. She still missed her dreadfully and would often just sit in her Mama's old bedroom where you could still faintly smell her perfume. Cecelia would chat to her as though she was sat next to her; she would tell her about everything and would even ask her questions and make decisions upon her Mama's judgement with her own reply, agreeing that that was a very good idea. The picture Cecelia showed Avia that morning was a very smart French gentleman in an amazing uniform. He was called General Pierre Dupont and was reportedly in prison after being defeated in Baylan in the Peninsular war that had started in May 1808. Olivia curtly commented that he will no doubt not look so smart and handsome now. Avia didn't really understand, but she thought the picture was very interesting, especially his medal. It was very elaborate and had intricate carvings of crosses set around a medallion, a little like her pendent stone, and it had a faint picture of an angel holding what looked like an anchor. Cecilia said it was the Order of Saint Michael - how she knew that was a complete mystery to Avia. The conversation then turned to Olivia's trip to stay with Thomas and his sister Edwina. Olivia was so excited she could barely eat her breakfast and just moved her toast around the plate. She had her favourite green dress on, and Avia thought she looked wonderful and complimented her. Olivia was surprised by her little sister's rare observation of someone's appearance, and it made her blush and giggle. Avia was not really interested in how she herself looked, it was an effort even to brush her hair; Martha the maid always struggled with her wriggling and protesting at the sight of a brush.

Avia excused herself after eating her bun and drinking two hot chocolate drinks. She wished her sister a wonderful time and disappeared as quickly as possible. Avia then raced down the narrow hall and stairs that led to the kitchens. At the bottom she bumped into Arthur, the oldest butler in the world, who cursed her speed under his breath, then shouted after her, 'Miss Octavia, be more careful, you best not fall'. Avia chanted back 'sorry and my names Avia'. She took a huge red apple from the larder and bolted out of the servant's entrance into the gardens. The air felt cooler than yesterday, but the autumn sun still shone. Avia's first job was to find Tomsk, so she headed for the kitchen garden where he would normally smoke his tobacco with a drink at this time in the old glass house. A huge new one had now been built producing an abundance of creamy, juicy white peaches; they tasted so delicious and were used for jams and puddings - Avia licked her lips at the thought of peach jam. Sure enough, Tomsk stood with Otto and Jack. Jack was crouched on the floor petting Otto's dog, a brindle bullmastiff called Benny. Otto was the game keeper, and Avia was a little scared of him and Benny until she got to know them better. Benny was so friendly, he just looked vicious. Otto said they both needed to look "real mean'uns" to keep the poachers away as they had deer, pheasant and grouse to protect for his lordship. Avia hated the hunts when they came, and she strangely would have preferred the poor creatures to be poached, at least then they went to the hungry. Avia couldn't understand why some had to be so poor and do without so much when they themselves had more than enough. When she was older she hoped she could change lots of things.

Out of respect, Avia had waited and went up to Tomsk after he had finished his smoke and he cheerfully bid her good morning. Jack immediately got up and grinned at her, while Otto eyed her cautiously. Avia asked straight away if she could have Jack to help her build her garden. Tomsk at first grumbled, then said one day a week and no more, which Avia accepted happily knowing full well that with the winter dragging its heels, Jack would soon have less to do and Avia could pinch him more regularly. Avia skipped off with glee towards the gothic cottage and her new garden.

The trench with its cavernous hole lay empty, and she decided to wait for Jack to help her dig. Avia was just about to start pegging out again when she noticed something strange; the little clay pots she had seen in the cavern were now neatly placed by the yew tree and even more strangely, they were washed out and shiny like they were new. Avia wondered if maybe Jack had done this, although wondered why on this earth he would have done so. Deciding to ignore the pots, she continued to work. Avia always forgot the rest of the world when gardening and time passed with such speed. A little robin followed her with curiosity as she dug here and there establishing planting places, although she would have to wait until the spring to plant most things. Tomsk had said she could plant out her hedging though, and she had already marked where the fritillary bulbs were to be planted. Avia had a very strange feeling though and all morning felt as though she was being watched. She began to feel a little uneasy so decided to walk back up to the Hall and have her lunch without being late for a change. As she walked, she still had the eerie feeling that someone was watching her, yet every time she turned there was no one to be seen. She listened hard and heard no footsteps, and as she got closer to the hall, she felt the presence was gone. After lunch she would go and find Jack and ask him about the pots, maybe some local kid was playing tricks on her. Avia, however, could not shake the feeling that she had company in the garden.

A few hours later, Avia found Jack by one of the temples. It was a steep climb, so Avia was a little breathless by the time she reached the top. The views of the lake and gardens from the temple were amazing. Avia loved the temple and its statues that stood proudly around the building under the arches, it was named the Temple of Apollo, dedicated to the sun god and true to its form, the lime stone look stunning in the golden sunshine. Jack was busy mulching the borders around the temple. Avia called him and he came grinning over to her. Avia reached into her pocket and threw him a large, freshly baked scone, and they both sat on the steps munching the stolen scones. Jack was a little confused when she asked about the pots, and it was crystal clear to Avia that he hadn't even been near the cottage or yew tree. Jack was a little concerned and said he would finish up quickly and come and have a look with her. Avia helped spread the mulch that Jack shovelled from the wheelbarrow. They were soon finished, Avia then got into the wheelbarrow and laughed hysterically as Jack pushed it down the bumpy cobbled path, while Avia pretended she was rowing with the shovel. They left the wheelbarrow at the bottom of the path and raced to the cottage.

When they arrived, just as before, six shiny pots stood by the yew tree, only this time it was even stranger, as two pots were full of a yellow liquid. Avia was worried Jack would think she was mad so she did not mention this extra phenomenon, but Avia was now really spooked. They both walked all around the perimeter of the cottage and up into the woods but could see no sign of anything, so Avia regrettably excused Jack so he would not get into trouble and tried to concentrate on preparing the earth for her hedges. Every so often she would glance over at the pots mystified. She went over to them and took a closer look at the potion, it smelt strange, and she carefully put it back and as she did, she saw something out of the corner of her eye. Avia gasped, and her throat tightened; she felt scared but was rooted like a tree to the spot. Sat on the yew tree branch was a girl. She wore a beautiful blue dress with delicate white flowers - her hair was black, and she wore strange jewels and looked to be around the same age as Avia. Avia stumbled to find words and bravely stuttered a demand of who her trespasser was. The girl quietly presented herself as Agnes of Stourton in the strangest accent. When asked her age she was unsure, and only gave the year fourteen hundred and eight. Avia gasped; she thought to herself, this can't be true, it must be a dream. Avia felt wobbly, and her head went all fuzzy.

The next thing Avia knew was that she was waking up in the parlour with everyone flapping around her. Avia had fainted, and as she came round she felt very strange-everything was a blur and she asked for Jack, feeling sure he had helped her all she could hear though was Nanny Maud's voice saying, 'she's coming round'. Avia was taken to bed and given sweet tea. Nanny Maud hardly left her side, Cecelia popped her head around often to check she was okay. Avia was very cautious of how to explain her fainting. The truth was absurd, and if Nanny Maud heard her account she would never let her out again. Luckily, no one asked her questions until the following morning. Avia had by this time come up with a story: it was simple she had felt unwell that morning and not eaten hardly anything. Her story was accepted, but she was made to stay in bed for the next few days. Avia was strangely happy to do so, unsure quite how to accept that what she remembered was true.

Stourton Castle: 1408

~~ * ~~

Stourton Castle was huge; its turrets reached to the deep blue sky and thick walls held endless courts and inner halls with elaborate rooms warmed by massive open fires. Fur rugs lay on stone floors with massive pieces of furniture carved in rustic oak simply scattered around; armour, swords and tapestries decorated the walls and placed proudly on beams, stag heads with antlers gazed over the halls. Outside, enormous courtyards with elaborate arches gave areas for different pursuits. Nearest to the castle were places of entertainment and seating. Arches led to stable stalls filled with sweet-smelling hay and the sound of neighs and stamping hooves. An army of horses stood in wait of action or dozed tired from their earlier pursuits. The grounds stretched for miles, filled with ancient forests full of deer and other game, hidden in the canopies of trees.

Lord Stourton of Stourton Castle owned the land, farms and villages all around for miles; his serfs had to pay him taxes and work for him farming the land-poaching was forbidden, and a death sentence of hanging was carried out if caught. Life for his tenants was hard. A bad year of weather could see many of them starve, while the Lord lived in luxury in the castle with tables laden with food, fires roaring and lavish furs to keep them warm. Serfs of the castle were badly treated, although treated better than many in the land-their Lord was only doing what was expected of him, and he had a kind heart and showed some thought for his people. They could feed on the leftovers, stay warm by the embers of the fires, wear discarded furs, and young children were free to roam. The servants treasured their jobs, knowing that they would not starve or freeze to death. The Lord also had an army of knights with powerful horses which he would send out to fight for the grand King George. The knights were skilled swordsmen; they took no prisoners and the King paid handsomely for his service. With the war still raging against France, the knights were never short of work or money.

A Rackety Cart

~~*~~

The year was 1408, and it was a cold October day. That day a market was being held within the castle walls. The stalls had a large array of farm produce, some sold hot pastries and mead served in pots, others had rustic clothing and tools. The market bustled with carts, horses and people, fire pits roared and the peasants gathered to keep warm. The market would go on late and games and fights would break out-this would happen every sixth day after the Sabbath. Every sinner could then pray for forgiveness from God in church the following day and then rest if permitted. The peasants, nearly all serfs to the Lord, knew each other well. They were tied to the land and not permitted to leave; they all had their complaints and arguments but generally they looked out for each other. A few were talented freemen and not hitched to the castle, these were mainly stonemasons and carpenters who often travelled for work. But folk would know them as they often came back to the same places for employment and had family scattered around, so when someone completely new pitched up at the market, the peasants were suspicious and not so friendly and the stranger would stick out like a sore thumb.

Agnes and her mother Avoca had arrived at Stourton in the summer, four years ago. They arrived on a warm, sunny day pulling their rackety cart full of their meagre possessions. They wore matching cloaks and pointed hats in deep blue wool, dyed by woad leaves. This was not sensible-it offended many as they were deemed poor and not worthy to wear such rich colours. Avoca though, knew it created work as she was skilled with dying fabric, and folk could not help but ask for a deep blue or vivid red garment. Avoca's cauldron bounced along, tied onto the cart with other pots, furs and wool. They had travelled far on foot, keeping mainly to the deep ancient woods hidden by the dark woody paths; they would camp late and rise early so as not to be found. Avoca ran from capture and torture by a sheriff of the King's own, who believed her to be a black witch who had murdered his brother. Avoca was in truth a white witch and she could heal with her potions and chants. The sheriff was nasty, and had a personal vengeance to seek out any who resembled a witch on his hunt, and with no trial he would have them burnt at the stake. He became well known; people were afraid and would quickly accuse anyone to save their own skin. Avoca and Agnes were lucky to escape and prayed to find somewhere less suspicious, where their skills could still be considered useful. When they stumbled upon Stourton, they felt blessed; the village folk were cautious, but they appeared gentler, and the lord who ruled the lands would soon find the healing powers by Avoca to be beneficial. She took a small stone hovel deep in the wood not far from the castle, and there she had spring water and all the ingredients and utensils she needed to make her potions, ointments, powders and dyes. Avoca and Agnes would set up a stall at the market every day before the Sabbath and, to avoid persecution, attended the church alongside the other peasants.

On that cold October late morning, Agnes and Avoca trundled into the cobbled marketplace within the castle walls. As always they went to the same spot at the end, a little away from the other stalls; although they had not encountered any animosity, they preferred to keep themselves to themselves and others seemed happy with their quiet presence. Many had begun to trust Avoca and took her potions for ailments, and since she had saved the life of little Tilly Feld from the sweating sickness, word had gone around and people treated her with gratitude. The morning felt uneasy to Avoca, and she was skittish and alert to everything. She discussed with Agnes that maybe it was because it was the Eve of Samhain, and later fires would be lit to ward off evil spirits at dark. Avoca herself would pray to her ancestor on this eve in a stone circle she made surrounded by candles and herbs. It was a time Agnes loved as her mother's dear friends would visit, and she could sit outside all night and stare at the skies with them, chatting of other times. Many stall holders were very busy that day and extra crowds gathered, buying produce to celebrate the evening. Avoca was not happy; she twitched and sniffed the air like a rabbit being tracked by a fox. It became too much for her, so they discretely packed up and left over a small side bridge that no one used as it made the walk a massive detour around the village. Avoca was happy for this extra walk and to be away from the gathering crowds. As they entered the woods, they could hear music starting to play and roars of laughter and they knew only too well this would turn to raucous bad behaviour later on.

Avoca settled herself down and held Agnes's hand firmly. She sang one of Agnes's favourite songs, and pushing the rackety cart they disappeared into the depths of the woods. Avoca and Agnes soon reached their humble hovel in the woods; where only the odd game keeper would infrequently pass and a young farm lad who they had found to be a friend. He bought her eggs and milk and in exchange Avoca taught him how to dye the wool he bought from the fields, fallen from sheep. Avoca didn't normally like many folks, but this young lad, Jeremiah of the Feld had a pure heart and was no trouble at all.

That evening they both busied themselves with chores and began preparations for their evening. A stone circle was made, and Avoca sprinkled her herb mixture around as she chanted little rhymes as she called them, rather than fixing spells. Agnes kneaded the dough, adding sweet berries they had dried from the summer. She added mashed hazelnuts and then left the dough wrapped in a cloth by the fire. She placed the cauldron on the fire and went outside to help her mother. The darkness had descended quickly and the skies were clear, lit up by the moon and stars. It was not long before the smell of smoke drifted through the air as the village and castle folk started to light their huge bonfires to ward off evil spirits. Many believed the spirits of the dead would travel, and they would set a place at their tables for their loved and lost ones who they invited in to join them in their feasting. Avoca though, lit no bonfire; she had no fear of any spirits, and she invited no spirits to her own makeshift table, instead she would greet her coven and they would talk long into the night and share knowledge, discoveries and spells. Agnes placed the dough on bay leaves in the dry cauldron, and added sticks to the fire beneath, turning her flattened bread until it cooked. She then placed water and chopped potatoes and herbs into the huge pot. Unlike the others, they would not feast on a sacrificed animal, instead they would pray for the safety of the woodland creatures.

Soon the others arrived, magically, just appearing from nowhere with only little pops of light flashing in the sky, and the wondrous evening began. The five witches sat inside the stone circle eating the thick soup and flat bread that Agnes had made. Agnes played contently while listening and watching her mother's friends; she was too young to be in the circle. Agnes loved to see her mother look so happy as she chatted in her own language. Agnes could understand some words, though many were spoken too quickly. Each witch was different in appearance, but all of them were beautiful and magical to Agnes. She loved Josina the best, not only because she looked just like her own mother, but because she also had the sweetest smile and spoke as though she was singing a song. Her shiny dark hair and eyes glistened, and she wore bright red clothes with pretty jewels. Josina always bought Agnes the prettiest dresses from far away and this year's Samhain dress was exquisite. Finely decorated in delicate white flowers, it was the most vivid blue in a luxurious fabric fit for a princess. Agnes loved it so much and she danced and twirled admiring the beautiful flowing fabric. She was complimented by the others, even jolly Lettice made a flattering remark. Lettice made Agnes laugh; she had funny freckles and curly red hair, and she wore many dresses in different colours all at once to hide her growing rotundness from an abundance of foraged and stolen food. She teased everyone with her drawl and at times was quite rude, chattering through her wobbly teeth. Avoca had told Agnes that she was extremely old and was born into a Viking family, hence her rudimental ways. Parnell and Wilmot admired her new attire and for Agnes this was indeed a triumph, for they were so beautiful, and she had always looked at them both with awe. They were identical twins, both fair and so pale they shone like diamonds. Both appeared shy and quiet and each spoke for the other; they were practically one person in two bodies. Avoca explained to Agnes they were the most powerful witches known in this realm, despite their demure and innocent appearance and soft gentle mannerisms.

The evening continued as normal with laughter and chatter, until it took a more serious note. Agnes was an observant child and she understood from people's tone of voice and expressions if there was any concern. That night, normally filled with joy, seemed to be taking a more sombre turn. The conversation grew colder and quieter, and the witches huddled closer. Agnes knew trouble was on its way; she stopped her play and went inside to the warmth of the fire, lying down in front of the flickering flames. She pulled a hessian blanket around herself and drifted off to sleep. Agnes did not sleep by choice; the spell had already begun to weave its magic.

Josina, her mother's dearest friend, had come with grave news. She was terrified by on of her many visions, she had seen a priest, a sheriff and a crowd and on the stake of fire, she had seen Avoca and Agnes. Josina knew a witch hunt was upon them and they did not have long. Avoca had to leave with Josina that night, they would take what they could carry and hide what was left behind. To Avoca's horror this included Agnes; she could not come as she was too young and would die in the crossing of time. Avoca begged her friends to find a way to take Agnes, but they insisted she would die. Parnell and Wilmot cast a spell so strong that little Agnes would not wake for hundreds of years, and she would only wake if the words were spoken of an ancient Indian spell. Her little sleeping body lay wrapped in hessian, with her favourite things in the chest, and with henna they painted patterns of protection charms upon the wood. Carefully they gave sleeping Agnes a potion, and there she would lie buried in a cavern underground. Avoca planted a yew tree for protection and so she would easily find the burial cavern on her return, even if it took a hundreds of years. Wilmot had promised her she would be safe and when she woke, little Agnes would be just the same, but for now though she was frozen in time.

With tears, Avoca packed, convincing herself she was doing the best thing. Josina had always looked after her and had come back for her. But Avoca could not shake off the feeling that something was very wrong. Why would the witches' coven not just take on the sheriff and priest? She had no choice though, and when she heard the sound of horns announcing someone of importance arriving at the castle, she hastened. The other witches helped pack up, making sure they left no trace in the stone hovel and they were gone-vanished into the smoky skies taking their spiritual paths and portals to their worlds in different times and places, far from danger and far from Agnes, all that was left on a faraway path was the remnants of a rackety cart.

Sheriff Dastin and the Priest

~~ * ~~

Sheriff Dastin had unexpectedly begun to quite enjoy his witch hunt. With a simmering rage over his brother's death, the search had given him the opportunity to seek out any wretched old hag he thought guilty of anything he disliked. He had gained good momentum, and had the company of a plump and vindictive priest who sought to rid the King's country of pagan beliefs and heretics and who was intrigued by Dastin's sorry story of his brother's strange death. They became very dangerous and unpleasant travelling companions. Each had the purse of the King as well as soldiers on horseback who had no empathy for others. Dastin had picked up a trail that headed west from Winchester, with many villages that seemed rife with paganism. After many cruel convictions, he continued his journey in search of more heathens and a castle that he had been requested to visit.

The track was well trodden and took the fearsome group past an extraordinary spectacle of stones. The stones stood surreal and proud in a circle on a plain of land that reached to the skies like the sea. The strange and huge statues of rock had a mystical eerie feel, and the priest commented that they must have had some ritualistic meaning in the way they were aligned with the moon and sun. They found unmarked graves and remnants of fires, the priest was nervous and pushed Dastin to move on as the night was the night when spirits and the devil's own were said to travel, and although his beliefs did not accept this, the priest had heard terrifying rumours of what happened to any found lingering too late at the 'Stones' on the Eve of All Hallows. Dastin agreed they should move on sensing danger.

They rode on, delayed by the stone circle, and did not arrive at Stourton Castle until very late. Dastin was there by invitation of the Lord who was inquisitive about his reasons for so many executions; he had sent a messenger conveying he had concern for his village and castle serfs, so he would like to be there when Dastin carried out his search of his land, The Lord of Stourton, it seemed to Dastin, was a very unusual man-he wished to protect his people rather than punish them. Dastin reminded himself he still sought justification for his brother's murder and no ground could be left un-turned. They were greeted with a little uncertainty as Lord Stourton had retired saying he would meet them in the morning, and they were provided with a humble supper and bed for the night. Dastin had hoped for a more lavish meal and chambers. He had heard amazing things about this castle, stuck out in the middle of nothing but woods. After an extremely uncomfortable night's sleep disturbed by screeches of owls and howling wolves, Dastin found himself in the morning sitting in a huge hall at a table with the Lord Stourton and many men and women, all of different classes, who bizarrely talked openly and freely about the day's work and discussed problems together. Dastin felt even more annoyed as he was ignored by the Lord; however, his ears picked up when they talked of a sick child in the village and someone suggested they call on the healer in the woods to help, which was agreed, and immediately a boy was sent to find her.

Dastin excused himself and followed without the Lord's permission or notice. Dastin found no problem in following the young serf who had no suspicions and was happy to hang back and chat; indeed, the folk here were friendly. He answered no questions that Dastin asked though, just saying he didn't know the honest answer, and the frustrated Dastin followed listening to his constant babble about the birds and trees. Knowledgeable as the young farmer called Jeremiah Feld was, Dastin had no appetite for such information and hastened him on, and they finally arrived at the stone hovel. Jeremiah called out to see if anyone was there. He tutted, 'how strange' and banged on the door, the door swung open showing the empty and abandoned room. Jeremiah scratched his head and excused himself running as fast as he could back to the Lord - he needed to tell him the healing lady had gone. Dastin looked carefully for any trace. He searched in every nook and cranny, but nothing could be found; the only small clue was a piece of ripped red fabric on a branch behind the hovel and he studied the silky texture knowing it was no poor hag's fabric. Dastin placed the silk in his pocket, a small trinket for his trouble and he did not know why, but felt sure that this wretched healing woman was his brother's murderer.

He paced back in anger to the castle to ask questions. Dastin would get no sense from anyone as the serfs and Lord were more concerned that they had lost the healing woman, who was clearly good at her job and had the whole castle and village under her spells. Dastin needed a plan, as these kind, simple folk would not respond to his brutal questions, so he took council in private with the priest and they agreed to walk into the village and see if they could help the young girl. The day was pleasant, the mellow air was fresh and the sun shone showing the stunning landscape, even Dastin had to remark on such a beautiful spot. He found Jeremiah and asked him to take him to the village, offering him a small cloth purse full of pennies. This to the farming serf was more than two years wages, so Jeremiah cautiously took the purse and hid it in his cloak. The walk was brisk and Jeremiah talked less but answered a couple of questions about the missing healer. He probably felt that with her disappearance he could now do her no harm. Dastin was even more certain that he had his witch, as she fitted the description; however, he did not bother to discuss this with the young and simple country lad.

The village was charming much like everything else and the folk friendly. Never had he seen so many pretty serfs; they all looked well-fed and in good health. He was taken to the cottage with the poorly girl and though Dastin had no care for the peasant and her family, he and the priest made a good show of concern. The child had a bad fever and the priest had seen this in many. He recalled a treatment that was successful in London and was simple enough: the patient would need to be dowsed regularly in cold water and given cold stew stock to sip and leaches placed on the skin to purify the blood, and he prescribed this with confidence and left. Dastin and the priest then looked around the village centre where the mellow stone rustic cottages were centred around a stone cross. There was a large green area where sheep and chickens roamed. An oval duck pond was sheltered by a huge old oak tree, and children played freely under its huge canopy, while some climbed up into the giant branches; carts came slowly along the rackety track, one full of straw for a cottage being thatched. Dastin and the priest watched the folk come and go, but there was no sign of the healing woman or any others alike. The priest noticed that most wore simple crosses made from woven dried grasses around their necks. Often they would make a sign of the cross on their chest, and he watched several pray in front of the stone cross and lay flowers, even though the day was not even the Sabbath. The priest and Dastin came away from the village feeling that the castle and village folk of Stourton were indeed god-fearing, kind people. Dastin had no place here. The lord of the castle was clearly ready to protect his serfs, and it was maybe a blessing the healing lady, as they had called her, had gone, for he had a feeling they would not have let her go without a fight. Dastin would find her some-how, he thought, and without a word they left the castle and its carefree ways. Dastin would make his way with haste to-wards the coast where he felt sure his witch would make for the coast and escape by boat. He wondered if she knew he pursued her and thought to himself, of course she did, she was a witch. Dastin, on the long ride, thought back to the stone circle up on the plains, something peculiar happened in that place; if only he had had more time to stay and watch, he felt sure he would find plenty of heathens there.

The Lord Stourton was happy to hear that Dastin and the priest had gone as he wanted no trouble and was pleased with his folk for causing none. He was frustrated though, for he felt sure that the healing lady in the woods had vanished because she had heard of Dastin's approach, he was an evil man and had caused widespread fear due to his conquests. Lord Stourton wished she had stayed; he would have protected her and her sweet daughter as they had been a valuable asset to his community with superb healing powers, he feared though his healer had fled for good. Sadly, the young child died in the village. As the Lord of Stourton suspected, cures were not only through prayers but through good treatment, remedies and ointments. Lord Stourton had his horse saddled and rode out to the village where he visited the family to pay his respects and had food sent to them. He then rode on to clear his head and to look at his land. He had not had the freedom of late to ride through the ancient woods and eventually he fell upon the stone hovel. He dismounted to have look around the room which, as found by Jeremiah Feld, was empty, although he could still smell herb scents faintly on the air. He walked the perimeter and saw nothing other than a yew tree that had been freshly planted in a part of the woods where only oak, elder and beech grew. He thought that perhaps the healing lady sought to grow it for one of her potions. Lord Stourton filled his leather pouch with fresh cloudy spring water that made a little stream and sat on the dry soft ground; it was so peaceful in the wood with not a soul around. He somehow felt though that he was watched. Was she still here somewhere? He felt a strong presence of something, but his thoughts were broken by the young lad, Jeremiah Feld, who strolled along whistling a bird song. He jumped when he saw his Lord sat on the ground and asked him if he was well. Lord Stourton laughed and bid him to sit next to him. Jeremiah happily sat next to the Lord on the soft grass, and agreed it was a strange business with Dastin, the priest and the healing lady gone. He then took his opportunity to explain to the Lord Stourton how he had been paid handsomely by Dastin for information and as a guide, explaining that he had not known he was a dangerous man. The Lord understood and instead of taking the peasants purse, he asked him what he might do with such a small fortune. Jeremiah explained he would like to buy some sheep and rent the glades of grassland in the wood. He said he had learnt from the healing lady how to dye the wool and thought he could sell the wool at the market. The Lord was impressed and granted him free use of the land. He would, however, take a small share of his profits in return, they shook hands and parted ways. Jeremiah Feld felt he was a lucky man, and he knew the healing lady or witch, as he thought she was, had helped him somehow. If Jeremiah could have looked into the future, he would have seen that this strange twist of fate, with a witch he once knew, would entangle his future generations once more.

Sage and Fern Leaves

~~ * ~~

Avia had not been to the garden for a few days, partly because she was told to have bed rest and partly because she
felt quite scared. However, the sunshine shone brightly
through her window and she decided she would at least go
to find Jack, so she wrapped herself up with more clothes
than normal and called to Nanny Maud that she was taking a
small walk. Nanny Maud came and fused over her, but
happy with her over dressing, she allowed her no more than
an hour with no digging. Avia couldn't find Jack so walked
towards the gothic cottage; she held the pendent in her
pocket, rubbing it between her fingers. The garden to the
cottage was just as she had left it, but the cottage was not
and had quite clearly been used, as herbs and flowers hung
from the beams, the smell of smoke lingered and a cooking
pot lay washed and discarded, drying in the sun. Avia turned
on her heel to go back, unsure whether or not she should
report this to Otto, when she heard the voice again, only this
time it sounded a little more timid and scared. The stranger
asked Avia if she would like some more sage leaves. Avia
replied curtly that she absolutely did not, then the girl Agnes
appeared from behind the yew tree. She said in her strange
voice that they were good for you when you were sick. This

time Avia held her ground and decided if the stranger was going to hurt her then she would have done so when she was flat out on the ground, instead though she had put some leaves on her head. Jack had told Nanny Maud he had taken them off when he found her as they had a funny smell and Nanny Maud had been concerned that Avia had taken to putting leaves on her head and wondered if they were the reason for her fainting. Avia asked Agnes what they were and why she had put smelly leaves on her head, and the girl replied they were fern and sage leaves soaked in peat water to keep her from overheating and to stop anything bad happening to her. Avia hesitantly thanked her and asked the girl where she was from. Agnes clumsily explained in broken words that she had lost her mother and everything was very strange. She couldn't see the castle, and everything was different - the deep woods had all turned into a lake with pretty trees and strange statues stood every where and even the hovel was different, then she started to sob. Avia felt sorry for the poor thing, but what was she to do with her? Avia comforted her and told her she had to go back, but she would come back with some things for her after lunch. Avia rushed back to the house and joined her sisters at the lunch table. Luckily, everyone was in a quiet mood; Olivia was day dreaming, no doubt about Thomas and Cecelia was absorbed in a book. Avia ate as quickly as possible, putting as much as she could in her pockets, and she then returned to the gardens, running along the high path that led quickly down to the cottage. She crossed over the bridge, where normally she would have fed the ducks and fish, but her bread buns had a far more important job today. Avia found Agnes sitting in the yew tree, so she climbed up and sat next to her passing her a bun. Agnes sniffed it and licked it then smiled, she liked the sweet sticky glaze and devoured the bun in seconds, so Avia passed her another to munch. Avia asked Agnes the last thing she remembered, and Agnes told her all about her mother Avoca and her coven describing each witch and saying how clever they all were, then she sobbed again because she truly was a lost soul. Avia began to realise that Agnes was a little witch. The more she told Avia of what she knew and how she had lived made Avia more certain that she was a real witch. The mystery still remained as to how on earth could she be here from four hundred years ago. Avia believed completely that she was from another time; she couldn't possibly make such things up. Avia had to be really careful and protect her, so she asked Agnes to promise not to tell anyone ever that she was a witch's daughter - she was sure it was still possible that she could be jailed or even hung. Avia studied Agnes. She had long, black hair and huge almond-shaped brown eyes; she was delicate and had the sweetest smile and a lovely way of expressing herself with dance-like hand movements. Avia looked at her bracelets and realised that the one she had found must belong to Agnes. Agnes said she could keep it as long as she wore it - she said it would ward off evil spirits and bad witches. Avia then asked her about the pendant which she timidly showed her with some reluctance as Avia did not wish to give it up. Agnes studied the necklace; she bit on the stone and then held it to the sky. Agnes said it was precious and she was lucky to have one. She said it was a moonstone and that Avia should keep it on her at all times, saying that it was much more powerful than her bracelet. She smiled saying she felt happier that Avia would be safe, because she really wasn't sure if the witches would come back or if they had ever gone and Agnes started to sob a little again. She said she felt scared of the witches and her mother now. Avia agreed it wasn't the best thing to do to your daughter, bury her underground and leave her for hundreds of years alone in a box. She held Agnes's hand and just sat quietly with her for a while. She would have to sort something soon as poor Agnes couldn't stay here all alone and scared. As Avia sat contemplating their predicament, she became curious as to whether her little witch could actually perform sorcery, although now was not the time to ask her. Reluctantly, Avia left her saying she would be back in the morning, and she told Agnes to hide herself well and she would be fine.

Avoca and the Fort of Chitrakut:

1300

~~ * ~~

The night Avoca left her little Agnes behind was hard. She left with Josina and travelled to another place and time. Avoca felt empty and missed Agnes's sweet little face and ways; it hurt to think of her lying asleep all alone in that box under the earth and Avoca prayed with all her powers she would be safe.

As time passed, Avoca started to enjoy her surroundings and felt welcome in Josina's colourful world where everyone spoke in her birth language, and she enjoyed the dry climate and heat of the sun. She lived in a magnificent fort called Chitrakut, where she worked with Josina making healing potions and beauty remedies for Queen Rani Padmini, who was the most beautiful person Avoca had ever seen - she loved her and was loyal to her service. Avoca felt safe and enjoyed a lavish lifestyle that she had once known before in the palace of her capture. Every day she was fed with the other servants who had a rich diet of rice, vegetables, spices and exotic fruits, and she had endless leisure time - free to wander the lanes of the great fort. In the evening the women would bathe in the warm waters to cleanse their skins, and, in stunning silk outfits, they would perform dances and carry out ritualistic chants, then sleep in exquisitely decorated chambers. Avoca now understood why Josina always glowed. Avoca grew more beautiful herself; she gained knowledge from the elders and became an even more proficient witch. Although Avoca was not named a witch or dankini, she was considered to have a profession in her potions and was needed and respected in the community. Avoca made friends and her life was rich and good; she thought less and less of Agnes and found it easier to try and forget her. One day she would go back for her but Josina said it was too dangerous to go back yet, so many things could go wrong, so they left Agnes while they considered what they might do. Avoca and Josina were content and happily went about their business.

Sometimes Josina would vanish for weeks and a few times Avoca travelled with her. They would meet the other witches from their coven in a chateau in France, owned by a strange warlock called Fabian. Avoca enjoyed the pretty gardens and sweet kittens, but the warlock she was scared of as he reminded her too much of another bad warlock. The others would stay with the warlock deep into the night, but Avoca would hide in her room discouraged from joining by Josina, who said she would find the subjects of no interest. Avoca never really knew quite what Josina did on the occasions when Josina was away without her, and Avoca never asked. Josina seemed very troubled from the last time she had been away and had been mumbling that she was too late and shouldn't have left. She visited the queen to tell her of her prediction, but even this could not stop the future, and Josina was correct in her fear and failure to stop the war she had predicted.

On a fateful night only three years after they had arrived at the fort, they were woken by terrible noises and the smell of gunpowder; others in their chamber started to wake and then an elder came in screaming for them to run - the fort was under siege and there was an evil plot against their king and queen. Josina as always took control and they quickly packed all they could in the chaos. They heard shouts coming closer, so Josina grabbed Avoca and they escaped narrowly as the solid door to their chambers was broken down. They ran in darkness down the tunnel that brought them to the river; from there they would escape to the mountains.

The night was clear and very cold, but Josina and Avoca dared not take flight in case they were seen; they could see many soldiers marching towards the fort that had once been their home, now a battlefield of destruction. They could not believe that their wonderful life and home was destroyed.

Josina would later learn that the fort was seized by Alluddin Khilji's vast army, that their king was gone and that their beloved, beautiful queen had taken her own life instead of facing the shame of her captor. The fort was said to be a place of horror and Josina and Avoca were lucky to flee. Josina never forgave herself for not being there earlier to try and stop the plot; she grew angry inside as they hid deep in the forests on the mountain slopes, waiting for the next Eve of Samhain.

Where to Keep a Little Witch

~~ * ~~

Avia had been looking after Agnes and had set the little cottage up as well as she could without too much suspicion; the gardeners would just think she was just making a playhouse. She had instructed Agnes to hide if anyone came and that together they would come up with a plan. She could not abandon poor Agnes, nor could she tell anyone about her. If anyone was to find her they would send her straight to the poor house. Avia had heard from Lucy that the poor house was an awful place and dreadful things happened behind those walls that were supposed to offer sanctuary. Avia continued to take food and clothes from the Hall, and in return Agnes helped Avia to make her garden; slowly the two became the best of friends. Avia's little witch was clever with plants and roots, and she taught Avia how to mix a potion - soon the two of them became quite industrious, making special plant food. Agnes would also practice her chanting of rhymes as her mother's book had been hidden with her in the cavern. Agnes started with simple spells at first and realised that she was good at sorcery. As she discovered her talents, she shared her growing confidence with her trusted friend Avia, who watched in amazement as Agnes moved things by pointing her finger at them and made potions that did different things; her favourite was the healing spell. One day they found a wild rabbit in a trap; the poor thing's leg was a mess but within a week Agnes had completely healed the rabbit and with joy they watched it hop away. All this still did not solve their problem, as Agnes could not hide in the cottage forever.

One day, Avia had a very clever idea. She had heard Jack saying that Rosy the scullery maid was leaving to marry a miller so perhaps Agnes could find work in the Hall, then she would be safe and they could still be friends - she just had to convince Agnes that she would enjoy working and somehow find a way to introduce her to Miss Bonneville. Avia explained to Agnes what a scullery maid did, and Agnes liked the idea of working in the kitchen, washing pots and floors. She said she would work on the tidy spell in the book and they both laughed - maybe she could do all her work with magic spells. Avia had to teach Agnes more modern ways of doing things and how she should speak as some of her vocabulary was strange and a little rude. She also said that Agnes would have to say she was eleven, as that was the youngest they would employ someone at Stourton Hall. The next morning, when Lucy was cleaning the fireplace, Avia asked Lucy all about how she got her job and Lucy said that she was employed as they knew her family and employed most of them - she was helpful by telling Avia that strangers needed a reference. Avia now had a huge problem: how would she get a reference for a witch who came from 1408. Avia needed help, but she could think of no one that she could trust. Cecelia would be perfect as she was so knowledgable - it was too risky though. Then she thought about Lucy's family, but could she trust a family of gossips to never give her secret away. Later, Avia walked around the lake trying to think, while Agnes played in the woods - she seemed to almost be flying from branch to branch. Avia was worried that they would not pull off her idea and was so deep in thought that she did not notice Jack come around the corner until he was upon her. Jack grinned saying, 'a tuppenny for your thoughts?' Avia jumped and laughed. Jack always made her happy and that was it, like lightning she knew: she could definitely trust Jack. Jack sensed she was up to something and presuming she was plotting for her garden, he enquired how it was going. Avia chatted away telling him all her garden news and they walked to the gothic cottage together. Jack was amazed she had done so much, and he was even more amazed she had grown so many plants in the depths of autumn; this became Avia's opportunity to mention her ward Agnes. Avia asked Jack to sit with her on the stone bench by the cottage window. Firstly, she asked him to swear on his life and his mother's life to keep a secret, then she told him about Agnes. She had thought to leave the witch part out and described her only as different and as someone who did experiments; however, the more she said the more she made her sound like a witch. Avia asked if he could maybe put a good word in for Agnes by saying to the cook that she was a long-lost relative who needed work and lodgings. Agnes had been sat on the roof listening, as Avia had told her to wait and not show herself yet, but Agnes became very excited as she had seen the boy called Jack in the gardens; he talked to the birds and sang lovely chants, so she was sure they would be the best of friends. Agnes scampered down and shocked poor Jack who went pale as a sheet. Avia held his hand and said it was fine and that she would not harm him. Agnes, uncertain of his reaction, quickly retreated behind the yew tree. Avia was suddenly not so sure this was a good idea as Jack looked most unwell. She called for Agnes to come back and introduce herself, hoping if she could show how sweet she could be he would like her, but Jack looked at the sun and excused himself saying it was time to go and he ran off calling back to Avia that he wouldn't tell, that her secret was safe. Avia stamped her foot and called Agnes who arrived with her head down. Avia was cross with her, but she remembered Agnes was different, so instead comforted her and said she was going to sneak her into the Hall for a sleep over tonight - her poor little witch would be warm and well-fed. Agnes's eyes lit up and she danced for joy as she hated being alone in the cottage at night.

Jack Run, Rabbit Run

~~ * ~~

Jack walked away from Miss Octavia or Avia as she liked to be called as quickly as possible, and once he was out of view he ran, and like a hunted deer he didn't stop running until he got home. His home was a small farm across the fields from the Hall; it had been in his family for centuries, and his ancestors had once been serfs to the lord of the castle - sheep farmers who dyed their own wool and did well enough to build the farmhouse and buildings over the years. His older brother, Bertie, helped his pa and they lived a reasonable life with a small herd of Devon cattle that grazed on the rich pastureland. They produced creamy milk that they made into cheese and butter for their own consumption and to sell at the market held every Saturday; they also sold anything else they could seasonally grow. Jack though had a real passion for the gardens and his Uncle Tomsk gave him the job and fair pay, which helped his family through the harsh winters.

When Jack walked into the farmhouse his ma was busy churning the milk. Jack offered to help, and his ma took a well-earned seat by the fire; the table was already laid for supper and the delicious smell of stew wafted through the room. Jack's ma looked quizzically at her youngest son and ask why he had such a furrowed brow. Jack asked where his pa and Bertie were, and as they were at market and not due back for a good hour, Jack felt safe to talk to his ma. Although he had sworn to Avia not to say anything, she had presented him with such a dilemma that he had no choice but to turn for help. He could not risk betraying the Hall - his family and other relatives were all dependent on the Hall for employment and homes; yet not to help Miss Avia was awful and to not help a witch could be dangerous. Although Avia had never directly said that Agnes was a witch, Jack knew straight away she was, what else could she be. Jack's ma was the kindest and calmest person he had ever met, and he trusted her with more than his life and so the tale was spun a little further, although that was where it would end. Belle, Jack's ma, listened carefully and was cautious not to comment until she had all the facts and when Jack had finished, Belle fluttered around the kitchen a little to calm her nerves. Jack waited patiently for her response. Belle took her son by the hand and whispered to Jack that the girl had to go as she was a bad omen. Jack argued that she wasn't and said Miss Avia had taken it upon herself to care for the waif. Belle and Jack decided to sleep on it; the men were back, and they both knew Pa and Bertie would go straight to the sheriff; they would have Avia's little witch captured and taken away and although Belle felt this was the best option, something in her heart and past made her think she should help. One thing was for certain though, Jack must not lie for Miss Avia or the waif.

The next morning Jack woke early and helped to do some chores on the farm, then grabbed a hunk of cheese and bread from the kitchen table. Belle was sat hunched over mending some clothes. She tiredly looked up at Jack, and Jack felt sad that he had caused her so much concern and wished he had kept his secret, but as always, his blessed ma knew what to do. Belle was still friends with the housekeeper, Miss Bonneville, and on their last meeting at the market, Miss Bonneville had told her how she sought a fine seamstress to design and make Cecilia's ball dresses for her first season and new frocks for the younger girls. Belle thought this position was far more appropriate than a scullery maid. Belle herself had worked up from a chamber maid to the Lady's Dresser so had many sewing skills herself. Belle began to tell Jack her brilliant plan. Firstly she instructed that Jack, Avia and the little waif had to follow her plan exactly. Agnes was to learn to sew, and Belle guessed that she would be quick at this before she had even met the girl; after all, she suspected she was definitely a witch. Belle would secretly teach her all the skills she had been taught by the old seamstress at Stourton Hall. Belle herself made elegant gloves from fabric scraps. Belle would help the girl if she promised to use no witchcraft and serve the Hall of Stourton instead with her fine needle work. The main part of Belle's plan was to be played out in front of the whole village on market day. Agnes would arrive in her exotic clothes, as Jack described them, with a basket of her fine sewing; she would linger at Belle's cheese stall at midday as that was the busiest time and Agnes would purchase a small piece of cheese while showing an enquiring Belle her fine work. The charade would be performed just as the housekeeper Miss Bonneville came to order the Hall's cheese, milk and butter for the week as she always did at midday. Such a coincidence of Miss Bonneville seeking a new seamstress and the young Agnes displaying such skills would surely result in her getting the position.

The next part of the plan and the most difficult part was for Agnes to say where she was from. They had to come up with a solid story and not one that divulged she came from 1408; she could not tell any part of her unbelievable story and this Belle thought was definitely the hardest part. From Jack's description of Agnes, she looked much more like something from an elaborate Shakespearian play. Belle had been awake all night thinking it through. Agnes would have to present herself as being older and she would have to adopt a foreign accent and declare herself a runaway orphan from Portugal, escaping the pending war and invasion from the French and Spanish. Agnes could say they had escaped Lisbon and travelled on a clutter class ship; she must say her parents had died while on board and that they were once tailors from Lisbon, known for their intricate laces and fine tailoring. Jack was amazed by his ma's incredible plot; quite how she had come up with it all he had no clue, but he hugged her warmly and ran to work bursting to tell Avia when he could.

The Past of Belle

~~ * ~~

Belle was born into French aristocracy in 1787, and by the time Belle was two years old, revolution had seized the country. It was a time of discontent and anger and as the poor people starved, King Louis and his queen, Marie Antoinette, lived an outrageously opulent life, spending obscene amounts of money in a senseless and bourgeois way - they would both eventually, without mercy, sadly face the guillotine. The revolution swept through France, executing and exiling all of its aristocracy. Belle's family was smuggled out by a trusted servant in the depths of a cold dismal night. They were bundled aboard a ship leaving everything dear behind and they sailed to a safer England where they were very fortunate to have wealthy family connections. Tragically, after only three years of living in England, Belle's parents both died of smallpox, having already suffered with poor health from their traumatic experiences and loss of a lifestyle so decadent and once glorious. Belle was left orphaned and alone and the house her parents had been kindly gifted was taken back by the Lord. He had little care for his French cousins and even less for their daughter and with no children of his own and no clue how to care for a child, he sent Belle away. She was sent to his cousin Lord

Richard Colt Hoare at Stourton Hall, saying his home was unsuitable for the child. Belle would grow up under the care and management of the housekeeper, Miss Bonneville, and was trained from a young age to work in the house as a chamber maid. Lord Richard Hoare was never informed by his cousin of the young girl's aristocratic family background; had he known, Belle's life would have been very different.

Belle was only young when Jeremiah Feld; whisked her away to his inherited farm, started long ago by his ancestor Jeremiah Feld. Belle would not have it any other way though as she loved her husband and sons. Her beginnings in a life of finery never left Belle though, and she was clever and elegant in her ways and her delicate features complimented her name, Belle. Lord Richard Hoare, being a man of great stature and wealth with his travelling and networking, one day heard of Belle's dreadful family tale through another French family who had suffered the same exile. He had never realised she was from aristocracy and was cross with his cousin for not informing him; he had thought her just to be an illegitimate child sent away to be hidden from sight and suspicion. The poor girl had grown up in the servant's quarters in service to his Hall and was now married to a farmer with a child or two; she could now never join higher society. Lord Richard Hoare, after long consideration, felt he needed to tell Belle and although he could not change the past, he could shape her future and her sons for the better. One day he asked Belle for her company to walk with him around his gardens. Lord Richard Hoare told her of her family background and said he was deeply sorry for his lack of interest in her case and was frustrated she had received such terrible treatment. Belle was content and had no wish now of mixing in the circles of the elite, and Belle knew her husband Jeremiah was so proud that he would never be able to accept that he had a wife from French aristocracy. Jeremiah came from generations of farmers before him, and she feared he would feel humiliated and unworthy. Lord Richard Hoare and Belle kept it their secret and sometimes he would invite her to walk with him around his magnificent gardens and she would tell her husband and sons how the lord liked to talk of his beloved lost wife, when in fact he mainly told her wonderful stories of his own travels, as if by doing so he was enriching her mind and freeing her from her low position in society.

So, Belle had easily found a story for Agnes the witch, for it was very like her own story and hers to give to another with hope in her generous heart. Belle met Agnes and Avia a week after the plan had been hatched. Avia was thrilled to meet Jack's ma, and Belle was very impressed with her bright and vivid character - she could now see why Jack talked about her so much. Belle felt nervous about meeting

Agnes. She was very superstitious about any kind of witch-talk and still thought it was the devil's work. Her catholic roots were embedded in her soul, but she also had a faint memory of something bad in her own past. Agnes though did not scare her; instead, Belle like Avia felt an immediate bond, so much so she worried Agnes had woven a spell of enchantment upon them all. She was sweet and funny and although her words were clumsy, she had a posture and grace more like a lost princess than a lost medieval witch. Belle did not waste time and set about teaching her eager pupil. Agnes loved it and she learnt quicker than a fish learning to swim. Belle would leave her with homework to do and the next time she visited Agnes, Agnes had elaborated her task, creating truly stunning work. Belle began to love her tutorials with the girls, even Miss Avia was attempting to learn to sew, although she seemed happier with a trowel and fork in her hand laughing with Jack. The little group set a date for the following Saturday. In the meantime, Avia had to teach Agnes how to speak well with a slight foreign accent. Agnes already spoke a strange and very different language although no one was quite sure what it was, including Agnes, who babbled away making them all giggle - their story was suddenly very convincing.

Avia The Teacher

~~ * ~~

Agnes loved staying at the grand Hall with its elegant furniture and lavish décor and she stared in awe at the paintings of all the beautiful people adorned in the most wonderful attire, each in stunning landscapes. She was fascinated with the collection of porcelain, clay and preserved animals, and she was particularly amazed to see a sweet pangolin in the collection - she had curiously heard of such a creature. Avia said it was an awful process called taxidermy and somewhere at the back of her mind, Agnes seemed a little familiar with the procedure. Agnes especially loved all the rich fabrics and wonderful tapestries that told stories on the walls, and she knew that to be found by Avia was the most amazing turn of fate. Avia taught her well, with such kindness and patience, and Agnes was forever in her debt and their bond was so deep nothing would ever stop Agnes from protecting her little saviour. Avia became an inspiring and dedicated teacher who spent hours with Agnes educating her on all the important and necessary things she thought a civilised young lady of the early 19th century should know. Music lessons were the most difficult as Agnes had to be hidden completely or the plot was ruined.

Avia had watched her household carefully and had made notes with all of the times each member of the house did different chores and where they were in the house. It was good her father was away. He was apparently on a dig with a whole team of archaeologists discovering amazing and interesting artefacts in Egypt. Avia knew her sister's routine and discovered the maids did all the fires in the house at 6.30am ready to be lit for the waking household, Avia had a window of opportunity at 7am - they had only fifteen minutes. Agnes was a special student though and had already learnt enough of the piano to satisfy anyone should she be asked to play, so Avia just had to build her repertoire a little more. Her speech and writing were excelling quickly, and Agnes was also helping Avia for some reason; by teaching, Avia learnt more herself and it was so much more interesting. Avia loved having Agnes staying in her room - it was such fun. Agnes was amazing at hiding, and when Lucy came into do Avia's fireplace, Agnes was gone - no sense of her being could be felt, seen, or smelt. Sneaking Agnes in and out of the house was always the hardest and most dangerous part of their days. Avia though had dressed Agnes in Olivia's old clothes, put her hair in a large bonnet and they would sneak out of window and take cover in a large leafy rhododendron bush, check the coast was clear and then dash to the ha-ha and stayed low until under the cover of the woods. On wet days, they were confined to creeping around the house and on

these days, the cook would remark on Avia's endless appetite and laughed that she would turn into a horse or that she
had hollow legs. Agnes had such an appetite for the Bath
bun - she found the brioche a delicacy. Avia told her the
story of Solange Luyon, a young French Huguenot who escaped the French protestants and fled to England. She arrived in Bath and peddled her buns on the streets from a
basket and it was not long before her buns and her beauty
made her famous. She married a baker who stole her heart
and her bun recipe. Agnes liked the story and would have
liked to have met her. Avia thought to herself, as her little
yew tree witch Agnes slept soundly on the other side of the
bolster, about whether she would be famous one day. She
had a very special feeling about Agnes, but for herself she
knew fame was unlikely, as a lady was unlikely to be recognised for her gardening skills. However, she thought again of
Solange Luyon and decided she must never be defeated. She
would, with Agnes's help, invent the most wonderful
designs. Avia drifted off to sleep dreaming of beautiful
dresses and gardens filled with exotic flowers; her dreams,
like always of late though, turned to the fires and chants with
strangers in bewitching dances.

Truth or Tale

~~ * ~~

Belle loved her new girlfriends. Having spent most of her life surrounded by men, she was now experiencing the joy of chatter and giggling over silly nonsense. Avia had the most wonderful sense of humour she could see the funny side of everything and Agnes she found fascinating, although she was unfortunately a witch, she was most definitely the kindest and most thoughtful one. Her sewing talent surpassed anyone's belief, especially given she had only just picked up her first needle. Belle insisted they must remain friends and an alliance grew strongly between the three unlikely companions, a little lady of gentry, a little witch of no fixed abode, and a French farmer's wife once of aristocracy.

Belle, though, had a small distant thought that ran through her head each night; she would lay awake and try to remember. It was to do with a folk tale and something that she had seen as a young servant, something she had blocked from her memory. Slowly the thoughts and the tales and the forgotten memories came together. Belle suddenly knew why she felt the little witch Agnes gave her that feeling of deja vu - feeling quite distressed, Belle remembered. She had arrived at Stourton Hall when she was six years old. She was tall and strong for her age, despite her delicate features, and Miss Bonneville, who was then the new housekeeper, was welcoming and kind and took the sad orphan under her wing, although a little confused as to why she was with them. Belle would have to earn her keep, so Miss Bonneville found her pleasant and easy tasks around the house and was delighted when she found Belle could speak French; the two, although in a working relationship, developed a fondness for each other. Belle would have to keep on her toes though, the housekeeper and mistress were very strict and insisted on perfection in performance, punctuality, politeness and puritan ways. In return for good discipline and obedience, the mistress rewarded her household favourably, and, although she ran a tight ship, it was a happy one with no grey areas. Belle did not mind any of this and enjoyed perfecting her work; she grew faster and more able and became at a very young age a competent house servant and was promoted to being the dresser to the lady of Hall.

Belle adored the wonderful Beatrice Hoare and enjoyed looking after her, Beatrice was pleased with Belle, and engaged with Belle's lovely tone and taste. Being the Lady's Dresser gave Belle a good position in the house and she was respected by the other servants; her position also gave her far more freedom and she was able to take walks around the beautiful gardens and lake with Lady Beatrice as well as alone. When alone, Belle tended to be a little more adventurous and she would ramble off the paths and through the woodland; she loved this sense of freedom. One day there was a heavy frost, so Lady Beatrice stayed warm by the fire afraid of a chill or a fall. Belle could not resist the beautiful, bright afternoon though, so once her chores were completed, she excused herself before the onslaught of the later dressing duties for dinner. Belle found the woods less slippery and was enchanted by the frosty beauty that glistened amongst the leaves and cobwebs; she had probably gone a little too far, carried away with her exploring, and she became lost. Beginning to feel afraid and to panic, Belle started to run, but this only led her deeper into the wood when finally, she a glimpsed a little stone cottage and saw smoke. With no fear of the estate or its occupants, Belle went up to the curious little cottage; she knocked gently on the door, she heard whispers and a rustle from within, and slowly the door was opened ajar. Belle apologised for her intrusion and explained she was lost and asked if she could warm her feet and hands by the fire. The lady who answered the door was dressed in strange clothes in a vivid red silky fabric with stunning embroidery that seemed more appropriate for a summers day; she wore several beads and bangles, had strange markings painted on her hands and exposed bare feet, and her face was made up with black around her eyes and red on her lips. Belle had never seen anyone so magnificent in her life. Sat by the fire was another lady, so similar they could have been sisters or twins, and they offered Belle a drink which she gladly accepted. She was given a stool by the warm ambers of the fire and every so often they would add extra twigs that seemed to burn far longer than a normal stick. Her drink was sweet and thick and tasted heavily of cinnamon, camomile and something else. Belle did not ask them many questions and excused herself feeling uncomfortable; they were very strange and spoke in such a funny way that she could hardly understand them; they both put on thick grey cloaks and offered to help her find the path. Belle did not argue as the night was bitterly cold and darkness had begun to fall. Confused, Belle saw them just disappear into thin air; she felt very strange and managed a few steps before falling and lay unable to move; she tried to scream but nothing came out.

Luckily for Belle, Jeremiah Junior Feld was using the top path to go to see the bonfire for Hallow's Eve at Stourton Hall. He had come every year since he could remember; his parents had both died, so at fourteen he was in charge of the farm and his two younger sisters. When he saw Belle lying there on the woody path he did not hesitate to pick her up; Jeremiah was strong, so her delicate frame was easy to carry and never did he walk so fast - he thought she might die in his arms. Jeremiah got her back to the Hall and took her straight to the kitchens, as he knew most of the servants of Stourton; with gasps she was well-received and he was sent to find the search party with news she had been found. Belle was ill for several days and she was kept warm in a room with a fire; they had the physician visit her who said it was as though she had been poisoned, and he did not know if her poor frail body would survive as she tossed and turned and cried out in her dreams. Then amazingly, one sunny Saturday, Belle woke feeling fine although very confused; she remembered nothing and never did until she saw Agnes who stirred up her past memories. Jeremiah always remembered everything of that night, and he called to see Belle whenever he could. Whatever had happened that night, to Belle it felt magical and Jeremiah was the kindest and loveliest man on God's earth to her. Belle and Jeremiah courted for a few years; he charmed her in any way he could find. For Belle though, it was mainly that he made her laugh, and they chatted for hours; he was the best friend she had ever had and on her fifteenth birthday, with the largest grin and smallest ring, he proposed. Belle missed the finery of Stourton Hall and her ladyship Beatrice and the housekeeper Miss Bonneville, but she was happy though to have a good husband who she loved and a pretty stone farmhouse with roses around the door.

The revelation for Belle to remember that night of her past was enormous to her. The villagers and Hall staff and family had questioned her for years about what happened that night and many told the stories they had grown up with about the witches in Stourton woods; young girls had gone missing from time to time and some like Belle had been found in a state of delirium and always on All Hallow's Eve. There were lots of different folk tales, and with horror Belle suddenly realised though that they were all quite true. Her mind reeled but she was certain of one thing: her fear of the dark and woods since that night was for good reason - Belle had met the witches and had been in their lair. She also knew if that it wasn't for Jeremiah finding her that cold night she would never have had the chance to survive. She thought back to the witches and how they held her as they walked her in the woods; Belle had a strange feeling they were taking her not guiding her home. She remembered they talked about something they had lost, they looked for something. Belle felt dizzy. Did they maybe look for Agnes all those years ago?

One Little Witch Goes to Market

~~ * ~~

It was a fine day, and Avia and Agnes crept out of the house after doing their final preparations, only this time Agnes wore her favourite blue dress with white flowers; she had altered it perfectly. Avia had set Agnes' thick, shiny black hair in ringlets that cascaded around her perfect little face and she wore the jewellery presumed to be hers that they had found in the cavern underground. Jack had created a dig and excavated many treasures; Avia and Agnes would catalogue each one and they hid them in the cottage attic. Agnes wore Olivia's old cloak and carried a basket with gloves and petticoats that she and Belle had made, each with exquisite embroidery, and, as planned, they met Jack at the gothic cottage on the morning of market day. Jack was faithfully waiting for them as promised - Avia smiled and lit up like a sun ray when she saw his smiling face and although nervous, they chatted as normal. Jack and Avia had shown Agnes the way to the market a few days before. She had plenty of time that morning and would be safe as lots of villagers and traders from other parts would be on the track to the market. Agnes was terribly nervous though that something could go wrong, but Avia had assured her she would be fine; she just had to be confident and remember her story and not say too much. They walked with her part way through the woods and got her to the track that led to the market. Avia also suddenly felt terribly anxious as she wished her friend luck and waved her off: what if something did go dreadfully wrong. Agnes waved and disappeared around the bend, and Jack reassured Avia on the way back to the cottage that Agnes would be fine, after all she was a witch.

Avia and Jack, to keep their minds busy, worked on the cottage garden. Avia had designed a wonderful wrought iron gazebo which had been made by Fred the blacksmith and the beautifully made structure now stood proudly in the garden with its intricate metal flowers. They planted roses at each corner of the Gazebo and then planted buxom in diagonals - Avia wanted to create a knot garden. As they worked, Jack and Avia chatted about their dreams and hopes and both laughed as they both wanted the same thing - to be famous garden designers. Avia enjoyed just being with Jack again; although she was terribly fond of Agnes, lately she had taken all her time and Avia hadn't been to see her friend Lottie for weeks; partly this was because she was on her guard and was afraid she would let something slip and Lottie, as lovely as she was, could most definitely not be trusted. Avia dearly hoped that their plan and all their hard work was working and that Miss Bonneville and Agnes had met. A hundred different scenarios, some quite silly, went through

Avia's mind, sending her into an oblivion of panic. As though Jack read her mind, he took Avia's hand and led her away from the cottage; they walked towards the Temple of Apollo. Together they ran up the steep steps and stood looking over the beautiful gardens and lake and prayed aloud for their plot to work. Avia wanted that moment to last forever, standing there with Jack, holding his hand, and looking at the beautiful view; she thought he felt the same because he just stood there with her The church bell struck twelve breaking their trances and both agreed they should go for lunch then meet back at the cottage and wait for Agnes; still holding hands they ran down the cobbled path then parted company. Avia ran back to the hall; her cheeks glowed from the bright sunshine and fresh air and she felt so happy to have Jack as her friend and wished they could be friends forever.

Lunch was difficult as her sisters asked her too many questions, intrigued as to what their sister was up to all the time. She explained about her garden and then spent the whole hour persuading them to visit it another day as she wanted them to see it when the fountain, pond and planting had been finished. They reluctantly agreed and then suggested they should call for the carriage and visit Thomas and his sister Edwina. Avia then had to worm her way out of the social visit, saying she had arranged to work with Jack; they were very persistent but agreed they would go without her and with relief Avia escaped, bidding them a pleasant stay at Dyrham and sent her regards to Edwina. Apparently Thomas had guests and Avia had the feeling it was more a plan to meet them. They were friends from Petworth in Sussex and Cecilia no doubt hoped to meet George Wyndham, whose father was a collector of wonderful art and they were very wealthy.

Avia ran down the path towards the cottage, she didn't wish for all the wealth and place in society as her sisters did, Avia fancied a simpler life and one in which she was always free to garden. Jack was waiting and grinned his lovely grin. They both sat on the stone bench below the gothic window and waited; if all had gone well and to plan, Agnes would have met Miss Bonneville at Belle's cheese stall. Their wait was long, but they were happy and just sat together spotting different birds and naming all they saw. They listened to bird song, which Jack was good at imitating, and to keep themselves warm they started climbing the yew tree. Jack help Avia and they sat on one of the big branches. As they looked up to the treetop, they saw hanging in the branches lots of metal charms, all with different symbols; they were old and rusty. Avia felt a shudder run through her as though they were being watched, although this time it felt different from when she had seen Agnes: this felt scary. Jack sensed the feeling too and they both climbed down. They needed to ask

Agnes if she knew anything about the charms and symbols, but there was still no sign of her, so they started to walk up to the track to meet her. Avia began to worry as the afternoon light started to fade; Agnes was really late now and she, like Jack, would have to get back home. They waited as long as they could; the woods started to grow dark quickly and still they felt watched. Jack was sure he had seen and heard something, and he glanced back to see a swish of colours disappear into the trees; someone or something was definitely watching them. Jack was worried for Avia's safety and walked her back to the Hall and once he saw her go through the door to the kitchens, he left for the farm.

When he got back his ma was back from the market: she had had a good day and they were all happily chatting and laughing. Jack was so pleased to see them - he felt blessed with his family and went to help clear out the cart as he listened to his ma gabble on excitedly about the day's events. She told Jeremiah the tale of the peddler girl with fancy gloves who came to her stall and met Miss Bonneville; who had employed her there and then for the position of a seamstress. She told Jeremiah about the stunning embroidery and the girl with the darkest hair and beautiful dress. Jeremiah listened and then said to Belle that she must choose some fabric; he would take her to town and this new seamstress could make her a fancy dress to wear on market days. Belle smiled with glee and said she would love that more than anything. Jack then dared to ask casually where this peddler girl came from and Belle just replied she wasn't sure, but it was not from these parts; she said he would probably meet her as she was taken by Miss Bonneville straight up to work at Stourton Hall. Jack smiled at his ma and muttered, 'thank the Lord'. Avia would know soon too he hoped, although in that massive Hall it was possible she would not. Jack was happy the plan had worked, and Belle seemed very pleased. Jack had a niggle though - he was worried. Something was strange about those symbols in the tree and something didn't feel good; both Avia and he had felt scared by their watcher in the woods. Jack had seen someone a few times now in the trees, but he only got small glimpses of ruffling dresses and a green cloak, he had felt uneasy for a while. He didn't want to scare Miss Avia too much, although he feared something strange was a foot and he hoped that himself and Miss Avia hadn't let the devil through the door with their plots and deception.

The Seamstress of Stourton

~~ * ~~

Agnes felt so nervous as she walked into the town; she could feel the town's folk and traders stare at her unusual looks and dress. She held her head up high and walked proudly with a smile on her face, just like Miss Avia had taught her in the library with books on her head; she looked at the stalls and showed her work and then went over to Belle's cheese stall. Belle gave her some cheese as planned and Agnes spent ages choosing a piece, then, when Miss Bonneville appeared at the stall, Agnes as instructed by Belle started proudly to show Belle her needlework and say how she sought work and somewhere to live. Agnes could not believe how well it went. Miss Bonneville instantly loved her work and was impressed with Agnes's knowledge and skills. Belle and Miss Bonneville chatted about old times, while Agnes stood taking everything in. She stared around the market and an old memory stirred of her stood by her mother at a stall with clay pots full of potions. There were other stalls all around and fires, straw was on the floor and folk were mainly dressed in thick furs; it was bitterly cold, and flurries of snow swirled in the air. Deciding not to settle, they went elsewhere that day, and Agnes remembered them packing up and going early. She remembered getting ready for Samhain and her mother with her friends by the fire and then nothing. Agnes started to feel a little panicky and angry inside. What had they done to her and why did they hide her and why didn't they come back for her; it was four hundred years ago.

Then Agnes heard Belle's sweet voice; she spoke to Miss Bonneville saying the poor girl must be half starved and with that it was agreed; Miss Bonneville asked Agnes that if she was able to retrieve her belongings another day, she should come up to the Hall straight away. Agnes, although nervous, got into the carriage with Miss Bonneville and they wrapped blankets around themselves. Forgetting her anger and panic, Agnes began to enjoy the carriage ride and excitement that she had done it. Avia and Jack would be so proud of her and how wonderful, she would have a room and food and she was to be a seamstress. Agnes decided that day she would do her absolute best and concentrate on creating the most wonderful needle work, maybe the odd little spell of magic could be sewn or seeded for Avia her most special friend. Agnes also thought to herself, as they trundled along in the carriage, if there was ever a need, she would protect her new friends in any way she could.

As the pretty woods and fields fluttered by Agnes felt an irrational sense that something bad was on its way and that she had best to be alert and ready - at least she would be safe in the walls of Stourton Hall. The cottage though - that was a place where trouble could come, and as soon as she was able she must find a way to put up a guarding spell to keep evil spirits or witches out. Agnes thought back to the memory of her mother, the market and Samhain. Whatever had happened and why Agnes was not sure, the only thing she did fear was that her mother and friends would come back for her, but Agnes wanted to stay here with Avia and Jack. She felt safe, a feeling she had never felt before, as with her mother, there had always been fear and persecution. Agnes began to suspect that her mother the witch, and her coven, were not perhaps as good as she had thought.

Agnes felt very grand as they arrived at Stourton Hall, even the servants entrance felt wonderful. The lower floor halls led to the kitchen, scullery, boot room and so much more; it felt warm and smelt delicious. She was taken to the huge kitchen and sat down at the large scrubbed wooden table; the cook eyed her up and down and called her a fancy princess, with a twinkle in her eye and instructed the maid Bonnie to give her a large bowl of stew and a huge hunk of bread. She was also given a pot of ale, but Agnes did not like the bitter taste and unafraid asked Bonnie if she could try another drink; Bonnie happily drank the ale and got Agnes some barley water from the pantry. Bonnie sat down and some other servants arrived and ate stew and bread; they chatted about the day as others appeared and disappeared, ate and cleared. Agnes was given a piece of apple pie with thick sweet cream; she then copied the other servants by clearing her plates and asked what she was to do. Miss Bonneville arrived instantly and took Agnes to the servants' bedroom quarters. Agnes had a room high in the eaves with a pretty window that looked over the treetops; there was a neat single bed, chair and a large dresser with a mirror and wash basin. A little fire crackled away with extra logs by the side and on the bed, folded neatly, was a uniform with a sturdy pair of shoes and on the pillow, a starched bed gown was folded with a knitted shawl. Agnes pinched herself to check this was all real. Miss Bonneville smiled seeing her delight and instructed her to change then meet her in her office opposite the kitchen; they could then discuss her wages and work schedule. Agnes waited until she had heard Miss Bonneville go down the stairs then gave a squeal of excitement; she had heard Jack talk of wages with Avia, and he had said Stourton Hall paid their servant the best wages. Agnes had not thought she would be paid - to have a room, a roof and a fire was more than a dream as well as the food they were going to give her. Agnes knew she was the luckiest girl alive and nothing on the earth would make her want to leave. She quickly dressed into her uniform and pinned her hair up neatly. Agnes looked at herself in the mirror, wiped her face and admired her crisp pale blue dress and apron all lined with delicate lace; she noticed the others wore a black dress with a white apron and the men a black suit and crisp white shirt. Agnes quickly made her way to the office, glancing back at her room so she did not forget the way. She found the office, knocked and went in and took a seat opposite Miss Bonneville. The office was neat as a pin with shelves of books on all sorts of things. Miss Bonneville opened a file and started to write and as she wrote she explained that Agnes would earn two pence a week and was allowed to take other work in her own time; she would work from seven until three and then be on call from six until eight for any fixing issues amongst the household. Her main work was completing a new wardrobe for Miss Cecilia and then Miss Olivia and Miss Octavia; they would go to Bath next week and choose fabrics. Miss Bonneville then asked her to follow as they walked up the stairs into the main house. Agnes already knew the house, so it felt strange to pretend she had never set eyes on its beauty before; she also knew they were heading for Avia's wing. Agnes felt a flush of nerves as they walked into the gracious sitting area. Avia was staring out of the window and turned trying hard to hide her instant surprise and pleasure to see her dear little witch. Olivia was concentrating on her embroidery and slowly looked up to see the curious newcomer, she smiled faintly. Cecilia immediately put down her book and walked over to greet Agnes When the girls realised she was to be the seamstress and make all their new dresses, they giggled with excitement and chattered and on learning they were to visit Bath to buy some fashionable fabrics, they bubbled over, even Avia showed an interest in having a new frock. Agnes was shown their dress collection and given a few that needed repair and a few that needed throwing away. On leaving the girls, she asked Miss Bonneville if she may make herself something from the discarded dresses to wear to Bath, and she agreed. Agnes sensed Miss Bonneville now knew she had no other possessions other than the ones on her back. Agnes was then led back over to the servants' quarters. They went up a little set of stairs that led to one large room with the most amazing half-sloped glass roof and windows that reached from the ceiling to the floor. There was a large table and shelves with every sewing thing imaginable in labelled boxes and a grand fireplace on the back wall that had just been lit. On its large mantle was a stone statue of a wild cat in a glass box - the wild cat stared towards the door as if forever on guard. Miss Bonneville then said her breakfast was served in the kitchen at eight, her lunch at twelve and supper at six. Miss Bonneville said if any questions she must ask her and not other members of staff and she was not to gossip or talk about others, then she went through a list of rules and finally finished by saying she could start work on Monday. This gave Agnes a whole day off and plenty of time to repair and re-design the discarded dresses. Miss Bonneville left her alone and Agnes set about hanging the dresses and finding all the things she needed to sew. Agnes looked at the wild cat on the mantle. When she had been the witch's daughter in the woods, she used to play with one just the same, she had called her Hestia as her mother had said they once had a cat with that name. Agnes couldn't help herself and carefully took the stone wild cat out of the glass box and breathed a little life back into her; soon Hestia was purring around her and sat dutifully next to her cleaning her paws as though she had always sat there. Agnes knew it was wrong to already be doing magic, but she knew Hestia would be useful and it was good to have a feline companion - every good witch needed some sort of pet. Elated, she started work and sewed by candlelight as the light had left the day far behind. Once the fire had died to embers, she left with her candle and went to the kitchen. Cook showed her how to make a cup of tea and gave her some sweet biscuits; she sat at the table joined by Bonnie, Martha and Lucy who seemed thrilled to meet her. Agnes had to be careful though and was very vague yet polite when asked questions about her past, keeping strictly to her story word for word. Agnes, exhausted, then excused herself and pouring a mug of milk she went to her bedroom. Hestia was curled up by the fire and Agnes gave her the mug of milk and chatted to her about the day. Sleepily, Agnes drifted off to sleep in her cosy room in wonder at her new life at the wonderful Stourton Hall.

The Past of Avoca:

~~ * ~~

Avoca didn't remember much of her childhood, other than always being hungry and travelling across deserts; each city or village they would pass through they would stay only for however long it took to replenish supplies, selling spices and charms. It was 1208 and they were traveling with the large caravans of desert people; safety in numbers was the reason in case they were ambushed by tribes, but they fought and spatted amongst each other for food and supplies, survival was hard. Avoca remembered looking at her mother and wondered how her frail body and furrowed face survived the rat race. She was kind to her children and fed them what she could. Avoca knew she stole to give them things; her hands were like lighting, and she seemed to disappear once the deed was done, so frail and bent no one could imagine her a thief or threat. Avoca's father though was strong and loud; he used force for any crime and would kill with his bare hands when times were hard. Avoca remembered the day her mother passed away vividly; she remembered setting her out in the burning boat on the river, the smell of smoke lingered in her memory for many years and even now a bonfire could stir emotion deep in her soul, where now only sadness lay deep inside.

Not long after Avoca's mother's death they arrived in a co-
lossal city with great white walls and a fortress that spread
for miles. It wound its way down to a huge river where elephants and locals bathed and boats larger than Avoca had
ever seen before appeared like monsters in the huge river's
mouth. Avoca was amazed by the huge citadel with its smells
and crowds of so many different types. She heard sounds
and singing that she had never heard and bells rang as they
toiled across the city skies calling out chants with words
Avoca did not understand. When nightfall came, they settled
by the river with other travellers who spoke to one another
relaying news of other lands and opportunity. Sadly for
Avoca and her sisters this bought news to their father of
payment in gold for good child stock and by the next evening Avoca and her sisters were taken from the wooden caravan, their home, and placed in a cold stone chamber beneath the ground. Avoca could see bars and no escape, and
her sisters cried for their father. He never came, and Avoca
knew he had sold them. She had seen the exchange of
money - if only she had known the terms.

Several days later with their sore eyes squinting from the
sun, Avoca, her sisters and other girls were bought to a pen;
they were ringed by the ankles to a rock and inspected by
their prospective owners. They looked at their teeth and
pulled on their hair and each child was taken. Avoca saw her

sisters go, all bought by the same lady and man, and she prayed that they were not cruel and would not work them too hard. Avoca was left to the very last and stood alone in the searing sun with no shade; she did not know why as she had good teeth and hair. She began to feel even more scared, then a woman arrived wrapped in silks and laden with jewels. Avoca had her ankle ring and rock removed and the woman bid Agnes to follow her. They got into a trap pulled by a donkey and were led through the maze of walls; eventually they arrived at a huge palace that sat on the top of the citadel and Agnes, with no word, was ushered along into a chamber where lots of other girls chatted and busied themselves and again, with no word, Avoca was left with the girls. Before long, a girl who looked just like her approached Avoca, and led her to a bathing area after which she was dressed in beautiful silks and had her face, hands and feet painted with henna. She then sat with the others in a large courtyard and older women bought them food on platters - she watched the others as they helped themselves filling their clay bowls. Avoca ate well and as she listened to the others talk, she began to understand their words were much like her own, with a slight difference. The girl next to her introduced herself to Agnes; she was charming, and her name was Josina. Josina seemed very curious about Avoca and stayed by her side and was helpful teaching her how things worked in the palace their prison. When Agnes asked what they were all doing there, she laughed and said that when she was older she would be taken to the prince to be his wife with lots of others. Avoca was shocked. Josina calmed her though and said quietly not to worry, as by then they would be long gone from the palace.

The palace chambers were comfortable, and Avoca enjoyed the gorgeous food; she loved swimming in the warm waters and wandering in the grounds with its scented trees and flowers. Josina had started to teach her many things. One was writing on slates with a chalky stone - she taught her how each mark made up her words and showed how she recorded her recipes on cloth that she painted with dye. Avoca was not unhappy with her situation, although she was a prisoner and property of the palace, but in time she yearned to be free and travel. Josina sensed her restlessness and asked her to be patient, she said it would not be long and explained to Avoca something that she did not fully understand. Josina told her she was born under a moon that gave her special gifts, that meant, like Josina, she could travel between times and places - this though could only happen on the special night of Samhain. When Avoca asked why she stayed prisoner in the palace, Josina admitted that she had been tricked, although she said it was ultimately beneficial to her. Josina travelled to the past of places and times learning others' knowledge and the palace it seemed had a wealth of scholars in apothecary and she had also learnt some wonderful conjuring. Josina then said though - they would be leaving the next night.

Although excited, Avoca was nervous as these walls had offered her protection and good health, although she knew escape was her only route - Avoca did not ever wish to be a wife. The Eve of Samhain, as Josina named it, arrived quickly and as the chimes were heard across the city calling for evening prayers, Josina and Avoca stood with their silk bags full of as much as they could possibly carry; they were dressed in so much they were stifled by the heat of the evening. Even though the temperature had dropped, Josina lit a small fire hidden in the ground and spoke a rhyme in her magical voice; as soon as the moon was aligned, they disappeared leaving only embers of sparkling dust. The guards of the palace who later searched for the missing prisoners, believed they had vanished into the flames to die, so no search or questions were asked - they were just two slave girls whose strange disappearance was of no consequence to anyone.

Avoca and Josina crashed onto the streets of London where the air was thick with smoke and the cold was unlike anything Avoca had felt before. Josina quickly found them lodgings above a noisy tavern; men whistled and called at them as they passed and Josina hustled Avoca along. They entered a dark room with a large fire that glowed in the open stone hearth and that had a small set of stairs that led to a bed; Josina opened the curtains that let in the lights of the fires from outside and the smell of smoke, Josina said they would take it and paid a grumpy hag some coins. She told Avoca the year was 1400 and that she would not stay long; they ate a bowl of pottage and slept in the lumpy damp bed.

The next morning, Avoca and Josina travelled by foot through the filthy streets to Fenchurch, where they visited an alchemist's shop; it smelt very strange and had deep shelves containing pots of different potions and stuffed animals that gazed through the dust a middle-aged gentleman neatly dressed with an apron who greeted them cautiously, noting their strange attire. Josina spoke weaving her story around him as a spider weaves its webs with silken thread. With no word from Josina and no clue as to what was happening, Avoca was left with the dumbfounded alchemist who showed Avoca to the back of the shop where he made his potions and pastes. Avoca watched as she was shown where to get water from and how to boil it; he seemed of a pleasant nature and was patient, realising his new assistant spoke no English. Avoca though was a very fast learner and she was obedient; Eliphas began to enjoy the company of his strange new apprentice and as she learnt quickly, he relied more and more on her skills and shared more knowledge with her. Eliphas let her look at his books and slowly Avoca realised Josina's plan: Eliphas was a warlock who worked his wizardry under the cover of his alchemist shop. He proudly boasted to Avoca of his history and of the generations of notorious warlocks before him; he knew secrets and mixes not even recorded in his father's works. He warned Avoca sternly of his younger brother who had been taken as a soldier for the king. Avoca understood this was a warning to keep her quiet. Eliphas looked after her, though he would often give her potions to help her sleep. Although most she would throw up, sometimes he would watch her drink and she would sleep with strange dreams. Most evenings, Avoca would excuse herself and record her findings at night in her little room above the shop on fabric scraps from sacks and using a dye from a paste she made. Josina would be pleased, and Avoca felt happier now that she knew of Josina's plan.

The next year arrived and so did Josina on the blast of a bitterly cold wind. Avoca was ready to leave, her little bag packed, and with no word to Eliphas. She intended to leave and not return. Josina was stood outside in the little courtyard her fire already lit and the girls greeted each other with joy; then Josina looked at Avoca with dread, the one thing they had not planned for was that Avoca would carry a child. Avoca had had no clue and cried that she must have been tricked by the warlocks potions that he had given her and now she did not know what to do. Josina in disbelief at her innocence, tried her best to comfort her but explained the travel would kill her - she had no choice but to go back to Eliphas. Josina promised she would be back, and after Josina left on that bitter night, poor Avoca crept back to her tiny bed and smouldered as she wept; Eliphas would pay for his trickery after the child was born. She kept to her word and as she worked, she stole and sneaked from her master. When Eliphas knew of the child that she expected he seemed not unpleased, and in a strange little church up on a hill, Eliphas married his apprentice so as not to shame himself and her. The baby was born late and Josina still did not appear.

Avoca tried as hard as she could to live the lie with her husband by her side; the infant was sweet and Agnes was her chosen name. Still Josina did not come, and Avoca could take no more. Eliphas had grown colder and crueller in his ways and one night she knew she would snap like a twig on the ground so, with a trick Josina had shown her, she would try to turn him to stone, she never meant to take his life away. Avoca hurriedly left with all that she could carry in a cart with little Agnes on the top; she pushed the cart through the streets and headed for the countryside where she could hide. However, Eliphas, as he had warned her, left her a trail of trouble, his younger brother was now a sherif of the kings a powerful man.

Dastin the sherif knowing that his brother Eliphas had taken a wife and had a child, searched for them, seeking permission from the king to find the murderer and have her hung. He was currently in great favour with King Henry IV after the defeat of traitors who had formed a rebel army to kill the King; instead, the traitors' heads would fall, including the leader of the conspiracy Harry Hotspur. Dastin was granted permission by the King to take another man and horses and search the land; he would bring the wife to trial for foul play in the matter of the strange death of his brother Eliphas; who was found literally a dead man standing, with no mark on him; there was also a matter of theft to deal with as all his money was gone. Avoca knew she would be hunted so she kept to the forest for over a year, travelling slowly with Agnes. She wanted to leave each night of Samhain, All Hallows Eve, but she never had the heart to leave her little Agnes with her sweet and precious little ways. Avoca struggled on until one day she found a pretty track by a stream and as she headed up the hill, Avoca looked over a valley of such beauty and charm that she knew she was at place that she could call home.

Yards of Lace and Fireworks

~~ * ~~

Avia woke up very early; it was Monday morning. She was so excited a she would go to Bath with her sisters and Agnes. She could not believe how well their plan had worked and she had nearly screamed out loud for joy when she saw Agnes with Miss Bonneville. She had been so stressed that Agnes was lost forever on market day, so to see her turn up in their sitting room was a pleasure beyond belief. Avia had spent Sunday in the garden with Jack and left Agnes to settle in; they also needed to be double careful they caused no suspicion. Avia had packed a special celebratory picnic with Bonnie's help, saying it was to thank Jack for all his help and hard work. Bonnie, being sweet, would not breathe one word and said how wonderful Jack was. Avia was unsure if she liked how much Bonnie went on about how wonderful Jack was, but she thanked her gracefully and left with the picnic. Jack was thrilled and they sat admiring their work by the new water feature with a large urn fountain and Avia thanked Jack so much for all his help.

Later, after they had giggled and chatted, Jack expressed his concern to Avia. He took on a serious note and told her of some of the old tales of witches in Stourton woods. He begged Avia to be careful at the cottage and asked her not to go alone. Avia was at first was defensive, proclaiming she was fine and could look after herself, but Jack grew a little cross, so she decided to obey his wishes. Jack thanked her and promised her he would visit the cottage as often as possible, so she would never be alone in the garden. Jack then told her Belle's story and how since seeing Agnes and for the first time in years, she had remembered that night and the witches and the cottage. Belle had asked Jack to tell Avia in confidence, as she was genuinely worried for her safety if the witches came back. Avia was shocked by his story although believed Belle completely. They both wondered if the witches would come back and if it would be Agnes they looked for. Avia said they must talk to Agnes, as she was surely in grave danger if they came back for her. Maybe they had taken other young girls instead of Agnes over the centuries. Avia shuddered with fear and thought Jack was right, it was no longer safe by the cottage alone. As if to confirm this they heard a rustle and a small screech from behind the cottage. Jack quickly got up and ran just in time to see the ruffle of dresses disappear and that strange smell lingered of pungent herbs and smoke. He came back to Avia saying they definitely had unwanted company.

Normally they would send for Otto and Benny, but they feared that would be of no help against a witch in the woods. Jack walked Avia back up to the house and he wished her a pleasant trip to Bath and he teased her for having fancy frocks made for her. Avia didn't mind; for some reason everything Jack said these days made her laugh or she found herself listening to him with the greatest respect. She waved him off, as always regretting they would not see each other for a few days.

The next morning arrived quickly, and Avia lay in bed listening to her sisters giggle with excitement while calling her to hurry up and dress for breakfast. The carriage waited for them with the horses impatiently stamping their hooves. Avia went straight to the horses and patted them giving them each a sugar lump from the breakfast table. Miss Bonneville and the girls put their travel blankets across their knees and soon they were off, with the wheels crunching on the gravel. Avia stared out as they left; she didn't like to leave and then she saw Jack by the walled garden waving with his infectious grin. Avia waved back and heard sighs from her sisters and little scolds for being so friendly with a ground's boy, Avia did not react and shared a little grin with Agnes who sat quietly next to Miss Bonneville. The journey was slow until they reached the turnpike to Bath and they arrived exhausted from being juddered around in the carriage. Their lodgings were at Sydney Place where they stayed with their great-aunt Eliza who had been widowed for many years; she still wore black and mainly stayed in her room and only talked of the good old days.

The house was not as lavish as the girls were used to, but they happily made themselves at home, engaging with their host. Cecilia was great-aunt Eliza's favourite, as she was the first born and she twinkled with joy when she saw her although she was just as happy to see the other sisters, only a little less enamoured. Avia was not put out like Olivia, and she gladly accepted the gifted pound each niece was given to spend in Bath - her great-aunt said she had no use for her late husband's stash. Avia had already decided she would save hers for seeds and bulbs and with hope, buy a book.

After a strange lunch of pease pudding, the girls excitedly set off along Great Pulteney, enjoying the crisp sunny afternoon. The streets of Bath were bustling with fashionable wealthy ladies from London. Cecilia and Olivia studied them in detail, considering this important research for their new wardrobe, while Avia walked with her head in the clouds admiring the architecture. They arrived on Milson Street and were directed by Miss Bonneville straight to the draper and haberdashery stores; even Avia was amazed and overwhelmed by the amount of choice. She wondered how on earth they would choose from all the fabrics, buttons and lace, but as soon as they walked in a little team of ladies in uniforms started helping the Stourton girls, which made their task so much easier. They were shown paintings of fashions and the latest pastel colours and complementary accessories, different styles and bustles - the process had begun. Agnes was engrossed in the paintings and she consumed every detail to the last stitch; she felt so important and hardly had chance to even look at her friend Avia.

Avia understood Agnes' work though and escaped asking directions for the bookstore, which was just a couple of doors down. As she entered, the bell rang and an old gentleman in pinstripes with glasses came forward to assist her; she explained her interest in garden design and said she would like the latest book. The gentleman scuffled off to the back of the musty shop saying very little and a little later he bought back in his clutches a large, red book. With gloves on, he put it on the table for Avia to look at and gestured she put some cotton gloves on over her gloves. The book was illustrated like her others by Repton, only this one gave a more modern approach, as the book was designed to reach a larger audience and not just the elite - it was perfect. Avia enquired for the price, noting to the book seller that it had a scratch on its jacket. He tutted and went away again, returning with a price written neatly in ink; the price was ten shillings which was half of her pound. Avia knew some people didn't earn that in a year; however, the pound was a gift and she would still have money for seeds and bulbs, most of which she could get for free from the garden. She cared not for buying anything else and her conscience, as if a completely different person, agreed. She thought of Jack and how he would love to look at the book, so it was decided and the book seller, a little surprised by her interest and wealth, accepted her pound. He wrote down her address and came back with her change. A younger man then came to the front of the shop and bid her farewell with thanks and added that if she should change her mind then she could bring it back. Avia thanked him and assured him she would not wish to return it. The young man then boldly asked if she would like to watch the fireworks in Sydney Gardens in the evening - he had free tickets. She explained they were a rather large party of five young ladies, but he happily gave her five tickets and said he looked forward to seeing her there. He handed her a receipt for the book saying it would be delivered later that day to her town address. She thanked him immensely and hurried back to the drapers.

Avia had to quickly decide upon her fabric, pretending she had been engrossed by the buttons; however, it was easy as Agnes had noticed her absence and covered for her friend choosing her the most beautiful, embroidered pale blue and white fabric, with complementary white lace and little blue buttons. As Avia would not be whirled out on the busy social calendar like her eldest sister, one dress was enough. Avia was thrilled with Agnes's superb choice, and she adored the painting of the dress that Agnes was going to make. Miss Bonneville was very impressed with Agnes and marvelled at how she helped with the fabric choosing and matching of things so delicately and well-coordinated; her girls would be the best dressed of the season and Miss Bonneville felt a flush of pride and that luck was on her side. They all then descended upon the Pump Rooms and had afternoon tea.

The room bustled, mainly with young ladies accompanied by their mothers and other chaperones. Avia, unlike her sisters who people-watched intently, looked with interest at the wonderful paintings by Gainsborough. She loved all the portraits she had seen by Thomas Gainsborough; his paintings made everyone looked so handsome or beautiful with stunning back drops - the landscapes and gardens were exquisite. Cecilia and Olivia ignored their little sister's comments, distracted by a group that had just entered the room. Thomas and his sister Edwina were among the fashionable group and Edwina came straight over seeing Olivia, bubbling over with excitement. Her calmer brother also came over clearly delighted to see Olivia; they all chatted and then Thomas mentioned the music and fireworks in Sydney Gardens later. Olivia sighed with disappointment, she was not sure Miss Bonneville would permit it - then Avia, to everyone's surprise, pulled five tickets out of her skirt pockets, declaring, 'I think she will if we can all go, and it is only over the path from our lodgings'. Everyone laughed in amazement at Avia and not one of them thought to ask how she got them. As if on cue, Miss Bonneville returned from her chores and happily agreed they could all most certainly go as long as they stayed close to one another; to have Thomas in the party would be even more appropriate. So it was settled, and they all met at the entrance that evening dressed warmly in their best. Never had Avia seen anything so wonderful and this was her chance to walk arm in arm with Agnes, as Miss Bonneville approved that each should have a partner; Olivia was even safer, as she had both Thomas and Edwina at her side. The park that evening was full of well-dressed people who seemed quite well-acquainted, music played from a bandstand and little stalls sold hot chestnuts, pies and other delicacies; drinks were being sold at long trestle tables, and pretty coloured lanterns and bunting decorated the trees and candle lamps. Exploring the well-lit park with all its oddities was very entertaining and at times a little scary; Avia felt like she was in some exotic country far away with all the colours and smells. When it was dark, the firework display was set off and the pretty lights lit up the skies, Agnes stared in disbelief and could not help to notice a tall dark over powering looking man who seemed to be in charge of the fire work display, who often starred her way, Agnes looked away form his piercing thundery eyes and clung to her oblivious friend. Avia clutched her friend quite terrified by the noises - she wished Jack had been there to see all this and could not wait to tell him. As they walked back, Agnes had chance to talk as the others hung back chattering. She babbled about how happy she was and how wonderful it was to be able to work and live in the Hall. Avia squeezed Agnes's hand and just listened with joy; tonight she would not ruin her pleasure by scaring her with Jack's story of Belle's encounter with the witches - they would have to do that another day.

As they walked towards the gates, she saw the bookshop man and thanked him graciously for the tickets which he happily acknowledged and bustled off with a pretty lady on his arm. Behind him a strange lady with a crooked back wrapped in cloaks approached them; she held a basket with wheat charms all intricately woven into different shapes of hearts, animals and people. She began her patter and tried to peddle Avia and Agnes the charms from her basket, saying they were lucky and would bring them fortune and love, but Avia thought she already had a fortune so was a little dismissive. The old lady looked up at her from under her cloak, then shrank away like a whimpering animal as if in pain, mumbling about curses and promises, then she looked at Agnes: bowing deeply she offered them both a wheat owl for free. Agnes felt some strange tension between her and the old woman, and straight away she could not explain but she heard words in her head and felt the urge to raise her arms towards the old lady; she managed though to not speak or act and somehow her eyes conveyed her message to the old hag to be well gone from her and Miss Avia. Miss Bonneville and the others rushed over when they saw their distress, but the old lady in cloaks had by now scuttled off into the darkness. Agnes looked shaken as did Avia. Avia knew something strange was going on and that her little witch was battling from within, so she tried hard to play down the whole event, proclaiming that the poor old lady was not of sound mind, and she feared she had been drinking too much gin. She assured everyone was fine and the party moved on, although Avia noticed that know Miss Bonneville now walked with her and Agnes, probably to check they were fine and also because Cecilia now walked with a tall gentleman named George from Petworth. Avia broke the ice and, giggling, said to her walking companions that all those beautiful dresses may be of no use after all as she thought her sisters had already found their suiters. Miss Bonneville tutted at her comment, although she would no doubt have to agree as the two older Stourton girls were already, it seemed, in the company of two very wealthy, honourable and well-born friends. All were exhausted from the party, and each bid their farewells retiring demurely for the evening.

Agnes managed to talk quietly to Avia about the old hag; she felt nervous about the situation and said she did not understand why she felt the need to be cruel to the poor old thing. Avia had already conspired her own theory: she thought, a little like society, witches also had a hierarchy and she thought Agnes was probably right at the top just like royalty. Avia made her giggle by saying she was a princess of witches. Agnes warmly accepted the proposition with gratitude and seemed more settled. The next morning was bright, and Avia could not wait to leave the bustle of Bath, longing to be back in the gardens and peaceful fresh air. Her sisters, however, had managed to persuade Miss Bonneville to allow them to stay and socialise, under their great-aunt Eliza's guidance and, with strict rules and instructions, they were left behind. This meant a roomier carriage ride was taken back to the Hall, but Avia was worried as her little witch looked drained and perplexed. She had to somehow talk to her with Jack, but it would be impossible for the rest of the week as she would be so busy sewing endless hems and tucks. The small carriage party home all seemed lost in their own thoughts and the arrival back to Stourton Hall was swift. Agnes whispered to Avia as she got out from the carriage, for her to meet that afternoon before dark at the cottage. Somehow Avia had to find Jack, and quickly she made her excuses and ran.

Failing and Falling

~~ * ~~

Life had become very hard for Josina and Avoca after the battle and seizure of the fort; the death of their beloved queen hurt them more than they could bear, and they mourned her loss as well their own. Hardship had fallen on many. Josina and Avoca lived in a cave deep in the mountain and hidden by the forest, living off what they hunted and foraged. Times had become violent, so they had to protect themselves as they waited impatiently for the next Samhain, planning to return to Stourton Castle. Josina was thrown off by the years and moons and her precious book of time had been lost in their escape, so their visit would be a random year. Josina could remember enough, though, to hopefully land them where Agnes was buried in the cavern and Avoca hoped that the witch hunt for Avoca was a long-forgotten mission.

The wait seemed long for their special eve and they became jittery. Josina made several attempts to find her book and other belongings. Avoca did not need a book to keep her findings and knowledge; she found she had a gift, and everything she saw and learnt she was storing away in her mind. One day she would record her findings for little Agnes, but for now she would carry them safely in her head.

Avoca hated this time; she often smelt foul smoke and heard screams, which reminded her of her own loss even more. Danger was all around them and they would do well not to be caught. She begged Josina to give up on her book hunt in fear she would be captured but Josina had no fear and carried on her search, each time bringing back books and treasure. One day she bought back a book that Avoca recognised. It was large and had a special clasp. She had seen it as a child long ago - an old lady had held it standing near a fire, chanting its mystical words. Her ma had said this was her great-great-nana Razia and that the book would one day fall to her by fate. Avoca was amazed that the book had found its way to her; she remembered the old lady who stayed hidden in the corner of the palace quarters, old and too frail to move or speak, she had clung to a book. Avoca shook her head with her thoughts that it could have been her nana Razia. Avoca stroked the books cover as though she had known and treasured it for her whole life. The book was written in Sanskrit, a language that Avoca knew. Josina thankfully had no interest and was glad Avoca liked the strange book. Josina never realised the power that she handed her friend and Avoca also did not realise it at first, until she started to practise some of the spells, secretly Avoca kept the knowledge from Josina, knowing it was from a very powerful and ancient witch, her own flesh and blood, her gift. Avoca a last had more hope of her own survival and going back to the gentle valleys and finding Agnes.

One day, Josina and Avoca decided to find supplies in the village as they needed spices and produce for their spells that they could not forage for in the forest. They wrapped themselves up well and keeping their heads down walked around the little market, gathering what they needed - Josina had plenty of coins from her thieving. As they approached one small stall, Josina saw a little girl much like Agnes who sat on a stool reading as her mother sold spices and dried leaves. This was by chance just the stall the witches needed. Josina knew straight away that it was her book of time that the little girl studied, and she quickly plottedhow to trick it away from the girl without suspicion or a scene. Avoca also saw the book and girl and began nervously to choose their needed spices. The girl was absorbed by the book and ran her little fingers over the words and symbols. The market grew busier as people came from the mountains and soon the little stall was overrun. Avoca bought their goods and turned to see that both Josina and the girl were gone. At first Avoca panicked, worried that something had happened to Josina, but she then realised something had happened to the little girl.

Quickly Avoca disappeared into the crowd and was soon in the safety of the forest. She had not walked far when Josina appeared gloating from behind some trees, holding her treasured book. Avoca was pleased for her and enquired where the little girl was. She need not have asked for stood behind her, the poor thing stood shaking. Shocked, Avoca asked Josina what they were to do with the child as she would surely tell, and they would be captured. Josina agreed and they took the little girl with them to their cave. Her name was Preeti, and once she had stop crying she seemed intrigued and watched closely as the witches made potions or pastes. She ate well and slept well. Preeti was clever and knew not to cause trouble or her captors could turn on her; instead, she was sweet and helpful. The witches enjoyed her company and taught her skills in making potions. Preeti would read their books and was able to remember so much that she began to consider this her opportunity to escape the village and her arranged marriage with the horrid boy called Rahul; she hated him in every way imaginable as he was cruel, greedy and arrogant. Yet her father said he was a good match and that she would want for nothing more in life. So Preeti stayed concealed in the cave. More than once she had the chance to escape and heard voices of villagers, but she stayed hidden and even warned the witches when she heard village people. Avoca grew fond of the girl and would be sad to take her back to the village.

One evening Preeti heard them talking of going and how they would leave Preeti outside the village. Preeti immediately begged them not to take her back to the village and when she understood she could not go with them, she made them vow to take her to the fort, where she could peddle potions for her keep and that way she would be free. The witches agreed, and so the plan was put in place and on the night of Samhain, the witches prepared Preeti with everything she would need. They then packed themselves up and hid their cave. They took Preeti to the fort and watched the sweet, brave girl walk in through the huge doors before nightfall.

Preeti was amazed when she walked into the fortress. It was a hub of activity and she was enthralled from the moment she arrived and never noticed the flame of light outside the fortress walls. Preeti quickly found herself simple lodgings in a room above the stables and paid in advance for a year with her jewels from the witches. She hid her other jewels and books and cleaned her new abode, then set herself up lighting the small fire for cooking. By morning, Preeti had enough potions to sell and soon she was happily curing and caring for the poor of the fort. Word spread, and she was even summoned by the wealthy, becoming a popular healer, trusted by many. The fort was now a settled place under a different ruler and Preeti did not lack admirers; however, she did not wish to be tied down and saw another plan - the witches had not been as clever as they thought. During those months of captivity, Preeti had hidden well that she herself was born under a black moon and although the villagers called her cursed, Preeti called it a blessing and she knew from a small child that she was somehow different and by luck or by chance, that day the witches had shown her the way. Preeti now had a life of freedom forever; she was free from the clutches of a matchmaker, the nayan, her parent's traditions, and the boy she could not abide.

The Visit

~~ * ~~

Avia had not seen her father for months as he had been on an archaeology dig somewhere, and he was coming back less and less and sometimes failed to even see the girls. This time was different and he came back unannounced, much to Miss Bonneville's horror. He was pleased with the house, and complimented her on how wonderful everything was. He met the new staff including the seamstress, marvelling at her wonderful work, and then went to find his children. Lord Richard Hoare did not think they would miss him or notice him gone, so he breezily walked into their parlour as if it was a normal occurrence. The girls were shocked and were glad they had had guests earlier as they were all well dressed and turned out. Cecilia greeted him with joy followed by her sisters. Avia was a little unsure, as he had never been very receptive towards her. This time though, he looked as though a black cloud had lifted from his brows, and he listened to their account of the interesting visit to Bath. Cecilia told him of her fashionable invitations and Olivia of her friendship with Thomas and Edwina. Avia had little to say, so she went to get her drawing book and showed him her own sketches and told him about her garden. She was thrilled, as he said he would visit it the very next day. Later they all sat and had dinner together and he gave them each a velvet necklace with a pretty cameo for their parties; they all agreed it had been a perfect day. Earlier that day, Avia had sat with Jack on the stone bench by the cottage. She had shown him her book and he marvelled at the drawings and information, and Avia said he could look at the book whenever he wished to. Both Jack and Avia felt safer in the gardens now. Since their rushed meeting with Agnes after the trip to Bath, they had taken down all the strange charms and buried them, replacing them with crosses made from straw. Agnes had sprinkled a concoction she had made around the garden and cottage and mumbled a rhyme, while Jack and Avia had planted St John's Wart and Hellebore to keep evil out. They all agreed, though, that they should only be there in each other's company. Agnes was told Belle's story, and they knew it was only matter of time until the witches would return. After looking at the book, Jack and Avia tended to the garden and talked about Agnes. They wonder if she could stay and they worried for her, as they knew Agnes did not want to be captured by a witch and was happy as she was.

The following day was bright and Avia's father, as promised, was waiting for her in the hallway. They walked briskly to the gothic cottage while her father told her interesting historical facts about the garden, statues and temples. Avia listened with interest and was so excited to show her father her creation. When they arrived, Jack was there and Avia worried her father would be cross, but instead he greeted him in a very pleasant way. Jack politely introduced himself as Belle and Jeremiah's son from Stourton Farm. Avia's father had not realised he gardened for them and seemed pleased, saying how fond he was of Belle and how she had been Octavia's mother's dresser. He summed Jack up and said he thought one day he could become head gardener at Stourton. Jack smiled and said he would like that very much. Lord Richard then drew his attention to his daughter's creation and was clearly pleased by the clever planting and introduction of a small pond, fountain and a wonderful gazebo. He complimented her on her roses and topiary and loved how she had planted hellebores gently all around the garden, drifting into the woods. Jack and Avia smiled at each other pleased, and also thankful her father did not realise they did more than look pretty, they circled the garden and cottage with a spell to keep out witches or any other unwanted visitors. Lord Richard then chatted about the gardens of Stourton Hall and he looked at his daughter with great pride, saying she was like her great-grandfather Henry the Magnificent. Avia felt so pleased she felt she was flying and dared to hug her father in glee and from that day on something changed for Avia and her father, they had something to talk about, so whenever he was not too busy, he would walk with her and tell her all he knew about the wonderful history of the gardens and his plans and desires for the place. He invited Avia to help and was impressed with her drawings and ideas - Lord Richard began to see Avia as his new partner in such matters.

Avia and Jack met again later that day and were pleased to see Agnes join them with her new companion, Hestia the large cat. The three of them carried on fixing their circle, planting St John's Wort and the scattering of lodestones they had found in the cavern. They then sat making more straw crosses, and although they spent most of their time protecting the garden now, they still played and had fun. The summer months spun ahead giving them chance to explore and enjoy lovely long evenings together. Avia could hardly believe that soon it would be a whole year since she had found her two best friends in the garden, Jack and Agnes. Agnes did so well in her work and her dresses had been the talk of the season that she had had to refuse some work requests, as even with a little magic she could not convincingly make too many without suspicion. Avia wished the summer could last forever; it felt so perfect with everything in place and she felt as though she did not have a care in the world. Yet around the corner, autumn would soon knock on their doors; something brewed in the stars and the moon had an eerie orange glow. Sorcery had begun and nothing could stop the future and forces that would collide and threaten Avia's summer of content.

Chitrakut Fort on Samhain: 1304

~~ * ~~

Avoca and Josina had watched Preeti disappear through the gates of the fort to what they considered hell - for Preeti, though, they knew it was safe. The witches now had their own job to do and although Avoca would miss Preeti, she had her own daughter to find.

They had decided to try and land in Stourton woods a hundred years on from in 1408. This was the first time they had come back, since leaving little Agnes and they saw great changes: a lot of woodland had disappeared, and acres of sheep grazed in its place. Josina and Avoca stayed at the cottage in 1508 for a whole year searching for Agnes; the land must have shifted though as something had changed and Agnes and her cavern could not be found. For some reason it stayed hidden, although the yew tree still stood there holding its deep secret. The two witches months at Stourton wood were mischievous; they made it their home and no one seemed to notice them. They thieved and caused jiggery-pokery wherever they went. Instead of peddling and becoming known for their potions, like ghosts in the night they would trick, steal and vanish. If they found a young girl wandering in their domain, they would keep her until they had finished teaching the child great skills considering that they did each one a great favour; some would return home when they were gone, others though would ask for freedom like Preeti and tragically a couple would die from a spell or potion that went terribly wrong, this was something that Avoca could not understand and she would partly blame herself and would worry deep down of Josina's part. Josina told Avoca that their hearts were already weak and that their time had come to pass on; whatever path they had chosen to take. Josina, however, also knew they would tell the village and castle of their existence, so with a pleasant-tasting cinnamon poison she let them go to a peaceful place.

In the year 1794, when the witches returned yet again, being tired of the world and wishing to rest at Stourton woods, yet more had changed. The castle was gone and grand stately home stood in its place, now lakes, lawns and temples adorned the gentle land where woodland had once been. Thankfully, most of the ancient woods still covered the valley surrounding the gardens and the old stone hovel was still well hidden. The witches had arrived early that evening, they settled in to the hovel planning a quiet All Hallows Eve with no guests. They had met Parnell, Wilmot and Lettice in another time at the chateau in France, holding meetings with a warlock. So Josina and Avoca planned a quiet night for witches on Samhain Eve. The earth was colder than they had ever known on that night and the frost played tricks in the woods. The glistening frost led a girl of high birth with an elegant face called Belle far off her path; it drew her in whispers to the cottage door and fearfully, as if in a trance, she knocked on their door. Josina knew immediately that she was of no use to them. She was from the grand hall where the castle once stood, and she walked from the land that was sculptured as if in a painting. Josina looked the pretty girl up and down and thought of Fabian her friend the warlock. He had lost his good housekeeper and castle so this girl of high birth would make him a lovely gift. The girl was dangerous though, so Josina gave her the poison while deciding what to do. They walked her to a path where no one would find her for days and then they would be gone. Josina thought to take her to the master warlock as a pawn that may win her some favour. Avoca, ignorant of her friends plans, just thought the girl was sleepy and that she would just wake up a little in the cold. Had it not been for the boy with the whistling tune and a little panic, Belle would have been lost forever to the warlock. For Belle was twice lucky; the witch Josina in her haste had made a mistake and added more parsley instead of more hemlock. The girl was poorly and nearly dead, and had the boy not come a long she would have been gone. Josina quickly left her frail body and she and Avoca ran back to the cottage; they vanished before they saw Belle being saved.

Back to Stourton by the Stones: 1810

~~*~~

After that evening in 1794, the witches had not been back to Stourton, worried they were becoming too well known; through the century's stories had gathered about the witches in the woods. Josina said this was their last chance to find Agnes, but she had to land them in the right year and she had practised until she had perfected her spell. Avoca had a very strong feeling that something bad had happened to Agnes and she needed their help, so although hesitant to return, as they had had so many failed attempts, she agreed as she always did with her friend Josina.

As they lit their small bright fire on the Samhain night and prepared to travel, they knew they would not be alone in the skies - others gathered to join them; they could see it in the stars. Something else was happening as well, something that Avoca was not sure about. The moon turned to red and the skies orange, and a warm wind blew in spirits from afar. Josina seemed nervous and unlike herself, as though she prepared for something unknown. Avoca felt worried and thought perhaps they could stay another year. The cave wasn't so bad and she could visit Preeti. Josina held her firm though and whispered the words; the fire and winds grew, and the time had come.

Josina and Avoca landed in a rather ungainly fashion, thankfully alone. They knew for certain they had been thrown off course by something and instead of the sweet oak woods of Stourton, they found themselves on a grassland plain that stretch for miles. Its gradient went up and down like a blanket blowing in the wind and in the distance they could see several fires in a ring and the flash of lights as others arrived like them. The harsh wind buffeted them as they walked, frustrated and fed up. Josina broke all the rules and with Avoca's hand in a tight grip she produced the feather of a buzzard and uttered a spell and with speed they flew, cutting through the crisp night air and landing not far from a strange spectacle. Josina knew she was at the place of sacrifices where a ring of sacred stones stood. The huge historic stones were very ancient, composed of sarsen and bluestone. The place had been used through the ages for burials and other ceremonies and for years witches had gathered here to celebrate Samhain Eve. It was told that with the sun and the moon you could read the future from the stones. Avoca had never heard of this place before and although this was not their plan, she saw no harm in following Josina and having a little look at their fellow witches celebrate the evening. As they came closer, she realised this was no normal gathering and began to think it was a mistake; she hung back and watched from afar hidden by the shadows. Josina then saw Parnell and Wilmot - surely they had not been knocked off course too. Cautiously they edged towards the Stones, gently calling their friends. Wilmot immediately turned and soon they were huddled together, greeting each other, each one as bemused as the other as to why they had landed here and not Stourton woods. They wondered where poor Lettice had landed, as she had not turned up, so they decided to make their way by flight to the woods; maybe Lettice had made it. Eventually they found the woods and walked towards the cottage and were soon intercepted by a cross Lettice asking where they had been, complaining that her perfect stew was drying out. They followed her, not to the cottage, but to an old wooden shed they presumed abandoned by a woodcutter by the amount of sawdust, axes and saws strewn around. Lettice bid them sit by the fire and she served her stew as if they were sat around a grand dining table.

After eating, Lettice began her tale. Lettice related that she had got in a muddle and arrived the year before and only realised her mistake when it was too late to travel back, so she had stayed in the woods. The cottage though was not safe, as a garden had been made and a girl and a boy were always there. Then she held Avoca's hand and told her that somehow Agnes had got out of her wooden chest and the cavern and walked the earth. The witches gasped. How could this be? And Lettice told all that she knew from her eavesdropping and spying. The witches did not understand quite how Agnes had been able to get out alone - had another witch broken the spell? Whatever had happened, Avoca needed to see Agnes and take her far away. Josina reminded her she would still be far too young to go through the port holes, but Avoca said they could travel abroad. Lettice thought Agnes had been taken as a serf to work in the Hall and she said everything looked different - a lot had changed. She thought she could get to Agnes through the girl who was always in the garden, though Lettice said of late she had never been alone and was always with a boy. Then she told them about the charms in the tree, of the planting circle and the stones. Josina was clever and quick. She knew Agnes had done this and she feared Avoca would become suspicious, so kept it to herself. Four hundred years was a long time to leave someone under the ground and although she would be the same age, Josina knew it was just too long and that likely Agnes would think the first people she met as her family; Agnes was no longer theirs to take. Josina, however, would go along with Avoca. She feared that Avoca would see their plan. It was no mistake that the witches and warlocks from far and wide gathered at the strange circle of Stones - this year was the year of the 'greatest plan'.

Belle and the Cauldron

~~ * ~~

Belle felt very twitchy on All Hallows Eves, but on this particular one she felt even more nervous than ever; there was a strange orange glow to the moon, faint, eerie howls could be heard and a stale smell stifled the normal fresh air. Stourton Hall was having a bonfire party and all had been invited. Belle looked forward to seeing her friends and with Jeremiah, Bertie and Jack by her side she should have felt no fear, but as they walked through the woods a cruel wind blew from the east carrying upon it a sinister secret, and still that strange pungent smell. Belle could not quite put her mind to it and as they walked deeper into the wood, the smell grew stronger and even the men commented on its strange aroma. They saw a trickle of smoke through the trees, and Jeremiah said he would investigate as he knew that since old Mac's death no one had lived in the woodcutter's shack. Belle felt uncertain and begged they carry on, claiming it would be rude to be late. Jeremiah though insisted, protesting that an unguarded fire could be dangerous. Reluctantly Belle followed but as they approached the shack she instantly recognised the aroma and saw above the little fire where a cauldron was hung. No one was there, but Bella knew that the witches were back. Jeremiah puzzled, put out the fire and tipped the cauldron out, closing up the shack.

He would send the gamekeeper Otto and some men out the
following day.

Jeremiah turned and saw his distraught wife and suddenly
knew; he remembered himself that night so long ago, the
strange feeling of fear and the ghastly smoky smell in the
woods just before he found Belle lying there near to death,
and now all those years on, that same smell and awful sense
of fear drifted on the branches and crumbling leaves. He
held Belle and bid the boys to make haste - they would try to
pick up the lane and stay at the Hall that night. Belle felt
such panic and walked as fast as she could manage; the
witches were back she knew it and she knew they came for
Agnes - she had to reach Avia and Agnes as fast as possible.
The wooded paths seemed to take forever, and the darkness
grew as roots and stones tripped them up and branches
lashed in their way. Jeremiah had them all link arms to keep
each one safe - they had to get out of the woods as fast as
they could. Never had Belle been so relieved to make it to
the Hall. They scampered up the gravel drive and joined the
others who gathered in the stable yard protected by its
walls. At last they felt they could breathe. Bertie asked what
was going on, but he was cut short by Belle who told Jack to
get Avia and fast.

Avia and Agnes were safely all wrapped up warm in the Hall. They stood in the library with its huge windows and from there they could see the fire and watch everyone having fun. Cecilia and Olivia were staying at Dyrham Park with Edwina, Thomas's sister; they were attending a lavish party. Avia had asked permission to watch the bonfire with Agnes and it was agreed that as the east wind was so biting, they could watch from inside the Hall; Miss Bonneville didn't want the cold air or smoke on Avia's chest. Jack arrived at the Hall and asked if he could relay a message to Miss Octavia from his ma Belle of a personal nature; trusted by the butler Arthur, he was escorted to the library. Avia and Agnes could not quite believe it when they saw Jack and excitedly chatted and offered him little cakes and cordial they had been given for the occasion. Jack stood with them looking over the lawns and the bonfire that burnt away from any buildings. He saw all the villagers and Hall staff gather with jugs of ale or spirits - music was played and some danced with joy.

Jack was so relieved to see them safely inside and once the main glow of the fire had died, he told them of their findings in the woods and how Belle and Jeremiah had reacted. He told them of the fire and the cauldron and the strange smell and whispered to them both that Ma Belle had mumbled behind their back: 'the witches are back'. Agnes knew they were here herself - she had felt their presence; she could almost see them so powerful were her thoughts. Several times over the last few months she had sworn she had seen someone in the woods and seen small fires. One day she had followed a young fallow deer so amazed by its pretty markings and sweetness. Her path had taken her deep into the woods and she had seen the image of someone she once knew. Agnes had hidden quickly flying up a tree and watched the person as she passed from above; there was no mistaking that it was Lettice and that meant the others would follow. Agnes remembered how she used to like and giggle at Lettice with her funny ways and many dresses, but now she felt nothing but contempt and fear. Agnes did not follow and had fled back to the safety of the Hall. When Agnes heard Belle's story and remembered her own life before, she felt so much anger. She listened carefully to Jack while she stood in the amazing library near her dearest friend, and she began to feel cross - she hadn't decided the best way to react if her so-called mother ever came back. Agnes asked Avia if they could speak with Belle. By this time Jeremiah had put out word that there was trouble in the woods. He did not use the word witches, but enough fear was stirred to warn folk to stay clear and that night they would all stay above the stables and in the barns. When Jack came and asked Belle to join them in the library she was grateful to get out of the cold, and after telling her husband, she went with Jack. Arthur greeted her with kindness and with the lord of the Hall elsewhere and the sisters away he saw no harm and arranged for warm wine to be sent for Belle with bread and cheese. The four of them sat in the library watching the fire as it lit up again and each told their account of what they had seen and of what they each thought. All decided they would sleep on their thoughts and Belle was invited to stay in the house near Avia, although she felt awful as she sent poor Jack to the stables and the cold. Avia walked through the Hall's long rooms with Jack, while Agnes and Belle went to the servants' quarters, Avia wanted to know Jacks thoughts. She was quite shocked and surprisingly pleased by his answer. Firstly he thought Agnes should meet her mother and send her away, he thought her strong enough and thought she hid her witch side well, and that she should stay at the Hall. Jack also said he would not like Avia anywhere near the woods or cottage and he made her promise to stay in the Hall and then he said words that she did not expect from someone so young. He said he cared for her and wanted her safe and didn't know what he would do if something happened to her - he was scared the witches might want to take her, as they had taken others before. Jack stood with a tear in his eye and said goodnight to Miss Avia.

Avia ran to her room as soon as he had gone. She was a bag of nerves and could never sleep with witches running wild in the woods, having Belle here to stay, thinking of Agnes and her dilemma, and herself brimming over with happiness that Jack cared for her. Avia was the most terrified and most gratified anyone could be and checked she had her moonstone necklace and bracelet firmly on. She found her poetry book that she had been given by her father that had come all the way from India; the poems were said to be ancient from Indian folklore and were translated to English with pretty flower drawings. She read her favourite poems and recited the one she always sang when gardening or when trying to calm her nerves.

The rivers flow flowers up to the moon, and trees like dancers glow with blossom in full bloom, mango fruits sweet and perfumed are sent to the skies, birds and bees sing songs of joyous times, with the wolves delighted everlasting howls The magical swans and peaceful turtle dove, are trusted to carry a forever secret of lasting love, So set free the little caged bird deep in the ground let it flutter and fly around, Sing the tune of joy little bird for freedom you can once again cry.

A Trick of a Witch

~~ * ~~

Before Agnes went to bed that night, she asked Miss Bonneville to make doubly sure that all the servants kept their windows and doors locked. Gossip and suspicious talk of strange happenings in the woods of Stourton had already reached everyone though and everyone locked their rooms. Agnes could not sleep and went to see Avia. She crept along the corridors in the dark afraid to light a candle as she did not want to be seen and as she approached Avia's room she heard her singing a poem, the poem that she sang when she was gardening and the poem that she had sung on the day Agnes was set free. When she entered the room, she saw the moonstone around Avia's neck and a memory flashed back to her - suddenly everything made sense. Agnes sat with Avia and spoke to her. The poem was ancient and although her mother had spoken it in another language, it was the poem that had set her free. Agnes declared Avia had, by some miracle performed a spell and she had been able to set Agnes free. She then asked her about the moonstone necklace again and Avia said she had found it. Agnes had already confirmed before that it was not hers, she had never seen it before. They thought of all the treasures they had found in the cavern, now hidden in the cottage, and decided it had probably been stolen by the witches.

The moonstone glittered and glowed as if it knew it was
been talked about. Agnes eyed it suspiciously and asked if
she could look at it, promising she would give it back. Avia
reluctantly agreed and Agnes studied the necklace. She
found engravings of tiny symbols on the back and from the
memory of her mother's teachings, she knew that they
meant it was a protection stone, and although Agnes did not
know what from, she felt certain it would be from witches.
Agnes said in the morning she was going to find the witches
and speak to her mother and ask them kindly to go away.
Avia was worried - she didn't think it was safe. What if they
took her? No one would be able to rescue her. Agnes sat on
Avia's bed as they wondered what to, and finally, both exhausted, they drifted off to sleep. Agnes dreamt of witches
flying over the Hall and sweeping down trying to find a way
in; she could see them clearly and heard them call out her
name - Agnes continued her fretful sleep and tormented
dreams. Outside the Hall, the witches had gathered while
everyone slept; they prowled around and at last they found
her - the little witch. First they tried to get through the windows with no joy. Then they saw the huge smokeless chimney pots some with broken tops and it was not long before
they were in, dusted in old soot and birds' nests. Lettice
stayed behind, afraid her physique would not quite fit the
narrow chimney descent. Once in the huge library they

knew which way to turn and soon they were outside the room of the sleeping girls, and quietly they crept in. Avoca saw her little Agnes lying there holding the other girl's hand, both of them so sweet and delicate. Agnes shone and looked so neat, unlike the Agnes she had left. The sleeping girls held hands and the witches gently reached for Agnes to carry her away but were thrown by some power straight across the room The thud of their witch bodies woke the sleeping girls who screamed and clung to each other. Hestia pounced out from nowhere hissing and growling at the witches. Shocked to see the ferrel cat back from stone, the witches were a little stunned, then Josina saw the sacred moonstone. The witches started tutting and cursing. Their plan- so simple - had started to go wrong. Agnes, realising the gemstone had worked, decided to take this strange and terrifying opportunity to have a little word. She recognised her mother and stared at her with hate and asked how could she have left her for four hundred years, in a chest underground, asleep. Avoca tried hard to explain, but Agnes said bitterly she would never go with them - her home was here in the Hall. Avoca was very shocked and felt terribly sad. Josina though was angry and started to make a spell. Agnes did not know how, but she began to make one as well. And while Avoca tried to unravel the muddle, Josina and Avoca were locked in a battle of mind spells.

Avoca started saying it was fine, they would just leave, but hoped she could just see Agnes before she went away. However, the other witches, unknown to Avoca, had a sinister plan to catch the young witch, born of a witch and warlock, and take her to the sacred Stones, where she would be a sacrificed for a far greater cause, giving all the witches more power and immortality. Avoca, reading Josina's mind, suddenly realised that she planned a ritual of horror. Desperate to save Agnes and the other girl, she had to come up with something quickly. She thought of her little Agnes and the sweet tricks she had played. From the spells she had learnt, her favourite was always to disappear from sight. Praying that Agnes would remember the vanishing spell, Avoca prompted her with the rhyme, Agnes knew straight away what Avoca meant for her to do, Agnes completed the rhyme, the spell was fixed and Agnes vanished into thin air. The witches sniffed and prodded, then Josina screamed that they would take the other girl and deceive the other witches and warlocks to whom they had promised to bring the special child. Agnes groaned inwardly as she realised she still held the moonstone pendant, meaning Avia had no protection. Avoca begged Josina to let her go; Josina cackled with the others - Avoca was a fool. They had no choice; a pact had been made and the moon and stars were aligned. This Eve would not happen for another thousand years and this child would do the trick; the other witches would never know until they died. Avoca sobbed and realised they had planned this all along; she felt so cross and foolish. Josina her friend had been up to chicanery for years. Everything Josina had done; was so that Avoca would have a little witch as a daughter, for the sole purpose of a special sacrifice. All her secret trips and strange meetings now made perfect sense. Agnes may have disappeared, but she heard every word and she listened with horror to the plan that had been made. Agnes fought back tears as she realised why she had been created and what they wanted her for and then she started to feel a rage inside her. They would not take Avia. She would rather die herself. Agnes heard her mother Avoca's useless plea to leave. Josina, Wilmot and Parnell had no intentions of listening to anyone though, they had planned this for hundreds of years and Avoca had fallen into every trap and plan they had made. It was no coincidence her father had sold her all those years ago, or that she had a child with the alchemist warlock, or that she had been hunted so she would have to leave Agnes. They needed Agnes to be ten years old on the Samhain Eve of 1810. Poor Avoca had had no clue. She thought of her life and how since meeting Josina, Josina had controlled so much and taken her to so many places and left her when it suited her. She recalled how she had helped her kill the alchemist - all the time everything was leading to this date. Agnes her sweet little witch, born on All Hallows Eve, was to be a sacrifice but she could not bear for either girl to die and she knew clever Josina would try to take them both if she could. Avoca had to think quickly - she had so many powers she had hidden from Josina over the years, and she had read and learnt so much. As Agnes reappeared, quickly grabbing hold of Avia so she still had protection from the moonstone, Josina made a final attempt to grab Agnes, and Avoca cast her spell.

Away in a Manger

~~ * ~~

Jack, his brother and his pa had an uncomfortable night lying in the wooden feeding mangers for the horses. Each time they moved, they shuddered with cold and winced with an ache, but they thought of what was out in the woods and settled back down, feeling safe in the courtyard of the stable, with the dogs, the gamekeeper and his gun about. A lot of the villagers had stayed, not wanting to risk the walk, so they could hear the whispers of those who chose to keep sleep from their heads. Jack kept waking. He had an overwhelming sense that something was very wrong but each time he would then fade back into a disturbed sleep. In his dreams he saw Miss Avia. He saw her floating in a manger on the lake, the cold waters surrounding her - she was still and pale. Jack woke with a shudder and, terrified that his dream was true, he ran from the stable barn towards the lake. The moon lit his way and although scared, he had to see if she was there. He gazed over the lake and could see no trace, but as he looked over towards where the cottage lay, he saw a flicker of light and with all his haste he ran stumbling towards the cottage, and as he ran, he screamed for help in hope someone would hear his cries. Jack never understood how he knew that Avia had been taken from her bed and as he ran towards the gothic cottage, he saw her lying, so still as if she was in his dream by a small fire that flickered suspiciously with no sticks. The ground was icy and with no hesitation he threw his jacket over her and lifted her from the ground and ran. From the corner of his eye he saw the witches. His mind flickered to Agnes, and he wondered if he should he have stayed and looked for her, but Jack carried on running - others could come back and search for Agnes, she had more chance of survival. Avia was cold and hardly breathed as he ran to the top path. A group of men came towards him, his pa and brother among them and he asked them to go to the cottage to look for Agnes, then Jack kept running. He banged loudly on the kitchen doors to the great Hall; Miss Bonneville was there in seconds as if she had waited for his knock. They quickly got Avia to the kitchen, where the range chugged the nights and days away keeping the kitchen warm, and they popped her in the cook's cosy chair, covering her with blankets, Miss Bonneville tried to wake her as gently as she could and slowly Miss Avia came around. Sobbing she asked for Agnes. Miss Bonneville and Jack comforted her, and she was given warm herb-flavoured milk with honey. Jack held her cold hands and asked if she knew where they had gone, but Avia sobbed that she had no clue. She said there was nothing they could do and mumbled about a plan about how they were going to take her little Agnes away. Avia was terrified and with her sister's and father away, and Nanny Maud ill in bed with a fever, she was kept with the servants. Belle came down to comfort her too and they all sat huddled in the warm kitchen, waiting for the dawn to come and praying for Agnes - nothing else could be done.

Still As A Stone

~~ * ~~

Avoca's spell had worked and within seconds Agnes, Avia and Avoca were by the cottage only Avia lay in shock as if she was dead. Agnes screamed to see her friend look so ill and Avoca quickly gave her a warming potion and lit a fire with spells. Avoca pleaded with Agnes that they had no time - Josina and the others would be with them in no time, and she was not strong enough to fight off all of them at once. All those days from being in the cave with Preeti had paid off that night, for when Josina went about her dealings, Avoca, like Preeti, learnt everything she could. She had read Josina's precious book of time and she understood how to use it. One time and place she had memorised was the cave near the fort. Avoca knew she had to get back to Preeti to warn her as well as to save her precious Agnes, because she now knew from her vision that both were in danger and that Preeti would have no warning. Poor Agnes did not want to go, and she cried to let her stay. She understood though that the witches would not let her go and their plan was not a good one. Agnes quickly put the moonstone around Avia's neck, she kissed her on the forehead and whispered she would be back, then Agnes and Avoca were gone - all they left was a sprinkle of glitter in the sky.

Josina and the others arrived at the cottage. They flew
around looking for Agnes and Avoca and screeched with
frustration, so annoyed by their escape. The witches saw the
girl lying there still as a stone; by Avoca's fire - they just had
to remove the moonstone from around her neck and she
was theirs. Hestia prowled around, scratching at the witches,
but each time they shoved her away. Lettice got a little stick,
knowing the necklace would burn her hands. She stood at a
distance and with magic she threaded it through the moonstone chain and was about to yank it, when she was interrupted by a boy who appeared from nowhere who grabbed
the girl so quickly and ran. The witches heard other voices
and lights and dogs barking. Both the girl and Agnes were
gone and now a witch hunt had begun; the sheriff had been
called and a search was on. The witches were defeated, and
Josina knew she had lost. She could not return to the Stones,
and she had less strength these days - she had needed the
power of the sacrifice. Then Josina, like lightning, suddenly
had a thought and with the other witches they took a quick
trip to another land - just one last chance to solve their dilemma. The hours of the night were passing fast but if quick,
they would just make it back in time.

Quick Sticks, Turn Around

~~ * ~~

Avoca and Agnes landed outside the Fort of Chitrakut from where Avoca and Josina had left. Avoca knew that Agnes was exhausted and confused, but she had to follow quickly; they had to find Preeti if they were to ever get back to the Hall. Agnes obeyed. realising it was her only hope. They easily got into the fort through an old damp tunnel without anyone seeing them and they quickly looked for Preeti; Avoca prayed she was not far. The streets bustled with wonderful colours and aromas of the bazaar, then Avoca saw her, and it was just as she had imagined. Preeti had a small stall and was selling her potions, just as Avoca had done with Agnes once. Preeti was shocked to see Avoca back so soon and she saw the distressed little Agnes and gave her a tonic. Preeti knew who she was straight away as Avoca had told her she had a daughter that she had to find. Avoca did not waste time; she told her quietly of Josina's plan and asked how they could protect Agnes.

Preeti quickly packed away her stall and led them back to her rooms where she lit a fire asking Avoca how she thought she could help. Avoca said she knew she was a witch herself - she had seen it when they were in the caves and knew she had powers that were much stronger than hers and her daughter's. Avoca told her she that had worked out that Preeti was born under a black moon. Preeti smiled and agreed she had grown stronger and more powerful and with each day she learnt more. Avoca told Preeti she thought Josina and her coven planned to take Preeti instead - she was a perfect fit for Josina and her wicked plan. Preeti acted quickly. She didn't need any second warnings, and had known from the start that Josina was bad and not kind like Avoca. Preeti's possessed lots of pretty charm stones that she sold, and each had different meaning. She took three black shiny stones with white dots, and put each little stone into the fire with powder. She then carefully took them out and welded chains around the stones and placed a bracelet on each of their wrist as she performed another spell. Agnes could feel the heat burn her wrist and Preeti comforted her saying the pain would pass quickly but that the burn would stay deep in her skin. The stone of Obsidian would always protect her from any spiritual force. The bracelet was impossible to remove unless by magic, and she would most certainly be safe now from witches and warlocks. Avoca spoke to Agnes and told her what they had to do and that they only had a little time left. Preeti gifted Agnes another charm on a pendant for her friend Avia. She said the little rose quartz would help Avia heal and give her love and protection.

The three witches, with capes pulled around them, walked back through the tunnel and out onto the hill. Avoca had written a note and wrapped Agnes's birthstone in it. She gave both to Agnes and said she loved her with all her heart, but they could not live as Agnes wished together, but said that one day when it was safe she would visit again, and if she ever needed her then she would be here with Preeti. Avoca told Agnes exactly what to say and gave her the potions to throw to the skies and with only a couple of minutes left she was gone, then Preeti and Avoca did the same ritual and disappeared as Josina, Wilmot, Parnell and Lettice all arrived at the fort.

Josina knew exactly where Preeti lived and where she held her little stall, so they would be able to find Preeti with complete ease and the sweet-natured child would have no clue, so trusting and obedient, unlike Agnes. They ignored the stares and comments and not seeing her stall ran straight to her lodgings, only to find that Preeti was gone. Josina screeched again to hurry - they had no time and as huge shadows grew over the moon and the wind blew dust from the sands, Josina and her coven realised their fate, the hour had past and they were stuck here in the fort with onlookers and guards. Each witch held their defence and with magical force stopped themselves being arrested - but the word Dayan could be heard. They began their escape and all but poor

Lettice made it out; she was too slow and her cries could still be heard. Josina though, had no thought of a rescue mission tonight. She was now the hunted instead of the hunter and with a weakness setting in and others in the witch world after her, she needed to lay low. She would not hang around to see Lettice's fate. Josina felt cross and cared for no one but herself, so she ran and intended to disappear off the face of the sorry earth; everything was ruined and she felt vengeful towards that annoying little witch Agnes and to Avoca who had turned against her - to hunt them though, she had no strength. Wilmot and Parnell were also fuming, as they had wanted to go home to their lovely lakeside home and now they were stuck in this hot, unknown land for a year with dwindling health. They parted company from Josina on bad terms after so many years of alliance, conspiring and planning; everything now seemed a waste of time. They had lost immortality and power beyond even their belief and the ancient scriptures that Fabian the Warlock had read, clearly claimed that these amazing prodigies could only take place every thousand years. Although witches could live for a very long time, they knew their time on earth was not for ever as they would have wished.

Equinox

~~ * ~~

Preeti and Avoca landed with a bump outside the walls of the fort. They both felt a little dizzy and Avoca was now very weary and felt sad and empty inside. Preeti was sad for her friend, but she was also glad of her friendship and of her warning. However, Avoca knew that the witches would be here somewhere and she knew they were now too late for the sacrifices at the stones, so with thousands of years to wait until the next perfect date, Preeti and Agnes would no longer be their victims. Preeti was also now very powerful so they would not dare try to take her and challenge Avoca. Agnes had gifted her mother a present that would give her more strength and life, a simple kiss - a spell to show her love.

Preeti and Avoca returned to the Preeti's home and Preeti made up a bed for Avoca and gave her food and drink; they then slept deeply with no fear. When Avoca woke late the next morning to the sound of prayers, for the first time in her life she felt free and although sad to lose Agnes, she knew she would find contentment here within the fort's walls and have a good life. She would make her life here with Preeti. She ate the flat bread and olives left for her and drank the warm goat's milk, then she washed and changed into

some of Preeti's clothes and went out into the dazzling sunshine and to the bazaar where she found Preeti, who admired her outfit with laughter. Avoca became her wise assistant and to others, they said she was Preeti's mother, who
was recently widowed. Avoca and Preeti were soon able to
move into a pretty stone house within the walls of the fort,
with a roof garden and lots of room; Preeti and Avoca felt a
sense of peace.

One day, not long after they had moved to the new home,
they heard lots of noise and jeering coming from gathering
crowds. With curiosity they walked to the forts centre and
the huge courtyard, and raised on four stakes they saw to
their horror, Josina, Parnell, Wilmot and Lettice in a sorry
state. How they had been hunted down Avoca could not
think, but she and Preeti disappeared from view, they did
not want to see what happened. Avoca half thought to rescue them, but she could not risk Preeti's life or her own and
why would she save the witches who had ruined her life and
nearly killed her own daughter and her best friend. Avoca
would not watch, and although she did not like it, justice
had to be served for the tricks and murders the coven had
played on their way through the centuries. Avoca could still
not understand how they had been caught as all were so
such clever and powerful witches. Avoca couldn't help thinking it was perhaps punishment dealt by the witches and war-

locks who had gathered on that All Hallows Eve at the Stones for the sacrifice that never happened; she was relieved that they had not seen herself or Agnes and that she had stayed hidden from view. They might have her name though, so she decided to call herself Petra for a while. Both she and Preeti would have to be careful. They set themselves up as alchemists hiding any sign of spells. The next day she heard something very strange had happened. Apparently the witches had just vanished into thin air. Avoca looked as shocked and aghast as everyone else, but later she looked at the dates. It was the first equinox of the year and not an uncommon time for a desperate witch to travel on such a day; it certainly came with risks of landing in a completely wrong time and place, but they had had no choice. Avoca felt uneasy that they were still present somewhere in the world. Preeti reassured her that they were all safe now, but said she doubted Josina and the others were safe - now hunted and on the run.

Back With a Bump

~~ * ~~

Agnes landed back at the gothic cottage with a huge bump and crashed into her old friend the yew tree and fell to the ground. Avia was gone and at this moment in time she did not know if this was a good or bad thing. The night was bitterly cold and the skies were clear. She sat for a few moments trying to digest all that had happened, then started panic: What if they had managed to take Avia? She did not know which way to turn and was about to take flight to travel to the Stones, thinking that maybe she could save Avia from the sacrifice and praying it wasn't too late, but she fell down, dizzy from her catapult through time. This was a lucky fall, as the last place Agnes needed to be near was the ancient Stones and had she taken flight, she would have instantly been spotted as witches flew searching the skies for their lost coven of witches and the child sacrifice.

Agnes, still reeling, looked to the sky and saw shadows of many witches flickering through the trees, so she quickly hid in the cover of the yew tree and in her mind she whispered many protection spells over and over again. Hestia appeared, purring and rubbing her head against Agnes's arm, appreciating her return. Agnes fussed her, comforted by her presence, but still petrified as she didn't know Josina and the others were far away, so she just kept repeating her chants and clinging to the charm that Preeti had gifted her. Agnes could still feel the soreness of the burn and she felt a strong reassurance that the bracelet stone was keeping her safe. Then she heard shouting and dogs barking and she knew they had come looking for her. She saw Jeremiah, Jack's pa, and ran to his arms and quickly she was whisked with no words to the safety of the Hall. Agnes carefully pulled her sleeves over her burning wrist and bracelet and decided like Belle once before, she would tell nothing of her night and journey to the fort; only with Avia would she share her story, when they were safe. Agnes joined Avia and Jack in the kitchen and Miss Bonneville squealed with joy when she saw Agnes and settled her down in the warmth and huddle of the kitchen. Folk were kind and did not ask questions - they were just glad that both girls were safe and seemingly unharmed. Agnes knew the questions would come, but for now she closed her eyes, so thankful that Avia was home and with Jack, she was back in her beloved Hall with her dressmaking and Miss Bonneville and Belle. She thought of her mother, Avoca, and was glad she could still feel love for her and feel no anger, but she was sad they could never be together; their worlds had grown apart through time, fate, magic and a lot of witch trickery.

A Family Occasion: 1811

~~ * ~~

Agnes and Avia often talked about their night of terror, but they did not share what they knew with anyone else, and Avia even held back on telling Jack some parts of it. Agnes's journey to the Fort of Chitrakut was too much for many to believe along with her burning bracelet and Preeti. Avia was completely intrigued and wished she could meet Preeti one day, she sounded wonderful. Agnes teased that maybe one day she would take Avia there on All Hallows Eve and they hoped this could happen. Both girls recovered well and people stopped asking about their ordeal. Avia's father of course would be furious and hunts were sent out regularly for any who matched Agnes and Avia's poor descriptions of their kidnappers. The story would travel, and England became very unsafe for any witch, although they would not have witch hunts and trials like there used to be, but other excuses would be used to persecute anyone who held anything that slightly resembled pagan beliefs or witchcraft.

The seasons passed quickly, and Agnes experienced a Christmas like no other. Embraced by Avia's family, she spent the day as a lady of gentry and was treated to a feast unimaginable for a poor witch who came from 1408. The cold winter brought ice skating on the lake with furs and cloaks. Agnes took pity on the ice boy called Rudy who had a hard life stacking cut ice from the lake in a huge bowl of stone and straw in the icehouse; she would often take him extra food and made him promise on his mother's life not to breath a word. She would tell him to have a little nap in the warm furs she brought and then Agnes would set to work and with magic, all the ice would be neatly stacked, giving little Rudy days to play and explore. Agnes kept her magic mainly to herself though. Her dresses were often made in magical ways. Her work was so outstanding that she became the most sought-after seamstress in the land. Agnes never took for granted the plentiful food, the warm room and a bed; she had heard servants in other stately households were not so well looked after, with freezing rooms, little food and a meagre wage. Stourton though was a special place.

Agnes often saw Jack and Avia - they seemed always to be together in the garden. Avia and Agnes would often have secret sleep overs in Avia's roomy chamber, and they would chatter the night away. One such night, Avia told Agnes exciting news: her sister Cecilia was to marry George and there was to be the grandest of weddings for years to come at Stourton Hall. Agnes was very excited, knowing full well she would be the lucky seamstress to design and make the special bridal gown. Avia and Agnes agreed they did not want to marry, although Avia sighed as she said it and she told Agnes her secret, that she would marry Jack but knew they would never be allowed to as he was low born and she aristocracy and never the twain should meet. Agnes felt sad for them. She saw how dear they were to each other and Agnes without a word muddled this over in her mind - she was a witch, so surely she could do something to help her dearest friends. The months leading up to the wedding were full of excitement. There were parties for the engagement, parties for the families of the bride and groom to be and for the friends and acquaintances. The Hall was forever busy - never had so many visitors wandered around the gardens.

Avia secretly could not wait for the wedding to pass and tranquillity to resume in the gardens. She had not visited the gothic cottage since the night of All Hallows Eve. She was still scared that a witch would appear. She often thought of how petrifying the night had been when the witches took her and although Agnes had brought the coven to her door, as Jack had feared, she had also saved her and remained her protector for ever more. Avia believed Agnes would stay here and weave her magic forever. Avia had watched her once at work with a dress and she laughed in amazement at how such a spectacle created the most wondrous gowns. Agnes would stay until she could no longer, although Avia wondered how long a witch could live for? Avia was excited for her sister's wedding and was dutiful in her kind remarks and pretence at her pleasure for her sister, she really would rather Cecelia stayed at Stourton. Petworth was so far away and she would miss her calming ways. Olivia would also become more demanding, taking away precious time with Jack. Avia knew though she must do as she was expected to keep the freedom she currently enjoyed, and of that she had far more than any other young girl did in her position.

When eventually the grand day arrived, Avia was thrilled. The sun sparkled and the pretty June flowers swayed in a sweet-scented wind. Dressed in the very finest attire, they travelled in decorated carriages to the beautiful little church in the grounds. St Peters was both part of the Hall and the village, so villagers crowded along the lane watching the distinguished guests arriving - it was a show of wealth, and all stood in awe. Avia arrived at the church early with her sister Olivia and, with her other relatives, who stood at the front. Avia, like her sister, wore a delicate pale-yellow dress with white flowers and lace, which Agnes said were like little daisies dancing in the meadow. Avia tried to peer around at as many guests as she could. Olivia gave a little nervous cough and became quite flushed when Thomas and Edwina and their respected family arrived. The church was packed and some lesser guests filled the back. Avia turned to see Belle, Jeremiah, Bertie and Jack in the crowd. She was shocked they had been invited but overwhelmed with joy, and she gave Jack an obvious huge wave to welcome him - he grinned in acknowledgement, not daring to wave back. The music played and Cecilia entered the church with her father, who stood proudly by her side. Olivia and Avia looked at one another and knew that each other were thinking how lovely it would have been for mother to have seen. Miss Bonneville caught their eyes as she also understood and reassured them in some way that their dear mother looked down upon them all. Avia was surprised how simple it seemed to marry, as the service did not go on for ages, it was quite quick. Soon they were all gathered outside, and a procession of carriages took the bride and groom and guests to the Hall, where the banquet began. Avia was pleased the service was short, but the meal part took forever followed by dancing and she felt dizzy from punch; she was glad to have Jack by her side. Later some of the servants joined in, including Agnes, who looked stunning in an unusual blue gown. Avia finally got chance to speak with Jack and he said tomorrow they must meet - he had some exciting news to tell her that for now he must keep a secret.

Isabella Maria De Bourbon

~~ * ~~

A month before Cecilia's grand society wedding to the adorable George of Petworth, Avia's father, Lord Richard Hoare, invited Belle and family to an informal meeting in the huge library, a place he often liked to hold meetings, full of wonderful artefacts and art where he could enjoy showing off his treasures while mixing business. It was a very wealthy time and his family profits soared from their banking and property empire and his gold business grew. He had also recently acquired the properties by inheritance from his cousin Lord Becklesford, who had no other family or heirs, not ever wishing to have children or marry. Lord Becklesford had been the cousin who had callously sent Belle to Stourton Hall with no information about her link to French aristocracy, or any clue of who the poor mite was or where she came from. Lord Richard had decided to gift Belle some of the inheritance. He also had news from France, where he had applied for her birth rights and money that remained in her family's name. During a short and hopeful restoration of royalty and aristocracy in France, Belle's link to aristocracy had been put on paper and she was the benefactor of a substantial wealth that had been held for her family. Lord Richard knew that Belle's husband, Jeremiah, would be shocked, but the wealth offered them considerable comfort and the opportunity to acquire Bonham Manor House that had recently come available. They would still be able to work their farm, as its land ran alongside the Manor's land. They would legally be able to take Belle's aristocratic name with its royal ties. Her full name was Isabella Maria De Bourbon. Belle of course had known her secret for years, but her poor husband and son Bertie had no clue. Jack seemed to find the news no surprise and, other than his thick Somerset drawl, he had always felt some sort of importance which allowed him to talk freely with his opinions. Avia's father asked Jack to stay behind after Belle, Jeremiah and Bertie had left with handshakes and kisses. Lord Richard said he feared it would be hard for him now to be a garden labourer under his employment and unrolled some papers of plans and asked if perhaps Jack would consider being a partner to help with the design and planting of his projects, with his daughter Avia's approval. Jack felt like jumping for joy but instead he remained composed and accepted in the politest manner he knew. Jack had to keep this secret, as the rest of the family did not want to cause a stir before Cecilia's wedding. Belle was delighted and was surprised how well her husband had taken the news. Jeremiah said he always knew she was something special and instead of a hurt pride, he took well to the thought of being lord of his manor, although he would always be the humble Jeremiah Feld, once of the sheep glade.

Belle's Hypothesis

~~ * ~~

Belle thought to herself often about Agnes and the witches and all that had happened. She wondered, if it had not been for the witches and Jeremiah saving her in the woods long ago on that frozen and sinister All Hallows Eve, and Lord Richard Hoare being so pleased with Jack for saving his daughter and Agnes, that maybe none of the good things that had happened would have come about. Perhaps their encounters with the witch Avoca had given them a little luck. It was a story told in the family of Jeremiah Feld, about how his 5th great grandpa had found his fortune through a witch who had taught him to dye wool the deepest red.

Belle now knew that Avoca was undeniably that witch, Belle thought of Miss Bonneville whilst thinking of witches and how well she had always treated her even as a servant, as if she somehow knew she was aristocracy. It was strange the way Miss Bonneville had taken Agnes in so quickly with no hesitation. She must have already known something.

She thought of Miss Bonneville and how she never looked any older and how she always knew things before they happened. She ran the strictest, yet happiest, well-treated household in England. Belle remembered back to the night she was taken by the witches and the way Miss Bonneville knew how to help her; she gave her a drink she had never tasted before, the drink she also gave to Avia and Agnes after their ordeal. Miss Bonneville always wore a pendant just like the one Miss Avia now wore. Belle asked herself a question, as she looked at the herbs she had been gifted by Miss Bonneville, who had taught her how to grind the seeds and mix the leaves; rosemary for pain, peppermint for colds, sage for sore throats, oregano for a boost of energy when feeling low, thyme and basil for healing, and many other remedies and recipes. Miss Bonneville was certainly an extraordinary character and Belle just wondered, knowing Agnes was a witch with such kindness and elegance, could Miss Bonneville be a witch too? The more she thought about it, the more similar they seemed - quick, intelligent, and always a little ahead of everyone, yet not obviously. They also both kept strange pets. Belle had often noticed that wherever Miss Bonneville went a magpie would follow, and Agnes had that strange, wild-looking cat that appeared from nowhere, so sleek and allusive. Belle thought of so many things; a scratch or a sore were no more when you visited Miss Bonneville, and any servant's trouble with another was sorted with no word. She remembered how chores could disappear and sparkling glasses and crockery shine like mirrors, the herbs and vegetable kitchen garden grew like no other at all times of year, admired by the cook, though not noticed by many. Belle thought of Miss Bonneville and the stories she could tell and the knowledge that she held. Belle had no proof, it was her own secret theory, but she felt quite certain that her friend Miss Bonneville was a witch of the highest calibre, if such things existed, and she wondered how much of their lives at Stourton Hall that prospered and bloomed were due to the loveliest witch of all.

The Surprising Thing About Miss Bonneville

~~ * ~~

Miss Bonneville had arrived at Stourton Hall quite by accident, blowing in on an autumn wind on All Hallows Eve. Her unexpected arrival extended to an interview with Lord Richard Hoare for the position as a new housekeeper, as her arrival coincided with a succession of applicants who had arrived and gone; none were quite what he was looking for. He needed someone he could trust to run a house and arrange social occasions at the beautiful Hall and gardens. Miss Bonneville had every answer and so much knowledge, she even had some understanding of his work in archaeology and antiquities, and above all, she seemed kind, fair and strict with high morals almost from another time; she was both immaculate and articulate.

Lord Richard employed her immediately, and from that day on the Hall seemed to have a bustle again; flowers filled the rooms, fires were lit, amazing food was served, delicate décor changes were made, and his lovely wife Beatrice was enchanted and more than happy with her new housekeeper. While Miss Bonneville was in charge, he was free to work and travel as he pleased. He did not ever feel the need to ask

Miss Bonneville her first name or where she had come from; she was so assertive and confident in her manner that it seemed an unnecessary need, but had he asked her, she would have most probably answered Mari, and she would have said that she came from a chateau in the depths of Normandy in France.

Miss Bonneville was not really sure of her first name as she was born so long ago and had travelled far with her old family. They had lived a simple life; her pa stole by night and her Ma sold herbs in the day and they lived in the woods and meadows. She faintly remembered her supposed parents, and a sister and brother with wavy curls and freckles, quite unlike her dark, tight ringlets and flawless complexion; they were also stocky and stout, while she was tall and slender. Miss Bonneville remembered kindness and love, all so long ago, and she tried not to think of her own loss and of theirs, banishing it from her mind - a pain her heart could not reconcile.

One stormy day they came upon a chateau and her pa asked for shelter for the night in exchange for some work on the land. The owner of the chateau had a face like thunder itself and scared the children, so they hid from him. They slept in the huge barn and stayed for longer than one night, working hard by day. They were fed well with a roof over their heads each night, and the children grew less fearful, enticed by the strange owner's pretty black kittens. They played in his gardens and watched his magical fire displays - the days seemed kind and they did not choose to move on. Sadly though, all good things must come to an end and one day the strange owner bid them farewell; he offered them a purse of gold, a cart and a horse in exchange for their eldest daughter and promised he would school her and that her life would be rich and free. That was the day they were all tricked and she, Mari, was captured.

She was kept by the strange owner with the face of thunder, who was a warlock. In truth, he gave her great knowledge, but freedom was something she would forget, and his remote Chateau de le Angotiere was a perfect spot, with no passers-by or questions. At the chateau he could create his firework displays and explosives. The warlock had studied in ancient China to gain his gun powder skills, and he sold the gun powder to whoever was in the market for the highest price, be it the French or the English. Both were always in need with the hundred-year war now raging on - it was 1337 and the war had only just begun. Mari realised she had been taken for a reason; he had been watching her and she was snatched because she was special. The warlock told her she was a supreme witch born under the blackest of moons and that it was her calling to stay with him. He trained her in

both magic and management, and she became his apprentice and spy as no one paid attention to a young girl, and as
she grew, he used her beauty as an enticement to further his
connections. He named her Miss Bonneville. She did not
count how many years she spent in his service as to escape
was futile, and although he was strange and dark in his
ways, the warlock called Fabian was respectful to her in
many ways and he taught her more than any person could
ever hope to know. Life went on for Miss Bonneville in this
way for an eternity. Fabian had many witches and warlocks
visit him over the years, some she remembered well and
some she liked better than others. The arrival of a witch
named Martiale Espaze, who weaved her path one winter's
day through the warlock's door, was the undoing of his long
success. Miss Bonneville warned him that this witch was evil
to her core, and when captured, her trial of horrors commit-
ted by witchcraft and worse dragged the warlock to the attention of others and the publicity of her execution, gave the
warlock Fabian only one choice, and that was to evanesce
without a trace. Without a word to Miss Bonneville he disappeared, and she was suddenly free. The law of the land
searched the chateau and found gun powders and more.
Miss Bonneville was under no suspicion though as she told
them of her long capture and with pity was let go; with papers in her hand and money in her purse, Miss Bonneville
was gone.

The Hiring of Nanny Maud

~~ * ~~

One small little matter Miss Bonneville also had to consider, with witches flying wild in the skies, was dear Nanny Maud. This indeed was a perilous time for her, and should she be spotted by a passing witch, it would sadly be game over for her. Previously Miss Bonneville interviewed many useless nannies. It was impossible to find one that fitted the description the Lord asked for - it was just unachievable to find a person with all those attributes. So Miss Bonneville took it upon herself to fill the gap in an alternative manner. She had watched the little mouse Maud whom she kept as a pet; so sweet, observant and a very clever little mouse, she knew the house, the children, the history and how things worked. So, for a well-needed temporary fix on a still summer's eve, the spell was cast, and Nanny Maud appeared. At first a little muddled, she worked hard and by morning was a shy and quiet little lady. By lunchtime her tail had fallen, and by the next day she was elementary and improving by the hour. Miss Bonneville was content and slightly smug with her creation. Nanny Maud was put with the children, who instantly adored her. Even Miss Bonneville could never had expected the sheer wonder of the mouse - a perfect natural in the nursery and devoted to the core; Nanny Maud would stay for a very long time as that temporary fix.

Fabian Benzlastien

~~ * ~~

Lord Richard Hoare was in full swing materialistically in the summer of 1809. He had yet another year of profits and it was well-invested by his bankers, but he had no interest in spending time making money. He enjoyed the freedom of his riches and his time was spent instead on his travels and archaeology. One such dig took him to the foothills of Nepal where he made acquaintance with a French explorer and although it was not customary to converse with a man whose country was not natural ally to his own, the two men had a wealth of knowledge and were intrigued by each other's great explorations and excavations. The explorer, Fabian, had the rare opportunity of a trip to London and asked if he might be able to visit Stourton Hall and its famous gardens. On a cold winter's evening on All Hallows Eve, Fabian arrived for dinner at Stourton Hall. He was amongst a number of important guests, as Lord Richard, on reflection, felt uneasy about spending time with an unknown explorer alone. The guests were well entertained with fireworks, a gift from Fabian- and by the light of fires and candles; they all had a spectacular evening and a tour of the gardens. Miss Bonneville immediately recognised Fabian. No one else in the world had such deep dark eyes and heavy black eyebrows; his face told stories with no words, and she felt a tremor of fear. He ignored her presence though, and looked through her as though she did not exist; Miss Bonneville returned the favour. However, she could not think as to what on earth he was doing here and what he was up to. Twice she saw him sneaking to different parts of the house pretending to be lost and while on the garden tour, and he hesitated for too long outside the gothic cottage. Miss Bonneville watched him from afar; he was up to something, she knew now from a night long ago that he had something to do with Belle's witches; she had seen them herself at different times in the woods and she remembered them well as visitors to the chateau. So, now it all made perfect sense - he had come to set his spells to make way for the witches' entrance. He must have known that Agnes was hidden somewhere near the cottage all that time and the short dumpy witch with freckles and a ridiculous number of dresses on had been seen around the woods all year, no doubt spying and informing.

After Miss Bonneville had seen Fabian that night in her safe hold at Stourton Hall, she had a busy time setting her own defences. She had already made sure that the moonstone was placed in Avia's possession, nervous of her playing by the gothic cottage and afraid Avia was now entwined in the story. She then set up a deflection spell by the witches' portal, sending them off course and she set little protection

spells all over the grounds; she also set a spy on the annoying witch whom she knew was Lettice. Nothing was more
easily trained and compliant than a chatter-pie, commonly
known as a magpie; these annoying raucous birds were a
wonderful witches' pet. Poor Hex, as she named him, had
been caught up in one of Otto the gamekeeper's traps, so she
freed him and fed him well on scraps and within a week he
was hers. Hex would arrive dutifully for his breakfast early
and be led to the wood chopper's hut where Lettice hid. Hex
would soon fly to Lettice and sit close by in hope of tip bits -
Lettice obliged well, as Miss Bonneville knew she would, and
all day and night Hex would follow and watch. Hex would
then fly back to his true mistress Miss Bonneville and she
saw everything through his eyes - she saw Lettice spy on the
strange little girl who had suddenly appeared and played
with Avia and Jack. Miss Bonneville was reminded vividly of
someone when she saw the strange girl with the shiny black
hair and when Miss Bonneville saw Agnes at Belle's market
stall, she knew it was a set-up, but she played along. As soon
as she saw Agnes close up, she knew straight away that
without doubt this was Avoca's daughter, the little witch of a
warlock to be sacrificed. She remembered now the witches
so clearly, all so beautiful and charming, and she heard their
plotting with the warlock Fabian at the chateau while Avoca
was distracted by the little black kittens or fast asleep from
the witches' potions. Miss Bonneville had tried to warn her

once or twice, to tell her that her friends meant her harm, but the witches and warlock were clever and she was given no chance to ever do so. Now all these years on she stood next to the daughter, with the knowledge that she was in grave danger. Little Miss Avia and Belle had created a perfect plot, and she could now keep the girl Agnes safe with her in the Hall, with the added bonus that she seemed to truly be a perfect seamstress.

Miss Bonneville had underestimated the powers and cunning of the witches and warlock; they had still managed to find their way back to Stourton with ease and into the Hall. She had been powerless, and it all happened so fast and she felt dreadful, but with thanks to Jack, Avia was saved and Miss Bonneville was sure Avoca had somehow saved her own daughter with a cunning trick - one day she would love to have a little chat with her and hear her story. For now though, Miss Bonneville felt a small glisten of satisfaction; she did not believe the witches or warlock were strong enough to come back for a good few hundred years, if ever, and she would protect Stourton when they did return and she could enjoy her place in peace. Hex, she would keep as he was very useful and he sat outside her office in the tree watching the gardens; Miss Bonneville saw no harm in having a permanent spy at such times.

Four Cross Witches and a Warlock: 1669

~~ * ~~

Tricked, banished, and nearly burnt at the stake, the witches managed to return to Parnell and Wilmot's favourite abode by the lake. They were all weakened by failing to not sacrifice Avoaca's child and appeared to show no shame of their plot. Lettice began to hide away - her time on the earth had been so long. The coven though, would struggle on and find other less successful prey to keep them alive and so, the witches of Siljan Lake stayed tucked away for hundreds of years. However, in their desperation to stay strong and alive, they had grown careless, and the city people of Mora started to talk and grew suspicious of their children's encounters in the woods. What once had been folklore and stories became an investigation and with talk of witches, Mora started a witch hunt. Not many would slip the net and the trials were brutal with many who were innocent accused. Josina, Wilmot, Parnell and Fabian were all eventually captured and found guilty, one though, would mysteriously disappear from captivity and never be found. The others would be hung quietly one cold winter's night. The ice on the lake reflected the rising moon and a phenomenon of coloured lights was seen as never before; it was told the spirits danced in the skies to celebrate the passing of evil and from the earth, others believed the witches spirits escaped and that they should have been burnt at the stake.

Prince and Frog

~~ * ~~

Belle loved her new home and wandered the rooms often
with her friends, Miss Avia, Agnes and Miss Bonneville. Entwined by all that they had been through together and apart,
they had a bond and enjoyed each other's company greatly.
Belle's family had taken to the good life well and the farm
prospered with extra land and a boost of labourers; Belle
would pinch herself that all this had happened. Avia could
not be more delighted that one garden labourer had
overnight turned out to be high born. Avia knew she had her
father to thank for this and now strangely found it easy to be
with him.

Avia had found the house strange without Cecelia since her
wedding and missed her; Olivia seemed to be always with
Edwina, plotting her own wedding day and life of comfort
with Thomas, who was now studying in London. Lottie had
now started working at the hall, so she managed to catch up
with her old friend and Avia had her special Agnes, the little
yew tree witch, who still worked hard and fixed little spells -
their fellowship would always be. Jack and Avia worked on
the garden plans and together they created wonderful ideas;
they would spend hours walking through the fields and
woods. Jack would joke that he thought Miss Avia must have

slipped him a quick kiss, because he, the frog, had turned into a prince. Stourton Hall felt safe and calm, and Avia was the happiest she could ever be and knew that now she could spend her life wandering these gardens and rooms - keeping their beauty and splendour for other lives to see. Hopefully with Jack by her side, laughter would always be close, and friendship would last for eternity. The yew tree now blossomed with beautiful though strange flowers instead of strange charms - an amazing spectacle that many would marvel at.

The End

~~ * ~~

The Stolen Winter

~~  ~~

With every falling snowflake,

another dream is made,

For Louisa & Ollie

May your wishes & dreams always come true

xx

The Beginning

~~ * ~~

*From the day they first met in the garden,
before their little witch Agnes came along,
Jack and Avia were bound together. Their
friendship and magical love could not be
broken, even by the cruellest wind and a
twist in fate that would bring more than one
witch and warlock to their door. Through the
sands of time and battles of other realms, can
they and their love survive?*

The Squall

~~*~~

The gusts of icy wind swirled around the gentle, wooded valleys leaving behind drifts of snow that sparkled and sprinkled onto the highest treetops and the bright moonlight flickered as the snow clouds turned and twisted in the sky. The houses and stables were engulfed in the endless siege of a wintery storm. As the dawn slowly broke, little signs of stirring and twinkling candles began; each maid and footman struggled to find their way - only those within the Hall could lay the fires and pray. The silence bought a peaceful time as the blanketed woodlands and meadows quietly hid; the birds took refuge in deep canopies and all that could be heard was the bark of a deer and the eerie creek of ice on the lake. The nighttime skies fell away, and a glimpse of sun gave hope.

Deep in the woods far from man, the artic storm had bought one more thing that was far more trouble than ice and white powder. She was dressed poorly for the weather in her silks and shawl. The strange girl with white hair and soft brown eyes hid in an old cave used years ago. She cursed the freezing squall that had set her off course, her delay would cost her dearly and the white warlock, her father, would be angered beyond belief. Afraid and exhausted from her travels, she lit her fire magically with no more than a few twigs; the strange concoction she made from herbs was sipped as though she had all the time in the world and as she stumbled into a tormented sleep she tried to unravel her predicament, as hopeless as it was. She grew sad and cried, then at last her eyelids grew heavy and in her dreams she escaped the coldness and fear to her beautiful land with its balmy breezes, blistering sun and the welcoming shade under the whispering leaves of the Great Banyan tree. So she slept in the darkness of the cave; no wolf or fox would dare enter - they sensed that something of grave danger hid in the lair once their cave.

Chime too Late

~~ * ~~

Avia woke with great excitement; the world had turned
white overnight. She called for Nanny Maud who she heard
scuttling around busily doing her chores. As always in a flash
she was there tending to her mistress, now a little old to
have a nursemaid, but still young enough to spoil. Maud
rambled on to Avia about how she must dress warmly and
not stay out too long and just as she had finished her witter-
ing, a snowball hit the window and below on the terrace
stood Jack, grinning like a cat with cream. They giggled and
Avia rushed to layer up and Maud ran for hot chocolate
drinks and buns, her mistress's favourite. Jack had slithered
into the kitchen for a warm-up. He knew the cook called
Bunty well though she hissed at him as he strew melting
snow onto the hard and now slippery quarry-tiled floor. She
complained that they would all break their necks slipping
and sliding about and still grumbling, she threw him a hunk
of bread and cheese. He sat with his hot milk and she asked
after his dear ma, Belle, who she had known when she was a
lady's maid. Belle had been kind to Bunty all those years ago
when others teased her for her poor complexion and lack of
hair. She remembered Belle's compassion and would always
thank her inside, and although she snapped at Jack it was
only in jest; like everyone she was very fond of his charming

ways and she secretly loved to see the romance that blossomed between Jack and Avia - it was a wonderful thought that they may one day, when old enough, wed. As Bunty daydreamed and cooked, Avia bounded like a puppy into the kitchen. She blushed and giggled when she saw Jack and glowed like a star all wrapped up as she urged Jack to finish his bread. Jack didn't hesitate and was soon pulling her by the hand; echoes of giggles could be heard through the halls.

They stepped out into a white wonderland and were quickly submerged in the snow. The sleigh was pulled behind them and they dived up and down the slopes, with Avia screaming for joy. They both would pause occasionally to admire the stunning views and the statues and follies covered in snow; the garden looked magical as the sun made flakes sparkle, while the frozen lake creaked and echoed through the woods, its spooky sound masked by giggles. Jack and Avia carried on until they could no more; both exhausted. They parted to rest and go home and get dry. Jack agreed to call back later - they had a garden design project to attend. They waved goodbye and all was well in their small perfect world.

A little later, Avia was warm and dry and she went to the library and spread out their designs for a stately garden nearby; exhilarated by the prospect of real work, Avia was bubbling inside. The fire crackled in the huge dog grate and the grandfather clock chimed as it did every hour, it chimed again and again, too many times. Jack was late and the hours passed and still he did not arrive. Avia began to worry; it was unlike Jack to let her down and with the snow so deep and the dark coming down, there was no way she could check or send anyone out. Avia paced the library unsure what to do. Miss Bonneville and Agnes were buying drapes in the city of Bath. Avia suddenly felt terribly alone and in desperation she went to ask Nanny Maud for her advice, although she was afraid it would stress her dear Nanny too much. She was right, Maud fussed and sniffled that something had gone awfully wrong as Jack was truer than the sky was blue; he would never be late for anyone, Avia could not bear not knowing where he was for one minute more so she sneaked away like a thief into the snowy night. Avia knew the way to old Jack's farm like the back of her hand and she followed the path that she knew Jack would take, in case he had fallen and lay hurt in the deepest snow. In useless haste Avia struggled through the now crunchy snow - the ice had started to set in for the night. The moon was rising so a little light showed the way and every so often Avia would call his name. She would then rest and listen for a reply, nothing replied and only a deadly silence greeted Avia's cries. Avia began to think she could not go on. The journey was so hard and with every step she took she became more exhausted; she bit back tears and told herself to carry on. Her father would never give up on one of his expeditions and she tried to think of him in the hot sun of Egypt and she dreamt of going to India and seeing elephants and all the wonders she had heard of. Avia felt a rush of happiness as she heard and saw someone coming towards her. Thinking it was Jack, she ran and fell forwards into the bitter drift; she felt strong arms picking her up like a fallen leaf. Avia tried to thank Bertie, Jack's brother without tears, she could not stop them though. He tried to sooth her sobs and got her back to the warm farmhouse where an empty place at the table was still set for Jack. Avia felt panic in her heart, when she realised Jack was not with Bertie and he was not at the manor and Belle and Jeremiah were away, travelling through France, following Belle's past. Bertie and Avia soon worked out that he had never returned from the earlier sleigh riding at Stourton Hall. Avia felt like screaming. He would be cold, very cold and hurt somewhere. Bertie made Avia promise to stay at the farm and close to the fire; he told her to keep the fire going and left quickly to rally help. Avia removed her wet clothes and found some of Belle's old farm dresses in a musty chest upstairs, itchy, yet dry and warm; she grabbed a shirt of Jack's just for comfort and returned to the fire feeding its flames, while waiting for Bertie and Jack's return. With no clock, she had no sense of time and afraid she would go completely mad with worry, she found a mending pile with Belle's old sewing box. Avia began to clumsily mend the holes in the discarded clothes pile, a small distraction while feeding the fire. Outside she heard an owl screech from the barn; tonight the owl would stay under cover to hunt as outside the snow fell and there was a stranger about.

Harini's Prisoner

~~ * ~~

Harini had woken to the sound of screams. She hesitantly left her cave and flew to the treetops to look for where the noise came from. A girl and boy about her age ran with a strange wooden contraption; the boy threw snowballs to hit the girl and pushed her hard down the hills. The poor thing screamed in fear, then there was silence and she thought the worse had happened to the poor girl; she looked but found nothing to save. Harini felt cross; why did males treat girls so badly here as they often did in her country. She carried on with her hopeless search for the boy she was supposed to find. Later on that day, she saw the boy who killed the girl; he strolled along with a smile on his face as though nothing was wrong. She spat at his smugness for what he had done and anger rose in Harini's heart. She came up with a very quick plan. She had been sent by her father the warlock to curse and capture a boy, the son of a witch, as her father was determined to entice the witch to his lair. She had been told to bring him to her father's castle in the Golden Fort. Harini, though, had no clue where the witch and her son were, since she had been thrown around like a rag doll in the storm. So, in desperation and in retribution, she would take this boy for harming the girl instead; the warlock would never know the truth. Harini braced herself for no reason, the boy was an easy target as he grinned at her and offered help. Harini cursed him - he would not have his next conquest with her. She hesitated a little though; was he some kind of demon as he just stood and smiled with charming eyes. The stupid boy was not ready for what was coming and had no clue and with a quick flick of her arm and a spell, he was suddenly dumbstruck and in a trance. Whatever she said he would do and like a puppet the boy followed her with his head held low. She led him deep into the woods that he once knew so well but where now he walked blindly, following his captor, with no clue as to who he was or where he would go. Harini impatiently took him back to her cave and she sat him like a stuffed bear upon on a rock and told him to stay, which obediently he did - he just sat and stared into the woods beyond the cave.

Harini had work to do. She had to work fast as the night of Samhain approached and she had to leave this frozen land. Harini took to flight, keeping just above the trees; she looked for traces of smoke and sniffed for certain smells as she had suspected in the woods so vast another dankini was about. She carefully circled and made for the top of a tall fir tree where she could hide in the branches and survey the situation, she watched in distaste as the scruffy old women pottered around moving things from one place to another, making more mess, after watching her eat, Harini tutted in disgust, wishing she had found a more elegant prey for her needs, as dusk fell she saw the witch retire to her hut, Harini moved closer carefully still in the tree tops and waited to hear the witch's hog-like snores, she landed softly and crept about noting the witch's supplies and cauldron that were strewn about on the floor where she slept. Harini, fast as lightning, cast her spell so when the plump, smelly witch would wake she would have no clue as to what had happened. She set about sorting the mess and found the herbs and parts she needed for her potion; the cauldron was soon bubbling away. Harini summoned her pawn from the cave and, while she sizzled and stirred, the boy made his way towards her alone. He walked at speed through the trees at an unnatural pace, pale and ghostly with no thought of his own, and with each step he travelled further from his home and the valley of the grand gardens, where his true love would wait in agony and not know his fate.

Harini was happy with her work; she would be ready to travel soon with the boy. The witch still snored annoyingly, something Harini did not have the time to sort. She sensed the boy was nearly at the hut and on his arrival she sat him in the warmth, not wanting all her efforts to become a block of ice. She fed him some bread and herbs while she ate herself then ordered him to get water in a pail from the stream;

he returned splashing the water as he went - Harini hissed at his clumsiness to no avail.

Time passed quickly and the morning approached with only a little moonlight left flickering through the trees, the witch and the boy made their way through the snow to the highest point that could be found. Harini found the perfect spot and looked over the bleak valley. She lit her fire and held the boy's hand telling him not to let go, then chanted her rhyme and in flash they were gone. Little fragments of light lit up the sky and the small fire died down leaving only embers that soon turned to ash in the cold; the only trace was a pair of brown, scruffy boots with their laces undone.

Bertie's Despair

~~ * ~~

Bertie left Avia in the farmhouse unsure quite what he was going to do. The snow and bitter cold was cripplingly hard for his task, but determined and desperate he made his way back to the Hall and went straight to the stable yard where he knew the gardeners and stable lads would stay. The staff at Stourton Hall were informed as Avia would surely be noticed as missing by now. Nanny Maud cried out and squeaked in relief that she was safe which was the good news, but the disappearance of Jack was terrifying on such a night, especially as it was All Hallow's Eve. Nanny Maud was panicking that Avia was alone and insisted she be bought back to the Hall or that she was at least sent a companion on such a scary night; everyone was too busy though searching for Jack, so Maud had no option other than to wait and worry about Avia. She thought to go herself but knew it was hopeless, she would probably not even make it to the garden gate. She called for Bunty, but even Bunty the cook had left to help find Jack, and soon everyone was out. A bonfire was lit on that eve, for folk to find their way back home. A young lad called Alfie stoked the fire with wood and after everyone left, he was stood looking around as he fed the flames when suddenly in the distance above the hill, he saw a strange flash of light that left sprinkles of light in the sky; he squinted in astonishment and wondered if he had imagined what he had just seen. The search went on and on and the men and women came back to the fire to warm themselves; gradually it became senseless - Jack was nowhere to be found. Bertie feared the worse, thinking that an animal or the lake had taken him, but the search carried on as no one wanted to ever give up. Bunty the cook knew the woods like the back of her hand and she found the cave that she had remembered that night - an instinct drove her there that she did not understand. She had played in that cave as a child; it was the perfect hiding place, where stories were told of witches and dragons. Bunty though never worried about such things as she was brave and tough having had a harsh upbringing. As she walked into the cave she saw remnants of a fire and footsteps could be seen, two sets, one tiny the other larger boots and on a rock Bunty found a button from a coat. She blew hard on her horn to call for help, and as she looked at her old witch's ring that mysteriously changed colour, sparkling violet instead of its normal colours of red and blue, she held her breath and waited in fear. Bertie and a few others were not far away and soon they were inspecting the cave floor and the button he knew was from his dear brother's jacket; he cried out loud to the others that he thought Jack had been taken and on All Hallows Eve it had to be an evil force. In sobs he panicked about Miss Avia being left alone and again sounded the alarm. Soon many were running towards the farm while Bertie prayed it was not a plan and that Avia had not been taken as well. Relieved and exhausted from their flight, they found her darning by the fire and Bertie gently told her what they had found and how they had searched so carefully all over the grounds and woods. Avia was in complete shock, she could not even cry; no one now could help other than Agnes and Miss Bonneville, who were scheduled to be back by now but were frustratingly held in the city due to the snow and had no clue of the drama and despair that unfolded at Stourton Hall. Avia could do nothing. They all had to wait for the morning and exhausted, Bertie fell asleep at the table. Avia put a blanket over his shoulders and returned to her darning while others sat around in disbelief that Jack had been taken. Knowing others still searched and with no strength left, they rested for a while. Avia thought and thought. Why would a witch take Jack? She began to worry that the coven of old were back, but surely they would come for Agnes. Nothing made any sense and eventually she fell asleep in her chair by the dying fire, where she dreamt of the witches and that fateful night when she had been taken and was saved by Jack.

The search parties scoured on through the night, yet they never quite went far enough to find the boots on the hill or the witch that still snored in her hut, where maybe a clue or two had been left behind.

The Golden Fort

~~ * ~~

Sonar Quila rose from the desert in all its wonder with sand-
stone that shone gold in the sun and a magical reflection fell
upon the lake that lapped gently on the sandy shore. The
fort was a vast expanse of temples and wondrous architecture, carved to the finest detail, where people lived and
worked. A bustle and explosion of noise and smells filled the
winding lanes within the thick protective walls. Rawal Jaisal,
the ruler, was an amazing and spiritual leader. He saw the
opportunity for his people from the silk road trade and his
wondrous city Jaisalmer prospered - he held a powerful and
enviable position. Rawal had many advisors and took council in his temples for situations both good and bad. As a fair
and kind man, he would only punish the extremes and
would keep peace if possible and negotiate terms. One of his
advisors was named Gedahard, an albino man that Rawal
was not fond of, yet he trusted his judgement on some of the
stranger things that he encountered. Gedahard would deal
with any black magic, dankinis or reports of meddling with
the spirits. He lived in his own castle in the fort and where
his wealth was displayed in a distasteful show, that mainly
only servants would ever see. He was secretive with
everything he did and the position he held commanded
great respect among many as they feared him and trusted

him to sort any occultists. No one knew where he came from and how long he had been around; his silver tongue could speak every language and his mind was a font of facts - it was as though he had walked the earth before, many, many times. Gedahard had few friends; no one from the outside knew him or whether he had a wife and children. Most of his servants stayed in his castle or were sworn to secrecy and would only scuttle out for food, most supplies being delivered through the huge gates forged in iron. Strangely no one ever bothered about their elusive occupant of the fort; he caused no problems and took solitary prayer. So when his white-haired daughter with her shawl firmly on walked in the shadows with a boy by her side, not a soul flinched or paid any interest as they entered the gates and were engulfed into the castle's walls. Harini was exhausted and feared to disturb her father at such a late hour, so she took her prisoner to a quiet and secluded open courtyard where he had shelter and a water well under some snarled olive trees; she would arrange for food to be delivered. Harini ordered him to eat when food came and drink from the well and shelter from the sun. The, boy glazed over, made no reply and just walked to the water well. Harini left him with no care and found her luxurious rooms. She called her maid to pour her a hot bath and fetch her food for both her and the prisoner. The maid Ynes would ask no questions and would complete her orders and once she had seen to Harini, she then took a large plate to the prisoner. Ynes spied through the peephole and saw he was asleep in the shelter, just lying with nothing but the sand and his clothes; she quickly placed the food by him and kicked him gently until he woke, then ran off and kindly bought him some old furs dumped for the rubbish. He looked at her blankly with no response and Ynes knew the poor boy had been cursed. She had seen them before and never knew who they were or where they went, but something about this one was different - he dressed quite strangely, and his skin was an unusual colour. His eyes looked soft despite his state, not wild and angry like others before. She gestured he should cover himself in the furs and told him her name was Ynes, then she whispered to hide the furs by day and that she would find him more food and fruit.

The next morning there was a huge commotion in the fort and bells rang out to call a meeting for all. Gedahard left the castle at speed to the temple of their ruler Rawal and while they all discussed important things. Harini slept in blissful comfort, oblivious to the harm she had caused. Ynes visited the boy with a huge bowl of fruits and breads. The boy hungrily ate each delicious bite and carefully took every seed out and placed them on a rock to dry out, then with an old shovel he found he dug the golden sand and eventual found a soil texture that he mixed with the left-over fruit and water.

Carefully the boy planted the seeds and each day he watered them and all the time he gardened he sang a song, a song he knew from far away. And he found that when he dug and watered and planted seeds that Ynes bought him, his mind could slowly start to think back to who he was, and with each hour that passed he remembered a little more.

Gedahard arrived back grumpy, shouting obscenities at any one he saw. He roared for Harini to get her lazy bones out of bed and show him the prisoner, the son of the witch Grettle that he had commanded his daughter to capture, so that he could finally settle a score with the plump, stinking witch that had tricked him. Gedahard was a warlock with so much power, but she had stolen a possession of his when he had journeyed through her lush green land. He had stopped for replenishment at an inn in a wall; the place was merry and served good ale and pies in the shape of a half leaf, and the locals played music and sang and danced. He had enjoyed his evening's entertainment. Groggy, he woke from a night of gambling at cards to find the wench he had thrashed had taken the winnings herself. Local folk laughed and said the old hag Grettle stole from everyone passing through and he would not see his winnings again - she would be long gone to her hovel deep in the woods. Gedahard could never let go of his anger towards the witch Grettle, for in the winnings she took a favourite trinket, a ring of special meaning that his father had passed down long ago. Its gem sparkled red by night and blue by day and if danger was upon him, it would turn a vivid violet. He valued it and could never forget it even after so long, so he had sent Harini to steal the witch's only son, who he had been informed was plump and red like his witchy ma and he thought his name was Redge. Harini was instructed to leave a talisman to link her to the fort and Gedahard believed the witch would come for her son, as he had been told he meant the world to her and was the only thing she cared for. He pondered all this while he waited for his daughter who at last had been of use, and he looked forward to seeing the fear and misery on the boy's face. Harini strolled down the stairs yawning and fussing at being woken exhausted from her trip, but her father growled that it was more than a day ago and reluctantly she took him to the inner courtyard at the back of the castle hidden from anyone's eye. Excitedly, Gedahard opened the door half expecting to see the witch there; instead, he saw a boy on his own who sang a song that was familiar while he hoed and who was tall and graceful with soft fair hair. This was no son of the plump red witch. What had Harini done? The boy did not even raise an eye to his captors and carried on with his own set of chores, getting water from the deep well. Harini frustratedly stamped her foot and said he was a murderer and her father roared that she should have been more careful, as now he would have to stay. They then looked quite puzzled at the green shoots that came up from the ground. Gedahard suspected she had stolen a wizard of the land. Intrigued he asked for his servants to let the boy free on his castle land where he could create an amazing garden - anything he wished for he could have. Exasperated, Harini instructed the boy, then turned to go, but her father pulled her back by the scruff of her neck and said her job was far from done - she would return and would not leave until she had the witch's boy. Harini cried tears of desperation, telling him how white and cold the land had turned and that she could not bear the stinking witch, that she never seen a son or the ring in the hut hidden from the world. Gedahard eyed her closely and examined what she had just told him; his rage was now tenfold. She had been in the witch's pad and had not the insight to find the boy or wait for his return; she had no defence and had decided to cry, but pity was not her father's gift and she was dragged by her cuff to pack and sort. He had to travel himself so would join her on the way, which made her feel a little more comforted as now she could tell her father where the witch Grettle lived, they could retrieve the ring and punish her in her own domain; they agreed a truce if she obeyed him to the word. They left the boy in a trance tending to his garden and singing the song that Gedahard had heard long ago. Harini called back not to forget to make the garden the most beautiful one in the whole of Jaisalmer if he wished for his life to be spared.

A Dark Cloud Over Stourton

~~ * ~~

Avia had not moved from her rooms; she spent her time hiding from the world. She could not face company and could not look at the gardens. Her sisters had sent her letters trying to comfort her and although she accepted the kindest words from Cecilia and a gift from Olivia, she still could not be bought out of her deep depression. Nanny Maud tended to her every need and knew that words were pointless, she could only care for her and would stroke her brow at night when she screamed through her nightmares.

Agnes and Miss Bonneville had returned a few days after the tragedy and knew before they stepped through the door that a heavy storm had ripped the heart from the house. They both first suspected Josina, although knew she would have hung around for Agnes and still days later nothing had been found, but Miss Bonneville could sense another witch within a few miles - they had to widen the search. Agnes, who had only had the smallest time with her dearest friend Avia, could not bear her pain or her own and had no time to be with her being in the desperate mission to find poor Jack. Agnes and Miss Bonneville had organised the hunt with maps, and all were employed to find the smallest trace. Bunty was praised greatly for her findings in the cave, and from just a small fragment Miss Bonneville could get a sense of the kidnappers' origins; she smelt spices and felt the heat of the sands. Agnes thought of her mother in the Fort of Chitrakut - surely she could not do this awful deed. Miss Bonneville was certain that it was a witch who had not travelled to these parts before as she could somehow just tell by the clumsy fall and poor uses of resources, even in a snowstorm. Miss Bonneville had a profile in her mind of a young witch sent by another from a land faraway and not that far from Avoca in her fort; maybe she could help.

The snow had started to thaw and left a muddy mess with yellowing grass, and with all snow tracks gone, they only had the scent that was left in the cave. Speed was their only hope and every stone had been turned over. When they began to feel that all had been lost, they heard a strange yowling from the window and sat on the sill was Hestia with a large boot by her side. Within seconds the window was opened and Hestia was fussed over and given milk, while Miss Bonneville studied the boot. Without hesitation, she commanded Hestia to take them to the place where the boot was found and though the witches did not often take to the sky, this emergency made them break every rule and by staying in the trees out of sight, Agnes and Miss Bonneville flew at full speed with Hestia in Agnes's arms to guide. Clever Hestia knew the way they were soon at the hill that looked over the wild valley, now drab and grey. They soon found the other leather boot stood alone in the mud, so now they had a pair and Miss Bonneville could get a fix on Jack. She decided upon a stakeout by the boots and the hill, around the clock - she had a suspicion that the kidnapping witch would return. The hours and minutes ticked away. Miss Bonneville did not care; she would have stood there for centuries just to get the culprits who stole away their adorable Jack. A little tear fell from her composed stance, and she sniffed and snapped at herself - it was no time for emotion or regret, she had to concentrate and remain composed to catch the dreadful snatcher and make them lead her to wherever Jack had been taken.

Miss Bonneville's time was up and Agnes stood in her spot. Hestia and she had decided to share their shift as loneliness was a thing Agnes could not do. Her fault, admittedly, was a great fear of being alone. Hestia purred around her shins, forever grateful to her for releasing her from being a statue in stone. They both waited for what seemed like an eternity. Agnes's tummy began to rumble and Hestia wished for her warm milk by the fire, but then they thought of poor Jack and stood staring at the boots Agnes felt something coming before it arrived and she shielded herself and Hestia with an invisible spell and held her breath. To her greatest shock a young witch and a warlock landed yards from her spot; they looked at the boots and then with haste they turned downwards to the woods. Agnes had sent her thoughts to Miss Bonneville who was very close by and the two witches, a magpie and a cat were all soon following the unsuspecting felons. They journeyed into an area of woods they had not seen for years, strange and dark with different trees, and they felt they were in an evil domain. They smelt the witch before the others arrived, and they spied and waited. The witch that they observed from the tree was small and plump with the reddest of hair. She reminded Agnes of Lettice - quite a strange coincidence. The witch called out the name Redge and as he walked out scratching his head from the hut, the white warlock and young witch suddenly appeared from nowhere. The witch Grettle gasped in fear, as she remembered the warlock from the ale house, and she felt utter panic. She knew he came for the ring, that she had lost in the woods many years ago on the night she had stolen his winnings. Grettle knew he returned for his possession, and he would not take gladly to the answer no. The onlookers, still hiding, knew they could not wait to listen to the narrative. Miss Bonneville recognised the white warlock from another time, and she knew their only choice was to fight - they had to find a way to bring a worthwhile negotiation to the table. Miss Bonneville and Agnes struck with force and no fear. They grabbed the pawn Redge, who squirmed and squealed like a pig until Agnes gagged his mouth. Grettle tried a fumble of a spell and was hurled off course by Miss Bonneville. Harini and the white warlock Gedahard were quite confused and thrown by the unexpected scene. Miss Bonneville immediately threw a protection spell and did not hesitate with her negotiating. It was Jack back or nothing – that was their only term. The great warlock laughed at her bravery and stupidity; however, he did not anticipate the strength and power of both witches. Agnes and Miss Bonneville were not mere amateurs like Grettle and her slothful son; they did not thieve and trick. The white warlock Gedahard realised quickly that he dealt with a supreme guard and questioned who or what they wanted in return. With disappointment he realised Harini had taken their wizard of the land, and now they had a huge muddle and mess that he did not want to be part of anymore. He ignored them and firstly asked the plump witch Grettle to show him the ring. She sniffled and spat that it was lost long ago on the leafy forest floor, at which the warlock roared in anger and with a bolt struck the witch Grettle hard and told Harini to get ready to return. Agnes quickly saw through their plan and thought of Jack as a prisoner far away in another land and poor Avia left heartbroken; a strength like a storm grew from within and she snatched Harini with force, her collateral for Jack's speedy return. Unfortunately, the warlock seemed not to care and with his roaring laughter he left in a flash, everyone stood silently, in shock. Agnes looked around for Miss Bonneville, but she had disappeared completely; she was now nowhere to be seen.

Miss Bonneville, having had years of experience with a dark and difficult warlock, knew that he would not care for his daughter's quick return, and she predicted he would take flight and disappear. The daughter might not ever be able to return if he blocked her path to protect himself, so Miss Bonneville escaped while no one was looking and flew back to the boots and waited silently. When Gedahard appeared he suspected nothing as he quietly lit his fire and scattered his potion and chanted his sleeven words. A loop, in the lightest chain of silk, was tightened around the warlock's ankle and Miss Bonneville's connection was in place and she was hurtled with him far back in time to the most glorious golden place as the sun set on the golden walls. Miss Bonneville followed the villainous white warlock - her only hope of finding Jack. The warlock entered the bustling Golden Fort and Miss Bonneville followed, keeping dangerously close so that she did not lose him in the vastness of the fort. She watched him disappear through a huge gate with a serpent and flower crest and narrowly managed to enter out of sight, quickly hiding in an ornamental statue of an elephant. She watched trades people come and go, but the warlock stayed cloaked within his walls.

When dark fell and temperatures cooled, Miss Bonneville still watched the gates. She was satisfied that after the evening prayer he would not move, so she left her post and wandered the narrow, bumpy and high-walled paths that circled his castle within the fortress. She passed a group of servants with tables of food, lit with pretty little candles that hung everywhere; music played from the strings of the veena, and all ages joined in with dainty dances. As Miss Bonneville watched, a young girl came over and beckoned her to join in. No questions were asked, and she enjoyed the night's Diwali festivities then left to her stakeout - the elephant with large stone ears and a jewelled trunk. Miss Bonneville saw nothing of the warlock thankfully, but she began to worry as to how she would ever find Jack in the vast labyrinth of walls. Miss Bonneville saw the young girl from the night before dashing about often; she seemed different and something about the way she moved made Miss Bonneville suspect she was one of her own, so she followed her and found herself in a strange garden where the girl collected assorted herbs and scented flowers - first she studied them and only seemed to pick a few of each. Intrigued, Miss Bonneville decided to take the plunge and stepped forward asking if she could look at the wonderful vines that grew. The girl at first looked skittish and nervous, but after a little more coaxing from Miss Bonneville she became more amicable and showed Miss Bonneville around. The young girl named Ynes soon had questions of her own and taking pity on Miss Bonneville's story, that she had been taken by the white warlock too, took her to her family and she was taken in.

Miss Bonneville spent her time in the gardens, with Ynes and her family, and was delighted to hear that the warlock's mistress sought a translator in secret for some scriptures that she had acquired. Miss Bonneville cautiously accepted this opportunity, although asked if she could dress like Ynes in a silk sari with a dupatta, Ynes painted her hands with henna in delicate stars and Miss Bonneville pulled down her neatly wound plaits in a tight bun and changed her hair style to be more similar to that of Ynes. With make-up and clothing she prayed that the warlock would not recognise her if by some chance they met and she added a veil to help with her disguise that many here wore for vanity's sake. Satisfied, she followed Ynes with her head firmly down.

Miss Bonneville felt nervous stepping into the warlock's hall, and she prayed he had not set a trap. She was settled in a cool room that overlooked the gardens that tippled down to the edge of the glass lake. The room reminded her of the Lord's study at Stourton with its deep bookcases with leather-bound books in sets, comfortable armchairs in scuffed leather, and tables filled with strange artefacts. The desk was ornate and the seat looked out onto the back gardens through grand windows, only these ones had shimmering voiles that blew in the faint breeze instead of the thick deep hues of wool that served to stop the icy chills at Stourton Hall. While Miss Bonneville waited and sipped iced tea, she glimpsed the back of a boy in the gardens. She could not be sure, but his build and hair, although shaded by scarves, could easily have been Jack's. Frustratingly, she could not get a good look and was soon interrupted by a young lady - to her relief the warlock did not come. The lady was dressed in traditional clothing, only her more elaborate fabric was laden in jewels. She curtly introduced herself as Princess Chandaria and asked a few simple questions, then she passed Miss Bonneville the scripts and asked her to work only in the room they were in; she would be escorted in and out by Ynes. Chandaria warned her that if her husband Gedahard ever saw her, she must hide the papers and lie convincingly - she was to tell him, if asked, that she was a dresser for the lady of the house. She would have to learn some Rajasthani words and play dumb. She was then handed a silk bag of rupees and asked to start immediately. Miss Bonneville agreed and sat down at the desk as she heard the key turn in the door; she was locked in, and the very young lady of the house had gone.

Left in the Mud

~~ * ~~

Agnes stood in a pool of mud. She cursed the plump red witch Grettle for bringing such trouble to their gentle woods and asked her to leave with her boy and not to return if she wished to keep her head intact. So furious was Agnes that she could not quite believe the words that spouted from her mouth. She then looked at Harini, who reminded her of Josina apart from her strange white hair, and she felt no pity at all for her tears - she had stolen her beloved friend Jack. Miss Bonneville had gone, so she decided to trudge back in the mud with the witch Harini under a tight spell of capture and as Agnes walked, she thought about what to do. Sick of the mud and the cold she again broke the rules and made for the treetops with Harini close, who seemed relieved to be off the sodden earth, as her teeth chattered and her lips were blue from the cold. Agnes had no choice but to get her back to the Hall or they would both die of hypothermia or far worse, so she struck a bargain with the snivelling witch - if she behaved she could stay indoors with a fire and food to keep her warm. She then grabbed her by the scruff and said that if there was any messing, she would find herself tied with chains in the icehouse for ever more. Harini sobbed and said she would be good and was now terrified of her captor, who seemed callous and quite mad.

Agnes managed to sneak her up to Avia's quarter, with relief that no one else was about. Nanny Maud slept, exhausted from the events, and Avia strangely sat by the fire and darned stockings and anything else. When she saw Agnes, she rose nimbly, then almost fainted as she saw the dishevelled and strange looking girl. Agnes calmed her understanding that she was still in shock. She asked hesitantly if they could change, both soaked and muddy from the day's events. Avia found them old clothes of her sisters that would only get moth holes if they were not used, then both girls bathed in separate tubs while Avia arranged for food to be sent to her rooms, vaguely explaining she had unexpected hungry guests. The three then all sat by the fire and sipped hot chocolate and ate Agnes's favourite buns. Harini pulled and played with hers at first then she decided it was delicious and went back for more. Harini started to study the girl and then stated she thought she was dead, killed by the boy who dragged her around on a torturous contraption in the white stuff. Avia went cold to the core as she realised Harini had taken her Jack; she bit her lip in response and looked to Agnes for help. Avia could not speak a word for her rage and ran to her bedroom in floods of tears; her mind was going crazy. Had the witch finished of Jack? Agnes's tough questions came hard and fast as she demanded truthful answers from Harini who twitched and looked to the floor - Harini's honest story of events was told. Agnes went to Avia with Harini close by who told her that he gardened for her father a warlock in the Golden Fort. Harini muttered an apology, realising the damaged she had bestowed on this girl. Avia accepted her story though did not forgive her and turned away.

Agnes and Harini talked into the night and something unexpected happened to Harini. For the first time in her life she felt understood and liked the girl Agnes, who was interesting and highly intelligent. Impressed by Agnes, Harini promised to help save Jack and she told her how he was safe making his magical garden. Agnes did not mention that Jack was no wizard - but wondered how he grew plants so quickly in the middle of the Indian desert, so she casually asked who the servants were and sleepily Harini described the ones she knew and spoke mainly about Ynes, who had been captured from Bengal. Agnes found her name interesting and asked Harini to describe her a little more and then she asked if she would have seen Jack, as Harini's eyes closed she mumbled that Ynes was in charge of feeding him and ordering his plants.

Agnes prowled around the room while the others slept deeply exhausted from the day. She summoned Hestia to bring her small spell book, which the cat brought quickly purring, then lay down by the fire. Agnes had become good at spells of the mind. She had been studying them in fascination and had found she had a real gift for reading and reaching others. She could now send a signal to Hestia and had used it on the young maids in a kindly way and now she needed to expand her distance and communicate with others. Agnes worked deep into the night, knowing that they had little time in reality to rescue Jack; the suspected witch Ynes, she was sure, would have a plan for the wizard of the garden. Agnes went to Miss Bonneville's rooms leaving Hestia to guard Harini and protect Avia. She looked for a personal trinket of Miss Bonneville's, something that she held very dear, and in a bedside draw Agnes found a pendant she would usually wear, but in her haste to find Jack, had left it behind. Agnes put the moonstone on; it was much like Avia's, and she went to her sewing room where she meddled with mixing potions and finally found the consistency needed. She placed both moonstones in the potion and took her spell book from her skirt pockets and read out loud. Strange lights flickered from the potion and in her mind she saw Miss Bonneville sat at a desk in a sunny room, with a boy in a garden; the sky was golden and blue, and a huge tree cast shadows as it swayed in the gentlest of breeze sending whispers on the leaves.

The Moonstone Connection

Miss Bonneville began to feel sleepy with so much reading of a text that was a broken form of English. She had made endless notes to decrypt all of its meaning and she had cross referenced it with many languages and thought she had broken the key - by the next day she would have solved it; however, she would not let on, and would explain the languages were mixed and it could take some time, giving her more time. She relaxed for a little and sipped the herb water, and gazing out to the garden she hoped to see the boy again. As she peered through the flowing drapes, she had the strangest sensation that someone else was in the room and from nowhere Agnes like a ghost stood in the room and hissed she had little time to explain. Miss Bonneville quickly got over the shock, grasping the importance of Agnes's amazing spell, and she listened carefully to Agnes, who told her that her biggest fears were that Ynes would run away with Jack and that she knew from Harini that the white warlock would never release Jack, unless to his death. Also, she said that Harini had cast a spell on him, so the poor thing had no clue who he was and was still under Harini's hoodoo. Miss Bonneville had not had chance to process Agnes's news when the key turned in the lock, and Agnes's apparition disappeared.

Miss Bonneville calmed herself and pretended to read more words as the voice of her new employer, Chandaria, asked politely how she had progressed. Miss Bonneville explained the difficulty of the languages, but comforted her agitation by saying it would not be long. Chandaria took the papers as Miss Bonneville sneaked notes away in her deep skirt pockets, and they arranged for her to come early the next day. Miss Bonneville asked if she could walk and sit in the beautiful gardens while she waited for Ynes to walk her to the living quarters, explaining that she always became very lost. Chandaria, eyed her suspiciously and then dismissed her irately as a nuisance, but granted that she could stay in the gardens if she was quiet.

Miss Bonneville sensed Chandaria's anger was more her desperation. Miss Bonneville had learnt from the scripture that it was in some way linked to Chandaria's family and her inheritance, which clearly had been stolen from her by the cruel warlock. One thing Miss Bonneville had not pieced together, though, was whether Chandaria was Harini's mother.

Miss Bonneville walked out into the gardens shaded by the old Banyan trees, and she could see lots of new planting and growth; someone had been busy. She sat on a bench and processed how Agnes had amazingly contacted her, her little seamstress had no bounds. She tried to piece together Agnes's thoughts and as she did to her amazement, relief and shock, Jack appeared. At first, she wondered if he was just another apparition or some trick on her tired mind but as she watched him, closely tending to his seeds and young plants, although he looked glazed and was clearly not himself, he was most certainly her Jack.

Miss Bonneville felt a rush of excitement but contained herself and stopped herself from calling his name. Instead she thought about how Agnes had connected to her just before; she had seen it performed by the old warlock Fabian a few times. She needed to give something to Jack that would link him to her and Agnes, then they could reach out to him with hope. She looked in her hidden silk purse and found a lucky charm that Agnes had given her the Christmas before, a tiny silk owl delicately embroidered with fragments of lucky citrine for the eyes and beak. Miss Bonneville walked up to the boy she knew as Jack and started to speak with him. She told him how they missed him and described the gardens at Stourton and Avia and Agnes, then commanded him to take the charm and keep it very safe. Jack took the charm and hid it in his pockets, but not once did he look Miss Bonneville in the eye, instead he kept his gaze firmly on the flower beds. Miss Bonneville thought hard of Agnes and tried to communicate with her, but her thoughts were broken as Ynes came flying around the corner. Jack disappeared deeper into the garden and Ynes urged her along to their quarters before she got called for more chores. She asked Miss Bonneville how her day reading had gone and if the Mistress Chandaria had been good to her. Miss Bonneville told Ynes little truth or information, yet satisfied her curiosity. Thanks to Agnes, she knew she had to handle her with great care, knowing that she could be of use if she did intend to steal Jack away, it would be easier for Miss Bonneville to reclaim him from her than the white warlock Gedahard.

Ynes chattered away on the way back and spoke of the gardener boy. She asked if Miss Bonneville had seen him or spoken to him, and cautiously Miss Bonneville said she had complimented him on the plants he grew and she shrugged her shoulders, saying he didn't even look at her and gestured perhaps he was mute or simple and did not understand her language well enough. Ynes, satisfied that she did not lie, as she had seen her speak to him from a tower, was happy, and she told Miss Bonneville about the boy who had arrived and how Harini had disappeared, that now the master Gedahard was gone, and the mistress was edgy and acting weird. Trusting Miss Bonneville, she asked her to keep a secret and she told her how she planned to rescue the boy and take him far away. She said her uncle ran a camel train that would take her to Kandiaro from where she would take a boat on the Indus River and travel down to where she could cross to Karachi and be free. Miss Bonneville tried not to react, doubting the young inexperienced witch would survive; she knew for certain poor Jack would not. Miss Bonneville did not discourage her though, and complimented her on such bravery and an amazing journey. She expressed that she would love such a venture herself and longed to travel once she had earned some money. Ynes did not reply and only smiled, unfortunately for Miss Bonneville, another companion was not part of her plan.

The Lonely Gardener

~~ * ~~

The boy sat under his shelter and as the darkness fell, he scuttled to the shadows and sat beneath a little crack of moonlight; he studied his gift. He liked the bird and its pretty colours and the tiny stones. He held it, smelt it, and studied it some more, then he remembered the words he heard in the garden from the strange lady, who talked of another garden far away and a name that made him feel some pain - his heart hurt and he did not know why. That night he dreamt of a girl laughing in a white world of trees and woke in a panic and then settled himself. He was still in his courtyard with sand and the few plants he had grown, he could not remember the girl who had taken him and thought in his muddled mind, that it was the girl who served him and tried to charm him with her smiles. He wanted to meet the other lady again, the one who had given him the charm; something about her made him feel safe. He did not sleep much more that night and spent his hours staring at his charm and little flickers of memories came to his mind and the name Avia hung on his lips.

When dawn came, he carried on with his gardening and acted the same way though something had changed inside him. He felt different and started to realise that things were very strange. He saw the lady who gave him the charm later in the study - he heard the key turn and knew she was a prisoner much like him. She subtly gave him a smile and sat to her work and the boy carried on his planting and watering and adding of potions that the servant girl made. She did not notice any difference, but ordered him to work well and fast and that one day soon he would be free. Confused, the boy continued his task of gardening. His small pet, a gecko he called Tibbles, ran from his arm to search for insects and leaves to nibble. The boy kept his head as low as possible, afraid he would reveal that his trance-like state was slowly lifting. He started to hear a voice in his head and then deep in the gardens by a fig tree he saw in the branches a girl who waved and said her name was Agnes and that she came to help rescue him. She told him to do everything the lady with the charm said and he would be fine in time. Voices approached and the girl vanished in a flick. The boy scuttled off now knowing he was being rescued from his fate, but he had to continue to try and fool them that he was still dumbstruck by the witch who tricked him, so when she came flicking her eyes with gifts of food and seeds he kept his eyes low and continued to not respond. She took his hand and said she would somehow break his cruel affliction when they were free from the castle walls. The boy was conflicted. Who was on his side? He had to trust his gut though and the girl in the tree was so familiar and it felt good to see her and again on his lips he said the name Avia. He would have to be strong and break the spell, so the boy started exercising at night He drew pictures in the sand of his memories that flickered like flames in his head and as the daylight broke with its huge golden sun, the boy carefully wiped his drawings away, in fear his captors would wash his mind away, like the grains of sand that blew through the cracks in the walls.

First Spell

~~ * ~~

Avia had still not been to the garden, and with Miss Bonneville gone and Agnes promising she was doing everything she could, Avia felt useless. For too long she had been stuck in her rooms and had struggled even to look out of the windows; her heartbreak and worry was too painful. Avia became cross with herself. She had to do something. She thought of the poem she had sung that had released her little yew tree witch, Agnes. So Avia went searching for her old book of Indian poems that her father had bought back years ago. She reached under her bed and found the dusty copy, and blowing the dust off, she began to look at the sweet verses, reading the meanings carefully. The poem that had released Agnes mentioned a free bird and as Agnes had been set free, she searched for a poem that would bring her Jack back. Avia read for so long that the light had faded from the skies and yet another day had passed of isolation, although she suddenly felt a little hope and slept in a world of strange dreams.

The next morning Avia woke to sunshine and a bright blue sky. She dressed slowly and taking her book, she wandered out of the house and into the gardens. The robin greeted her and hopped along the hedgerows, the noisy ousel bird sang out, whistling its tune, and rolling tears flowed from Avia as she thought of Jack and how he used to sing with the birds and knew every call. Avia carried on towards the gothic cottage holding her shawl tight around her. She went up onto the little stone bridge with its grassy path and looked at the ducks and fishes that darted beneath, their expectations of a crumb or two from the shadow above were disappointed and Avia thought she would visit the kitchen and feed them later. She carried on patting statues like they were old friends and talked to the birds as though they understood her ramblings of despair. When she arrived at the cottage, it looked much the same. Avia lifted the pot and found the big iron key and she let herself in. She could see with relief that it had not been touched, and she clambered up the rackety ladder to the tiny roof space where they had hoarded the contents of Agnes's box or tomb. She found some pots and jars of herbs and the leather-bound book of spells that Agnes had once used. Avia then immersed herself in finding the spell that gave her a connection to something special. She remembered some of the words that Agnes had taught her when they played by the yew tree, and she remembered Agnes trying to connect to her mother Avoca with a spell she thought had never worked. Avia though began to think it had, but it had just been sabotaged by Josina and her evil plots. Avia then began to collect her herbs, although she was missing lovage and it was the wrong time of year. She knew where it grew though, but would have to wait as the light was fading and another day gone.

Avia made her way up to the house, feeling hungry and with a little colour on her cheeks. She went to the kitchens and asked for a meal to be sent to her room. Bunty was thrilled to see her up and about, but held her tongue, knowing she was as fragile as an autumn leaf in a swirling, wintery wind with Jack still gone and everything feeling so spooky and surreal. Avia returned to her room where there was a note on the mantle from Nanny Maud apologising for her absence at such a dreadful time; she had some emergency at her old home. Avia found this most peculiar and a puzzle; in all the years she had known Nanny Maud, she had never once mentioned a family or been anywhere. Avia dismissed it though, too busy with her own thoughts and grief. In some way it was a relief; she could bring the spell book, pots and herbs to her room, where she felt safe and warm. Avia ate every morsel of her food and again slept full of dreams, which became more vivid. She walked in a hot garden shaded by strange trees. She could see golden temples and carvings of elephants. Avia tasted sweet fruit from a knife, and as the person handed her the fruit, a strong hot wind of blistering sand blew the person away - little speckles shattered and then there was nothing, just the cold, hard ground.

Avia woke feeling strange yet refreshed, despite her dream. She felt some hope that she was in some way connecting to Jack, and she made her way out via the kitchen, grabbing some buns; the kitchens were quiet and no one was around. Avia guessed that they were all enjoying the free time, although she could not help feel that something was strange. Avia looked around and on the side dresser she noticed Jack's unmistakable pocketknife, with the handle he had carved and the leather sheaf Agnes had made; he must have left it on the morning of the snow. Avia pinched herself to check she was still not dreaming and walked out into the crisp, cold sunshine and went to find Tomsk who could help her by lending a trowel. Tomsk was glad to see her and was the only one who dared mention Jack. He spoke of Jack's ma and pa who knew nothing still and could not be contacted as they were still in France. Avia thought it was a good thing that they didn't know - poor Belle would nearly die of worry, and she prayed that on their return, he would be back. She gave Tomsk hope and felt better herself.

Avia now knew she had to be strong - it was her duty. She had to start running the house and gardens, what with Miss Bonneville gone and Agnes in hiding somewhere close by. With more purpose than ever Avia ran to the bridge and quickly fed the ducks and fish who frenzied with their rewards. She then went to the spot where she knew a huge clump of lovage grew and she began to dig and scrape the cold hard ground until she found the roots. Pulling a few out, she put them in her apron pockets and walked via the temple for the view of the garden and its stunning lake. She forced sadness from her mind and prayed, like she once had with Jack by her side in that very spot, that her plan would work. Avia then ran down towards the cottage around the lake and through the trees, unlocked the door with the key and went to get the book, pots and herbs. Avia grabbed the things but felt uneasy, as though she was watched. She sensed someone had been in the cottage, then dismissed it - she had the only key. Avia put everything in her basket then locked the door behind her. She looked around and saw nothing, but sensing something was still there and hearing a faint rustle, Avia bolted towards the Hall.

Afraid, Avia bolted the huge front door after herself and ran to her room. She checked that her moonstone was firmly around her neck and checked that her bracelet from Preeti still clung to her delicate wrists, then she read a protection spell and sprinkled dried comfrey around the room. Avia then began to make her first potion. She carefully followed the recipe in detail but again the light began to fade, and another day was lost in her inexplicable and lonely world. Avia slept again with her dreams becoming much more vivid, and each time the hot sandy wind dumped her back on the hard, cold ground.

The following morning brought a thick fog with ice and an eerie chill. Glad she had everything hidden in her room, Avia wandered to the kitchen through the huge empty rooms. She saw Lottie and caught up with the gossip from the village and of the staff, then Lottie sobbed about Jack. Avia felt cold hearted not to comfort his cousin, but she felt her own pain so badly, and could not bring herself to share her feelings or feel empathy for others. Avia now understood how her father had felt when her poor mother died. Avia inhaled a large breath and in her strongest voice promised her that Jack would be found, she hugged her and then asked Lottie to let all the staff know that a meeting would be held in the library, with tea and cakes, at three o'clock sharp.

Avia then went back to her room and sat with her hot chocolate and biscuits sat by the fire. She held the warm cup and vacantly looked out at the gardens immersed in a thick fog that she doubted would lift. Avia looked at the grandfather clock. She had six hours or less to perform her first spell, so she got out the potion and placed it onto the hearth, then she put side by side the pocketknife of Jack's and her gloves that she loved with the little robin embroidered on, gifted by Jack. She warmed the potion and read the spell as she sprinkled it onto the items and herself, she did this again and again and then she read the poem she had found:

Lotus Dream

*Under the Banyan tree lies the shade, thick
glossy leaves of leather and luck, with woody
roots that wind and fade and take the
dreams of love far away.
Gracious lotus flower with purity and
serenity concatenate your illustriousness upon
distrait.
Petals of roses blow in the breeze and float
daintily upon the seas, your scent reveals.
Sing to the treetops koel bird with no re-
straint, your song will find my lost and in
your flight on blackened wings, bring back
on the fall my heart and my dreams.*

The clock struck two, and Avia said her poem one more time, then hid the ingredients of her spell well and lay on the bed thinking of Jack. She talked to him as if he lay next to her under the yew tree on a hot summer's day; she almost felt his warm breath and heard his drawl - he said her name over and over again and Avia called out to him to come back. Avia was certain she felt his presence as he felt hers, but the moment of connection was suddenly lost, as though a hard wind slammed the door, and the clock struck the half hour.

Avia got up in a dash, and she splashed water on her face as though nothing had happened and she had just woken from a nap, then she marched with assertiveness to the servants who waited on time. Avia began giving instructions to all - the house would be treated as though it was full. Avia ordered flowers, food and fires, then organised an event that all the families could enjoy, her gift to them; the hall's wonderful rooms would be filled with refreshments and music. Excited and thankful for her stance, the staff all scuttled off with purpose, while Avia stood and wondered if she could make it work. A banquet for Jack's people and the poem read should surely, with a secret spell, call him from wherever he had been taken. She prayed the more she did the more he would fight to survive.

The Witches Hunt Witches

~~ * ~~

Agnes was hiding out at the manor house where she knew there was a strong connection to Jack, with his belongings and family ties. She had bought Harini with her, mainly because she could not concentrate with her out of sight and also because she had shown remorse and wanted desperately to help. Avia was best left alone for a few days to realise she had to fight back. Agnes knew her friend was strong and would eventually find a way. Agnes was pleased she had connected with Miss Bonneville and that she had managed to get through to Jack enough to break his trance a little. Harini was trying with difficulty from a distance to undo the spell she had put on him that day in the snow. Agnes sensed something else was going on though. She felt magic in the air and when she spied on her friend Avia, she was both shocked and impressed to see that she had made a spell and had a plan herself. Deciding it could do no harm and that she would not really be able to do anything as not being a witch, she left Avia to her tampering in magical affairs and felt proud that she was doing something. She had also heard the rumour of a party at the hall - another effort by Avia to lift spirits. Agnes was proud that Avia had such strength and guided the village who all depended upon the work and life the Hall brought.

There was something else though. Agnes felt something more powerful, so Harini and Agnes went on a little hunting trip in the thick fog. They travelled by treetops and looked over the estate. Above the gothic cottage they could see a strange light and on closer inspection wisps of smoke. They quietly climbed halfway down the yew tree and sat like wild cats ready to pounce on their prey. Agnes felt a certain amount of protection with Harini by her side, two witches were far stronger than one and she began to enjoy her company; she was quick, clever and funny in her ways. The icy cold fog only sharpened their senses and every single sound could be heard - even a brave little shrew was spotted, who surfaced for a flash before disappearing back to his hole. The witches waited patiently, and the hours ticked by. The moon started to shine on the icy lake and shadows danced in a wind that grew, blowing away the thick fog and lighting the night. Agnes was about to call their stakeout over, she needed to get back to concentrating on Jack as his world would be waking while hers went to sleep, when creepily a faint image appeared like a ghost. The figure made a fire and tried the handle of the gothic cottage door, which was then opened by some other force - the cottage had a visitor and not a welcome one. Agnes knew she had seen the image before, but she could not quite place it so different in its ghostly form; she needed a closer view without the hooded cloak. Knowing they had more trouble, Harini and Agnes gently disappeared into the night and leaving the spectre, they went to the Hall. Agnes had to protect Avia with dangerous company in the grounds.

Harini and Agnes had a busy night ahead, so while the house slept, they worked through the night connecting with Jack and researching more spells. Hestia the cat returned from her nightly hunting early with news of her sighting for Agnes and so by morning Agnes knew her ghost was no ghost at all - instead, it was a struggling and weak wisp of Josina, who came, Agnes feared, to fight; her last chance maybe to survive. She told Harini the story and they agreed they needed Avoca and Preeti; this battle could not be fought alone - there was too much to lose.

Red Sky

~~ * ~~

Miss Bonneville saw the dawn arrive with a red sky in the east and it glowed across the fort turning the stone a strange pink. She had heard the phrase 'red sky in the morning, shepherds' warning' and thought 'witches warning' was more appropriate that day. She had been up all night and had thought over and over about what Agnes had managed to tell her; she had promised she would be back soon and would get word to the Fort of Chitrakut, which was amazingly not so far from the Golden Fort.

She sent her message with Ynes's brother who travelled there with rugs made in Jaisalmer. He promised to go there as soon as he could and Miss Bonneville handed him a part payment which he happily accepted. He liked her - she was witty and bright, she had taught him to read some letters and he hoped she would stay, as with her, he felt some hope. Miss Bonneville's note was simple and did not give too much away. It just read Agnes was seriously ill and needed her mother Avoca as well as Preeti, she hoped they would understand and not panic too much for Agnes - unnecessarily. Miss Bonneville had thought to bring them to help her with Jack and had Josina not showed up at Stourton Hall, she may well have done so, but she worried at the thought of Josina in the cottage and was even more eager to get Jack back to his home.

Miss Bonneville sat in the office again, translating and deciphering the scripture, and now understood the full wrath of the document. Chandaria had been sold by her uncle to the warlock, who now controlled and owned all her wealth from her royal parents who had been murdered. She was bound to the warlock in every way and had no hope of escape, unless she left India with nothing but the clothes on her back and even then, she would still be his to hunt down. How she would explain all this to her she did not know and wished she had a solution, but for now she could not help Chandaria, she had to save Jack. Ynes had become worrying, as she was becoming more secretive, clearly not wanting Miss Bonneville to join her on her escape with Jack. Not knowing when she planned to go was a challenge, as Ynes knew her city and the fort well in addition to its escape routes. She was so deep in thought that she nearly jumped out of her skin when she saw Jack's sunburnt face at the window. Scared they would be seen, she gestured to the sun and pointed to the west where it would start going down and pointed to the sun dial. She hoped Jack understood that she would meet him after her work - he gave a strained smile and Miss Bonneville knew then that there was hope.

Eager to finish her work and meet Jack she rang the bell for a servant and a young girl much like Ynes arrived, but when Miss Bonneville asked her where Ynes was, the girl just shook her head and said, 'gone'. Miss Bonneville felt utter panic. Had Jack come to say goodbye? Had he already gone? She waited for the Mistress Chandaria and all too quickly, and perhaps a little harshly, explained the meanings and consequences of her uncle's actions. Chandaria sobbed and asked Miss Bonneville what she was to do. Miss Bonneville decided a bargain was her greatest ploy, so she carefully explained that she recognised the missing boy in the garden who, she said, had been taken from an important English family of aristocracy. Miss Bonneville said that if she were allowed to take the gardener boy, then she would help Chandaria escape - she promised she would come back if no word of the boy and her connection was ever told. Chandaria had wondered about the boy and his strange state and the disappearance of Harini, her daughter, who she was never allowed to see - she had only ever had glimpses of her when she played outside. So Chandaria agreed and sent for the boy; they waited and waited but no boy came, and after the fort had been searched, Miss Bonneville realised her greatest mistake - Ynes had gone.

Chandaria was desperate as she now had no bargain and only the truth of the scripture, so she sobbed even more.

Miss Bonneville said she had to go but promised she would come back, then hesitated. If she left this poor young woman, hardly old enough to be a mother, in the hands of the barbaric warlock, she would never escape, so she quickly wrote clear instructions of a date, time and what Chandaria must say and do. She gave her a small clay pot of powder and checked she understood, explaining it was her only way out; she must take flight. As Miss Bonneville rushed out of the office and through the gardens to a side gate, she saw a temple in the distance and on top stood a figure who looked her way and pointed. At first she thought it was Jack, but she followed her instinct that Ynes would have taken him out of the castle gates and on to the lanes. Miss Bonneville had glimpsed the warlock's return to the castle and just as she was looking at him, in a flick she missed a camel train that turned the corner bound to the desert, with two young riders at the rear, wrapped in silks with only their eyes visible.

Miss Bonneville rushed to Ynes's family within the warlock's castle walls to warn them; they were in grave danger she told them because of what Ynes had done. Relieved the brother had not yet left, she asked to join him on his journey to the Fort of Chitrakut, while the others frantically packed and cursed their foolish child. Soon, Miss Bonneville and Ynes's brother Yari sat wrapped in long white linen scarves as they set off on the dusty tracks. Miss Bonneville waved sadly to the kind family who had been so hospitable and now they too had to flee. Yari told Miss Bonneville not to worry for his folks - they were nomadic and rarely settled in one place for long, so it was good they escaped the warlock's walls, but said he would miss the Golden Fort and its good people.

As Miss Bonneville sat on the cart with the donkeys pulling in the blazing sun, she thought of Jack and wondered how he would manage on the long camel trek that his keeper had decided upon. She thought of poor Chandaria, the princess locked in the castle with her family's fortune stolen and all her freedom gone. Miss Bonneville began to miss her home herself and wished more than anything to be back with Jack. She looked over to Yari, who was silent, respectful and a good driver. He did not stop much, only to feed and water the donkeys. His patience and gentle manner was received well and the journey, despite the terror of losing Jack and the worry of Josina at Stourton Hall, was quite unexpectedly pleasant. Yari was good company and the scenery spectacular. Miss Bonneville began to calm and to think more clearly about her situation. Had she and Chandaria begun the exchange of Jack, the warlock Gedahard would have come back to find them with the boy and the scriptures, and the outcome would have been disastrous for all. She suspected

Ynes had known the warlock would return, hence her quick escape. Miss Bonneville thought about what to do but could not decide and longed suddenly for her meeting with Avoca and Preeti. In her wandering thoughts she fell asleep and woke to noise and chatter everywhere as they rode through a place packed with traders. The enormous fort stood on the hill, its walls defending those within, an imposing and daunting place. Yari carried on to the fort entrance with no fear or hesitation; the guard looked at his seal and at Miss Bonneville - Yari just shrugged, his mother had come and far too easily they let him through with his delivery for the Maharajah. As agreed, Miss Bonneville dismounted in the square and began her search for Avoca. Yari wished her luck and hoped to see her again in the humble life he led, and Miss Bonneville hoped so too.

The square was both vast and busy. Miss Bonneville wondered how she would ever find the pair whom she had never met, having only seen Avoca from afar a long time ago. Just as she began to panic, she saw a crowd around a small stall in the far corner and what had to be Avoca, as she looked just like Agnes, only older. Avoca touted her audience with some sort of potion for healing, and Miss Bonneville joined the onlookers and offered to purchase a pot. Avoca took her money and sent her to Preeti who gave her a small green pot of the ointment. Miss Bonneville handed Preeti the note she had intended Yari to give. Preeti was quick and, glancing at the note, called to Avoca they must stop selling today and a rush of purchases flooded in and soon every pot was gone, then with no word, they were packing up the stall. Preeti gestured that Miss Bonneville follow them and she was taken back to their neat stone house a little way from the square where she was smuggled in checking that no one watched. Preeti quickly explained that the guards searched for a dankini as a succession of bad things had happened. Avoca mumbled that it was an illness and no witch was at work, but they still had to be careful and had thought to leave for a while. Miss Bonneville then explained everything as quickly as she could about Jack and Josina. Avoca listened without speaking a word, and they agreed to pack and leave before nightfall. Travelling light, the three women separated and arranged to meet outside the fort away from the crowds and prying eyes.

Miss Bonneville felt very nervous and suddenly saw Yari; she waved and he stopped his cart - she hopped on, relieved. She just sat with no explanation as they trotted out of the fort and through the crowds who seemed to endlessly pour in and out - never had she seen such a busy place. The bumpy track led them away and as the crowds faded, they stopped by a shallow river for the donkeys to drink and Yari to sort himself out. He arranged his rugs that were left over from his sales and tucked his money safely into his boots, then asked Miss Bonneville if things were all right. Miss Bonneville was beginning to trust Yari and decided it was time, so she asked him yet again for his help. She told him all about Jack and Harini and how she had tried to rescue Jack and now Ynes had him on some camel train, when she was supposed to have Jack by now, and she explained that she needed her friends Avoca and Preeti, who she knew could help. It was no surprise to Miss Bonneville that Yari wanted to help her and not once did he flinch or show any worry for himself. He just expressed concern for his foolish sister and the boy Jack, who he feared stood little chance when faced with the dry deserts and endless thirst.

Avoca and Preeti arrived on the river bend and petted the donkey's much to Yari's delight. Both of them thanked him profoundly as they quickly slithered onto his cart, hiding under the woven rugs. Often they would look out as they passed the mountains and herbaceous scenes and not far from the village where Preeti once lived, a missing child who escaped or was captured. She briefly wondered if her parents were still alive and felt some pity for leaving them all alone. Born a cursed child she did the best for them, but she could never have married their chosen suitor. Preeti winced at the thought of her life if she had gone back. While Preeti poundered, Avoca sang songs and asked questions about how long the journey would take and where they would go. Yari politely answered, giving little information away, he just clicked at the donkey's and chatted about the birds and the trees that they passed.

Several days later, the donkeys and cart rattled into the ancient caves of Atdo where Yari knew his uncle would arrive with his camel train. His uncle always stayed in Dayapar for a few days to do his dodgy business trading with disreputable types, before travelling onto the border. Yari was certain Ynes would not know of his dealings - she did not know enough to be safe. He was glad he knew of her plans and hoped he could save his sister and the boy Jack from a dreadful fate, as he knew his uncle would not care for either of their lives.

They found a good spot for the donkeys in the shade of a cave covered in hay and as Yari went off to find water, he called out that they were all free to roam - there would be no trouble from the quiet and gentle cave folk. While he tended to his beloved donkeys, Avoca and Preeti clambered out from under the rugs and joined Miss Bonneville at the water well, where they drank thirstily and then made a fire to boil their rice and herbs. Several passers-by chatted with them as though they always sat there and ate their supper. Yari said the cave dwellers were the friendliest and kindest of sorts;

they lived off the land and cared for no trouble and were descendants from an ancient tribe called the Cornovii, who long ago had become nomads, leaving behind the sea and fish. Miss Bonneville was curious as to why his uncle would turn up at the caves, but he just replied they would soon see, and Yari pulled his robes over his face and bundled his bag up laying it under his head and soon he was fast asleep. Miss Bonneville, Avoca and Preeti went to a hilltop where they could not be overheard and they started to make their plan. It was decided with some difficulty that only Preeti would travel back to help Agnes at Stourton as Miss Bonneville needed Avoca's help to find Jack. So, after many goodbyes and solemn words of advice, they lit a fire and the verses of travel were spoken. No longer did they only rely on All Hallows or an equinox to travel; Preeti could go anywhere whenever she pleased. Avoca and Miss Bonneville stood and watched her disappear, leaving just fragments of sparkling dust and although they were worried, they knew Preeti was a strong witch. With Agnes and Harini, Josina would now surely struggle to get close for a while. Avoca and Miss Bonneville just had to wait and hope they could see and snatch Jack back, but how possible that would be they had no clue.

They set up camp and watched, and just as Yari had promised, a camel train arrived - over fifty camels loaded with goods and people trekked in by moonlight. Their first and most dangerous part of the desert was done - no snakes, bandits or desert demons had taken anything or anyone, and with each camel loaded with goods, the procession headed straight for the large watering hole, a hidden oasis in a dry and sandy land. The cave people were gifted many supplies for the use of their caves; water and food were provided and soon a feast was made and delicious smells rose as the stars and moon shone down. As they watched the travellers make camp, Miss Bonneville looked in desperation for Jack, but it was impossible as every man and woman looked the same in the dark, and with their cloaks and turbans. Miss Bonneville needed help from Avia or Agnes, so she started to chant her spells - reaching out to those who would listen.

Jack's Dreams

~~ * ~~

Jack was sad not to have been able to speak with the kind lady who gave him the owl charm. He was confused as he still did not understand everything that had happened and only knew that if he escaped with Ynes, he was at least free from the prison he had found himself in. He did not trust Ynes though and was not keen on her method of travel - it was hot, smelly and uncomfortable. Horses he loved, camels he did not. They were too high from the ground and too hard to control, but he had no choice as they were all tied together in the endless camel train. They slept in makeshift camps along the way, uncomfortable, scratchy and cold by night or sweltering by day. Jack hated that Ynes tried to always lie close to him; he felt irritated by her presence. He was grumpy from the heat and hunger he felt during the day and the shivering fear he felt at night - he thought they must have been travelling for months, when in reality it was only days.

At night he had had dreams of gardens with a lake, and he could faintly see a girl who called to him; each time, though, she faded into the misty lake. The night again came around and he struggled to sleep as the sky was so clear and the ground so cold; he stared up at the stars and in his mind he heard a voice, as though it lay next to him. The voice was familiar and made him feel happy; she talked of valleys, gardens, and birds and said her name Avia, again and again, and in his dreams he held her hand and they stared over the lake. Jack woke with a jolt as he was gently nudged by Ynes to wake; they needed to eat and go. Again he was back on his lumpy, stinking camel; somehow though it seemed easier, as he daydreamed of Avia, and the more he thought of her, the more he started to remember. He began to look forward to each time they would shelter from the sun or cold night, for then he would find her voice and dream of her - everything she said came to life in his mind and Jack knew he was getting closer to her. Then one night she came to him, and he saw people that he was sure were familiar; they were all smiling and singing - flashes of people bought him even closer and Jack woke knowing who he was. He remembered Avia's words to come home, but he knew that he had to remain cautious and pretend he knew nothing until he was found by Miss Bonneville again. Jack felt angry that he had been tricked by Ynes and taken further away. He swallowed his rage though and carried on in his dumbstruck ways - as his hate for Ynes grew. Jack had to be careful, so he decided not to speak or even look at anyone, keeping his head down and soon Ynes became bored with her boy; she left him alone and went off with the others she had met.

They came back later making lots of noise and laughter. Jack watched Ynes from the corner of his eye and wonder with dread what she plotted next. Had she decided to leave him behind, or had she decided to try and sell him; he had heard her boast of his gardening skills, and Jack felt nervous and worried. Maybe he should escape the camel train, but he had no clue in the vast desert which way he would go. The journey seemed endless, and Jack began to wonder if he could survive much more. His thirst and hunger was gnawing away, his sight was blurry, and he trembled when he was hot and when he was cold. This ride was the longest ever, and just when Jack felt he could no longer last, they set camp in a rocky and hilly place - he could see caves and people started to appear. Exhausted he slept and woke to the sound of music and smells of food. He was handed a massive bowl of rice and a spiced drink; hungrily Jack ate and drank as he watched the dancing and fires. Jack stayed firmly where he was and just ate food as it was passed around, and later, as the music and fires died, Jack still stayed rooted to his spot. He lay down and waited for his dreams of Avia to find him under the cold, moonlit and starry skies.

Preeti at Stourton

~~ * ~~

Preeti arrived in an elegant manner, prepared for the cold
and rugged terrain, landing on her tip toes in fur boots in
front of the Hall. She brushed off the snow in a dismissive
fashion, as though she had seen snow every day; indeed, the
cold white flakes she had seen high on the mountains, but
never so close to the door of a home, she was far more used
to sand and heat. Luckily, Preeti had been well-advised by
her dear Avoca on what to put on her feet. She walked purposefully to the door, her feet hardly touching the ground
and leaving no footprints. Preeti tapped as hard as she could
and the door was opened by a grey-haired butler and she
asked to see the seamstress of Stourton. The butler looked
her up and down; unsure of her and with so much strange
business around, he did not invite her in but instead left her
stood out in the cold. Preeti did not let the incident ruffle
her and instead patiently waited and looked over the gardens. A girl approached up the long stone steps; she seemed
faintly familiar in some way, although she knew she had
never met her before, and wrapped up in so many layers
and muffs it would be hard to decipher quite who she was in
any event. The girl looked afraid, so Preeti called out she
was a friend of the seamstress of Stourton. Unsure, the girl
hesitated and looked around for which way she should turn

to run, then with relief the huge door opened and a concerned Agnes stood calling out firstly to Miss Avia to come straight in or she would catch her death from the cold and she shouted again with a giggle - their guest was Preeti all the way from India. On these words, Avia bounced like a puppy towards her home and shivering with cold ran into the hallway. Soon, they were all sat in the library with hot tea by the fire. After the excitement from their meeting, Preeti began to check out their guest, the snatcher Harini, for any more cheating. She listened to Agnes and discovered what she had found out and how things went with poor Jack, she then looked to Avia and asked her how her spell had worked, a little shocked she could perform spells at all. Avia said they went well; she had felt a real connection with him and knew that he heard her. Agnes eyed her dear friend and asked her what spell she performed and how, while Avia asked how Preeti knew; Preeti just smiled and shrugged. Avia explained to Agnes about her Indian poem book and how she remembered things she had seen Agnes do and that she had used Agnes's old spell book that they had found in her shallow grave. Impressed, Agnes looked more closely at Avia and looked to the witch Preeti for an answer. Preeti had seen it straight away; the girl who had stood scared in the snow was no mere mortal, though whether by accident or birth it was unclear. Agnes could not really believe that her dear friend was now by some strange miracle one of her own sort. Astonished at first, she then laughed that now there was four of them with so many spells that surely Josina stood no chance. Preeti then kindly explained to Avia how she knew everything - she could see a person's thoughts and things they had done and things they planned to do. All were impressed and a little nervous. They sat and listened to a story Preeti told them of when she was small and how she had realised her skill and not known whether it was a hinderance or gift - she was never sure. Preeti recounted the tale like it was happening all around her - the girls felt that they were in some play, so rich were her descriptions and words.

Rolling Stones

The village lay at the foot of the mountain, dusty and dry from the heat; the rains had not come and rumbled elsewhere, leaving the village to fend for itself, with a river that barely babbled over shingles and fish that did not visit. The grasslands tinged brown swayed little and even the trees bowed downwards from the sky.

Her home made from rocks and mud was nestled into the huge rock face much like the others; their settlement had stood for hundreds of years as her people were not nomadic like many, they were instead dwellers that stayed and whatever the gods brought, good or bad, they would accept as their path. Preeti remembered the rolling stones, the day of the monsoons. She was only small as she watched them tumble to the water's edge – that was the day she found she was different and the day she first saw something happen before it did. So young, she could not help or understand her curse gifted from the black moon she had been born under. The rocks fell slowly at first from the top of the mountain then suddenly more and more joined them and at speed they hurtled down towards the people. Preeti had cried out, screaming before it happened and with luck this bought her mother and father out from the mud home, and as they ran to her thinking a mountain cat came, they were saved from the rocks that crushed many others. From that day Preeti began a life of precognition, and as she grew older she found ways to prevent bad things happening, always with great care, as if seen or suspected they would kill her for bring a jadoo or worse. As she grew older it became in some ways easier but in other ways harder to control her growing powers. Preeti found the other children in the village boring and she played with them only to mask her true self; she practised kindness, sharing and giving as taught and was praised for her quick cleverness, patience and resolve.

Preeti loved to help her mother mix the herbs for dahls and medicines, and she would help make the food and breads for the day, then sweep and clean before her freedom was allowed. Her older sister had gone, married by arrangement to some ogre and her younger sister and brother were also gone, taken back to the gods. Her family said that was how it was meant to be, the gods needed them elsewhere and although she was lonely, in some ways for Preeti it was good, she had her mother and father and she saw that they loved her. She remembered sitting with them by the fire outside with the starlit sky and them singing old folk songs, but as the years past the embers died, and she saw something black in their hearts. Because of her reputation and their purse, she had to be married. The boy that the families and match maker had settled upon was good; he lived in the village and his father had money so she would be well-fed and cared for. Preeti knew the boy well, as he teased her like the others and stood at the well pinching chapati. He was round with small eyes, and he snuffled like a wild hog. Preeti knew well before she was told and saw the image of her wedding day: a simple affair with pretty rose petals floating away and herself stood there with tears as he stood over her, greedy and selfish. Preeti pretended not to know and went along with the facade of her loving family and cosy life, but inside she burnt a candle to escape.

One day she explored a woody path that she had not been on before – she had seen some strangers come that way. Intrigued and curious, she took a look and found herself in the tallest grass upon a plain. She climbed a lonely juniper tree and from its branches she could see for miles into the sky that faded to pinks and oranges; she saw the soft grey and white geese in flocks arrive to rest on their journey to higher ground, and they swooped and hallooed to the valleys that the journey was calling them. Preeti took their graceful charm as a sign that things would soon change. When she felt the warm winds she turned towards home and as she climbed down from her hiding spot, she saw a strange book and a small collection of pots. Preeti studied the items they were covered in dust and look as though they had been lost or left for a while, she thought, if they had been left on purpose by someone, they would have hidden them, Preeti decided to take them and one day she would return them to the tree, hiding everything under her skirts, she ran like a chinkara to her hut, Preeti carefully hid the things under her sleep mat just before her mother called for help to cook and light the fire. When the first light of the new day shone, Preeti looked intrigued at her book where she saw symbols and words she had never seen before. Afraid it would be found, she bandaged it to her body with scarves and helped her mother pack her pots of herbs and plants for market day and was snapped at many times for not paying attention and packing the cart all wrong, setting the stall too slowly and placing the pots on a tilt. Preeti hardly listened though so engrossed in her thoughts about her book and when all the chores were done, she sat on a stool not far from the stall. While her mother peddled away, Preeti began to understand the words and symbols; they danced in the air and made patterns in the sky. She moved them with her mind and saw that these spells could take her far away. So entranced, she did not foresee the witch look over at her with anger and contempt and as the stall grew busier and the crowds pushed in the dust, Preeti felt a strange uncomfortable pain and suddenly she was walking without telling her feet to move with the arm of a strange lady hiding her in her cloaks. Preeti could not speak or change direction; she was truly captured and stuck. At first she felt sick and panicked inside and tears rolled down from her huge brown eyes. They stopped and waited for the other witch and soon they were in a cave high in the mountains, near to where the mountain cats prowled and growled. Preeti heard the villagers' cooees in the distance, fading away upon the wrong paths and at first, she thought about how to break free. At times, it would have been simple, as she was often left alone with the kinder witch, but in time they became friends, and together they made potions and she learnt how to mix and grind the ointments to heal and the spells to certain things. Preeti knew she had a life away from the village with a ghastly marriage; she would miss her mother and her father and felt sad to never see them again, but in Preeti's heart she was gone; her life was to take a different path and she knew the gods would not care. With a black moon as her sign, she was set free for eternity.

Preeti finished her tale with her account of Avoca and Josina and the fort and how she knew so much about Josina and all her tricks and of the spells she had learnt. She was stronger now than any one of the coven who came to take Agnes and Avia, and she would train them hard - the four witches would fight to the end. The girls had all listened with fascination, and even Harini who came from India herself, could not believe how brave Preeti had been. Harini thought of her protected life in her room of luxury, with her father the warlock in control and her mother who she was never allowed to see, and she began to realise that her life was a prison and her poor mother's too. When this was over, she swore to herself that she would somehow break them both free and like Preeti, be brave like a tiger's roar.

Fiesta at the Hall

~~ * ~~

Avia stood and looked over the huge ballroom that she and her friends had decorated with simple woodland branches and ribbons. Agnes had added a touch of magic with lights that most would puzzle over, and even Harini had made a spectacular display of entwined frosted twigs that shimmered along the centre of the huge table that was filling quickly with pies, meats, and pickles and a huge cake took centre stage. Drinks were ladled from huge, silver bowls, the local musicians played the piano and strings, and soon the room was bustling with every villager and member of staff. Avia wished Miss Bonneville and Jack could see her work and as if Agnes heard her thoughts, she was over in a flash and the two held hands while quietly chanting their rhymes to connect with the ones that they had lost. Agnes hoped their connection would be so powerful that Jack would re-member his home and fight with all his heart to get back; no one noticed their strange trance, they were each so en-tranced with the wonderful night as the musicians played. And as the villagers and servants sang, an intoxicating spell began. Harini and Preeti, dressed by Agnes in new dresses as not to cause alarm, glided around the room chatting and charming with a confidence such that no one suspected or questioned a thing. Preeti kept her eyes peeled and did not let her guard down; the door and every entrance was hexed to the hilt, so no witch, warlock or demon could pass, and she gently blew a haze around Agnes and Avia who reached out to Jack.

Preeti had at first found the Hall strange; it seemed so dark and cold, But, as the fires roared and music and feasting began, she realised these folk where much like her own. However, she could never relax as she had been sent to work and protect the most precious thing to Avoca - her daughter, the little abandoned witch, who now seemed to be growing into a strong and sensible lady with airs and graces like royalty. Harini loved the party and she chatted with the youngsters from the village. She had never in her life had so much freedom and fun and at the back of her mind she kept toying with ways that she could run and leave her evil father the warlock for good.

Gradually Agnes and Avia left their trance feeling sure their work was done. Avia knew she had felt Jack close to her, and she knew he understood somehow it was to bring him home, to where his family had lived for centuries before. Avia busily chatted with as many as she possibly could; she thanked and praised the staff, making a special thank you to Bunty for all her hard work and endless wonderful food as the drinks flowed and food was still in abundance, Avia saw no need to stop the party. She had thought it would trail at eleven, so instead she retired and left them all to decide when they wanted to go home and had a feeling that she would hear music and laughter late into the night. Avia loved it though; the noise made her feel safe and warm inside, she had some hope at last. Like bodyguards, Agnes, Preeti and Harini escorted her to her room. Preeti checked Avia's room was safe then left her alone, as the others wished to return to the party. They watched and listened, gathering little snippets as they skipped and danced; they heard the gossip of villagers, who gave them clues to what seemed like insignificant events that had been happening in the last few weeks. Agnes had jotted a few down in her small notebook and Preeti and Harini added any they thought were curious. The list grew longer and soon they realised they had more than one witch about, with stockings and other garments being stolen from washing lines, eggs and chickens missing despite no fox attack, Mr Combe's spade had vanished into thin air and the blacksmith, Peter, reported firewood had been thrifted and so the list went on. Even Bunty the cook had chatted about how the potato sacks went down so quickly, yet with hardly any mouths to feed and she had asked Otto, the gamekeeper, to set a rat trap. The most certain clue of all was when Otto said he had seen smoke in the woods and how Benny his dog was mighty cross and always growling and grumbling; he told the tale, of how one evening the poor dog had come flying out of the thicket, as if he had been kicked by the devil himself and the poor thing shook for days afterwards.

Later Preeti and Agnes studied the notes by the fire in the library. The hour was late and the fire still crackled away; the last guest dwindled away, singing and swaying down the huge drive lined by aged oak trees. Harini had retired to her bed, but the other witches could not let go of their puzzle, like a dog with a bone they gnawed at their clues and decided Josina had most certainly enlisted help, why else would there suddenly have been a descent of displaced witches. Agnes thought of that annoying smelly, plump witch Grettle whom she had evicted from the valley, and who had most definitely come back with help; they must have known Miss Bonneville was not at the Hall. As Agnes thought, she showed no fear, and she wondered who the other witches were that Josina had congregated on her turf. Agnes and Preeti agreed to finally try to sleep, deciding the next day that they would organise a witch hunt.

Avia's Dream

~~ * ~~

On the night of the party, Avia fell straight to sleep exhausted from the evening, and she tumbled into a dream that felt so real that she could feel and touch the things around her. She was riding on a large animal with a strange pungent stench, following many others across a huge expanse of endless sands, further than the eye could see. Huge birds circled, descending low upon the trail, waiting for death to find its way, and she heard voices in another language and smelt strange spices. The orange sun blazed like fire in the endless skies - her mouth was dry, and her lips felt cracked and sore, her head hurt from lack of water and food, and she felt as though she clung to life. The endless strides in the sand carried on and on and Avia felt herself drift in and out of a disagreeable drowsiness when suddenly she was snapped from her dangerous slumber by voices and a commotion; they had arrived at some rocky pass with high walls on either side and a hill of rock caves. Curious people looked out and smiled and waved, and next she was pulled from the camel and laid down by a fire; food was passed around and gradually she managed to eat and drink, then Jack was in front of her, and they were together - she held his hand and led him away. They walked towards the hill; no one else noticed or cared, all were full of food and mahua.

The path was rocky and the night skies bought cold air; shivering from the chill, each step was painful and felt like the last, then they joined two others that they somehow trusted and camped by their fire that still roared warm, where they settled down - at last something felt safe. With a jolt Avia had a falling sensation and left behind her dream of hot sands and cold night skies. Instead, she plummeted at speed into the soft branches of trees and a familiar smell; soil and leaves were under her feet, she heard the bird song and smelt the fresh and delicate breeze that carried a smell of wood smoke and herbs. Avia walked down a mossy path that tossed and turned her back and forth by the brook and into the rocky valley where the black and white eagles roosted high. She saw a tiny cottage well hidden in a thicket, and she watched it from behind a strange yew tree; the cottage was much like the gothic one and a lake was nearby, yet it was not her dear Stourton - the place was more rugged and not manicured. She then glimpsed herself riding with her sisters through the valley and trees and they picnicked by the lake in the woods. Avia was then back by the yew tree much like the one she met Agnes at and as she watched the cottage she saw four witches gather by a fire. Next she was bolting through the woods on her pony Mulberry, as black as the night skies, and her sisters calling her to stopped. Avia fell to the ground with a bump, but from the corner of her eye she saw a strange foot that stuck out from the bush, painted like a decorated jar, and she glimpsed the woman with the long dark hair and silks of the deepest red.

Avia woke bolt upright and knew she had found the coven in her dream. She prayed in her heart that she had delivered Jack to his desert saviours and hoped that Miss Bonneville and Avoca had found him well. Avia sobbed to herself that they were still so far apart, but she had to be strong for him and all of Stourton. This time she felt Josina was up to something more and she wanted more than Agnes - now she wanted it all.

The Witches Hunt Witches

~~ * ~~

Avia wide awake and nervous went down to assess the damage and mess from the party, which strangely felt like ages ago. She, of course, need not to have worried, her loyal staff had cleared and scrubbed any trace away and all was neat as a pin. Back in their place, the huge ornate vases of great fortune stood on the grand marble tables with carved oak legs, silver candlesticks and bowls glistened, and statues stood staring as they had always. The musty morning bought a surprisingly warm air and open windows let the scent of pinewood lift any staleness. Avia continued to the kitchens to thank everyone and to find food - she was ravenous. After laughter and tales of the evening before, Avia made for the library and was soon accompanied by her blurry-eyed fellow witches. Avia had not really thought much of her newfound talent and she was still unsure if it was just her desperation to find Jack that had bought on an unusual phenomenon, or if just hanging around with Agnes had rubbed off on her. At the moment, she could only think of saving Jack, and she had become surprisingly tolerant of Harini considering it was her stupidity that had taken Jack away. She somehow understood that Harini was only under instruction and that the wrath of her father the warlock was clearly to be avoided, and anyway, Harini was trying desperately to help her find Jack.

They all sat in a circle with their legs crossed on the floor and let Agnes lead the discussion. She informed Avia of their eavesdropping and information that they had acquired from the villagers, which was proving to be invaluable. Avia went straight to her father's drawer; she could still smell the faint smoke of cigars and sandalwood as she sat in his huge chair. She wiggled with the lock and rustled around finding the plans of the estate that included a detailed map. Avia returned to her friends and told them of her dream as she straightened the huge map out on the floor. Agnes and Harini gathered paper weights and candle sticks to hold the map in place, while Avia studied the detailed drawings. She found the lake that they had ridden to as children, and she marked it with a pin. Agnes then did the same for the witches' hut and they marked the location of the reports of the thefts. They soon found that there was a cluster of activity at the north side of the lake that ran close to Egbert's Stone and King Alfred's Tower, both within easy striking distance of the village. Avia return to her father's desk and opening another drawer she found the huge iron-carved key for Alfred's Tower. Her grandfather had had the tower built to celebrate the end of the war against France and the accession of the King who still reigned their land; it was the only key to the tower, and they all agreed that it would make a perfect look out. Avia arranged for the horses to be saddled. Preeti and Harini were doubtful of horses and the skill of handling them, but they decided to give it a go as Agnes convinced them the horses were of kind nature - unlike the camels they would listen to their commands and obey them.

Appropriately dressed, the four marched to the stables and the stable boy merely nodded at them, not wishing to say the wrong thing. He only dared look at Miss Avia and accepted her thanks as he scuttled off to the safety of his barn. The horses, fresh from a warm night of hay, oats and water, were keen to be off and clattered out of the cobbled yard regardless of some of their riders awkwardness. Agnes could not help but giggle at Preeti who juggled with the reins and clung to the saddle for her life. Avia kindly helped her and rode close holding her horses reins, while she sorted her balance and stirrups. Harini's chestnut mare was flighty and as soon as its hooves hit the grass, it took off with Harini calling out that she wanted to ride forever. Soon the four all closed in and after cantering over the meadow, they took a wooded path that curved and climbed and then descended into the next valley. They often disturbed fallow deer who grazed and nibbled peacefully on the foliage, then bounced off with their white bob tails bouncing. Harini was charmed more and more by this strange, cold land, and she began to feel that if she could ever adjust to shivering constantly, she could stay forever. The horses trotted on over the soft mossy grass, and as they turned a corner, the tower could be seen reaching to the sky. A striking mix of limestone and clay brick with a single turret rose up elegantly. Powerful and imposing, it told of wealth and support for the King and the country it resided in.

They tethered the horses and Avia opened the huge door, and above the entrance, a statue of King George looked out with a superior gaze over the valley. The girls began their ascent of the splendid stone steps that curved to the very top, and on the roof they looked beyond the turrets and towards Stourton where they had ridden from and then towards the wild lake in the woods. Although hardly visible, they managed to pick it out and sure enough from the valley of lime rocks and wilderness, they saw puffs of smoke, gentle and white like wisps of clouds, hardly noticeable. The witches below were busy in their hiding place creating something and as no one lived there, it had to be the coven that they sought to find. They all rode back on the horses, heading back to Stourton as they could not risk going nearer towards the valley on the horses as they would alert their suspects; instead, Preeti and Harini agreed they would take to the tops of the trees and go to spy on the thieving coven - they could then hopefully discover how many of them there were. They rode back quickly; the ponies seemed to sense the urgency and bolted home. After Harini had fussed over the chestnut for as long as she could, she set off with Preeti to the woods, with Agnes calling to stay out of sight. Avia was relieved to stay at the Hall with Agnes, agreeing they needed to connect with Miss Bonneville and Jack. Both glided up the huge staircase to Avia's wing, where they threw off their cloaks and made for the fire and Avia's hidden box of tricks.

The Snatch and the Jakhs

~~ * ~~

Miss Bonneville and Avoca watched from their small camp, so engrossed in their mission to find Jack that they had had little chance of small talk. Avoca had so much to ask about Agnes and Miss Bonneville had many questions about the life that Avoca now lived with Preeti; they both felt anxious as they had little hope of finding Jack until the morning came. The hours passed and Avoca could bear it no more so, in broken Tamil and English, she took the opportunity to ask the immaculate well-spoken and intelligent Miss Bonneville about Agnes. She was a little afraid of a snub, as Miss Bonneville would know Avoca was nothing more than a peasant and not high born, unlike her daughter Agnes, who had her father's royal connections running through her blood, so she stuttered out her question asking after her daughter's well-being. Miss Bonneville was distracted, staring at the group below them who sat around the fire, but she suddenly turned when she realised that her gentle, quiet companion had asked after her dear Agnes. She had avoided the conversation so far, not wishing to upset Avoca with such difficult matters, but was thrilled to tell her all about her and how wonderful she was, with her endless talents and beautiful gowns that she produced. Miss Bonneville complimented her daughter Agnes on every single thing she did and totally shocked Avoca by inviting her to the Hall when the awful business was all over – she knew Miss Avia and Agnes would love to spend time with her and Preeti, she said, they had the perfect cottage in the grounds where they both could stay, hinting in a friendly way she had perhaps been there in the past. Avoca grinned from ear to ear to receive such warmness. It was not how she had expected the conversation to go and not wishing to ruin anything, she thanked Miss Bonneville and lay down exhausted to sleep.

Miss Bonneville dozed sitting up; sleep was a luxury she could not risk, anything that happened she had to see. Her attention was drawn to a girl who she quickly realised was Ynes – she hoped this meant Jack was somewhere near. She watched Ynes talk with her brother Yari – they seemed to argue, no doubt over Ynes's return or escape, then Ynes stormed off and fell into the arms of a tall thin boy, but she could tell it was not Jack. She began to feel panicky – what had she done with Jack, had she grown tired of him and found another escape. Miss Bonneville watched Ynes and the tall boy go to join the others by the fire, while Yari went over to his donkeys and seemed to make a bed amongst his rugs and cart so he could return to his sleep. Satisfied all was still, Miss Bonneville thought to move closer, worried as to where Jack was, but just as she began to walk, she saw a figure start walking away from the fire and towards the hill, he walked like a shadow with his face was down; it was as if someone pulled him by the hand towards the hill. He stumbled and fell a couple of times and seemed to walk blind and each time he had his hand out, as if a ghost took it and pulled him closer to Miss Bonneville. As he grew closer, she knew it was Jack and her heart skipped several beats. She quietly sat down and let what was happening be, and Jack just slumped down by their campfire.

Miss Bonneville had no time to lose, she must snatch him straight away and so, with all the powers she could muster, she pulled and pushed and rolled him towards Yari's sleepy donkey cart. Quietly as possible she stuck to the shadows and wrapped a protection spell around Jack so he would become almost invisible to the eye, then she hauled him up into the cart where the sleeping Yari sniffed and snorted and she carefully rearranged the rugs, hiding Jack well. Then she went to sit at the front from where they would normally drive the cart. Miss Bonneville took vigil like a desert wild cat, ready to pounce. Every movement that night was seen, from a desert jird to a Bengal fox - Miss Bonneville missed nothing. She watched a few cave people go to hunt, just as their ancestors would have long ago and she watched the mesmerising geckos as they made patterns in the sand. The caravan of travellers though did not stir, and exhausted they slept finally silent. Just before the light broke from the night skies, Miss Bonneville stirred Avoca and grabbed her things. Avoca trusting and complying with no questions rustled up her stuff and quietly followed without a sound. The two witches harnessed the donkeys, and Avoca wiped them with an ointment of lemon grass to ward off the flies and patted them with tulsi, then they let them drink and put feeding bags over their nuzzles.

The two witches then slowly drove the cart out of the rocky pass towards the air that blew from the west. Miss Bonneville headed for the coast and the port of Jakhau. Her short time in Chandaria's study had not been wasted, and she had found and studied maps and sea crossings. She planned to be in Muscat within the week, but she had to get Jack fitter or they faced a six-month journey by ship back to England, which she did not fancy and was determined, with Avoca's background in medical cures, that the two of them could somehow protect him until the next equinox so they could travel home. Miss Bonneville had heard Muscat was pleasant enough and she was sure they could lodge some-where quiet, without too much suspicion being aroused. Miss Bonneville stopped herself thinking ahead as they had to get to the port first, then board a ship; her impatience was agonising as she was so used to things being sorted with a snap of a finger or twist of a twig. Miss Bonneville also needed to wake her slumbering crew - her little sleep spell needed to be lifted as the heat grew and all would need water.

The donkeys faithfully pulled the cart up a hill and through an arch decorated with curious figures, each with flowing yellow hair and white robes. Miss Bonneville quickly calculated there were exactly seventy-two. Each one stared down at her as if to question her business and goodness and she immediately felt something surreal and beautiful about the small hilltop village named Kakabhit. A temple stood that seemed to honour these strange fair people with its delicate carvings, and flowers were laid all around the steps with a water fountain dribbled like magic from a mouth of another solitary carving. Miss Bonneville watched some locals lay down little charms and then took a drink from the temple and went inside. She decided it was safe to wake her fellow passengers and each came around stiff, hot and grumpy. Yari was very confused, although seemed happy to have a drink. He then flustered around his precious donkeys, worried that they had been harmed in some way, but seeing they were fine, he quickly forgave Miss Bonneville. Yari then looked at Jack, who sat hunched amongst his rugs; he took water over to him and wondered how he could look so pale. Miss Bonneville was also worried for him - he was not strong enough to travel by any means and she asked Yari to keep watch over Jack.

Avoca had gone straight off to find herbs to help with Jack's poor condition. Miss Bonneville needed a local healing person, so that they could hide their cures without any doubt or suspicion of their presence. The hilltop village was silent and still, and the stone homes were tiny and seemed to prop one another up, each made from crumbling rocks. In the shade she saw people on their haunches either praying, resting or eating and they curiously watched her as she walked around the small church or temple. From behind a crumbling stone wall she heard a voice hiss, then saw a hand wave for her to follow. A little cautious and ready to retaliate, Miss Bonneville pursued the waving hand She went down some crooked stone steps that led to a small stone and straw cottage that stood alone. A large, graceful Shailendra tree, full of sweet singing shama birds, gave a subtle shade, and beneath the tree a young girl with a golden skin and glowing locks of fawn sat with her bobbin, making lace from the threads that she magically wove. Miss Bonneville smiled at her, but the girl ignored her presence as though no one stood before her at all. Miss Bonneville then took a step back in a little fear - near to the cottage an old woman suddenly appeared, her old bones were bent and her face was distorted with what looked like burn scars on her face and arms, her hair was gone other than a few patches of grey, and as she smiled her teeth had stains and cracks of time. The old, bent woman spoke, not in Hindu as Miss Bonneville had expected, but in pidgin English, and she spoke in a pleasant enough manner. Then, much to Miss Bonneville's shock, the old woman walked towards the pretty young girl and vanished into her body, continuing her greetings as the young girl's face took on an older expression. Miss Bonneville tried to remain calm, as though it was the most normal thing to see, and the now beautiful witch beaconed for her to sit by her side under the welcoming branches of the musical tree. Afraid of such a peculiar spectacle, Miss Bonneville sat down, although she politely refused the old witch's herby tea. The witch laughed, teasing that she wouldn't poison her just yet. Miss Bonneville ignored the jibe and asked directly who the girl was and how the spell was possible. The old, bent witch began her story, looking up to the tree as she spoke, as though she read the tale from the leaves that stayed so still.

Beliccia

The name of the witch that you sit before is Beliccia. The bent, ugly witch was how she had begun life, as a child crippled with nothing other than a cup in her deformed hand, abandoned by her own mother. Beliccia was

always kind though and had a gift to heal.
In exchange for her cures she would fill her
cup with coins. But many were suspicious
and cruel and often she would be kicked
aside and left for dead. Then a kind old
couple saved her from the streets and bought
her to the cottage now her home.

One awful day she was captured by an evil
albino warlock who now knew who she was
– He knew the child's mother from long ago
and remembered her beauty and grace. He
had the cripple, now a young woman, burnt
to her death calling her a dark witch, yet in
truth, he could never risk the threat of her
powers, which were stronger than his own.
Yet as he walked away something amazing
happened and she was saved from the fire
and was turned by the gods into something
beautiful and forever young.

The cripple thought her end had come in the
flames and smoke until she had a vision of
the seventy-two Jakhs. She told how they
circled above her reaching out their arms
and she reached for the skies and as the

small crowd thought her body sank to the flames, she instead floated to the arms of the white gods and was sent down to earth in her saintly form, as Carmenta the healer. Carmenta had since spent her centuries healing and travelling the globe, though she took care when spreading word of her cures and methods that the Jakhs had taught her so as not to show anything was too paranormal.

Beliccia now Carmenta then related how she remembered when the Jakhs had ridden in from the sea, with their golden hair and robes of white – seventy-two of them. The people were at first fearful, but this turned to complete wonderment and they began to see these people as gods from the skies and seas as they proved to be kind and gentle and lived amongst the people. For the land and lives they did only good and never harm; everyone loved them dearly and the once bent, old witch remembered each of their names. Two of the Jakhs, Sayari and Sah, became her friends and they taught her wonderful things. They showed her the power to change the way things were, to turn bad to *good and make the ailing well. These gods, the Jakhs, knew everything. They came from far away and one day they just returned to the stars and skies. After a hundred years of calm, giving and teaching, they thought it was time for the humans to continue alone.*

It did not take long for war and greed to sweep the land once again and soon, other than the temple and shrines, the Jakhs with their peaceful ways were forgotten and lost in time; they became legends, just stories swept aside. The beautiful witch you sit before has cried many tears over the years, but she carried on trying to teach and keep the work of goodness going; her efforts though we're all in vain and she had been thieved of her greatest gift.

Carmenta stopped her story, although Miss Bonneville sensed it was not the end and the witch then cackled that every year she would return to this sacred place to honour her beloved Jakhs, as one day they had promised to return and then she silenced herself again, as though she had already said to much. She studied Miss Bonneville and proclaimed that she had seen her coming - she had had a vision of her and the Jakh. Miss Bonneville protested that Jack was no Jakh, tutting at the confusion of his blond locks and name. Carmenta ignored her and hissed they must be quick; he needed her help and without any further words Miss Bonneville was soon following her up the steps and through the dusty tracks to the donkey and cart - where Yari proudly stood guard. They led the donkey and cart away from the village and up towards a bigger hill, following Carmenta, as the sands swirled around their feet and the sun scorched down on the earth. Avoca had by then reappeared and followed them; she cursed and wittered, unsure of their helper who they now followed - she saw no reason to trust some hill witch and feared she had put a spell on Miss Bonneville, who repeatedly assured her this was not the case as she had protected herself well from such spells. Still Avoca was not happy, and she watched Carmenta like a hawk.

Avoca could never trust anyone other than Preeti and Agnes as Josina had broken her trust in all beings; ever since, she had feared the world of friendships and acquaintances. She had begun to like Miss Bonneville though and felt certain if Agnes trusted her, then Miss Bonneville could trust her too.

Avoca felt her mind wander and a twinge of excitement despite her efforts to concentrate on the hill witch; the thought of seeing her daughter again was a wondrous thought and she prayed to herself this would all work. She missed Agnes so much and hoped that Agnes and Preeti would be safe despite the despicable Josina running wild in the woods.

Avoca's drifting thoughts were broken as she heard Yari's sharp shout; they had reached the brow of the hill and he called for them to turn and look to the growing golden skies and as they did they saw an apparition of saintly figures approach. They swirled towards the cart and reached for the boy, one of their own or so they thought, and as Carmenta offered their Jack to the godly Jakhs, Miss Bonneville was quick to realise what was happening and screeched as she desperately threw herself on the clueless Jack using every power she possessed. Avoca realised in panic and quickly concentrated on holding back Carmenta who ran to free Jack to the gods. Stopped by Avoca, she screamed in anger as she saw her precious Jakhs turn and fade away. Miss Bonneville cursed Carmenta in anger; they had waisted precious time in saving Jack.

Carmenta soon vanished and could be heard wailing down the hill, while Avoca and Miss Bonneville tended to Jack on the rocky hill in total despair. They soon discovered by luck that the hill Carmenta had led them to turned out to be the perfect place; it had spring water and caves that gave shelter from the sun. Avoca quickly set about making her potions and pastes while Miss Bonneville muttered her healing spells and gave water to their patient. Yari went off to find food as the small group settled into their temporary and unusual accommodation. Several days passed and they began to recover from the shock of Carmenta's plan to give Jack to the gods - the Jakhs and that the unearthly phenomenon was real and not a tale.

Jack, oblivious, began to come around and the curse that had been put on him by Harini the young witch was completely lifted from his mind. Rehydrated and healed, he gradually responded and remembered fully who he was, and his first reaction was to ask after Avia. Miss Bonneville chose not to tell him about Josina just yet, afraid the worry would send him spare and instead reassured him that she was fine. Keen to be off the sacred hill, they decided that Jack was strong enough and they would travel again with Yari's kindness to the port.

They trundled and clattered down to the bustling harbour of Jakhau and watched the huge sailing ships cut through the waves towards the small harbour, where traders and groups began to gather as colourful hubs of silks, cottons and spices grew in number. Jack purchased their tickets and as planned, he said that he travelled with his servants to Oman. Each one of them waited in fear. Never had they sailed, and their nerves jolted, even Miss Bonneville's calm nature was a blur as pulsing heat, shouts and smells descended upon the small group. Scared stiff, they boarded the creaking ship, and they waved goodbye to Yari who had offered to accompany them, afraid for their safety. Miss Bonneville, however, insisted he went to find his family - they would be worried and had already lost so much including a daughter to goodness knows what fate. Yari waved back with huge tears in his eyes, Avoca called out that she promised to find him on her return, and he managed a smile. In his heart, Yari wished to be with Miss Bonneville, Avoca and Jack as he felt a sense of loyalty he had not felt before. Yari would travel back to his family to check they had managed to find safety, then he swore to himself, as he watched the tiny ship upon the glazed horizon, that he would find his way to England with his handsome payment from the wonderful Miss Bonneville.

Miss Bonneville and Jack stared out to sea for as long as they could, each wishing their feet were on solid ground. Avoca though slept happily in the crowded cabin and her cot swung in tune to the sea, unlike her travel companions, who feared to sleep, eat or lie on what they thought were diabolically treacherous slings between planks. For them, the voyage would be tedious and long and when they arrived at the stunning harbour of Muscat, with its backdrop of mountains and glistening white forts, they felt exhausted and drenched with sea sickness, while Avoca looked as fresh as a daisy in the morning dew, well rested and fed. The three travellers stepped off the ship with trepidation. Jack tried hard to look like the master and ordered both Miss Bonneville and Avoca around. He boldly asked for lodgings in a quiet place and was swiftly taken by an elaborate carriage pulled by Arabian horses, while his supposed servants followed with his somewhat meagre belongings by donkey and trap. Their driver was not unlike Yari in looks, but his nature was harsh and he cared little for his donkeys that he whipped - he seemed to have a cruel heart. Miss Bonneville glared at him and gave him a small spell of kindness and care for a tip, he stopped his donkeys and gave them a fuss and they were dropped at the gates of a gleaming palatial place they were hustled in like sheep to the courtyard where Jack stood grinning like a cat who had got the cream. Jack dismissed and paid off all of the servants and once left alone they celebrated their success. The lodgings were very pleasing and full of luxurious furnishings. A huge terrace and garden of flowers stretched to the sea, and at the end of the day a stunning sunset sky melted into the night, they heard crickets and geckoes cry their nighttime call. Tired, they each retired and sleep took each one to another place and time, they would wake to a different world and a free life for Jack, with some hope at last for his return.

The Secret Witch

~~ * ~~

Avia spent her days on highs and lows; she felt all at sea and rolled on under Agnes's command. Her hope for Jack's return grew stronger, yet her fear for his safety during his journey home made her desperate with worry. She had lost him from her dreams and could only now pray that Miss Bonneville and Avoca would bring him home to her in one piece. Avia longed for his smile, laughter and flash of blonde hair, his voice and funny nature - now a distant memory. She feared he would not be the same - his absence and abduction would surely scar him in some way. Avia managed to walk around the gardens, although it hurt with every step, she needed the air and everywhere else was not safe for her. Harini always followed her. She reminded Avia of a curious little ousel bird, as she fluttered and rustled around behind with a boldness and a disregard for silence or solitude, yet strangely Avia enjoyed the presence of the one who had taken her love away. She screeched in silence, yet partly forgave her, understanding Harini's life was more complex than most. Avia grew curious about Harini's different ways, and she wished to understand her customs and beliefs, her land and life, but she held her at bay, afraid the anger of her loss would explode and cause harm beyond repair, so she choose to ignore the fluttering in the trees and walked with purpose around her lake while she thought. Avia then had the best idea; she would travel to see her sisters. No more could she wait in agony and risk the wrath of Josina. To see Olivia and Cecilia in Bath would be a joy and distraction from her pain - she knew they would be shopping and staying in their great-aunt Eliza's old house as Agnes had mentioned she would have to meet them at some point for measuring dresses for the season, and Avia now enjoyed staying at their great-aunt's house in Sydney Gardens. Happy with her decision, she thought about asking the others to accompany her; Avia began to love the idea of showing them Bath. Excitedly she made her way to the house to announce her plans. Agnes and Preeti were unsure of Avia's plan to visit Bath, as they feared leaving the grounds would give Josina to much freedom to carry out her plans, whatever they were. Avia hid her disappointed, going alone was no fun, so she agreed to wait and took Agnes's council that she must remain quiet until Jack was back. Agnes worried that her sisters would tell others if she fuelled them with any more news - it was bad enough that they knew Jack was missing.

Avia hid her dismay as well as she could and went to the library where she searched for any books she could find on India - in some way she hoped if she gained knowledge about the places and customs Jack had been living in, then she could relate to Jack about what he had experienced. Her books took her far away and she read of the distant land - she studied the maps and wondered where Jack had been and where he went. Curled up in the chair with the warmth of the fire, Avia fell into a deep sleep and in her dream she found herself upon a hill that looked over golden sands and huge trees; she saw temples and statues and huge gates that swung shut, she felt fear and saw burning and people grabbing all they could and running, she smelt the thick smoke and tried to scream, nothing came. Avia woke with a start and saw the skies had turned to dusk, the clock struck five in the hall and everywhere was silent. Avia knew something was very wrong; the fire had died and she heard no voices or movement - she just knew the Hall was empty. In an instant, Avia grabbed the huge library door key and bolted the door, then she checked all the huge windows were locked and raced to the cupboard where they kept the spell books and powders. As quickly as possible, Avia circled the whole room. She drew the curtains and lit the fire with a protection spell and then listened. Not a sound could be heard. Avia then remembered the secret corridors her sisters would play hide and seek in as children. She felt for the little handle under the dusty bookshelf and slipped through the secret door, closing it softly behind her. Avia took off her laced boots and crept along the corridor towards the kitchens; she knew it came out in the parlour where the servants sat for their meals. Curious as to where they all were, she quietly approached, then peeked through a tiny gap in the floorboards into the parlour down below. She saw to her horror that Preeti and Agnes were tied to chairs with some strange rope, each gagged and floppy; she then saw a strange, cloaked person and her heart skipped a thousand beats, the bad witches were in the Hall. Avia strained to look but she could not see Josina or any others or even Harini - she hoped that the little ousel bird was safe. Avia then climbed the tiny staircase up towards her own floor and followed with small steps the long corridor; several times she stopped dead to listen and stayed silent like a hunted deer.

Deciding it was too dangerous to go to her own room, she peeked again through a tiny hole in the door behind the bookshelf, and gasped inwardly as she saw Josina the ghostly witch was storming around her room. She looked for something and Avia was thankful that they had moved all the spell books and potions to the library She felt for the moonstone around her neck and felt the bracelet on her wrist, then she crept away without a sound and slipped back towards the library. To Avia's great surprise she found Harini in the hidden corridor - she had followed her but become lost. Without a word they made it back to the huge library and in whispers they discussed what they could do in this dangerous dilemma; both agreed that if they tried to escape they would be easily spotted. If they stayed, they could do their best to fight off the witches and wage their own silent war. Their priority was to save Agnes and Preeti from the clutches of the enemy; neither one of them could understand how they had been caught and this worried them more than anything. Josina must have some unknown power, but what had she found to overcome two witches as powerful as Agnes and Preeti and how would they ever be able to stop them now.

Carmenta's Mistake

~~ * ~~

Carmenta felt like sometimes she was the oldest witch in the universe. Her knowledge was so extensive, and she would become excited to find something out that she did not know already. She had travelled all over the world looking for new remedies, and she would often be drawn to witches like herself to find more knowledge. One star-filled night in France she came across a chateau that she had visited a good few years ago when it had been owned by a powerful warlock who called himself Fabian. She remembered his clever and beautiful young assistant. Now both were long gone, and she instead found a grumpy witch who was dishevelled and desperate as she was on the run. Carmenta remembered her and her coven, once all grand and full of life and beauty, and she felt pity when the witch told her story of how she had lost the child of a witch and warlock on the epic night of Samhain and how since then she had been the victim of foul play, and she had said how she missed the child that was taken from her.

Carmenta felt understanding and empathy for this spent witch who had lost her child, and she showed her a trick or two to help her fight back those who had hurt her, but there was one powerful element she should not have shared, known only by the Jakhs, which was how to disable a powerful being for just long enough to read their minds or disable them from action for several hours. The two witches stayed in the dusty chateau reminiscing about the glory days and the great Fabian and his fireworks and kittens. Then, without much thought they went their separate ways.

When Miss Bonneville turned up on the dusty tracks of an Indian village, Carmenta knew who she was straight away and thought it very strange to see two witches in one century both linked by a warlock and a tale. This once housekeeper to a formidable keeper of gunpowder and wealth, had a secret in her cart - she smuggled the boy that Carmenta had sought for many years. She searched for her son, that was born on a golden moonlit night. The baby boy had not long been born when he was stolen away she feared by the evil white warlock she once knew. Carmenta saw the boy in her dreams and knew he had to be the one that had been taken from her and held in a hidden prison. She called for the Jakhs' spirits in fear the warlock would return to take him back - she felt sure the Jakhs would keep him safe in their world, and she knew, in her heart that he could never be hers.

Carmenta had called for the spirits in the skies and like a dream she saw them come for the boy with the golden hair - her son would soon be free with the kindly gods and go to a good and honest place. Carmenta had not realised that the witches were so powerful that held the boy, she began to fear that she stood no chance and doubted her actions. They protected this boy who they called Jack with such fearlessness and conviction. The Jakhs also left very quickly, and she began to wonder if the boy was not who she thought he was. Although she cried and felt cross inside, Carmenta knew she had a puzzle to unwind - something was amiss - and she pondered about what she had done, and as she looked at the stars, Carmenta saw a pattern she had never seen before. It made her think of Josina, the fallen witch, and the spell she had shown her, and Carmenta groaned inside. She had been tricked. Josina was not the girl's mother, she was the one who sought to sacrifice her, and Carmenta had given a bad witch a way to get her own back and now she was the one to blame. She had to find this girl, born of a witch and a warlock, for it was Carmenta's fault; her life was once more in grave danger. Quite where the boy Jack and Miss Bonneville fitted into this strange movement of events she was not sure.

She would have to look again for her real son - she deserved her time with him on this earth if only for a day, but Carmenta now had an evil white warlock to find as he knew something of Josina and her plans. First she would seek the missing girl Ynes, who she had once met under a banyan-tree, when she was a small child, seeing her talents she had set the girl to work, to help find the white warlock and her son, her spell was strong and the girl Ynes she knew would find him somehow and while all this whirled in her mind, she also sought revenge; the witch Josina had been deceptive and had tricked her, but she knew Josina's trail would never be too hard to find - as a mess would always be left behind.

The Storm

~~ * ~~

The warlock Gedahard returned to his castle, to find complete bedlam; his young wife had written an angry letter and hid somewhere - he decided that he would find her later and punish her, his useless daughter was still gone although this he was pleased about, and he presumed that the maid had absconded with the prisoner, as the boy who was a magician in his garden had vanished. He also still did not have his ring or revenge upon the witch who he sought to punish for her tricks and theft. Gedahard growled and grunted like a lion.

He picked up his wife's letter and read it - she rambled about how he had stolen her life and all her inheritance, and he wondered how an earth she had found out such secret information. She was clever, but had no understanding of other writings and his documents were kept safely in his rooms. He could hear the servants' whispers of gossip and fear and he felt brewing so much uncontrollable anger. The staff and prisoner were fortunate that day, as he had no choice but to leave his own dilemmas behind - the King had summoned him for his answers on another bewildering topic regarding a war that brewed - a nasty conflict that would damage their whole existence. The white warlock felt explosive and raged around the castle and everyone dashed for cover as he left to speak with the King and his council.

Gedahard could bear it no more, and as the skies grew darker and redder, he delayed attending the summons and gathered some belongings of importance and went to find his only true friend, Fabian, who would guide him through this hell. Yet, as he trod the familiar stones of the golden fortress, he sensed a strange feeling like never before, and as the skies got redder he began to think he should turn back to the council, but he was drawn away from his duty, pulled by some force as he stepped out of the Golden Fort's protective walls. He walked towards the lake boat where Fabian now lived, but as he approached Fabian's mooring nothing was there other than the lapping lake with a fiery red reflection from the skies above; the beautiful boat and his friend had gone.

Fabian was no fool he would have read the stars and seen that Jaisalmers peacefulness would soon be gone and only years of torment were to come. Gedahard felt an unusual dismay and he started to think of his last few years and how turbulent they had been. His liaison with the beautiful witch was a distraction he should never have taken and one he had started to mistrust. What game did she really play? Did she use his connections? Gedahard started to worry for the first time in his life. Had the witch betrayed him and used him for her own gain? He then realised that he had been a fool; the witch Josina had charmed him for information.

Gedahard was now on a trail of revenge and as the great storm swept over the Golden Fort, it cleared his mind; he would find Josina as well as the other thieving witch and both would fall. The boy in the garden he felt certain was somehow linked to the Hall, a property with land that his dear friend Fabian wanted for a secret he said he would share. Harini had not returned from that wintery land surrounded by sea, but it would not take long to find his daughter and the night was perfect for travel. The thunder and lightning cracked and pounded the skies and the rain tumbled down; soon torrents of water ran like rivers through the sands, washing away whatever stood in their path.

Gedahard turned to look at the Golden Fort that he loved so much, and which would soon be lost to war. He thought of his imprisoned wife, who would be captured again - her beauty and wealthy position would once again be her downfall. He counted his losses on the night of the storm and knew his run of good fortune was temporally suspended.

The boy who he had imprisoned would stay hidden as ordered, and one day soon he would return for him and gift him to Fabian. He would escape and reappear before the war. The forked lightning that bought fire gave him his chance to leave and he suddenly had a vivid image of his daughter, cowering in a room of books - a powerful link that he could follow. Gedahard concentrated with all his might and held his blackened candle to the red moon; tonight he would travel as never before, and in a whirl of spells the storm lifted him to another land.

A Message from Maud

~~ * ~~

Maud scuttled around hopelessly; she needed Miss Bonneville so desperately. Her tail had grown back and although
she kept her human form, her ears were growing and she
saw tufts of fur, and she craved cheese so badly and
scampered off to the parlour unseen. The last few weeks she
had hidden out in the attic knowing she could not be seen.
With a lie she said she went to visit a dying relative. Poor
Maud was in such a terrible muddle, she had never thought
there would be a problem, but Miss Bonneville had warned
her to stay hidden from witches who meant harm, as just
their presence would make her turn back into a mouse. In
horror she realised the Hall was swarming with witches both
good and bad. When she reached the parlour and saw poor
Agnes bound with her friend, she nearly squeaked out loud.
Maud scuttled off. She had to find Avia to check she was not
harmed. As she ran along the hidden corridor she felt herself getting smaller and smaller and eventually poor Maud
scuttled along the floor. With salty tears streaming down her
now small furry cheeks she made it to the library and
squeezed through a gap in the wood panelling. To her relief
she saw Avia and their visitor who seemed to mean no harm,
and seeing the protection spells, Maud found herself a comfy

spot in the underside of an old leather chair where she could watch and listen.

As there was little else she could do, exhausted and traumatised, she had a little snooze and when she woke she saw the girls were busy making potions; unsure what they planned, she just watched fascinated. Maud heard a tapping noise from the window and saw Hex the chatter-pie fluttering around - he no doubt missed Miss Bonneville and her tasty snacks. Then Maud had a thought; the magpie was connected to Miss Bonneville - it was her pet, so she had to try and show the pesky bird what had happened. Frustrated by her form, she could only squeak and scratch, and she was unsure if magpies understood mouse. She scuttled over to the window and raised herself up on her hind legs looking at the bird; it tilted its head and pecked on the window louder, causing Avia and Harini to turn and stare at the mouse and the magpie. Harini raised her hand to do something, suspicious that they meant some harm, but Avia quickly stopped her, explaining that the magpie called Hex was always around Miss Bonneville and she studied the mouse and strangely thought of Maud. Avia, no longer surprised by anything, went to pick the little mouse up, who sat tamely in her hands, still looking and squeaking at the magpie. Avia stroked the mouse and, putting it gently on the chair. She then went over and quietly opened the window to let the magpie in. She explained to Harini they had to show Hex the magpie the captured friends. It was worth a try. It was their only hope to send a red alert that they needed help. So they all crept into the hidden corridor and made their way back to the kitchen where Agnes and Preeti still slumped, tied up. Hex could see it all: the parlour door was wide open and a witch in a cloak stood guard. He flew along the corridor and came out into Miss Bonneville's study where he sat in her chair pecking at her pen. This alerted one of the witches who saw Hex and went to catch or cast a spell on the vexed bird. The witch in pursuit was short and round and stumbled clumsily. Hex flew over her and out to the trees, his work was nearly done. Hex then flew back to Miss Bonneville's window again and sat on the sill as trained. He pecked and pecked at the bell - a talisman to reach Miss Bonneville and he squawked and screeched madly at the invader in Miss Bonneville's room and knew his job was nearly done.

The Coven and Josina

~~ * ~~

Since escaping the Fort of Chitrakut, Josina had faced an endless category of disasters. Her once blessed life had taken a turn for the worse and should really have temporarily ended like the others on the northern town by the lake. The night she parted company from Parnell and Wilmot went badly, she had stormed around with a vengeance in her heart and had no care for her discretion - she sought revenge for her failings and the betrayal of Avoca. Josina was unable to bear the thought of Fabian, and that the others no longer walking the earth as before, and at her own ghost-like form. She knew from old tales that something at Stourton Hall could save them all and Fabian knew the key, so she had found there dwindling spirits and helped Fabian and worked hard with his help to raise them all to come back to fight for one more chance of eternity. To help her plan, she needed a boost of power and touch of evil, so Josina sought out a warlock she had met long ago in the company of Fabian. She remembered this warlock bragged about his powers and the great Golden Fort, and eventually she found it and tracked the cumbersome Gedahard down. She found him uncouth and did not like his ways, unlike Fabian, who had always been a charming gentleman. Gedahard had a ruthless nature and ran a harsh and unfriendly home. His castle was easy to find, brash and showy as described; it was also poorly guarded and she easily blagged her way into the huge court-yard, where she waited to meet the white warlock that all seemed to fear. He recognised her instantly, although com-mented she looked like the walking dead and seemed eager for her to be gone. Josina had ignored his harsh yet honest comments, as she had some useful leverage and wanted help in return for her long silence - his weapons dealings with Fabian would be unwelcome news to his peaceful leader Rawal at that time and she dangled the carrot of Stourton Hall, the grandest property with something magical in its vast land. Annoyed and intrigued, Gedahard the white war-lock played her game. She was given board and lodgings for a short while to temporarily regain her composure and looks, for which he gave her a little help.

Josina used her time well in the fort and charmed the fool Gedahard. She stayed longer as he enjoyed her reckless company, and her extended stay and freedom to roam al-lowed her to gather lots of useful information. She knew all of Gedahard's nasty dealings and his underworld. He had more contacts than she could believe and when she dis-covered his dealings with a few unsavoury witches in the rolling valleys of the south of an island, she was overjoyed, her plan formed quickly - Josina would have her revenge and take that grand Hall with its ornate lake and wonders for herself. She dreamt daily of throwing Agnes and Miss Bonneville to the dogs - she would have their pinnacle of power and place, but she had to have patience. One lesson she had learnt was that if she started a little ball rolling, it would collect and grow, ending up just where she wanted it to go.

Josina, on her return to England, soon found Lettice in a deathly state hidden in a cave, and with apologies she rejoined her to the coven. Lettice, happy with the plan, headed straight for the woods. Now Josina had to find the witch that Gedahard wished to avenge, and while she searched for Grettle, she fell into the company of three other witches who she secretly found quite hateful and horrifying; they seemed to have no morals at all and no care for any living thing - they were, however, perfect for her plan. Josina easily recruited them, and they rubbed their hands in glee at the thought of living in luxury. So, Josina fixed and planned her plots, then she gathered her coven by the wild rocky lake and the five witches became inseparable: not in friendship but in greed and hate. Josina first met Lil, Mo and Prim in an ale house not far from the dreaded open plains with circled stone. The crooked black and white drinking establishment sat in the wall by a huge cathedral; ancient tunnels led from the house of gambling and ill-repute, used to hide, escape or cause mayhem, a perfect place for the three witches who had a passion for gambling and theft. They earned a pretty penny from their skills and by cheating. Josina that night looked for the witch Grettle, who was said to frequent the place, typically that night she was nowhere to be seen, so the frustrated Josina took a jug of ale and settled herself in the shadows. She watched the three witches from her dark corner and liked their style; they played a game of deception. Towards the end of the night a fight broke out and the witches were accused of cheating by their opponents, but they would not back down; instead, they severed the accuser's hand and threw it to the fire where it sat grotesquely between the grate and the wall. As the witches left screeching with their gold, Josina followed them, impressed by their sheer braggadocio. She stood blocking their pathway in the tunnel and gave them a choice they could obey her and they would get gold and more riches than they could ever imagine, or if not she would turn them to stone, with little choice the witches agreed to partake and in turn Josina served them a spell of alliance to her that they could not break. The three witches cackled in glee and skipped behind Josina each one for now was entranced.

Josina had to quickly learn to ignore their constant arguments and fights between themselves; she would occasional though pay attention, as in their outbursts of anger the fools often let many a secret slip, all of great use to Josina. It was in one of these spats that Josina heard of Grettle, who had been taken in a drunken state to the jail house, accused of unruly behaviour. Josina quickly went to find the jail house and returned with the awful, stinking witch - Josina had easily broken her out of jail. Grettle though would pay a price for this favour for life. Each one of the witches Josina found unsavoury and she knew once her quest was completed she would be rid of each one of them. She would never share her Hall with such rude undesirables, for now though they were invaluable and rotten to the core. They all spied on the Hall and the young elegant witches that lived there, and although they feared their prowess, they knew that they stood no chance, as the young witches would not put into their estimations quite how ruthless and cruel Josina's coven could possibly be. She hit them hard and captured two with ease using a new spell she had learnt; annoyingly, the other two seemed more elusive and she could not find their hiding place. Josina was fuming; she ordered the witches to keep guard of the others, while she figured out how to handle any mortal servants that would approach. The staff would have to go - she would disguise herself as Miss Bonneville and dismiss the lot of them on the spot. Josina cackled at her pitiless plot as she ran to find Miss Bonneville's room where she would dress and wear her unique perfume - the fools would never guess. Without hesitation she called a meeting and each and every servant was told to leave immediately, no one was to ever trespass on the land again; with tears and protests each dragged their feet away from the Hall. The maids all cried and the footmen, gardeners and grooms raged on. Tomsk though remained calm as always and he looked back at the house and noticed something strange - he did not buy the dismissal and did not believe that the strange lady was Miss Bonneville, he believed she was an imposter, so he walked a while and pondered what to do.

Josina clapped her hands, applauding herself on her handy work, and she then went to search through Miss Bonneville's possessions; she felt sure she could find lots of helpful things. Smugly she looked around, feeling sure she had won this time - it would not be long, and as she laughed at her success, she picked out a pretty paper weight from the dresser draw and caught her reflection fading in the mirror, looking dreadfully old and haggard and thought it would not be long until she was beautiful again. From the corner of her eye she saw a magpie sat cheekily on the windowsill; he squawked and hopped like something possessed. Josina shrugged at the strange behaviour of the bird, maybe it disliked the real Miss Bonneville, then something strange started to happen. She suddenly felt something tighten around her neck and despite battling, she found herself frozen to the spot - her reflection now a stone statue that gawked into the mirror above the fireplace that lay stone cold.

A Distant Statue

~~ * ~~

Miss Bonneville woke bolt upright in her bed. The breeze blew the silky white drapes and she smelt jasmine and roses from the gardens floating upon the heavy heat. She felt clammy and a slight panic, and she was not sure if she dreamt or not, as in front of her she saw Hex her chatter-pie. At first she thought it was a bird from the garden, then she realised he floated above in a strange image on the ceiling fan. She spoke to him kindly as she always would and held up a scrap of date from the bowl. Hex then showed her his image and in shock she watched. She saw Preeti and Agnes bound up in the scullery and Avia and Harini imprisoned in the library. She then followed Hex and he showed Josina in her room, touching her things. The connection was strong so Miss Bonneville began the most powerful spell she had ever learnt from Fabian the warlock. It involved immense concentration. Hex gave her the connection, as he fluttered and pecked madly at Josina from the window at the Hall, and as Josina in her frail state glimpsed in the mirror and clutched Miss Bonneville's paper weight, a gift from Agnes, Miss Bonneville fixed her spell on the wretched witch Josina and her ghostly reflection, and with all her strength she turned the witch to stone. Satisfied she collapsed upon the bed, Hex and Josina faded away, and she prayed her spell had worked. Miss Bonneville lay exhausted in a trance.

When Avoca discovered her she at first panicked thinking she suffered from some strange illness, but Miss Bonneville, despite her state, managed to explain. While Avoca patted her forehead with water and fragrant petals, she knew one thing was for sure, they had to get back to the Hall. Miss Bonneville though needed time to recover, so Avoca, with pride, set about her task to nurse her patient noon and night, and with no thought for herself she laboured to help her recover so that she could help save Preeti and Agnes; but all the time she felt anger in a rage like never before - this time Josina was going to suffer, surely this time it was her end.

Chandaria's Strange Gift

~~ * ~~

As Chandaria lay on her day bed, she dabbled her fingers in the water that splashed from the fountain onto the mosaic's delicate pattern. The jacaranda tree gave shade to her balcony; its delicate lilac flowers had begun to bloom, and she thought of the forests near her real home. She dreamt that she rode her horse Bali through the paths and forest of flames - she could almost hear Bali's hooves on the shingly path as he trotted along, agile and strong, his gorgeous, dappled grey coat shiny and his mane flowing like silk on his withers, tacked with a beautiful, elaborate flower-filled bridal saddle. She was dressed as a true princess in her colourful riding sari on top of her pair of harems, she wore her tiara and her face was painted and behind her, bodyguards rode at a distance with watchful eyes. Chandaria then thought of the beautiful fortress of Bojairpur and of her mother, father and brothers. Tears rolled down her cheeks as she thought of the brutality, the murders and her loss. Taken, she had never known her family's fate - only that they no longer ruled. She prayed by some slim chance they had been saved. She had been captured and imprisoned in the Golden Fort's castle - for how long she had forgotten. The master Gedahard made sure she was given no information and kept her hidden from the world. Chandaria managed to stop her tears as the servant girl entered the room. Ynes had run away and she already missed her only friend; the new girl was stubborn and acted stupid to avoid too much work, she had no conversation and no heart, glad when she had finished her chores. Chandaria checked the doors were closed and felt in her deep pockets, hidden from the master. She carefully took out the little pot and opened the folded paper that Miss Bonneville had given her, and she read the instructions again and again and learnt them, so she could never forget should Gedahard find them and take them away. She knew she risked her death if caught, but she wished more than ever to escape, knowing that Gedahard had taken away her only hope of freedom in this land, once her home.

Chandaria walked around her vast rooms and touched everything gently as she said her goodbyes. She packed a few of her favourite saris and shawls and wore as many clothes as she could, knowing she went to a cold place, and she carefully placed many jewels of value deep in her pockets. Chandaria then climbed up the little marble steps that led to the huge roof terrace, and there she stood and stared at her homeland. She breathed in the warm heady air and smelt the perfume on the breeze, she looked at the gulmohar tree, knowing this year she would miss its bright orange flowers that sprouted amongst its white canopy. She gazed out to the rest of the Golden Fort, as the sunset glowed and hues of pink lit the delicate skies, and she heard in the distance, the rumblings of a storm that that came her way. Chandaria hastened as thunder approached. She no longer waited for the dark to engulf her, and she bravely stepped into the unknown. Fear rose in her throat -she had not been out of the castle walls for years. Freedom called her though, and she thought of herself and Bali galloping through the forest of flames, then Chandaria lit her fire and sprinkled the concoction from the pot, then she spoke the words with faith and held her hands tightly together as she vanished into the skies, with only a sparkle of dust left where she once stood.

Deep in the castle grounds, as the thunder rumbled, the hidden boy in the temple - kept a prisoner - sensed a flight of freedom nearby and he began to wish for his own escape and prayed to the gods for a way out.

Ynes Alone

~~ * ~~

Ynes felt the strangest pain - an emptiness like never before. She looked to the skies as the sunset turned pink, then whined, as she felt a sharp pain from her ankle. She crawled into the cave for protection and prayed and pondered what she was to do. Things had not worked out well - she had been foolish and knew she was in a mess. The master Gedahard would no doubt kill her if she ever made it off the mountain alive. The poor dumbstruck boy she had taken would probably die thanks to her stupid plot; she had endangered her family and everyone. He was lost to Harini's spell and stood no chance, and she wished she had taken her brother Yari's advice and gone with him, instead of the man she thought to be a good and trustworthy friend with his promise of another land and fortune that were far from the truth - he had sold her as a slave and turned away with no care, not even a backward glance or goodbye. For days Ynes had travelled in tears to where she had no clue. Bound by chains in a cart with other girls like herself, she found her small repertoire of spells useless and realised she was not really a powerful witch as she had wished, she was just clever with old cures and tricks she had been taught. Ynes knew she was deemed for an awful place and life. Had the cart not lost a wheel she would never have been set free. The cart had lost its balance and capsized, and as it started toppling down the hillside, she had made her break and prayed it would work. Her move had been both brave and idiotic as she threw herself towards the bushes. Scratched and sore, she had stood in agonising pain, the chains had gone but her ankle was badly cut and with little on, she struggled to bind it. Ynes had stayed hidden in the bushes all night, too terrified to move. She heard someone calling and other voices that became muffled and went away. The first night was freezing, so the next day she hobbled to the cart, where she found the large heavy sheet that they had covered them with. Ynes was not sure if the others had survived or had just been taken, but as there was no sign of anyone, she dragged the heavy sheet behind her, limping until she found a small cave she could hide in, away from the cart should they come back again.

Ynes drifted into a feverish sleep that she tried hard to stave off, afraid she would never wake; each battle was lost. Ynes mumbled aloud in her delirious slumber. She dreamt of the witch who she had met when she was a small child, under the shade of the ornamental gulmohar tree, its flowers fallen leaving stained petals in the sand. Ynes saw through her beauty and recognised the snarled body inside. She felt no fear though and knew that the witch had put her under a spell. The legend told that Carmenta the witch of the winds did only good. This day though she sensed a different beat, but Carmenta's words echoed through her tormented mind – *'steal the boy with lemons in his hair, eyes like the sky and the skin of pearls, take him to the desert, give him up to me, and you will be free from the warlock forever'.*

Ynes dreams blurred back and forth, and she remembered being a small child wandering the castles walls and she saw a boy not much older than her dressed in formal Indian attire, his striking pale skin, yellow hair and eyes bluer than the sky made her stare as he disappeared like a god into a temple. She often looked for that boy - it had made her feel special to see his face; she sensed him forever near, yet she never glimpsed him again in her conscious life, then the temple and the white warlock all flashed in her head and the golden boy in the garden, then Carmenta was back in her mind with her she reached out to her and cried for help. Ynes lay struggling in her sleep as the pain was so strong and she knew she came too near to the end.

Wagons and Ponies

~~ * ~~

Carmenta knew she had little time; she sensed that Ynes, like a flower, wilted in the hot sun. She knew that she would have to follow the routes of the camel trails across the deserts and the paths used by the slave traders; they would travel through the mountain pass on the silk road towards Leh, where all the treachery and exchanges were made. So many dangers awaited any traveller along the route including mountain cats and thuggees, who waited ready to ambush their victims; desperate cries for help were only forgotten breaths in the wind and their belongings gone, only the circling vultures would hear their hollow end. Carmenta was unafraid of such things - she took to the hefty heights of the hanging rocks and, like an eagle, she studied the dusty tracks looking for any clues. Her instinct told her something had happened nearby and on the pass she saw a discarded wheel and remnants of clothing on the mountain road's edge. She levitated down to get a better look and followed the cart's unfortunate end. Easily finding the stripped and abandoned cart, she carefully searched and found where the girl had jumped, a brave move she thought - much better to die in flight than in the clutches of a killer's grip. Carmenta found her quickly in the cave, where she lay still as though she was departed, the smallest breath left in her timid body.

Carmenta quickly saw to her wounds and poured life back into her limbs, with potions and prayers, and she then worked quickly.

She found the two sturdy grey mountain ponies, who drank by the river, both injured. She healed their wounds and found them food and with gentle persuasion she bid them to follow. Slowly she attached them to the now mended and much improved cart, and they began slowly at first on the winding river road. Ynes slept covered by the shaded canopy of a wagon-like structure that Carmenta had created, as once seen on the prairies of Montana. After checking on her patient, she gently urged the ponies on. Her journey was long in regions far from any watchful eyes so a little magic would speed up their pace. They would follow the Zanskar River towards the plains. The mountain ponies obediently trotted along blissfully unaware of their pace. By night they sped on the dusty rocky tracks and as the pink dawns floated behind them in the mountains and rose golden to the south, they rested in the caves and drank from the hidden water holes. Still the patient, Ynes, slept. Carmenta rested by her side and thanked the Jakhs for saving her from being at fault and causing the girl's death. Ynes would be fine now, she had got there just in time, and had one more job to do and she would as promised set her free, although she hoped the girl would stay in her safety from the warlock for a little while.

Carmenta felt a pang of hope and a need of a friend like in the old days and she brushed away a tear or two when she thought of her dear friends the Jakhs.

The hot day passed, and rested and eager to move on, the wagon and ponies again set off at an uncanny speed - their journey was quick and undisturbed. Carmenta knew that again she had little time with the skies rumbling and the threat of war; she was both anxious and relieved to find at last the Golden Fort. It loomed from the desert in crimson red on that night, the storm was growing, and people fled from the citadel walls, once a safe haven - now a trap and prison with the enemy only hours away; the fear was written on their faces, with their humble belongings strapped on sticks and backs. Carmenta wondered and worried where they would flee to escape being persecuted in their own land. The archway and entrance to the fort was open, and any could come and go in the storm and thick smoke from fires. The ponies carried on, steadfast for their new master, and entered the walls, sure-footed over cobbles and they arrived at the castle - the warlock's home. Carmenta knew he had gone; the warlock would not risk being discovered by a war and a new ruler. As they entered the castle, the servants were burning rooms and smoke filled the halls - they hid any evidence of the warlock as they fled in fear themselves. Carmenta tied the ponies firmly away from the fires and quickly ran to the temple that she had seen in Ynes' mind under. The temple stood alone, away from the castle, and realising how far it was, Carmenta went back for the ponies and wagon and crashing through the ornate garden path, they made their way to the temple that stood simply decorated not far from the boundary.

Carmenta ran towards it, climbing the steps, but the huge carved door was locked fast. Carmenta knew it would be no simple task, so looked for another entrance higher up, and she was easily pleased as she saw a small window open on the temple's walls. Scrambling up with ease, she squeezed herself through the tiny gap and was in; she scurried down the endless spiral stone steps passing many small side rooms that lay empty with views of the castle, lake and desert. As Carmenta entered the ground floor, she followed the rounded hall down some more steps that led to a door, again locked. Carmenta drew her breath, there was little time to lose, and whatever lay behind the door, she would have to deal with. The door slowly opened revealing a darkened room, which at first looked empty, then from the shadows she saw a figure rise, his hands held over his eyes as he grew accustomed to the seeping light that poured into the room. Carmenta saw endless pots and potions stacked high and books upon books as high as the huge, vaulted ceiling, she beckoned the scholar to come forward. Carmenta froze for a moment, as she knew it was him - the son of the Jakhs - the boy who should never have been born, her stolen son.

Carmenta panicked inside but beckoned him to grab anything that was of great importance, then she ushered him out with no explanation. Using her magic Carmenta sealed the door. Both left by the small, open window scaling down the temple walls. Carmenta did not even consider that the boy couldn't achieve the drop, as she suspected he managed everything with ease. Still with no questions, he got into the wagon alongside Carmenta and the two steadfast ponies pulled them out towards the lake. The boy finally put down the huge book he held. He took of his cloak, then he just stared longingly at the endless views around him. For a while he studied the Golden Fort as it faded from view - a mirage in the desert - his prison and home, the only place he knew that was not in ink on papyrus. As he began to see the mountains, trees and rivers, he reached out to each, still in silence. Carmenta sat quietly and drove the ponies towards Kakabhit, the village on the hill, the place Carmenta called home. She wondered whether the boy had the gift of speech. Had he been kept a prisoner for so long with no interaction that maybe he knew no spoken words? The books, Carmenta thought, told a different tale. She kept her silence, afraid she would scare or torment him with idle chatter and so the quiet journey carried on. Under the cover of night two grey ponies and a wagon rolled into the sleepy village, and still the boy observed everything - not once had he slept, Carmenta thought maybe he feared sleep would steal his new world away.

They arrived at the cottage and Carmenta instructed him to help lift Ynes inside. He responded immediately and still with no words - only a look of concern. Carmenta explained the girl's rescue, and they placed her in a cot in a cool room. Carmenta left the shutters closed and a jug of water and pot with camomile flowers sprinkled in, then she left the door ajar and asked the boy to follow her. She led him up a rackety staircase to an attic room, the boy stooped in the rafters, while Carmenta magically cleaned. She flung open the shutters and pulled out a large bed, throwing the unused items out of the window where they mysteriously disappeared. She again bought water and a pot with camomile and then left the boy, with the door open - here he was no prisoner. Carmenta then went downstairs and busied herself making chapati and chana; she happily chopped and stirred. She laid the table and then went to wake Ynes - she left her with a bowl to wash and fresh clothes, then left her to come around on her own, she would be hungry and Carmenta suspected she would come out for the food. She then threw a stone hitting the boy's shutters and gestured to him to come down and eat. Carmenta then wandered off to check on the ponies who seemed to wish to hang around, she fussed over them and fed them, then left them free by the small stream. She suspected they would stay and thought to call them Zani and Kari. Pleased with herself, Carmenta went back to the front of the cottage and much to her delight, she saw the boy and girl sat opposite each other, with their bowls filled with food. Carmenta sat down and filled her own bowl and the three sat and ate in silence.

Ynes eyed her two dining companion. For now she needed no explanation. She knew she had been rescued from the cave by the witch and she presumed the strange boy was the one the witch wished her to find. Something made sense to her and her relief to have no pain was a bonus on top of being alive. There would be time to talk, but for now she was tired and afraid of the world; Ynes had no reason to rush off anywhere. The ponies, the boy, and Ynes stayed with the witch. The boy opened his shutters wide every morning to the pretty pale skies and birds that sang, and he wandered freely in the mountains and always came back to Ynes and Carmenta. He watched them make food together and laugh and he thought them to be mother and daughter at first, then he heard their conversations and soon realised the significance of their link. The boy began to get curious and to the shock of Carmenta and Ynes, he began to talk and asked them who they were and why they had set him free and how. Carmenta told him their story and slowly he realised she was his maker, and he was a child of the Jakhs. He felt sadness and anger that he had been stolen. The white warlock had lied to him all those years, feeding him stories about how the witches hunted him to boil his bones and how he would give them life for eternity, so he stayed hidden and protected he thought in his temple, safe and secure. The warlock taught him and gave him many books and the boy devoted his life to learning. He had learnt and learnt and practised and practised the warlock's spells, afraid, though he pretended he could do no magic, so he could stay hidden from the witches that sought his heart.

As the days passed by and the boy learnt more of the Jakhs, he was fascinated and listened intently to Carmenta's tales, the three became a family and the boy told them more and more of his life with in the walls of the fort and how the warlock waited to use him for something special, Carmenta shuddered. The boy explained that he had discovered that the something special was his own sacrifice and that the witches and warlocks sought his heart. Carmenta kept quiet, for a while here they were safe and Ynes and herself would protect him. She could have sent him back to the gods; to see him each day though made her feel joy as he enjoyed his freedom, he reminded her of his father whom she still loved.

Gedahard's Landing

~~*~~

It was a cursed thing to be blown off course and to land at the dreaded sacred Stones of sacrifice that sat on the huge plains with no cover; he stood out like a sore thumb with his golden robes embroiled with jewels and silk scarves flowing in the wind, even his tapestry bag gave him away full of all he could take. He headed quickly to a cluster of trees and sat and waited for the dusk to come. He watched shepherds herding their sheep and peasants pushing carts on the track and then to his annoyance a group on piebald ponies arrived and sat in a circle at the Stones, where they painted themselves and began a strange dance. Deciding they were harmless and would cause no bother, Gedahard moved on. The ground was hard and frozen, the snow had nearly gone, but still he was grabbed by a wintery scene; an east wind blew cutting into his bones and Gedahard felt a twinge of sadness as he remembered the day his heart had turned to stone. The day he vanished to the deserts of India and shores of the Arabian Sea and called himself by another name, not to hide but to think and create his revenge.

998 The Schleswig

~~ * ~~

The day was cold with a bitter twist on the wind; they had come from the sea and waited for the waif with straight white hair. She held a basket to collect shells along the shore, but instead of skipping and laughter, she just lay there, so still and quiet. That was when his beloved sister, Auriela, had died centuries ago - killed by a coven, enemies of his ancestors.

The family had lived on Gotland and life had seemed perfect, with a small holding and freedom. Gedahard could still feel the shiny pebbles on the beaches and smell the salty air; he felt the warmth from the damp, burning logs on winter nights in the cosy dwelling, protected from the icy winds and snow. Gedahard and his sister had never known that their parents hid from a revenge killing and that they knew Auriela was in grave danger; a curse that went back centuries, and nothing could be done.

In an ancient Byzantine scripture, scrawled in messy ink was as sinister legend of a princess who married a ruthless king who slayed their first-born girl, wanting only a boy. The princess was the daughter of the King Schleswig; she was no normal princess and came from a coven of ancient witches.

Her pain was so deep she sought a bitter revenge for the King Whiteshank and all of his descendants. The coven of Schleswig created a curse that the princess put upon the king. No other Whiteshank would have the joy and charm of a girl, each one would be found and slain. The scroll told of many revenge killings and then faded as the blood line thinned and the ancient tale became a folktale a scary story for those whose bloodline they did not know

Gedahard had since made it his life's work to find the coven and the killers. The centuries turned slowly like a clock and with each hour that passed he grew no closer to a clue.

Gedahards travels took him far and wide and his world grew darker with each turn; he grew more sinister with his obsession of wealth and dominance. He did many, many wicked and callous things even to those who were his own - too long had he walked in vengeance, but his wrath could not be stopped, and his treachery became more malevolent and pure evil struck; when he captured others for his devilish plans to entice covens and possess more knowledge, with the thought to double cross those more powerful. Gedahard the white warlock was by far the most villainous and vile to tread the earth.

The Fortress of Books

Harini and Avia remained in their fortress of books. Harini
had even disguised the library door as a wall from the hall,
so she hoped the witches would not find them. The windows
were also hidden from the outside, and although the spell
wobbled and faltered at times, they hoped it was still
enough. They saw the three spooky nun-like witches searching for something outside and heard the muffled calls for
Josina; they cautiously watched and saw them head towards
the gardens and woods beyond. Avia and Harina took their
chance and ran along the secret corridor towards the kitchen. Harina jumped in and stood guard by the door, while
Avia quickly grabbed a kitchen knife and cut the rope. They
dragged their fellow witches into the secret corridor, and
Harini locked the door to the kitchens and put her finest fixing spell on it, while Avia dragged the dazed Agnes and
Preeti one by one. Harini busily went around sealing off the
house, then exhausted she returned to the library, happy
she had given the witches a problem and her new friends the
best chance.

Poor Agnes and Preeti were deathly pale, they were glazed
over and looked out with empty stares. Harini quickly recognised the spell, although she could see it had been done

very badly. It was the same spell she had put on poor Jack, only these were protected witches. Harini puzzled on how they had cast it and how to lift it. As she thought and thought and tried to get through to them, Avia rallied back and forth along the secret passage grabbing food and drink and any other useful items in the house, not knowing how long their forced lock-in would last. She was in such a fight mode she had not had chance to think of their perilous situation and she had not even thought of how Jack was doing and if he had been saved. It was only when she stopped later that she prayed with all her heart that he was safe and with Miss Bonneville, and that he would soon return.

Both girls were terrified they would not be able to fight off what lay outside in the woods. The days and nights felt so long, and both began to fear where everyone had gone. They thought of the frozen lake and gardens lying abandoned and all the house staff disappeared, with empty rooms and unlit fires, caused them both worries and questions. What had the witches done? Their only choice was to stay in their own prison. They at least had run of the house with the witches temporarily gone and at times they began to have a little fun. Avia would read to Harini and teach her things that young ladies in England did, and in exchange for Avia's gift, Harini told stories of her own culture and experience; embroidery or lace, the piano or string, an odissi or cotillion dance -

they giggled and loved each other's different and wonderful ways. Avia watched Harini as she slept and felt she had found a friend; though she still was not sure whether she could still accept her if Jack did not return. Avia went over to the mouse that sat upon her father's chair and she talked to the little creature as though it understood every word.

The Gardener Smells a Rat

~~ * ~~

Tomsk left the grounds with his spade over his shoulder and a bag of gardening tools. He strode straight over to find Jack's brother Bertie, who was working hard as always on the land; he looked pale and sad. Bertie looked up and did not hide his pain. He missed his ma and pa and was worried sick about Jack. He feared the worse like most, and the hurt would only get worse when he had to tell his folks that Jack was missing, presumed dead. He hadn't been over to see Avia. He couldn't bear to look at her grief-stricken face and although he felt guilty, he knew he could bring no comfort - he had never had Jack's charm or looks, so instead he did chores upon chores. Tomsk greeted him with sympathy but got straight to the point and told him about the strange happenings at the Hall and how he hadn't seen Miss Octavia, Avia, for a few days. He had seen strange visitors who the maids had told the village were cousins of Agnes's from overseas. Tomsk, though, had seen others and was sure they were no relatives of Agnes. One was plump and had curly red hair and she dressed like nothing he had seen before, then the other three were hauntingly similar, each with the straightest mousey brown hair; they were pale and skinny and had again the strangest attire - they looked more like scary nuns. He went on to describe the other, the prettiest

woman he had ever seen, a little like Agnes. Bertie remarked
that maybe they were all connected to Agnes. Tomsk though
was not so sure, he had seen the other two with Avia and
Agnes - they were sweet and young and much like Agnes,
but these others were different and so much older in certain
ways. Bertie talked of strange things he noticed happening
and rumours that spread in the village and then Tomsk told
Bertie about Miss Bonneville firing the lot of them and how
no one was allowed to go back to the Hall or gardens. Bertie
looked truly puzzled. He knew Lord Richard Hoare would
never get rid of any of his staff; he had even kept one maid
who pinched some bread, he had given her more money to
feed her bairns. Tomsk then described how strange Miss
Bonneville seemed and how she had lost her sweet ways and
he said how the house had a strange glow. Bertie had now
heard enough. The two men walked briskly towards the village to find the sheriff and ask for a meeting, something had
to be done.

The sheriff named Brodie was a scary man, he had no patience and little emotion, something was wrong or right and
a wrong was punished with no doubt and harshness. They
heard him shouting before they arrived at the small court-
house; the stocks were empty to Bertie's relief, he hated to
see even a villain in them. A young man came flying out with
a bloodied nose. He did not hesitate and ran as the sheriff

came out and bawled at him to go find another town. Brodie had a generous waistline and his hair thinned on top. His pallor was flushed from too much ale or whisky and he spat tobacco from his cheeks. When he saw Tomsk and Bertie he changed his grimace and grinned, greeting them as old friends whom he trusted to abide to the law. He had no problem with them and he sat and listened to their story and agreed something was strange and with the Lord away, he would gather a rally of some burly men, and so with a hand shake it was agreed. Bertie and Tomsk took a pint of ale in the small ale house by the stream. Nervous though, they did not stay as long as they normally would with so many strange folk around, and both made their way home in the light of day before dark; they shook hands and agreed they would meet at the yard after dawn.

Lil, Mo and Prim

~~ * ~~

Lil, Mo and Prim were an unusual force. Triplets that were sadly orphaned at birth, they never knew their poor mother who didn't stand a chance, as she gave birth to them in a corn field alone. The babies were found by the farmer and taken to a local nunnery named Wilton Abbey in 1280, where he left them in the safe hands of the lord. The girls grew up strong, although they were always as thin as rakes and by the age of six they had started to show signs of mischief and peculiarity. Over the years they would cause trouble beyond belief, so much so that the Benedictine convent was investigated and found guilty of misconduct by the crown. Lil, Mo and Prim took this as their cue to scarper and started their devilry and tricks elsewhere.

They found that they had a talent at playing games with dice and through the centuries they got very good at the game of cards, gambling became their foray and the way that they survived, each one ruthless to the core - they seemed to have no mercy or conscious. When the wicked three found the tunnels and the ale house, despite their very religious beginnings and proximity to a cathedral, they began their business, and they stole and cheated every traveller or drunk who thought he was going to have an easy time stealing and winning over the amusing nuns. Each one was dressed so primly in their habits. The sisters were joined at the hip and blood ran thicker than water even in their case, and although they scrapped and scratched like ally cats between themselves, they would protect each other to the death - they would lash out with such viciousness that most would run or die a nasty death.

Their meeting with Grettle was unfortunate as she made them worse if it was at all possible. She had run a nasty game of thieving for years and only gave them support and more ideas. The day that they met with Josina was an even darker day for the gentle valley folk. The reckless witches now had some brain power and a plan that they liked.

Every step of taking over the Hall seemed to be going well until the morning Josina fired all the servants and she had not been seen since. Now they had no plan or person in charge, and afraid they would be captured for their crimes, they retreated to the hut by the wooded rocky lake and waited for her return and instruction. Knowing the two witches were tied to the chairs and the others hid in fear, the three witches soon got bored of waiting and decided to go off and have some well-earned fun in their favourite ale house and so they left the scene. Their timing was impeccable. Just as they ordered their pints of frothy ale that they drank with greed, an albino man of stature walked in behind them in a strange-coloured cloak embedded with jewels, his skin as pale as marble and his hair as white as snow His silhouette in the doorway caused a few to leave, but for Grettle and the others it was too late for any hope of escape.

Chandaria's Fate or Fortune

~~ * ~~

Chandaria landed hard. As an inexperienced traveller with little instruction from Miss Bonneville, she was lucky to survive. By some fortune she fell upon some hay in a barn full of horse stalls; she smelt a sweet smell and found it to be very clean. Her heart lifted when she saw a pair of large, dappled grey horses hanging their heads over their doors; both eyed her suspiciously but with no alarm; they snorted a little and shook their heads. Chandaria got up slowly, checking she was not injured, and quietly made her way to the horses; so long since she had felt the soft muzzle of a horse and the greeting of their huge kind eyes. So engrossed in petting the pair, she did not hear the young man enter his barn armed with a rifle.

Bertie held his pa's old riffle firmly - there was no way he would let one of those witches take his best horses. Whistle and Whisper were his pride and joy and his only large spend since his family's huge inheritance. His arm shook slightly in fear as he could not decide if he should attack her by surprise or wait to see if she ran away, the latter his preferred option. His greatest fear was soon extinguished as she turned and screamed a little and fell to the floor. She had fainted in a heap. Bertie was confused. Was it a witch's trick or did she really faint? He warily walked closer, and gripping the riffle, he gently moved her head with his foot, still pointing the riffle at her head, but she was out cold. He then began to worry that maybe he had killed her with shock. Bertie put down his riffle and carefully lifted her and carried her to the farmhouse. She wore strange clothes, and her face was decorated with little jewels. He looked at her delicate hands and features and laid her down on the bench in the kitchen and propped her head with a cushion and waited. His mind reeled; he had only just returned from the village meeting where they had rallied a witch hunt, and a small army was being gathered to check Miss Avia was not in any danger and here he sat with this strange lady in his parlour. She was fragile and beautiful and for some reason he wanted to stay with her, yet he had never seen her in his life before and had no clue where she came from and how she had ended up in his horse barn.

Bertie waited and when someone knocked on his door he nearly fell off his chair. He realised he had dosed off while staring at his ward, but to his shock she was no longer there, and the knock grew more urgent. He then heard Tomsk's thick drawl. He shouted they were off to the Hall at six and to meet at the crossroads, then he heard other voices as they marched away. Relieved Bertie sighed, and then panicked as he wondered where she had gone. He was about to flee to the barn when he heard a voice behind him. She spoke in a strange, broken language and she held out a plate of some strange flat bread she had made. Bertie took the bread and without thinking ate it and then hoped she had not poisoned him. She then sat next to him and started to point to things naming them in her language. Bertie realised she wanted to know the name in his language, so they went all around the house and outside and each word she repeated, copying everything that Bertie said. They went to the barn and she again went to fuss the horses. He told her their names and she said them in her strange accent, they laughed together, and Bertie began to think that she was no witch but was just somehow very lost, then he looked at the light creep under the door. Bertie explained with his hands and voice that he had to go and would be back, and he asked her to look after his horses. She smiled and immediately started to fill the horses hay nets. Impressed Bertie left, and as he turned and smiled, she demurely smiled back with her stunning eyes - something about her made Bertie feel so happy. He shook his head, it was ridiculous; Bertie realised he had fallen for her in the shortest time. He double prayed she was not a witch and concentrated hard on a more important and per-haps dangerous task.

Bertie joined the group of men who rallied with pitch forks as they approached the Hall. Bertie was out of breath from running to get there on time. He held his riffle over his shoulders in hope he wouldn't ever have to use it. Bunty the cook was in the crowd; she looked red with anger and ready to take on any imposters, and she was the first up the steps with balustrades that led to the grand front door of the huge Hall. There was no reply to her loud knocking, so they all gathered and walked around the building, but the kitchen lower door was firmly locked and even Bunty's key could not unlock it. They continued to walk around trying to peek through windows, but some no longer seemed to be there and when they reached the library, they all wondered what was going on. The huge windows could not be seen and a strange wall of creepers grew over the Hall. Bertie became very concerned at what had happened. Poor Avia. Had she been taken as well? The group of vigilantes became nervous; to try and break in would be considered unlawful even with the sheriff on their side, so they had no choice other than to wait and watch. Brodie the sheriff ordered them all to posts to watch. Their alarm was the cry of a buzzard, and each post settled themselves in and waited in the hope they could help. Many were in the surrounding woods, while others hid in the gardens and stable yard - they would do anything to protect their Hall. Mainly though they did it for Avia, although most feared they were too late. Bertie did not stay. He made his excuses that he would be back and all understood his farm was his world and he could in truth do little at the Hall. Tomsk joked he was off to cuddle his precious horses.

Bertie ran from the house. He didn't like to leave Avia, but knew he could do nothing, just as he could nothing more to find Jack; he had a hope though that his new friend may just be able to help. As he approached the farm he saw Whistle and Whisper were being ridden around the big paddock at the front. She sat there with no bridle or saddle and both did just as she asked. She waved madly when she saw Bertie and cantered them as if they danced towards him. He walked with her alongside the fence and chattered about the problem at the Hall and how Miss Bonneville had fired the staff. Chandaria to his surprise burst out when he mentioned Miss Bonneville and waved her arms around. After dismounting and putting the horses back with water and food, she tried to explain with her broken English and by drawing pictures in the dusty barn floor. She drew stick people and a large castle, and she pointed to the people, one she called Miss Bonneville, another Ynes and the other the boy, and she pointed to Bertie's face and the stick boy's face, until he understood they looked alike, she then waved her hands around and Bertie got she meant far away. Slowly she started to learn the language more and in a stumbled way they communicated. She drew more stick people and named them and by the time darkness had fallen, Bertie understood there was a dangerous man called Gedahard who was as white as Whisper, and that she had a child called Harini, who she was not aloud to see. Bertie asked if she knew of Avia and she shook her head, but she said the boy was saved from Gedahard. Bertie was so confused. He understood some of what she said, and he suddenly had a little hope that Miss Bonneville was with Jack. He knew now that he had to get into Stourton Hall and he asked Chandaria to help him; bravely she accepted in return for a coat as she gestured to the row of hanging furs, he laughed and handed her one. Bertie locked up his house, although this was not something he would normally do. They got Bess out of the barn - an old bay cob he had had for years. She was as gentle as a kitten and as sure-footed as a mountain goat, sturdy and strong. They both sat on her and travelled through the woods and all the time Chandaria learnt new words. Bertie could not believe how she managed to remember them all; she understood him sometimes just by his expression. Bertie was more than impressed and when she explained with drawings and words and sign she had been locked up for years and taken from her family who she had never seen again. He understood she had been captured by someone very cruel, who had given her a child who she never saw. A child herself when she was taken, Bertie felt pity and pride in her ability to escape. And on that strange, still, cold day that the sun never reached, something happened between

Bertie the farmer and Chandaria the princess. A bond of friendship and fate was made and neither one wanted to be without the other.

Bess snorted and whinnied as they rode up the drive to the Hall. They dismounted and led Bess up to the stables where a few congregated, waiting for news from the ones who were staked out in lookouts, but nothing had been seen or heard. Bertie introduced Chandaria and fibbed that she was looking for her lost sister that she believe to be in the Hall. He took her hand and led her up the drive as though they visited for afternoon tea. He explained to her what they had seen as best as he could, and he knew she grasped the situation. She looked at the Hall as though it was a friend, and she smiled with such pleasure confusing Bertie. Chandaria then ran up to the building. She knocked on the door with a certain tune and sang a strange poem, and the door started to open and Harini stood there with her brown eyes and white hair. Bertie hesitantly followed her into a Hall that was different, doors and things had disappeared. Baffled Bertie stood there, Harini just stood there dumbstruck that the woman she believed to be her mother stood in the hall thousands of miles from the Golden Fort, she had only glimpsed her once or twice but she felt sure it was her.

Bertie called Avia's name loudly repeatedly and was about to give up when he saw her walking towards him. She walked cautiously and then ran to Bertie's arms sobbing and telling him all she could in drifts of tears. Chandaria had by now stopped starring around and noticed her estranged daughter now slightly behind the door. Cautiously they eyed each other up and down. Both had glimpsed each other in the castle, both afraid of each other from the warlock's poisoned mouth. After a few moments of the realisation that they had never had anything to fear, they both spilled tears and gently hugged each other, both frustrated and saddened by what they had missed and been through.

Still afraid of the witches, Avia asked everyone to move into the library and Harini resealed the front door and library door. She believed they could take no chances, especially with Preeti and Agnes still out of action. Chandaria saw the girls' glazed eyes and showed great concern and asked Harini why she had not broken the spell. Harini explained as best as she could that it was truly impossible, and they had searched and searched to find a way. Bertie stared dumfounded by the scene. Unlike his brother Jack, he had avoided the realms of the witches, and he now felt as though he was in a nest of vipers. Miss Avia seemed more than comfortable and acted as though she were one herself. He looked to Chandaria, who fussed over the two young witches in a daze. Bertie just prayed that the lord of the manor did not return home early and surprise them as he normally did - he wondered how he would react to the scene in his precious library. He wished Jack was by his side to support him. Bertie then sat down overwhelmed by the surreal events and loss of Jack, he did not yet dare share the news he had got from Chandaria - afraid to give false hope if it was not to be true.

Avia sensed his despair and came to sit with him, she encouraged him to go back to the farm and protect his horses. Bertie took little convincing and Chandaria, who felt useless, wished to go with him; they would return in the morning. As they left the Hall, they found Bunty stood by the door asking to come in. She wanted to help and cook for them and so it was agreed, if she promised to turn a blind eye to a few things. Bertie eagerly left with Chandaria, and he gave instructions to the group of villagers to carry on from the stable clock tower watching the Hall. He asked them not to wander in the woods anymore but to stay in the stable yard, reassuring them that Miss Avia and her friends were fine, but not out of danger. Bertie bid them good night and said he would return first thing. Chandaria was already sat on Bess waiting and soon they were trotting quickly along the track. Bertie was eager to get back to his horses and farm, away from the woods, with each twig that broke he felt fear, and he remembered the night with his family when they found the woodcutters abandoned hut and his ma had muttered in a thick slow whisper, "the witches are back".

The Boy Who Named Himself

~~ * ~~

The stolen boy grew more confident and felt safe with Carmenta and Ynes. He understood that he was connected to Carmenta the witch and although he was not quite ready to call her ma, he felt content and trusted her. Carmenta had told him her story one starry night by a crackling fire, so he now knew his grandfather by blood was the white warlock his captor. Carmenta warned him that the white warlock must never know; Solly was surprisingly calm and mulled the possibility of such a twist in his clever mind, he felt an anger like never before, despite his years of captivity he felt more aggression for the warlocks evil to others, in turn he told Carmenta the story of the curse on the white warlocks sister and bloodline, he handed Carmenta a scroll he had found with the name of the princes of Schleswig and her coven, this he had kept from the warlocks hand, knowing how much he wanted the information; before his escape he had thought it a bargaining chip for his freedom. By sharing the scroll Solly felt some relief and enjoyed that he could tell Carmenta anything. Carmenta's response was calm and she carefully placed the scroll deep into her folds of clothing commenting Solly had done well.

Solly found great pleasure in his new found freedom. He would walk for miles and return often the next day choosing to sleep under the stars. Carmenta worried about him, even though the once defenceless baby boy that was taken was now a skilled wizard of words and powers. He had devoted his whole life to learning and the albino warlock who had kidnapped him no doubt thought he could use such a talent. His prisoner, though, had been clever from the start and as soon as he babbled his first words in the arms of a nurse-maid, he was protecting himself and sharing nothing. At two, he was charging around his elaborate prison with gardens and huge rooms, and he had servants running around after him. He would learn all day, then sleep in his hand-crafted crib that swung in the nursery with the fresh scented breezes from the garden. It was only when he would not comply to his master's commands that he was thrown in the temple and kept under lock and key until he would oblige with some magical spells that the warlock knew he could do. The boy had a predicament: to escape was futile, the warlock would hunt him down forever, but to kill the warlock was not a thing he felt comfortable with, so he bided his time and read everything - it was the one privilege the warlock would allow.

One day when captive, the boy read a book of Nordic legends - he liked the pictures that showed people that looked like himself. There was one fable he particularly loved, and he read it often to keep himself assured that he did the best thing to wait, to be patient, kind and calm and in the legend he found his name and called himself Solly.

The Waddenduivle

The settlement of Ribe sat on the shores of the Wadden sea. The driftwood huts sat on a plateau slightly above the grass marshes and mud flats – it was a place of cruel tides, ice rocks and the black moon of birds. The Nordic folk with fair and aqua eyes were hunters of the sea and many farmed the shores like their ancestors before. Life was both harsh and gentle. The seasons gave them shallow waves and sun kissed winds or ferocious waves as high as mountains and endless darkness with bitter winds. The changing seas were not their main fear though – deep in the marshes there was a sea creature called the Waddenduivel, the devil of the Wadden.

Solly lived with his family in a small wooden hut, and he hunted just like his brothers and pa. His ma had gone to the longest sleep that she would never wake from, but he sensed in his heart she was still there, and her sensible thoughts and commands still stayed in his mind. Unlike his father and brothers, he would take different paths and listen carefully for telltale signs, bubbling water or no tide at all, and always stick to the rock paths and never the sea mud. Solly became a loner from his tribe, and he spent hours wandering the flats of Wadden. It was here he could hear his ma's sweet singing voice, and often, in the warmer months, he would sleep in the towans of grass and sand, although always he would take with him hemlock to scatter around and dig himself in for a safe night by a fire. The deer from the forest would venture down to the marshes and skittishly avoid his bed as they took their early morning sea grass nibbles. His fear, though, was from none of these – it was the fear of the Waddenduivel. It came from the depths of the cold northern sea and took its prey with no care for its heart or family left on the shore.

Solly had always obeyed his dear ma's instruction and he quietly lived at times near to the creature. He smelt his foul pungent aroma as it often snaked around him. Instead of panicking like many did, Solly would stay calm and stand his ground keeping to his rock bed paths, where claws could not grab his ankles and pull him beneath.

The Waddenduivel became obsessed with this strong creature that avoided his wrath time and time again with only solitary quietness and no fear. Solly felt a strange connection to the creature and unlike the others, who always failed in gangs with traps and axes to try and capture the beast that took their kin, Solly decided he had to help and thought of a plan. He patiently watched the creature's moves, recording the times that he came, and each time he would gift the beast an already dead animal or fish. The Waddenduivel took it each time and often Solly would smell its stench as it began to wait for his gifts.

Solly carried this on and the folk of Ribe started to notice that no kin were taken, and they looked to Solly who wandered the shores and called him to ask if the Waddenduivel was dead, believing he saw everything. Solly told the people he did not know if the Waddenduivel was dead or alive and he continued to train the beast with patience and each time he fed the Waddenduivel, he led him further away from the people of Ribe. One day the Waddenduivel was absent; there was no stench, and he never came for his food offering. At first Solly feared he had gone back for the towns folk, so in panic he ran to the settlement to warn the people that the Waddenduivel could be back in the marshes, the people eyed Solly suspiciously, as no one had been taken and no Waddenduivel had been seen. He still suggested caution and Solly watched and waited, walking the shores of the marshes, yet still no Waddenduivel came.

One day, he walked far out on a low tide, and he watched a peculiar fisherman with an old cobble boat; the fisherman spat and grumbled a growl, and he waved in a strange sort of way. He looked closely at Solly and recognised his clever friend, just as Solly got a hint of the pungent smell. The Waddenduivel, now the fisherman, pulled his boat away, and Solly watched him disappear into the sand towans. Solly knew the Waddenduivel was now gone from the town. He now fished on the shores for muscles, shrimp and his favourite new dish of hake that Solly had often gifted, and the town folk were left alone.

Solly smiled to himself. His plan had worked; patience and kindness had paid off. He glimpsed the strange old fisherman a few more times in his life, but never did he ever get quite so close again, not wishing to tempt fate.

Carmenta Takes Council

~~ * ~~

Carmenta watched the boy, and she grew to adore him; she could see he turned each day to look more like a Jakh and his father, her beloved Sah. One day, while they walked in the hills, she asked him for his advice and how she could stop and solve a problem that she thought she had worsened with her meddling. She told him of Josina and talked about his captor Gedahard and how she thought that they plotted something horrible once more; she feared if she just let it be, that the consequences would come knocking on her door and others dear would fall. She feared that the girl was still not safe and that the warlock and witch would still want Solly and Agness as a sacrifice. The boy reassured her that they could no longer take him, he was stronger now, and with her and Ynes by his side he was also free and no longer hidden. He also felt the Jakhs knew where he was and look down on him. Carmenta looked concerned and said she didn't want him to leave this precious time they had. The boy did not answer, he instead looked to the skies, then later he said, 'we will go together, when our time on this earth is done'. Carmenta felt a happiness inside that she had missed for a very long time. She encouraged the boy that he needed a name and he simply replied that he called himself Solly, a name he had found in a story from long ago. Carmenta clapped and said she could never have chosen such a good name. He patted Carmenta gently on the back and said they should go find Ynes, they had a witch and a warlock to chase. Carmenta cackled out loud, liking her friend and son called Solly. She repeated the name and felt a glow in her heart.

Later on, when the moon swirled in the sky and wisps of cloud flew by, Carmenta took from her box the small charm of Josina's that she had found in Fabian's chateau and had kept in order to return it to her one day - it now became a useful hex to take them to the place they had to be. They concocted a spell and the three stood around the cauldron of flames. They each chanted and sang, holding hands firmly, and they found the place they needed to be. Carmenta knew they had little time for preparation, and that she would see a sign when the time was right for them to go.

Gedahard and the Serpent Bite

~~ * ~~

Gedahard rode along the cobbled streets on his stolen piebald cob that he taken from the travellers by the circle of stones. The night grew colder and the chilling eastern wind still blew. The sign of the ale house in the wall creaked back and forth, dominated by the huge cathedral that was lit with candles, the singing of hymns floated on the squally gusts. The Haunch ale house was still a dingy place with thick, poorly fitted wooden beams and crooked walls; small steps led off to different cramped rooms, and the fire roared away in each fireplace, one of which was particularly gruesome - with a strange bone hand stuck behind the iron grate. Tatty leather hide seats were strewn around with beer barrels as rackety tables, while antlers randomly hung about. A separate room was used for gambling, this was a place the white warlock Gedahard had visited before.

Gedahard walked into the ale house of disrepute and lingered in the doorway. He could not believe his fortuity, for as soon as he strode in, he saw the plump witch with tight curls of red that he sought revenge upon, and with her, leaning on the bar, stood her freaky threesome of nuns. She was trapped and she knew it. They all eyed him and one of the nuns flew at him like a coiled serpent, so quick and forceful like a snake she bit him hard on the hand. Gedahard was too quick and strong for her though and she was pushed and held on the door, spitting and cursing she writhed, desperate to be rid of his spell. Next the other three were frozen as onlookers started to casually disappear. The bar boy shook in the cellar and all that could be heard was the relentless protests from Lil, Mo and Prim, who screeched from their frozen spots, while Grettle, petrified shivered in silence.

A most unfortunate visitor came in jeering with his friends. Redge would regret his calling to his regular drinking hole that eve, as he saw his mother, Grettle, and the others stuck to the floor like breathing effigies. Gedahard recognised the boy straight away and fixed him to the spot, while his friends ran screaming for help. Gedahard peeled Prim off the door and stood her like a pawn next to her sisters, then he went to help himself to a jug of ale while bolting the bar boy below. He put a silver coin on the shelf and went to sit by the fire. Gedahard sat there as though he had all the time in the world and not a care. He put his feet up and closed his eyes for a little while then drew another jug of ale, and again left a silver coin, then walked around the bizarre collections of statues he had created. Pleased he patted each one on the back, and began his questions and he expected answers. The first was his ring - he wanted it back or the boy would die an unpleasant death. He secondly wanted to know what had happened to his estranged daughter, and thirdly he wanted to talk with Josina urgently, alone. Grettle spluttered out all she could, stammering in her stone façade. She had seen the ring in the Hall on the hand of a servant she did not know, the cook she thought and a dangerous type. Gedahard laughed out loud at her calling someone dangerous. He strangely believed her though. He boomed out 'next', and Mo slurred, as though drunk in her rich drawl that his daughter was at the Hall with the Lady Octavia whom they could not catch. Again the warlock laughed out loud, he could not decide if it was the ale or the comedy of the scene and the replies - such incompetence.

His daughter was good then as he had always suspected. It was a shame in a way that the Viking coven would come for her, now she was not being lazy in her room and the safe walls of the castle. He chuckled with a strange unfamiliar tinge of pride and drank more ale. The witches then rolled their eyes, knowing he again would be entertained by their pathetic demise. Josina was missing; she had not been seen for days. She had looked for something and then had disappeared. Each witch in turn confessed that without Josina they had no plan, so they had come for a beverage or two, for medicinal purpose more than anything else. Again the albino roared with laughter and took to his seat by the fire.

He felt quite content that all was well for him and as he sat he had a thought. Instead of ridding the world of the pests he had caught, he decided the vermin could be of use, so while they were stuck in the mud he told them of his proposal and offered twice what Josina had promised. Each witch was now excited and, easily fooled, they agreed on the spot and the deal was done. Again, the warlock chuckled away as he said it was set in stone - any misbehaving or disloyalties then they would be statues for good. So he released the witches, who twitched and stretched and clasped their claws, holding back their instinct to attack, and he called the bar boy to serve them ale and pie. The hatch was unlocked to set him free and the bar boy gulped when he saw the strange group sat in a corner, with Grettle's boy Redge shoved under the bench - Gedahard's insurance policy until he got his ring back.

Gedahard asked them many question, and they told him many lies. The strange alliance was complicated, with each one cheating the other in their mind. The only thing that was certain was that they were off to the caves near Stourton Hall, where Josina had said Fabian and the others would join them when the time was good. The warlock Gedahard rubbed his hands, everything was working tremendously. As the poor bar boy nervously filled their jugs and put down their pies, he heard many things he should never have heard.

The witches and warlock, who thought themselves so clever and above the rest, did not think the lad would have a clue, but the youngster was clever and unbeknown he had doused them with spiked ale and huge helpings of pie filled with magic mushrooms. He took the warlocks silver he was owed, then he quietly disappeared into the dark, cold night. His pony Lucky was a sturdy number bred by his favourite cousin Bertie. Jerome rode him hard towards the woods and fields that eventually led to Stourton Farm. He flicked his blond curls from his face and wiped away tears of fear from his deep, blue eyes - he had to hurry. Jack's Avia and his friend Agnes were in true danger.

Fallen and Back

Agnes began to come around a little. She could see Preeti sat next to her in a strange trance-like state. She could not move but she knew she had her mind back. She saw Avia and Harini working on something on the rug by the fire, she felt the soft lambswool rug weaved by Tess in the village and she saw the endless ceiling to floor shelves of neatly organised books with wooden ladders on rungs reaching to the top. She felt the warmth from the fire and saw the Lord's artefacts, ornaments and statues around the room, many that were displaced from other parts of the house - Avia and Harini had been busy. She then saw Bertie, Jack's unmistakable brother, and another much like Harini, only her hair was dark like her own. The stranger seemed to stand closely to Bertie; she was nervous and her eyes flitted around the room, and each time they rested on Harini. Agnes began to feel they had a connection, but unsure, she concentrated on other things.

Agnes could not help it but as she kept staring at Bertie, she thought of Jerome. She had not seen him since the end of summer, when he had been dragged back to work in his pa's ale house that he hated. He said the place was dangerous and full of frightening thugs, but he had no choice until he freed himself and his ma from the violent clutches of his so-called pa. Agnes thought of the wonderful days she had spent with Avia, Jack and Jerome. They had swum in the lake, climbed trees and played endless games of croquet. To Agnes, it felt like the childhood she had never really had. Her love of Stourton Hall and everyone was so strong and she had felt herself falling for Jerome. He had the looks and charming nature like Jack's and something else she sensed; he was also worldly from his travels with his pa. As dodgy and ruthless as they were, Jerome was kind and they had often talked until late of how he could escape, but his ma was frail and needed care. Agnes had talked to Avia and knew with Jack that they would come up with a plan, but the danger was Jerome's pa, so they were bidding their time.

Agnes thought back to the happy golden days again and she felt tears falling down her cheeks, and she began to sob as she had sobbed when she realised that her mother Avoca had abandoned her buried in a hole hundreds of years ago. Agnes could not stop. She feared losing everything she loved so dearly and that she may never see Avia, Jerome or Jack again. As her tears fell hard, she started to feel something, her hand could move and then her arm and gradually, although painful and stiff, she started to stir - she felt a little like a puppet on string, but gradually Agnes came back to life.

Avia turned when she saw her dear friend in tears and ran to throw her arms around her, elated she was coming around despite her sadness, and slowly Agnes began to speak; the others came over and with great relief they got their Agnes back. Agnes felt exhausted and asked for food. Soon Bunty the cook was cooking a hearty, humble meal for her hideouts in the library. When they had all refuelled, Agnes drew her attention towards Preeti, who still sat dumbfounded. They could not understand if the spell had worn off or Agnes's mind had won. Agnes thought Bertie and the thought of Jerome had bought her back from the brink, so Agnes started singing old songs that her mother would sing - the songs were old and sounded strange, but Agnes knew how Preeti loved Avoca as though she was her mother and Agnes knew she looked just like her, so holding her hand she kept trying, but Preeti still did not respond. Agnes stayed with her never giving up, they had little else to do other than protect themselves and wait for whatever came next.

Miss Bonneville Back-to-Back

Avoca felt pleased with her work, and as she wandered around the heavenly, scented villa gardens. She thought of the Chitrakut fort and their little stall and cottage and wondered if the time had come to go back to the woods and valleys of the small wet island she still thought as home. Although she had been born under a hot sun and had spent most of her life in the mountains and deserts, she still found the rolling valleys with gentle folk the place she would truly like to be, and she thought of being by Agnes and teaching Preeti the ways of a simpler life. Avoca sighed and snapped herself out of her daydreaming and ran her hands along the huge fig tree, then picked the ripe juicy fruits. Wandering back to the pristine white villa she saw Miss Bonneville reading on her balcony and Jack staring out over the gardens on the veranda, she waved and smiled. Avoca had grown to adore Jack - he was smart and witty and as he had slowly come back to being himself, he showed how quick thinking and knowledgeable he was. He was charitable with his kindness towards her and never made her feel awkward or stupid with her blunders and instead he helped her to understand and taught her how to say things in a more acceptable way. Jack and Miss Bonneville had in fact turned out to be her tutors on etiquette and she was learning fast. For too long she had hidden away, always feeling like she was hunted, although in truth she still was, as Josina had never gone away. She panicked a little inside, then rushed towards the house - the thought of Josina made her feel scared, knowing she was waiting in the shadows for her daughter and Avia.

Miss Bonneville had looked up to see Avoca's distressed face. She did not need to ask why, she felt tense and worried herself. Miss Bonneville looked out over the gardens and above the canopy of scattered ghaf trees that shaded the pretty garden from the scorching sun, to the mountain peaks beyond. Each night, the crickets sang and fireflies danced in patterns around the beautiful frankincense trees. Striking black iris grew in circular clumps and scented roses, much like home, grew around the house. Miss Bonneville sighed as she thought of Stourton Hall that stood all cold and alone - she had begun to prefer the long dry heat of India and had also become fond of Muscat very quickly. She loved the sounds, sights and smells. Miss Bonneville wondered if it was time she found a new life for herself; however, she would always be torn. Then she looked down at Jack, who took seeds with care from the pod of the black lily and wrapped them in his handkerchief and careful placed them in his pocket - always the gardener. Miss Bonneville knew before she could think of herself that she had to get Jack back and sort out Josina, then just maybe she could live a different life 'First things first', she scolded herself, and determined to get her travelling spell perfectly correct, she went back to the book that was once Josina's, that Avoca had kindly lent her.

Miss Bonneville struggled as they needed to travel together, this was a challenge in itself. Their location also had to be very precise as they could not risk being seen by anyone at all until they had established what was going on. Miss Bonneville intended to land at Belle and Jeremiah's manor house, as they would still be in France. She continued to mix the coordinates and dates and times, but the process was complicated and she thought of the strange small clock in a silver casement that Fabian the Warlock would carry everywhere; she remembered him tuning the dials this way and that. Miss Bonneville would have given a lot for that silver contraption in that moment of time. She paused and thought of Fabian and how she had spent so much of her life as his servant and prisoner. She sighed again, maybe it was time to find her roots and she had the strongest feeling they were in India, something about it felt so familiar and homely to her.

Jack placed more seeds in his pocket and placed Tibbles the gecko on a plant explaining he would be happy here in the sunny garden. He sensed the time was near that they would go, and his land was too cold for a little harmless gecko who was used to the warm sand. He looked up at Miss Bonneville who studied something of importance and difficulty by the grimace and seriousness of her look. He smelt the air and longed to be back in the fresh air of Stourton Hall, with the gardens and valleys. He could not bring himself to think too much of Avia alone there and afraid; it broke his heart they were apart and in such a strange and dangerous predicament. As Jack wandered around the paths, he looked to the mountain tops and thought of his time in India. In some strange way he wished he could have stayed longer in those castle gardens and he would have liked to have talked to the boy he sometimes glimpsed, and disappeared. The boy had looked much like himself, only there was a strange aura around him, and he noticed when this boy walked, his feet almost did not touch the ground and the sweet little flower pecker birds with their blue coats and white bibs would always follow him. Much like the robin, they were cheeky and bold, but how they loved the boy; he would hold out his arm and there they would land. One day, Jack called to him and his call was carried on the hot sandy wind. The boy had turned and nodded his head once and smiled. Jack though was then still in a trance-like spell and he began to wonder if it was all just a dream. He wondered if many things were - the girl and the camels and the caves. Poor Jack had no clue in his head what was real, he only knew he had to get back and that the present was real.

He certainly had stories to tell, however, of ships and sea creatures that rose from the depths, jumping and arching back into the inky waters. He had heard the name 'orca' shouted as the crew pointed excitedly and prayed to their god, and buckets of fish were thrown to them and many bowed; the orca, it seemed, were a lucky sighting and a party began. The huge blue creatures swam at speed along-side entertaining the onlookers with gigantic loops, and cheers were raised from the elated audience. Jack could have stood on that ship deck for an eternity watching those sea wonders and he swore, as soon as he got home, he would draw pictures of his memories and write everything down for Avia to read. Jack just wanted to be home now and as if she had heard his thoughts, Miss Bonneville called both Avoca and Jack. She asked them to gather whatever they could carry and told them the time had come, they had little time. She had nearly missed the perfect date and the next time would be a good six months away; she grumbled, feeling no desire to board a ship again.

Solly's Dreams

~~ * ~~

Solly's newfound freedom and happiness had also bought with it vivid dreams. He often dreamt of the castle and fort that had become his prison. He walked the stone steps in his dreams and always he found walls to the sky with no way out, then the white warlock would terrify him, waking him in cold sweat, and he would fall back to sleep, but soon other dreams would find his mind, tormenting him with riddles he often could not understand. In these dreams he met people he did not know and saw places he had never been to and each time he would wake feeling a connection to another world.

Solly spoke to Carmenta about his dreams and she became more and more intrigued at his description of the world and at some of the people he described and names she heard fall from his lips - these were names she knew from her own travels and meetings. Carmenta decided it was time to act. His dreams were surely the sign to go and she would take Ynes and Solly with her, her own little army. Carmenta had prepared her troupe and they could now go into battle unharmed. Solly and Ynes she suspected would once again meet the white warlock Gedahard, so they needed to be more than ready.

When Carmenta told them it was time to go she was surprised by Ynes and Solly's reactions. Both were very keen and their own instincts had sensed that something was brewing in the skies and that they were somehow entwined. They had worked hard and listened to every single word, spell and potion that their teacher taught them; Carmenta was satisfied with her crew.

She took them to the hill where she called to the Jakhs one day so Solly could see the strength of his beginnings. The day was soft and the sun watery and a dusty breeze hazed the view, and as Carmenta called the Jakhs, she held tight to Solly's arm and asked Ynes to hold tight to his other arm in fear they would take him. Soon the skies filled with the beautiful beings and one by one many settled to the earth. They touched the boy in amazement - a child born half-Jakh and half-human. Carmenta cried when she saw Sah, Solly's father, and he too shed tears. Sayari, her dear friend, was there to comfort them all and for hours, long after the others had left, Sah and Sayari stayed to talk to Carmenta and Solly. The night skies became cold and full of wondrous stars, yet still they talked not wanting to leave, but when the dawn began to rise and the embers of the fire began to die, Sah and Sayari sadly said their goodbyes, although this time Carmenta knew that they would be back as they agreed that Solly should stay and not yet return to the skies and seas, until his time on earth was over. Carmenta felt such relief. She knew he had centuries left to share with her and now that he was blessed and known by the Jakhs, he could never come to harm as they had found his heart to be true and pure and encouraged him to do good on the earth. When they had gone Carmenta no longer felt sadness; instead, she felt joy that she had Solly and her friends the Jakhs back, and she thanked Solly for being so wonderful. They then woke Ynes, who slept in the cart, and with the last shadow of darkness they all disappeared, cart, ponies and all had vanished from the hill, leaving tracks and ashes for the rising sun that glimmered through the sacred Butea tree. The leaves fell to the dusty ground, while a golden eagle swooped on the warm wind, its gentle whistle calling to its forever partner that the gods had visited earth.

A Neat Return

Miss Bonneville was more than pleased with herself and clapped, praising herself for such skill. They landed neatly in Belle's beautiful drawing room. Elegant drapes covered ornate windows meeting with grace the shiny floorboards. Beautiful hand-painted walls with silver birch and doves complimented the elegant furniture, gifts from France. Each one smelt the fresh air and sighed relief. For a short while they could enjoy the tranquillity and pleasure of knowing that they had Jack back on English soil. He was home, but not yet safe, and although he desperately wanted to run to Avia, Miss Bonneville knew this was the most dangerous thing to do, for now they had to remain hidden from all. Jack showed them to the guest bedrooms on the left wing of the manor and both were more than happy with their stunning, spacious rooms.

Avoca had spent the entire time since landing just staring dumfounded at the glorious home and gardens, where everything was so neat and tidy. Miss Bonneville laughed at her expressions. She had grown fond of Avoca's non-assuming ways. She expected little and took nothing for granted and seemed thankful for the smallest of things, and she was learning fast. Her manners were becoming impeccable, and she spoke more eloquently by the hour. Miss Bonneville asked her to put a maid's uniform on instead of her silken sari, as she looked a little strange in the rolling iced valleys, and so she also had a cover should anyone see them. Miss Bonneville did the same thing in case a visitor should call or the maid herself came in to clean and check on the house. She knew Belle had paid most of the staff to stay on in their absence and her niece Lucy would be in charge. Miss Bonneville and Avoca then set to work on trying to communicate with Agnes, as she had been lost to them for days now.

Avoca planned to go out in the early evening to track any activity, and the two witches busied themselves with their plans and plots to find the other witches. Miss Bonneville to-date was the only one who knew it seemed where Josina stood, and she hoped the statue in stone would stay set for long enough. Jack listened to the witches' plans, he was still suffering from the journey and ordeal, he felt weak and tired, so he retired to his room away from witchy things; he just wanted his family back and to see Avia, and he wanted to wander the woods as he had all his life, and work on the gardens design. He looked around his grand room, a far cry from his tiny attic room in the small farmhouse that his brother and he had shared all their lives. He then studied the globe that his mother Belle had given him and turned it around. He found Jaisalmer in India and where he thought the Golden Fort was. He then studied his journey across the deserts of Rajasthan, the Aravalli mountain range; the glorious Kumbalgarh Fort with its endless walls, the cooling hills, forests and lakes of Mount Abu, and the sacred Lakhadiya hill, then the bustling port of Jakhau. His finger trailed across the Arabian sea to Muscat and he thought of the stories and experiences he had to tell Avia. While he waited to see her and frustrated by the danger, he took his ink, feather quill and paper from his desk. Jack began to write and draw every memory he possibly could. He only stopped occasionally to look out over the garden. He longed to go out each time though, so every time he had the urge to run to Avia, he would start to write again. He was both obedient to Miss Bonneville's advice and aware of his own fear to stray out alone, and only when the light faded did he stop. He watched Avoca in her dark cloak walk across the lawn then disappear from sight. Jack shuddered and wondered what had happened to this world that he loved. He realised that the valleys had been home to the occult for centuries, and for some reason they gathered, and he hoped that maybe their time was to come to an end. They sought something though, and it was more than woods and lakes. Jack's whirling mind then slept, while the world of witches and warlocks brewed a tempest and his dearest Avia was in the eye of the storm.

The Jakhs & Punvara

~~ * ~~

The year was 1028, and a storm had tumbled over the land and sea causing great destruction. As the people wandered along the shore to salvage parts of boats and drifting flotsam, each one saw a strange light appear from the horizon out at sea; afraid they retreated and watched the lights move closer. Soon they could see figures, and as the visions came to shore, the people froze in fear. The strange ones were tall and slender, each clad in white robes, with striking lemon hair and piercing turquoise eyes. The terrified onlookers counted seventy-two of the strangers, each one looked powerful and had a saintly ambiance about them. They all stood on the beach and lifted their arms to the ocean and from the waves' crashing foam came seventy-two dashing white horses. The figures quickly mounted their steeds and galloped away towards the hills. Many thought they had seen ghosts of the sea and others believed that the gods had come to earth, others just said it was a shipwreck and they were foreigners from a far off land, the latter was the less-believed theory and many were truly convinced that their prayers had been answered. They became known as the Jakhs and turned out to be a good thing for the land and sea. They were soon loved and respected by all, apart from one, who cursed their arrival.

Punvara the White thought himself as royalty of Kera and the golden gods seemed to now control what he considered to be his land and people. They also seemed to possess a power he did not understand, unlike any magic he had ever seen. Punvara tried many times to have them persecuted, yet each time the people would rise to protect them and insisted they stayed - they had many loyal disciples.

Punvara needed a plan, so decided he would take a bride, the daughter of King Sindh. This daughter would bring him more power and a son, and he believed he could then gain more popularity. So he began his campaign of being generous to his people and parading around with his beautiful wife. He felt some success and although he had no real love for his wife, she had proven to be a reasonable accessory to his scheme. The time passed though and there was still no child. Frustrated he went to the seven devotees of the Jakhs and asked them for help to give him a son. The devotees who disliked the cruel Punvara told him he must first take an oath and sacrifice his most treasured possessions as a mark of respect to the Jakhs. Punvara gave them his prized white stallion and took an oath of respect to the Jakhs.

Time passed and still no son appeared. Punvara raged that he had been cheated by them and he sent their devotees in chains to trample the corn, cutting and burning their feet in the scorching sun. A kindly passerby named Burba the baker was so saddened by the sight that he let one of the devotees go, taking his place. The devotee, Aval, ran to the hill of Lakhaydiya and called for the Jakhs to help. The Jakhs came as always and asked Punvara to release the devotees. Punvara just laughed and jeered at the Jakhs. They warned him they had no choice but to banish him to a prison, until he could find kindness in his heart. He was sent to a cave and imprisoned and left to live a lone in the strange underworld.

The devotees were freed and cured from pain and a peaceful life returned to them. The Jakhs disappeared to the skies with the promise of returning should they be called upon. The queen, Punvara's wife, eventually had her child secretly in the village where the Jakh's sacred statues stood. The poor infant was born a cripple and at birth her given name was Beliccia, after a kind old dakinin who helped the queen give birth. The queen was saddened by her child as she grew and she could not bear to look at her, so she left her alone sat on the village track, in hope someone would take her in.

Poor little Beliccia sat there abandoned and still she did not cry, she just waited for something good to come along. The kindness of mankind was never far and an old couple with bent backs and no children of their own would take Beliccia

to their cottage, she was given an attic room with a spectacular view of the hills, she was cared for well, much loved and
protected. Bellicia in turn would grow to be a charming and
very kind daughter, who kept her adoptive parents well to
the end of their days.

While Bellicia grew in happiness and her childhood left her.
In the shadows of the underworld a creature lived in the
dark. Once he called himself Punvara. The evil remnant of
the man had clung to life and within his hellish capture, he
had found a nest of rare white Krait snakes and with his
magic spells, Punvara transformed himself with their
venom. Slowly he made himself stronger than ever before
and escaped the Jakhs prison; without a kindly heart. Punvara was now if possible, more evil than before.

He wandered in the villages where he had once lived and
watched the crippled girl with curiosity, there was something familiar about her and he heard in time the gossip, that
she was Punvara's daughter abandoned by the queen, so he
had watched her grow from time to time. He felt no pity for
her ailments and no pride for her care to others. As she grew
he watched her more carefully seeing that she was very gifted in theurgy, Punvara began to realise she could never find
out who she really was and he became obsessed with the
thought of her knowing and feared her powers, he could not

bare for her to live, so he decided she should die by his own hand - he captured her and had her burnt to death, Punvara walked away from the burning, satisfied she was no more than dust.

Unbeknown to Punvara, the Jakhs returned to save his daughter, who by a miracle survived. They saw her heart was pure and kind and they pulled her from the flames and turned the beauty from within to show on the outside. She became a heavenly sight, more beautiful than her mother the queen, and they gave her the name Carmenta and taught her their ways.

Her father Punvara; oblivious of her new existence, would again reinvent himself and become Gedahard the White once again, in his truest and most powerful form he would carry on with his malevolent way.

One night, Gedahard had a haunting dream of his dear lost sister Auriela, who pestered him to remember that he sought revenge for her death. She showed him a golden fort with a castle and a princess far away on a beautiful white horse. Auriela told him to snatch the princess for their own revenge and to take the princess to the castle far from her valley of woods and kings and queens and that her daughter, like all their families before, would be killed on the day she turned fourteen. Auriela screech wildly in his dream that then the trap would be set and she could return.

Gedahard woke from his vivid dream and followed his sister's instruction. He found the princess and made a deal with her uncle that he could not refuse, he then took the princess to the castle in the Golden Fort and his plan was cast.

Auriela would haunt him again in his dreams and she told him of a baby boy that had been born of the Jakhs, and that he would become the most powerful wizard of all time. Auriela hissed he must take the child and keep it secret and use its talents for their vengeance. Again Gedahard woke and obeyed her commands. The small baby was stolen from a beautiful woman who he felt he knew from somewhere. The baby boy became his prisoner, and a temple was built to hide him from the world. And when Gedahard's Golden Fort was invaded he had no choice but to leave and follow a path that no legend tells in this world.

The Farmers Yard

~~ * ~~

Carmenta knew full well her landing at the grand Stourton Hall had to be very precise. Josina had taken occupation, so too close was too dangerous and too far was a nuisance. A little way off would be perfect, under the protection of trees, with a stream, on a slight hill with shelter was everything she would need. However, she felt a powerful talisman throw them off their course and clinging tight with all their might they landed ungainly in the back of a famers yard - their landing was not soft and discreet as she had planned. She suspected she may as well have landed with trumpets and drums, and was furious with the spell some other witch had made that had sabotaged her careful planning; she muttered and uttered many foul words in her ancient tongue of Sanskrit. Solly and Ynes shook off the hay and muck and looked to sooth the poor ponies Zani and Kari who shivered and whinnied in shock - the poor mountain ponies were petrified and Carmenta wished she had been less ambitious and left them behind. Solly was very skilled though and slowly they calmed down and rested their heads in his open arms; they pawed at the cold ground with their hooves, then stood still and waited for food.

Relieved, they all sighed, then looked behind them to see that a man and a familiar lady watched on. Ynes called out, 'My lady is that really you?' And relieved, Chandaria ran to her lost maid. She hugged her and kissed her forehead in relief, thinking that poor Ynes, her dear friend, would surely be dead. Bertie gently put down his riffle and stepped forward to greet his peculiar guests. Chandaria explained who Ynes was and looked with curiosity, the boy who Ynes had stolen and another she had never seen, and she gently nudged Ynes for an introduction. A little awkwardly Ynes obliged and introduced Carmenta and Solly as her dearest friends, although she chose not to elaborate on their status or history. Bertie said Solly reminded him of his brother, and he wiped a tear from his eye. Everything was more than peculiar, with so many visitors from far-off lands and his poor Jack still nowhere to be found. Ynes went to him seeing his distress and feeling guilty as she had made things worse. She told him that Jack was safe and he would be back soon. Carmenta told him they had travelled to Muscat and Miss Bonneville and Avoca guarded him well. The extra confirmation of Jack's well-being was thrilling, so, with some hesitation, Bertie invited them all in. Firstly though, he saw to the ponies and admired their thick grey coats. Zani and Kari had never had such a soft and sweet-smelling bed, with food and company in the barn of stalls. Content the ponies were settled, they all went to the house and sat around the old kitchen table while the fire roared and spat fiery embers onto the hearth.

Bertie served bread, cheese and ale and they all talked as though they were long-lost friends and Solly found that he knew the language well. He felt something strange, a connection to this world that he had seen in his dreams. Carmenta found the company more than useful – they had knowledge of everything that went on in their valley and Bertie gave a thorough account of the recent events. Poor Ynes began to cry knowing she had harmed this poor boy's brother by taking him far into the desert thinking he was the other one who turned out to be Solly. She felt confused and over-tired with everything, so was settled down to sleep, while the others chatted on. Soon each one found a place to sleep, and it was agreed that tomorrow they would visit Stourton Hall at first light.

By Chance

~~ * ~~

Avoca felt good to be back in the old wood with the familiar smells and sounds; the cold she did not miss, but the air felt good and she felt this land was her home. She still held guilt for Agnes and anger at Josina for her trick all those years ago, and now they were back, only this time she feared it could be far worse than before. She tried not to panic at the thought of Agnes and Preeti captured and she had promised Miss Bonneville she would take no action. The woods were quiet and only a distant owl hoot could be heard as it echoed over the silent valley. Avoca shuddered, it was a bad omen; she wrapped her cloak around herself and took to the canopy of the trees. Avoca knew the valley well and was soon close enough to the Hall to get a sense of what was going on and who came and went. The wind was kind and settled as Avoca found a comfortable spot where she could spy, spectate and listen - still the owl hooted calling to its mate or calling out their fate. Avoca heard something on the forest floor and watched as a herd of deer tracked deep into the woodland for the night and then silence fell like a curtain on the stage and she looked out at the changing scene as the moonlight played tricks on the shadows. Avoca thought of the old castle and kind lord. If only she and Agnes could have stayed safe in their hovel in the woods and served the gentle people with her ointments and cures. She sighed it was not meant to be. Avoca stayed so still and hardly dared to breathe in case she missed a sign or sound. Silence though was not needed as she heard them coming along the track long before she saw them. As they appeared in silhouettes under the arched branches basked in moonlight she could hear their roars of laughter and as they grew closer, she saw a drunken group of wenches with a master. They were trouble in the making - she could smell the stench of spirit and foulness from a mile. The three women looked like nuns and the tall man reminded her of a warlock she had met many years ago. Trailing behind, muttering and slouching, was a rounded witch who was the spit of Lettice, only she was a tad taller and her hair was a brilliant red. Avoca's mind raced and she hardly dared to take a breath; she watched them and carefully and followed them as they carried on their raucous chants unaware of their spy. Avoca studied the figure who trailed behind, so like Lettice who was once her friend. So similar it was uncanny and impossible to be true - she thought of Lettice who had been captured. Avoca brushed the past from her mind and concentrated on her assailants, as she suspected they made for the old cabin by the wild lake far from any eyes. Certain they were there, she decided to head straight back and report to Miss Bonneville - she could not risk this news not travelling fast, a warning of who they dealt with. Avoca turned quickly and flew at speed, and hurtling through the foliage and moonlit leaves she landed briefly at the gates to Stourton Hall. Sensing all was calm, she ran back towards the woods, faster than a deer and more nimble than a fox. Avoca trod the paths she had known for centuries before.

A strange mist gathered amongst the trees and in the distance Avoca spied a waif running, her deep blue cloak was buffeted by the growing wind. Cautiously, Avoca grew closer and closer until eventually she flew above her in the trees, and she watched the girl, feeling protective - this was a dangerous place to be with so many witches hunting in the woods. Avoca thought it was too perilous for the young, cloaked imp to be alone and to her horror she heard more laughter. The warlock and witches still drunk appeared back on the path. Like wild cats they had smelt the girl's scent and within minutes they grew ready to pounce upon their easy prey. Avoca thought fast and she heard the girl let out a gentle scream as she saw the onslaught of the others in her path. Quick as flash Avoca swooped like a bird - she gathered the girl and was gone at such speed the still drunken wretches stood bemused and laughed off their apparition as a joke and by chance Avoca escaped with a girl she knew nothing about. Straight to Jack's manor they flew while the girl stayed very still, petrified by her ordeal.

Snatched

~~ * ~~

Avia stomped around the library. She was bored and scared and sick of the situation, and it had begun to feel that there was never going to be an end. She felt the deepest sadness inside and hated the way things had turned out. Avia felt cross towards all the witches, including Agnes and Harini, and she argued silently in her own mind. She wanted no part of this magical world, she wanted to be normal and free. She looked at Agnes and Harini who continued to do their protection spells and poor Preeti who was still in a trance, and she lifted from her pocket the mouse that slept and gently popped her in the velvet box on her father's desk. She left the lid open and wondered if she was her Nanny Maud. Had she been bought up by a tiny mouse? Again, she felt grumpy and confused and paced and paced the endless shelves of books. While the others were busy, she slipped through the door that led to the passage and made her way to the kitchen. She saw Bunty asleep in the rocking chair by the hearth, holding a pistol tight in her hands. Quietly Avia stole a favourite Bath bun and popped it in her cloak pocket that she took from the peg in the scullery hall, then like a mouse she crept to the wood bunker and lifted the lid. She propped it open with wood as she had seen the servants do and lifted herself, carefully she closed the ligand went out into the cold night air. Avia then ran hard to the woods and to the track that would take her to Jack's manor; she knew she would be sad that he would not be there, but she just knew she had to get out and be free. The air on her face felt fresh and she began to feel alive. Breathless she pushed herself on to run, knowing full well that what she did was dangerous for everyone. The track grew misty and deadly still - all she heard was the owl who screeched and the odd crack of a twig in the deep foliage. She told herself it was only some animal who hunted or scavenged for food. Avia ran harder as the mist thickened and then to her horror, not far in the distance, she saw the three nun witches, the red head and a tall white-haired man; she shuddered as she whispered the name, 'the white warlock'. In her despair she screamed then stopped herself; the nun-like witches moved forward quickly - all she could do was stand there on the track like a rabbit in lights. Avia felt sick and did not know what to do. The group of witches and the white warlock began to move with such speed towards her. She turned on her heel to run the other way when she felt an arm fling itself around her and she was lifted at such a speed, she felt dizzy. Avia felt herself go all strange, the days flashed before her to when she first saw her little yew tree witch then she fainted - she was out cold in the grip of the arms that flew her over the trees.

Panic Room

~~ * ~~

Agnes and Harini had searched every possible place that Avia might have gone. They felt sick to the stomach. Had she been taken from under their noses? Afraid, they headed quickly through the empty Hall back to Preeti in fear she too would have gone; however, poor Preeti still sat in her chair glazed over. Huge tears rolled down Agnes's face. How could they have lost someone so dear and poor Preeti still sat there - the situation felt desperate. Agnes and Harini saw no way of escape. If they had taken Avia, then surely they would come for them next. The huge library their prison became terrifying - all their spells and fixes seemed useless. Agnes pulled Preeti off her chair and lay her on cushions next to the fire, then they moved furniture around themselves and pulled the huge rug over the furniture. Agnes remembered playing this game with sheets in Avia's nursery room and she thought back to the rainy day when they played for hours making dens. Agnes had never been so happy - this Hall was her safe place and Avia and Jack her family and now she felt everything was slipping away. She gulped and felt panic rise in her throat, and she felt like screaming, instead she managed to calm herself and got busy feeding the fire. She then urged Harini to help and they again with little strength, put a protection spell around themselves. Agnes now knew she had to get Preeti out of her trance - they were weak with one down and heavens knew how long it would be until Miss Bonneville and Avoca returned with Jack, if ever at all. She wished she could call back Bertie and Chandaria. Harini tried but felt no connection, so they stayed in their panic room. Agnes stroked Preeti's forehead, while Harini chanted a spell in her wonderful language. Agnes knew it was same language that her mother Avoca and old friends, Josina, Parnell, Wilma and Lettice had spoken, she understood and recognised so many words. Agnes thought back to those times by the fire in the woods, she knew she had been happy then; Josina though had tricked them all.

Time seemed to move slowly for the young witches and Preeti did not respond for ages then Agnes saw her eyes flicker and slowly she moved herself and soon she was sat up and looking around the room confused. Harini and Agnes gave her time, then gently explained how she had been in a trance-like state for days. Preeti thanked them for saving her, although she had little clue quite what to do - she was afraid they were just sitting ducks. Preeti thought they should leave as there was no sense in them just waiting like stuffed puppets. She knew that any powerful witch, especially Josina, could break their seal and with Avia gone they had to do something. Each one quietly prepared themselves and wrapped in cloaks they crept out along the passage and went to Agnes's sewing room where they found a very cross and hungry Hestia who had managed to get trapped. Agnes settled her feline friend and lifting the huge sash window they climbed onto the roof and as Agnes had many times before, clambered down the drainpipe to the garden bed. The garden was dark, the only movement - the darting of tiny horseshoe bats. The night was still and no breeze blew. An eerie mist clung to the tree edge, and the shrill of an owl broke the silence. Agnes shuddered. It was as though the gardens and woodland beyond held their breath in fear. The three witches stayed close to the shadows and decided to go with great speed towards Bertie's farm.

The Captured

~~ * ~~

Avoca was glad to be back at the beautiful manor house. The mist grew thicker and was growing around the valley - it rose from the woodland floor, submerging all. She gently put her captured girl down in the hall, calling for Miss Bonneville, who seemed to just appear from nowhere. Avoca told her about the three witches and the white warlock and the other trailing one, who she swore was some relation to Lettice. Miss Bonneville gently pulled back the hood from the young waif who had fainted, and was in disbelief when she realised that it was Miss Avia lying on the floor. Miss Bonneville praised Avoca again and again, not daring to think what would have happened to Avia in the hands of those rogues. She gently carried her to the parlour and as she had once before bought her around with her special milk and herb mix. Avoca went to get Jack warning him that Avia had fainted in shock. Jack ran to the parlour and just as Avia came around she saw Jack running towards her and Miss Bonneville standing over her.

Avia's last image was of the witches and warlock that approached and felt she was still in a nightmare. She thought she had been captured by them when she was pulled from the icy ground, then darkness engulfed her.

Slowly Avia came around and saw Jack, he flung his arms around her, and Avia sobbed both tears of joy and relief. Miss Bonneville calmed her and she looked over and saw Avoca grinning in the corner and knew at once that she had saved her. Avia was overwhelmed to have Jack back and he relieved that he looked the same, just thinner, blistered and bronzed from the desert sun. He was still her Jack, and for now she would wait to hear all his tales, they had forever to be told. They all had to decide what they should do after hearing Avoca's terrifying news of the night and discussed how they would rescue the others and fight. Miss Bonneville knew one thing for certain, she had to get Jack and Avia away from the boundaries of Stourton Hall - they had to go somewhere where they would not dare to look.

The Journey to Dyrham Park

~~ * ~~

Jack and Avia sat with fur rugs over them; they held hands and hardly spoke. Miss Bonneville and Avoca drove the grand carriage through the bumpy tracks in the wood. They travelled swiftly - their sure-footed horses knew the route well and soon they reached the main turnpike towards Bath. They all knew they could sigh with some relief as they came out from the woods and the realm of the witches and warlocks. Not many saw the carriage that misty cold winter's morning, although plenty heard the hooves that trotted at speed and echoed through the depths of the fret, an eerie awakening to a strange, obscured day, and many, for no reason other than a sense of fear, stayed close to their neat cottages and did not stray. The carriage hurtled on towards the streets of Bath and beyond they heard the huge abbey bells strike six and could just view roof tops - all else was veiled. Avia clung to Jack's hand, she would not feel safe until she was in the safety of her sister's abode full of the king's cavalry, servants and family.

The trek out of Bath was steep and difficult for the horses to manage, steadfast though, they sensed the urgency, and with all their power and loyalty pushed on. Finally, they arrived at the gates of the huge deer park and wound down the gracious drive to the magnificent house, passing stags that stood and watched like paintings in the early dew - they snorted and turned to their herd. Avia felt excitement. She longed to see Olivia - it had been too long. They had to rehearse a story scripted by the clever Miss Bonneville. Avia was to say she had become unbearably lonely with the absence of Agnes and Miss Bonneville, who had both taken a long-deserved sabbatical to India in which they wished to find Agnes's heritage, then she said Nanny Maud had been called away on urgent family business, leaving her alone in the Hall. As more snow was forecast, she took her chances, bringing the safely found Jack, who was more than keen to see Dyrham's splendid gardens and deer park.

Avia gasped with excitement as she saw her sister come flying out of the huge doors hugging a huge fur coat around her slender body, waving and jumping up and down. She hustled her sister and Jack into the warmth, the carriage was unpacked, and Miss Bonneville and Avoca disguised as footmen flew off back up the drive. Not wishing to be seen, they would rest the horses in the nearest village. Avia performed her scripted and dramatic spiel, lowering her eyes to her boots as she fidgeted. Olivia eyed her suspiciously - she knew her sister lied. Something was going on and Jack looked most peculiar, each of them held a secret. Olivia, however, was glad of their company as her husband Thomas was in London on business and she had found no one to invite. Her sister she knew normally preferred to be at Stourton Hall, so she was shocked that she was lonely. Avia would normally prefer her own company and a trowel, but Olivia accepted the tale seeing no point in arguing. Instead, she called the maid to show them to their rooms, where their trunks had been taken. Olivia followed chattering about this and that and all the engagements she had been to and how she was invited to so many more. She was disappointed Agnes was away, wishing she could have fitted her for a few more new dresses. Avia promised she would send her as soon as she returned. Olivia left them in the rooms and asked them to join her for breakfast, then they would walk to the viewpoint - she could not wait to show off her land. Avia went straight to her window and pulled back the shutters and stared out over the garden.

She could see the long, stone oblong fishponds, the neat knot garden and perfectly trimmed roses that waited silently for the hard winter to pass. Avia could just see the spire of the tiny chapel on the side of the garden. She looked around half expecting to see witches in cloaks, but nothing was there, only a few wood pigeons who pecked around at the bushes and trees. She glimpsed a cat shoot after something small that dashed under the wall and for the briefest moment she thought of Nanny Maud. She tutted, still in disbelief, and turned to concentrate on making herself present-able in such a grand house, and she sighed with relief; for now she was safe. The last few weeks had been hell, and she prayed that the others would not be in a state and felt guilty about her flight. However, she knew she could no longer cope and though it was foolish to have walked away, she now knew that she had gone to find Jack - she must some-how have known he was home. Avia tried to ignore her new talent and ability to dabble in spells and decided it was just fate and luck that bought them both back together. She heard a gentle knock on the door and found Jack outside her room with his famous grin, she grabbed his hand and they dared a hug, and both besotted they walk towards the stairs.

Jack admired the amazing paintings and grandeur of the house, and he chatted away to Avia as though nothing had ever happened. Jack had bought into Avia's story well, she thought. Perhaps it was his way of coping with what he had been through and imagined time would heal and allow him to talk. For now though, she would let him babble away in his lovely way and she would listen and agree and support almost everything he said - her sole job in her mind was to care for him and make sure he was well and safe. Avia briefly thought back to her encounter with magic and perhaps thought she would practise a spell she had found in the book and seen Agnes and Harini perform. What harm could a protection spell do to keep the ones she loved safe. They all sat around an oval table adorned with porcelain, flowers and silver ware, and they feasted on a delicious breakfast, then they put on cloaks and muffs and walked briskly up the hill away from the house. The treacherous mist had not reached Dyrham and a low winter sun glistened on the sprinkling of frost; iced spider web patterns hung on the fences, and leaves crushed under their feet. Jack walked excitedly ahead with his binoculars, a present from Avia's father Lord Richard Hoare, while Avia and Olivia walked with arms linked supporting each other up the hill. Never had Avia been so glad to be in her sister's super intelligent company. Her bright conversation and knowledge of the current times was a fantastic distraction for Avia, who admitted that she knew nothing at all of went on. Olivia sighed at her sister's lack of attention to the outside world. Avia then asked her many questions - anything to stop quizzes on herself. The morning was perfect, they could wander freely and absorb the elegant beauty. Olivia left them in the gardens near to the house - she had social engagements to arrange. So Jack and Avia enjoyed studying the planting and design. While they wandered, it felt as though everything was normal. They walked up to the little chapel and lit candles. Both prayed silently for the same thing; they wished for Stourton to be saved from the endless torrent of an unwelcome and evil enchantment.

Bertie the Bearer

~~ * ~~

Bertie woke to the smell of spices and cooking. He looked out to see the house was surrounded by a thick mist, he could not even make out the barn. He dressed quickly and avoiding the crowded kitchen, climbed from the window - as Jack and he had as children when they snuck out to explore the woods on summer evenings. He remembered them climbing the steps of Alfred's Tower and watching the world go dark. Bertie and Jack had no fear then, but their ma had been right. She knew the woods were dangerous and he remembered vividly one night when they had seen smoke and crept to see what was happening. From behind a large ancient oak they had watched a gathering of five, all dressed in vivid colours who danced around the fire - terrified they had crept away and bolted to home. Both scared, they never went out at night again. The next day though, Bertie's pa Jeremiah had taken Bertie to that same part of the wood, and as they looked at the embers of the fire, his father had spat on the ashes and cursed, blaming poachers. Bertie had kept his mouth shut - they were no poachers; he had known what they were.

Bertie walked over to the barn and concentrated on his chores and tried not to think too much of his past. He heard

Chandaria call his name softly from the yard, he paused and looked at her, now dressed in his ma's old woollen clothes. She had put a scarf around her head and her dowdy greys looked a far throw from her bright silks - she was still a beautiful princess though and he as always was glad of her company. Bertie washed his hands in the stone trough full of fresh spring water. As he wiped his hands from the freezing cold water he heard a rumble behind him and the clattering of wheels pulled by the unmistakable speed of trotters. He turned to see his ma's carriage, pulled by her horses, the two greys, Orlov and Olga, a gift from a relative who lived in Germany. Bertie was puzzled as to what his ma's prized horses and carriage were doing in his yard and by whose permission. He saw the footmen and went to steady the horses who had been driven hard. He was ireful for their irresponsible actions and began unharnessing the horses, with Chandaria's help. As he ranted crossly, they rubbed their flanks with hay, put thick blankets on them and walked them slowly around the yard until their breathing slowed; again they were rubbed down and the rugs put back on, then Bertie and Chandaria led them to a stall in the barn keeping them together, and they rubbed their legs while they munched on hay. Bertie then walked them around the barn checking neither was lame; he then cleaned out their hooves with care and eventually let them drink small amounts and gave them a small feed but continued to monitor them. The horses calmed and cooled and he prayed that they would be fine. They seemed settled, so he put more straw and hay in their stall and left them to rest - feeling secure and well cared for it was not long before both horses lay down to sleep exhausted from their ordeal. Bertie smiled and thanked Chandaria for help and they both went to find out what excuse the footmen had for such behaviour. When Bertie entered his own parlour he was shocked to find Miss Bonneville and another strange lady called Avoca, who reminded him of Agnes. Miss Bonneville was equally shocked to see a rather drab looking Chandaria and greeted her with formality; not forgetting her place in society, even if they were in a farmers parlour. Bertie sensed a little tension in the room and a few snide remarks came surprisingly from Miss Bonneville towards Carmenta and Ynes. Carmenta returned with a hiss - no harm had been done, all would soon be well and they would be thankful of her help. Bertie scratched his head and warily greeted them. Very confused and bewildered by all his guests he asked if someone could tell him what went on.

Miss Bonneville stood as though she was in some grand hall and began her speech She immediately had everyone's attention and poor Bertie, still seething about his ma's horses, began to realise that his breakfast table had become a place for the gathering of what he hoped were the good occultists.

He sat down and ate the delicious spiced food, deciding he was just a farmer who needed not get involved in these strange affairs; he wanted Jack back for sure though. Then he heard the magical words, 'Jack was back', and with Avia. They were hidden away from danger. Together they were safe in one of the most guarded houses in the south - Bertie guessed that they were at Dyrham with Olivia, although kept his thoughts to himself. Elated they were safe, he began to forgive the mistreatment of the trotters and calmed himself. Jack was back and safe and Avia was with him - he felt such relief and everything else that Miss Bonneville said became just a sound and he heard nothing, all he cared for was that his brother and the recently elusive Avia were free from the witches. He looked at the company that he held and thought of all that had happened, and he knew they could never rid the valley of these types, though he wished that things could go back to an occasional glimpse or presence unknown. Bertie decided to ask about this world he did not understand. He needed to know why so many witches gathered, now he knew Jack was back. Carmenta, for the first time that morning answered. Her thick accent was hard to understand at times and often she would slip back into her own language. Bertie and the others all listened though and understood much of what she said. Carmenta spoke of a warlock named Fabian who had been, she suspected part of an ancient tribe called the Cornovii, he had lived in the valley long ago be-

fore the castle of Stourton was built, the tribe were descendants of fishermen who came from deserts. These people
were far more advanced than any other tribes of their time
and seemed able to write and run a civilised settlement.
They called the land that they had found sacred and Carmenta believed that they had found something that gave
eternal life - the witches and warlocks holy grail. Carmenta
believed that Bertie's precious valley had drawn the witches,
not for that reason alone, there was a pull, a connection
from the past of the Cornovii, the beginning of them all,
sometimes called the wickers.

Bertie grumbled a muffled thank you and went to check on
the horses. He was shocked and was finding it hard to take
in. Chandaria came to find him in his barn and just sat
nearby as he worked. She knew it was foolish to speak, he
was like she had once been, a person who did not believe in
such things, it was heretic and against her god. Chandaria
also felt scared and had no clue what she would do and
where she would go, so their silence continued in a comfortable and understanding way, both grappling with the events
that surrounded them that were spiralling out of control.
After a while Bertie came and sat next to Chandaria, he held
her delicate hands and apologised for ignoring her. He knew
he had no need to say sorry though, he knew she empath-
ised. Bertie then told Chandaria he thought he knew exactly

where this ancient sacred thing was buried. It was an old legend and folk story he had grown up with that he had never thought was true, but now maybe he thought perhaps it was. Chandaria followed him into the house where thankfully the coven of witches and wizard had disappeared. He went up to his room and then came down with a small tatty brown book that his ma used to read to them as children; they had loved the story, but now he was not so sure. Bertie had one problem though, he could not read much, just a few words, so he went to find Solly who always had a book in his hands. Solly was sat on his ma's old bench where she would sit in the summer and sew, the others he said had gone to spy on the Hall, and he had been told to stay. Bertie thought Solly looked as confused as he did, and he trusted him somehow. He preferred him to all the others, so he asked him if he could read his story. So, in the winter sun, the three sat together with Solly in the middle and he began to read. Bertie would never forget that day when Solly read the book - it came to life, the words stepped from the pages and danced around. Bertie felt he could touch and feel everything, he could see the characters like never before, he felt he had stepped into another time - long, long ago.

The Legend of King Cornovii

Once upon a time there lived a tribe of travellers. They came from a land far away, a land of golden sands and turquoise seas. The possessions that they carried were paintings and scriptures of their cultures, beliefs and way of life. Detailed illustrations, giving clues to their world of fishing boats, temples and shrines, were all rolled carefully – the delicate papyrus was sacred to their tribe. The Cornovii, as they were called, had left their land in search of a prophecy that pulled them across the great desert and seas. One day, they found a beautiful valley with lush green woods that densely covered the land. It was full of spring waters and lakes, and a shallow babbling river wound its way through weeping willow trees that clung to the banks and surrounded small shingle bays. Perfect reflections swayed in the gentle breeze on waters where fresh fish, otters and king fishers fluttered, skimming the water in glorious colours. The tribe settled and made their homes in the huge arms of oak trees, safely away from the marshes with its thick guzzling mud and from the wolves and bears that paced and howled in search of food. They lived on fresh fish and herbs, instead of salted and spiced sea life as their ancestors had. Theirs was a simple life rich in good-ness – they were the way they wished to be. Contented, the Cornovii lived in peace and calm; a secret tribe that hid when they heard others pass through with their armour, swords and rough brawling ways. The thugs would leave once the deep mud marshes, fierce wolves and brave bears had had their say, and scared, they would run faraway and it became a place to avoid by word.

As time passed, the Cornovii tribe found that their good way of life worked well and as they grew in size they chose a king to rule and settle small disputes, over trees and fish, simple yet important things. The king was called Momolou, and his people loved him deeply. He was kind and understanding and lived among them; humble yet saintly, he was true to everyone. King Momolou had a younger brother who he adored, and whose name was Aethelbert. Aethelbert liked to think of himself as a great explorer and he grew to know the valley and woodlands well. One day, he walked out beyond the tree line and found a rock formation unlike anything he had ever seen. The rock was glistening white with crystals running through its veins, and unlike the golden ochre of the natural stone, this shone brightly in the morning sun. Aethelbert lay on the smooth rock in the warmth of the sun, he felt the gentle wind and listened to the birds sing their songs. Aethelbert fell asleep and when he woke, the sun had left the sky and hardly any moonlight struck the earth; instead, he lay in darkness, surrounded by the strange echoes of the night and the terrifying howls of the wolves. Afraid, Aethelbert stayed on the stone not knowing what to do. From the woodland shadows he saw a bear approach, it growled deeply and pawed at its prey. Aethelbert curled up defensively and prayed, then Aethelbert felt the strangest sensation as if the stone appeared to levitate and swirl. The bewildered bear ran lolloping to the woods, and all night the stone protected him from wolves and others who looked upon Aethelbert as an easy supper. When the morning came bringing glorious light, Aethelbert picked pretty blue flowers and lay them on the white stone promising he would never forget the passing of the night. Aethelbert ran to tell his brother the King of this amazing stone and his tale of the night. The King had been panicked by his absence all through the dark and relieved he was safe, went with him to see this amazing stone. From that day on the stone was sacred and was blessed by the King; anyone who wished for anything would seem to get their dream, but the Cornovii people kept their wishes simple, and the tribe lived full and happy lives, with no hunger or illness and for years this prosperity went on.

A group of the tribe, however, became obsessed with the stone and while the others slept in their cosy oak canopy of beds, the Wickers, as they called themselves, began to gather and create rituals around the stone. With the stone's help they made potions and chanted spells with strange rhymes and soon they could make things happen that shouldn't have been happening at all. The group grew in number and often some would leave to practice their newfound trade in other parts. It did not take long before the King found out about the Wickers and their rituals and mischief. He was most unhappy that they mistreated the sacred stone and had it guarded night and day, but with much sadness he lost many guards, as the Wickers retaliated with fury. The King began ridding his tribe of the Wickers, who he considered to be evil and they were banished from his land. Each of the Wickers felt cheated and angry and left with their spells and potions.

The King Momolou grew older as any mortal man would and when out walking one day, he asked his brother Aethelbert why he never aged a day. Aethelbert told him his story of the first night he had discovered the stone all that time ago. He told him how he had prayed when the huge bear placed his paw upon him and the wolves circled with their snapping jaws; he had prayed to be saved and to live forever; Aethelbert began to cry, he did not want this curse of eternal life. The King was crushed and felt his brothers utter despair. He asked him though, why he had not asked the stone to take away this wish. Aethelbert said he was afraid to live and afraid to die. The King sighed and thought. He told Aethelbert how it was so wrong for any man or creature to live forever; they should only ever pass through; too much knowledge and power was a dangerous gift. The King ordered that a hill be made and within it a tomb to cover the stone; there he would be buried and Aethelbert could be by his side guarding the stone for eternity always by his side. Aethelbert could not believe his request, for him to live forever in darkness, which he called hell, and they saw little of each other from that day. Aethelbert ran away the night his brother died with tears streaming down his face. The King Momolou was buried by his loyal people in his tomb upon the white glistening

*stone. The Cornovii people were heartbroken
and many moved to go back to their land of
golden sands and turquoise seas. Some
though would stay in the valley to keep the
legend alive and some of the Wickers would
return to live peacefully in the valleys and
woods. The hill had a fortress mysteriously
built upon it and it was said that Aethelbert
would visit and lay blue flowers on the site of
his brother's grave.*

Once Solly had finished reading the story, he took a long pause while the others digested the story. Bertie was the first to break the small reading group's thoughts. He thanked Solly and explained that his ma had only ever read parts of the legend. He then talked about the hill and the old fort and how, when it was being repaired, strange things had happened there and rumours still circulated about the fort being haunted, Bertie said he was certain that was the hill where the king was buried on top of the sacred stone. The fort had been built by one of Avia's ancestors, maybe for more insurance so the stone would never be found again. Did the witches and warlocks still search for the stone? Solly was concerned now for Bertie. He was suddenly the bearer of the key to dangerous information as was Chandaria and himself. He knew he could keep this safe, but Bertie if captured could disclose all the information that Solly had read. Solly had a feeling Carmenta knew something of this sacred stone and was now sure it was what the white warlock looked for in these parts - he had to get Bertie away from the farm and fast. Bertie protested, his horses would not be safe, so it was agreed they would take them to the manor where the grooms still lived above the stalls, the others they would ride to the hill and then towards the coast, to a farm Bertie's uncle once lived in, now empty. It was a good place to hide that no one knew anything about as his poor uncle had died.

They set off quickly, only grabbing a few belongings, riding and leading the horses who seemed pleased to be going and eagerly bounced along the wooded track - the grooms were thankful to receive the trotters. Bertie gave a brief explanation that the carriage was being repaired and he needed to go away and would appreciate the good care they would give to his horses, they then turned and galloped through the woods to the fort on the hill. Bertie had always thought the hill had a strange typography; it sat unnaturally as though it had just landed from the sky. The fort was poorly made and had always looked more akin to ruins than a folly. Solly dismounted while the others stayed on their horses who stamped nervously at the ground, they sensed the tension and maybe something more. Bertie tried to sooth them, but they still remained skittish. Chandaria had impressed him with her riding skills, and she grinned from ear to ear, so happy to be upon a horse again, riding through woodland and over hills - she kept pinching herself to check it was true. Solly came back with a grave look of concern, someone had been digging at the side of the fort and remnants of a fire was left, activity was definitely here. He feared it was too late and that the wickers were here from long ago, because surely only they could know. Solly asked Bertie and Chandaria to go on alone, he would come and find them when it was safe to return - they took Solly's horse as he asked and were gone with little encouragement needed.

Solly watched them disappear and he found himself a comfortable hiding spot. He thought over the story and wondered who Aethelbert was in this life and if it was true that he existed. He had to be a good man surely or the stone would have resurfaced and been used years ago, and he thought of the wickers and who the eternal ones could be. Did they keep the secret or spread the word? Solly thought of all his years of capture and learning and searched his memory for any mention of the names in the books he read. He had found references to eternal life in vampires and demons, but never had he read of the Cornovii tribe. Solly got the feeling they had maybe not shared their secret. He felt differently about them - maybe they were not evil like the poor King Momolou had thought. Solly would have dearly liked to have met one of the Cornovii, especially Aethelbert. Something about the name reminded him of something from long ago, to a face he had seen through history cropped up in illustrated references. Solly had one theory that fitted. A face he seen many times in portraits, and each time it seemed the person was different, yet to Solly that person looked just the same, as a lord, a king, a prince or member of state, and the last time he had seen that face was in portraits upon the hallways of Stourton Hall. In his portrait he looked pale, yet still those dark eyes and distinctive features stared out at Solly. The picture had stared back as though the portrait knew he had recognised him and the game was over. Where did this great man of reinvention hide he wondered.

Return & Retreat

~~ * ~~

Lord Richard Hoare felt some excitement on returning to Stourton Hall. He had missed Avia and Jack, who he found to be wonderful company and he had a guest arriving in a few days, the adorable Lady Bee. He had decided it was time to let go of his dearest wife - he would never forget her, but he needed to let someone else into his life. By chance, on a fascinating cruise of the Nile, he had met an amazing person called Lady Bee. She was a perfect companion who wished for no children and only to travel and see the world - her passion. She had inherited a fortune from her American family and was greatly interested in archaeology and it seemed, someone who was not after her money. They had already travelled far together and now he wanted to introduce her to his daughters and if she was not put off and did not run a mile, he would propose on Christmas Day; he felt the box deep in his pocket and felt content at last. So far away in his thoughts, he did not notice that they had turned onto Stourton drive and had pulled up to the great Hall, his home.

He stepped out into the bright day and sighed with pleasure to breath in such fresh air after the smog and filth of London. He looked up to the Hall with pride as he always did and thought maybe to walk the gardens first, while there was still a string of light on this cold winter's day. As he looked up though, he felt unsure. The Hall seemed cloaked in a strange mist and the windows looked black and gloomy. The Hall that normally sang out its glory and grandeur, instead seemed shadowed in darkness. Lord Richard Hoare approached the door and was flung straight back by some strange phenomenon. He began to worry what had happened - the place was deserted, no staff milled around, no butler answered the door, the even immaculate Miss Bonneville seemed to not even be in residence. Lord Richard began to panic, what had happened? Where was his beloved daughter Avia? He decided to walk to the stable yard and was relieved to hear horses and voices. Lord Richard quickened his pace and was greeted, with what looked like an army: all his servants and the village folk stood with any available weapon from pitch forks to spades and worse, the local sheriff Brodie, the game keeper Otto and Tomsk the head gardener drew plans on a large map. They were calling out orders to the groups and went deadly silent when they turned to see the Lord of Stourton Hall looking at them in disbelief.

Tomsk bravely walked up to his master and gave a brief yet as informative account as he could. Flabbergasted, Lord Richard stared at them in disbelief. Had everyone gone completely bonkers? He then turned to see Miss Bonneville looking a little dishevelled compared to her normal self. She shook herself off and did the normal formalities, then poured into some of the facts, being careful to skim a few of the truths and her involvement. She informed him that Avia had been taken to Olivia's at Dyrham, Jack had accompanied her and they were safe. She then asked him to go to his daughters too, for his safety. Lord Richard Hoare felt cross; the situation was ridiculous. He could not get into his own home, his daughter had fled, Jack had been kidnapped and returned and some strange cult threatened to take his home and land and they, the servants, instead of calling the king's army to protect his empire, decided to protect it with spades, pitchforks and broomsticks.

Miss Bonneville took a deep breath. That final comment was a little too close to the truth, and she glanced over to Avoca who stayed hidden in the laurel bush, holding firm to her broom. Miss Bonneville agreed it was a mess but feared the army would not come and only cause more damage. He at least agreed to that, then he looked at his servants who cowered in fear more of his mood than those who threatened his estate, and he looked at Miss Bonneville and thought of all the times she had been right and how well she had handled that strange night, when Avia and Agnes had been taken from their room. He had always suspected that

Miss Bonneville and Agnes were slightly strange and yet somehow he felt protected by their ways, but he knew she did not tell him everything. The valleys had always held secrets that he had been told as a child, stories of witches in the woods and children disappearing, some never returning. He remembered faintly the tale of a king and Wickers, but he did not remember how it went. It had been read by his great-great-grandfather Albert who had long ago left; he had strangely vanished, to where no one knew, a very strange affair, but he left a legacy of wealth and clauses on the estate. Some said his ghost still roamed the gardens and grounds checking his estate was treated well. A story from many years ago told of an ice boy who had nearly drowned and was mysteriously saved. He had described the man to be that of the deceased Lord Albert, but there were so many tales of strange events that Richard had grown up ignoring their worth and now, stood before him, was a small army who looked for his guidance, or permission to follow Miss Bonneville's instruction.

The day began to fade and get colder as the time ticked by. Lord Richard had a great curiosity about the happenings and asked Miss Bonneville to let him stay and help, but he needed to get to his library, where he knew he could do what he did best, research. So, escorted by his faithful staff he wound his way back to the Hall. No ghosts, demons, or witches seemed to lurk about, at least not in sight, then as he stood looking down from the steps of the grand entrance, he saw hooded figures approach. Each one held a small candle and sang an enchanting song that he was sure he recognised as it was sung in Sanskrit. He was at first afraid, then he saw the face of Agnes who beamed to see her Lord; she broke ranks and ran to greet him. Miss Bonneville shot her a knowing look and Agnes who understood not to tell all, was glad to see her well. Lord Richard gave her a warm welcome, as he would his own child, they then all poured into the Hall and introductions were made and he met Harini and Preeti, Agnes's long-lost cousins from India, who he was charmed to meet. Miss Bonneville sheepishly walked to the library ashamed of the poor state of the Hall, still with the hidden hexes, talismans and spells in place. She felt some relief though that the Lord was home, for some reason it gave some normality to the situation - to fight for what was theirs. Lord Richard called for everyone to gather in the library, despite its strange smell. He had a story to tell them of long ago, a story he had forgotten until then. He found the hidden copy locked in a box, the old cover was brown and tatty and he knew that only two copies were ever printed and that one was misplaced, so they sat and listened to his tale about a king who ruled the Cornovii tribe.

Avoca's Vision

~~ * ~~

Avoca stayed hidden in the bush; she had had the strangest vision of a man stood in the darkness on a hill, he held his arms to the sky and cried to let death come to him. He yowled like a creature in pain, and she saw Solly walk towards the screaming man. Avoca knew what she saw was real and she grabbed a horse from the stable and galloped towards the hill that she knew so well, where the fortress lay. Stories had been told for centuries of the Wickers and how it started all those years ago. Avoca knew that it would not be long until the end of the siege was over, whoever might win, but she had to get to Solly and the man in her vision. Solly was the answer - the only hope for them, he had held the secret safe.

As she approached the hill from the woods she heard the howls of wolves and other roars. What strange phenomenon had happened? Why did they hear wolves in this century? They had been banished long ago. She tried to remember the legend she had been told as a child, about how the brother of a king was saved from the wolves. Did he get his wish? Did the wolves come to get him this time? Solly stood by his side, with a flame threatening the wolves as they snarled and snapped at their prey, Avoca cast a spell to rid the hill of wolves, but the wish was stronger and still they stayed. She chanted to stop, to stay alive for the sake of his beloved valley. Avoca knew it was Lord Richard Hoare's ancestor; he had been lord of the valley for centuries, coming and going with different names, but always the same. He looked at Avoca and remembered her as the healing woman from long ago and how she had disappeared with her sweet daughter when the evil witch hunter came. His mind thought back over the long, long years. He thought of the good and not the bad and the wolves faded away; exhausted, he fell to the ground. Avoca and Solly ran to his side and threw him on the back of Avoca's horse. The time had come for this legend to tell his tale.

Avoca felt she had to know the Wickers somehow, she had been around forever and knew these parts and all who were entwined. She thought of Fabian, who was obsessed with eternal life and Gedahard the white warlock that they all feared. She paused at Miss Bonneville and Carmenta; somehow though they did not fit. No one but Fabian really fitted the part, yet he had passed at the hands of a witch hunt on the lakes of a Scandi scandal. Avoca breathed in deep and thought of Fabian hard. She had never dared before in case she raised his mind - did he still live and tread the wooded paths? Had her fear been put to rest foolishly? She panicked inside and thought of Agnes, so vulnerable despite her merge of witches.

Solly noticed her change in pace and enquired why she seemed so flustered. Avoca liked Solly, she trusted him and knew he was good. He was a little like Jack, only he was scholar of the world of the superlunary. She told him she thought she knew who one of the old Wickers was and if she was right, they were all in such danger. Fabian was more powerful than any and he was evil to the core. Solly touched Avoca gently on the shoulder and told her not to worry so. He said that Fabian may well be powerful, but he had not yet met Carmenta or himself and the Jakhs if need be - he would summon them to be near if they were needed. Avoca looked to him and thanked him for his reassurance, but still her pace was faster and she could not be comforted. Solly let her race towards the Hall. He was concentrating more on the elusive man they had on the horse, the man he had seen throughout history in his books, who, no matter what he did, became successful and supreme in everything he touched. Solly had heard of Fabian, an acquaintance of his keeper the white warlock, so the story of the white rock appeared to be a truth - the power it could give was beyond anything and even Solly began to fear how they would hide such an inestimable object. Its dominion over man could be both incredible and disastrous. The great King Momolou had been right all those years ago, he saw the outcome of the future. Solly could not think though, how such a thing could be hidden forever; it perhaps needed to leave this world and return to where it had fallen from.

A Message from The Haunch

~~ * ~~

Lord Richard Hoare stood in his library with his artefacts and endless shelves of leather-bound books. He warmed himself by the fire and smoked his favourite cigar with a glass of brandy in his hand and an audience of the occult - he felt strangely comfortable and captivated. He listened to Miss Bonneville and Carmenta, whom he presumed to be the superiors. He held no fear whatsoever of Miss Bonneville, or the beautiful Carmenta, although her rattling breath and strange ways he was indeed wary of, but he felt happy to have her on his side. He had heard of the dankini on his travels in India and it seemed the tales were true. Lord Richard listened to what they had to say and eventually agreed that he would leave to visit his daughters and the safety of Dyrham; he would travel at first light. Miss Bonneville felt relieved. She had not expected his return and was not prepared for the fact that her patron would know she was a witch; she felt though he must have already suspected something strange. Confused over his lack of reaction, she became suspicious of Lord Richard's part in this conspiracy.

A loud knock on the door broke everyone's thoughts and Miss Bonneville nervously went to see who visited, and she came back asking Agnes to sort their visitor out - it was Bertie and Jack's cousin. She hissed to get rid of him. Agnes blushed and ran to the door, she opened it and slid out onto the terrace and immediately hugged Jerome, so pleased to see him she did not even think to hide her joy. He too seemed elated, although soon his ebullience turned to a more earnest mood. He told Agnes what he had heard and seen and he had been to find Bertie, but the barn was empty of horses and Bertie was gone. Agnes looked around sensing his fear. She ushered him in and took him to the kitchens where she heated milk for him. They then returned to the library, and held each other's hand in support of one another. Agnes boldly introduced Jerome and asked him to tell his story of the happenings in the ale house in the wall called the Haunch. Jerome nervously looked around and began his tale leaving no detail out, he then sat exhausted on a large leather chair and politely asked if he could sleep the night out in that very spot; he was too afraid to venture out with his pony, Lucky, who was stabled in the yard. He closed his eyes and was soon asleep. Agnes went to find a blanket and lay it over him; she gently touched his forehead and sat at the foot of his chair. Her cat Hestia was by her side, and the two like guards sat in vigil, while they listened to the plan that formed.

Again, everyone was interrupted by a large bang on the door. Miss Bonneville again went to check who their caller was at this hour. She saw Avoca and she ran to let her in. Poor Avoca was stressed and mumbled many strange things. Behind her, Solly climbed the steps with a man in his arms; a man that Miss Bonneville recognised, but could not quite place. They took him through to the library and lay him in a neighbouring chair to the sleeping Jerome. Avoca ran to hug Agnes and she joined them on the floor. She looked at the present Lord and cast her eyes to the ground, afraid of what would happen to them all. Lord Richard stared at the man in disbelief. He slugged back his brandy and looked to the young man Solly, who he had never met before, for some explanation of why and how it was possible for his late ancestral great-great-grandfather to be lying on his chair. Solly, of course, could not explain it all - and he left out the most crucial part about the sacred stone and the location of their encounter. He did, however, present the man to be Aethelbert - the legend that lived.

A Heart of Stone

~~ * ~~

Miss Bonneville felt satisfied as she closed the huge door. She had watched the carriage thunder down the sweeping drive towards the track driven by Jerome, who she had only just learnt was of great importance to Agnes. He was loyal, and she trusted him. Agnes rode in the carriage for extra protection, with the excuse to see Avia and Jack and that Olivia needed new gowns.

Glad they were all gone safely, Miss Bonneville hoped she could concentrate on all the theories and plans. Aethelbert still slept and it had been agreed by Lord Richard that it would be best at this stage, if they did not meet; the ancient ancestor had a job to do, if he could ever wake himself up. Miss Bonneville went to the kitchens to find Bunty, who had become a more than a cook. She needed to know if she could trust her, but something about a ring on Bunty's finger made her doubt her alliance with the Hall. If Bunty was a traitor, then they had a huge problem that unfortunately Miss Bonneville would have to sort. Bunty was stood at the table chopping vegetables; her strong hands quick and skilful soon had each root chopped. Miss Bonneville again looked at the ring and was certain now it was the ring of Gedahard's.

Aware of her opponent's strength, she carefully addressed her cook ready with a spell. Bunty looked up and knew immediately that Miss Bonneville had something more than stew on her mind, and she shuffled her feet asking how she could help. Miss Bonneville studied Bunty's face, its ruddy complexion lined with character of a good few years. She showed no guilt though, and Miss Bonneville felt a little more at ease to ask about the ring. She did not dally and asked her directly how, where and when had she acquired such a jewel. She could tell Bunty thought to lie, then decided to be truthful, much to Miss Bonneville's relief.

Bunty told her story. She thought that when it happened, she was only nine or ten. It was the winter and she had been playing out all day, avoiding the chores at home. She looked sad and explained that her parents were in charge of the Berkshires, that the old folk at the manor used to own. As a girl she was expected to earn her keep from a young age. She said her parents were quite cruel; they weren't kind or generous people and only had children for their free work. Miss Bonneville interrupted to ask what a Berkshire was. Bunty grinned, saying it was a large pig. She then carried on. She had been making her way home that day and every so often she would climb a tree. The particular oak she was climbing at the time was by far her favourite, and she could get really high. She sighed saying the view was spectacular on that dreamy day and despite her hunger and fact she should have gone home, she had instead sat and watched the sun fade away. Bunty then lowered to a whisper as she recalled the vivid encounter. Her daydream from the branches of the oak had been broken by a voice from below and she looked down to see a strange-looking woman in very peculiar clothes. She wore many dresses and had the brightest red hair. She swore like a fish wife and kicked and cursed at the ground, then she started muttering about how the white warlock would kill her, saying she should never have stolen the ring and she continued to kick and curse, then she was on her hands and knees sniffing the ground like a dog. Bunty had done all she could not to laugh out loud and she waited until the dog-like thief had gone, then clambered to the ground where a ring was to be found. Bunty began to look. One thing she had always been good at was finding things with her eagle eyes and although she didn't find it that day, she returned whenever she could and searched for the ring. For some unknown reason she became obsessed, and her search carried on whenever she could run away. It was not until the next January that she found the treasure. The cold, bare land gave away its hiding place and Bunty popped the strange ring straight onto her finger and ran hard for home. She hid it from her parents and wore it in bed, until the day her parents had both passed away, and now she wore it proudly all the time. 'Finders keepers, losers weepers' she said with a shrug. She then explained to Miss Bonneville that something about the ring made her seem stronger and sharper than before, although this she was not entirely sure about. She also said that the ring changed colour and since the troubles it had glowed a lilac shade. Miss Bonneville asked to look more closely at the ring and Bunty removed it from her finger and hesitantly handed it over. Miss Bonneville studied the jewelled crest set on a gold band. The crest had a serpent that curled around a rose, she did not yet know the significance although felt she knew someone would. Miss Bonneville asked Bunty to show it to Carmenta.

They left for the library, where the girls Preeti and Harini studied books, and Aethelbert slept. The room felt much quieter with Lord Richard, Agnes and Jerome gone. Carmenta sat at the desk and studied a map, while Solly was on ladders in ecstasy with so many books of knowledge to read. He had permission to help himself on the promise he would return each to the exact spot, so Solly left a bright red silk scarf dangling in the empty spot should he forget. Avoca was nowhere to be seen. Miss Bonneville imagined she had escaped to the woods, preferring the outside. Bunty confidently strode over to Carmenta and asked her to look at the ring. Carmenta sucked her teeth and drew in her rasping breath. She studied the ring and called Ynes who was curled behind a drape with a child's picture book of flowers and woodland creatures clutched in her hands. Solly climbed down and came over too. In turn, they studied the ring and gave it back quickly to Carmenta. Ynes said that she best hide it with the white warlock on his way for it was his old ring for sure and he still searched for it. Carmenta thought it could be a useful talisman to the white warlock Gedahard. She smiled and asked Bunty if she could care for the ring until they were rid of the witches and Gedahard. Bunty felt she had no choice preferring not to have a warlocks ring for now, and with relief she returned to the kitchen, then turned as she had forgotten to mention a strange statue in Miss Bonneville's old room at the top of the house. Miss Bonneville let out a surprising squeal of delight. Her spell had worked and with all the commotion and comings and goings, she had not yet had time to check. She asked the girls to follow her, while Solly and Carmenta were left with the sleeping lion.

It felt strange for Miss Bonneville to walk through the halls that were so quiet and cold, no fires were lit, and no staff busied around. The Hall was like a museum that had been closed to the world and she dearly hoped soon things would be normal again. They went up the back stairs to the servant's quarters. Miss Bonneville now had a large sunny room at the front of the house. Her old room was small and was tucked away from sight under the eaves, where she still had a few belongings. They carefully opened the door and, stood in front of the mirror was Josina turned to stone. Miss Bonneville's chatter-pie Hex waited on the windowsill for more orders to come. She went and opened it, giving the eager bird a well-earned tit bit. She then looked as the others did at the stone figure of Josina. How long it would last Miss Bonneville had no clue. One thing was for sure though, they needed to somehow find her a prison should she come around. Ordering Preeti and Harini to take the feet, they carried the statue to the garden and along the lavender paths to the icehouse, and with a rope they lowered her to the depths and then pulled up the ladder. She now lay hidden under a sheet in the deep basin of stone and ice. Miss Bonneville then locked the iron gates, while Harini and Preeti fixed a spell to stop her getting out - the heart of stone lay in the cold darkness, hidden from her coven.

Another Blunder

~~ * ~~

Ynes had decided to go out and had been wandering the woods for some time. Strangely, she was enjoying the freshness of the cold air and the dampness beneath her feet. Many years of heat and stuffiness in captivity made her realise what freedom felt like and it was certainly not trekking across the desert on a camel with a bunch of criminals. She had Carmenta to thank for her life, despite the fact that Carmenta had set her up to do what she had done, but she knew she would never have escaped from being a slave if she had not. Ynes thought of Carmenta and how strange she was in her ways – she adored her though and had learnt so much. And Solly, who she thought of as her dear brother, like Yari, who she hoped was safe and had found her family well. A tear escaped and rolled down Ynes' rosy cheeks. She wiped it away feeling embarrassed even though no one stood there. She had not thought of her family or Yari, afraid she could not cope, knowing that she had left them with no word. Maybe one day they would forgive her, if she ever saw them again. Ynes concentrated on Solly and how he had become such a friend. Both of them prisoners of the white warlock, they had a bond, an understanding of their captor and a fear they could not explain. The thought of the warlock wandering the gentle valleys of trees made her wince, yet here she stood alone in the woods looking over the lake and exquisite gardens; she wondered at the beauty and how it was possible.

Ynes felt a chilly wind blow up and decided she should head for the Hall; she did not want to be caught in darkness. She heard a rustle in the trees so hastened her step, her small feet in neat, laced boots quickened on the gravel paths - she felt panicked. Ynes knew something tracked her; every instinct in body told her to run faster than she had ever before. She tried to think of flight but was not yet proficient in the craft, she looked at the icy waters of the lake they were no escape, just a cruel, long death. Ynes saw the Hall and let out a yowl for help, no sound came, as her breath was taken by her running and the sharpness of the air. Ynes pushed herself faster and she felt something grab at her cloak - she was being pulled back. Ynes saw the Hall and with all her known power kicked out at the force behind her and muttered the spell Carmenta had taught her to protect herself, concentrating with all her mind and no fear as she had been trained, but the force still pulled at her. Then she felt herself being lifted in the air, and she saw Solly's face, not the face she dreaded; he held her fast while he roared at the force that tried to take her. Ynes still felt the pull, but Solly was strong and his talent was more than that of a witch. Solly of the Jakhs that day showed the capability of his power, that the white warlock Gedahard had tried to use and capture all those years ago, From nowhere a swirling wind carried Solly and Ynes into the air, stones flew and a darkness fell. Solly returned to the ground and whatever had tried to take Ynes went howling into the depths of the woods.

Solly and Ynes stood bedraggled and cold from the hail and wind. They watched the darkness turn lighter, and as the gentle last rays of sun streamed through the clouds, a small group had gathered behind them. Carmenta clapped, while Miss Bonneville ran to Ynes ushering her inside. Ynes did not want to though, and she reached out for Solly who seemed intent on following the perpetrators. He called back that she must go with Miss Bonneville and stay inside. Ynes reluctantly obeyed his orders and waved faintly at him, and Solly gave back his unfaltering smile. Carmenta joined him and they both disappeared from view towards the woods, leaving a trail of devastation. Miss Bonneville tutted, although accepted there would be a clean-up after the war of the witches and warlocks had been won. Ynes hung her head in shame and her latest blunder and returned to the Hall that was looking far more homely; fires were lit and flowers stood on tables, doors to rooms were back to normal and the windows were no longer shrouded in darkness. She looked to Miss Bonneville, afraid it was not safe, but Miss

Bonneville ignored her and ushered Ynes to Cecilia's old room where she was given warm tea and a change of clothes; the fire had been lit and Ynes felt the warmth start to fill her frozen body, she felt exhausted and weak, her old wound ached. She looked to Miss Bonneville and repeated whether it was safe to open up the house. Miss Bonneville, seeing her concern, reluctantly explained, wishing she could concentrate more on helping her to heal, as she knew Ynes would suffer from the attack for days. She began to tell her, however, that they had decided that instead of being hidden in a cave, they would made the Hall an inviting fortress of traps. The roaring fires in each fireplace all over the house each burned with a clever invention of Preeti's that would be fatal for any intruder, and the windows also concealed a cunning trap unseen to any eye, each would turn to stone just like Josina. Hestia the cat purred, missing Agnes. She had taken to following Miss Bonneville and she liked very much that Josina had been turned to stone, a long awaited pay back for her own feline misery. Miss Bonneville briefly fussed the cat and continued to say that every door was alarmed and rigged and the whole perimeter had again been covered in talismans and hexes that would throw and warn them of an assault. Ynes asked sulkily why they had managed to get to her. Miss Bonneville sighed and trying not to sound curt with her, she explained that Ynes had been beyond the border of safety. Ynes hung her head and began to cry - she had caused trouble again, it was her fault and now Solly and Carmenta were out in the woods to chase her predators. Miss Bonneville soothed the poor girl, she could certainly do no right it seemed and she was still annoyed with her for taking Jack and costing them so much precious time. Miss Bonneville knew it was now pointless though to torture the girl anymore; she clearly had the greatest guilt for her actions. Instead she soothed her and gave her a warm herbal drink and sat holding her hand until she slept. Ynes felt her body relax and the warmth finally clear her chill as her tears faded, and with gulps of breath, she closed her eyes exhausted. She muttered a sorry as she felt Hestia jump on the end of the bed, where she curled up at Ynes's feet, and Ynes drifted away with relief. Once Miss Bonneville had checked she was fine, she instructed Hestia to guard her and closed the shutters, then she quietly left the room. It was time to wake Aethelbert - he had slept long enough avoiding questions and his responsibility to his ancient domain.

Avoca & The Cloak

~~ * ~~

Avoca could not stand the stuffy library. Miss Bonneville went around lighting the place up with fires and candles and turning everything back to how the Hall should be, only full of spells mostly invented by clever Preeti, who was so absorbed in her mission that Avoca had hardly had chance to see her. So, deciding she was of little use, she went out to find Ynes, who had been gone a little while. Avoca had that feeling, like so many times in her life, that something was very wrong. She heard the voices of the past whispering in her mind and felt a strong urge to run away and leave all the mystery and muddles to the others. Avoca then began an argument with herself - she could not always run away, and to leave would mean abandoning her loved ones and she could not repeat that ever. As she debated her natural instinct to flee and consciousness to stay, she walked towards the lake and gothic cottage, but her mind was all over the place instead of concentrating on finding Ynes, she walked blindly in thought, she arrived at the cottage with the realisation she had not once looked for Ynes.

Avoca looked at the cottage, once a simple hovel, her home so long ago, and at the yew tree where Agnes had been buried in her tomb. She looked at the charms that blew in the wind and feeling the chill, fumbled for the key in the huge clay pot. She let herself in. The cottage smelt strange - someone had not long ago been in there, and this made her uneasy as she knew that they all stayed in the Hall. She went to the fireplace and felt the ash that was still warm. The old clay pots had been used, and smears of herbs and potions were left on their rims; whoever had cleared had done a sloppy job. She climbed up the little ladder to the room once filled with her belongings and to her great surprise, she found a straw bed and belongings of someone else. Something was very familiar about the small, messy ways, and left strewn on the floor was an old green cloak that she was certain she knew of old and sure enough a broach clasp gave the identity away. With the symbol 'Aegishjalmur' or 'The Helm of Awe', the broach was made from old silver and bore eight spiked tridents surrounded by the three serpents - a broach of protection, just lying abandoned on a cloak that once belonged to her dear friend Lettice. There was no mistake who it belonged to, Lettice the Viking witch with the unruly ways and rogue tongue, thought dead by many. Did she still live? Or had she had her belongings filched?

Deciding some other witch must have acquired the cloaK Avoca did not hesitate; the broach was powerful. She grabbed the cloak and ran from the cottage and took her place in a beech tree that looked over the garden and cottage and that was back in the protection zone of the Hall. She had to keep watch to see if the cloak thief returned. Avoca wrapped the thick wool cloak over her own and clamped the broach shut. She almost felt its power as it sealed around her. For all those years it had protected its wearer - forged by the Vikings who fought and pillaged, and who with no pity took great stretches of land. She wondered whether Lettice was one of the original Wickers. Avoca thought of Ynes, wandering around with such peril, but she could not leave her post now and prayed Ynes would have the sense to turn around. So Avoca stayed and watched in camouflage under the branches of the solid beech tree. Like a gecko, she clung to the soft bark, her stolen cloak draped over her; she became part of the branch.

Not many hours had passed when Avoca heard the unmistakable mutterings of Lettice. She grumbled and growled under her breath using foul language, spitting and swearing. Avoca listened carefully and managed to hear her rhetorical conversation and despite Lettice's clear betrayal of Avoca and Agnes, she could not help but feel happy and amused to see her old friend. Her question remained, did Lettice join the white wizard and his coven or did she fall by chance into this plot. Her mutterings seemed to be about strangers taking over the place and the shear arrogance and insults, then she continued about someone who seemed to be a distant cousin, Grettle, whom she clearly hated. Her descriptive words were unrepeatable, making Avoca giggle to herself, as she only described herself. This, however, indicated that the white warlock and his clan had upset the very old witch and if Lettice was alive, and Josina, then surely Wilma and Parnell were too and maybe even Fabian. How they were she could not understand.

Avoca continued to listen as Lettice stirred her pot throwing in potatoes and herbs while still she grumbled about how she should be dinning on mutton and carrots, not old potatoes stolen from the store. Once Lettice had finished her meal, she lay down next to her fire and was fast asleep within minutes. She snored like a hog and Avoca could not quite believe how she exposed herself to the elements with so much danger around - did this mean she was part of the plan? Avoca cursed her foolishness for doubting that she was not involved in Josina's plotting. Careful she slid down from the tree. She went up to the sleeping witch and sprinkled upon her fire a little spell to keep the flames roaring and the sleeper to stay as she was. Avoca then left. She did not return to the Hall though, but made her way to Dyrham - there was only one person she needed to warn and that was Agnes, who she knew would return soon from escorting the lord and visiting Avia.

Avoca by flight on her broom soon reached the dazzling lights of Dyrham Park, and she made her way straight to the stables and gently petted the cavalry of horses all gleaming in their well-kept stalls. Avoca found the Stourton horses and nearby in a barn the carriages. She climbed into the carriage that Agnes and Jerome would return with in the morning. Hiding herself, she nibbled on some apples and oats and waited for the morning to come. Avoca did not sleep. She sniffed the air all that night like a fox on a hunt - Avoca was on guard. She knew the scent of Fabian and his witches; it was engraved on every sense of her body and mind. What she was to do she was not sure, but just being there made her feel that she protected Agnes from their wrath.

With Lace and Cake

~~ * ~~

While Avoca hid in the carriage, listening for trouble, her daughter Agnes dallied in the great rooms of Dyrham Park. The girls had gathered in the beautiful orangery with Sicilian oranges and lemons in Tuscan pots. A huge table was laden with the remnants of an amazing super, while bowls of fruit and tiered cake stands were filled with delicately iced treats. Olivia paraded around in the most beautiful dress of delicate pink with lace and flowers, a colour normally worn by men; she had heard it was all the rage for the Parisian aristocracy from a letter Agnes had received from Belle. Jack moaned he had not heard from his ma in months, yet both Avia and Agnes had received letters. Avia laughed and removed the letter that she held dear from her skirt pockets. They had only recently received them. Agnes had found the poor messenger at the Hall lost by chance and in such confusion and fear. Although receiving letters had been their last concern, she was glad she had found the messenger before leaving for Dyrham.

They had spent the day in Bath, and the girls had had a wonderful shopping trip. While the boys had scuffed their feet waiting, they decided to visit an ale house to warm themselves, and each one ordered a brandy and hot chestnuts. The ale house wench knew Jerome and asked after his ma with a little hesitation, knowing that his father would visit on his trips from abroad and give her a hard time. She also had some strange information. The sheriff had not long been in handing out drawings of a dangerous prisoner who had escaped and was not to be approached. Jack asked for the picture and quietly folded one into his pockets. Something about the description of his crimes made Jack uneasy. Why would someone kill a librarian and steal several books and then purposefully be caught and then escape? Jerome and Jack left the Saracens Head and looked at the sign depicting a painting of a Turk crusader returning from the Holy land. They felt uneasy. The strange escape of a prisoner who stole books of no worth was indeed a puzzle. They managed to retrieve the girls from the haberdashery and escaped in the carriage. Jack nervously watched all the way home to check they were not followed; maybe they had been foolish to step out with such danger around.

Since their Bath trip, no harm had come their way, so he hoped the librarian's murder and the books were not linked to their case. Something niggled him though about the picture. It was someone he had once seen; he could not place him though, and he choose not to show Avia and upset her as she seemed so rested and happy. As the girls admired Olivia in her new dress and giggled, Jack felt an urge to go out and check around the stables and yard. He had a sense something was wrong, and he cursed them for being so foolish as to go into to town. Something struck a chord about that picture. He thought he had seen the very man watching them as they had eaten lunch in the assembly rooms. He had tipped his hat and moved on when he saw Jack see him and still Jack had that niggle that he had seen him before. All of a sudden Jack wished he was back at Stourton; at least there he had the protection of a full coven.

Jack pulled his coat around him and held fast to a small hunting gun he had bought with him. He walked through the horse stalls - they all dozed and seemed quiet and he made a special fuss of the Stourton horses. While looking over at the carriage in the joining barn, his heart shot to his mouth as he saw a piece of green cloth caught in the door. Jack removed the gun from his belt and walked behind the carriage - he bent down and walked slowly and quietly, trusting in the element of surprise. He was, however, thwarted as the coach door flung open and an irate-looking Avoca stood with her stick ready for a fight. So relieved, Jack knelt on the floor and held his hands up in retreat. Avoca walked over to him offering her hand and gave him a grin. They talked for a while exchanging news. Jack showed her the picture of the escaped prisoner. Avoca's reaction was not great, she looked white as a sheet and said he should be dead like the others.

Avoca was now even more nervous knowing it was true, and she accepted Jack's offer to join them in the house. When they went back, the orangery had been cleared and they had all retired to an inner drawing room where a fire was roaring in the hearth.

Knowing Lord Richard had retired after all the excitement of his return and visit, Jack boldly walked in with Avoca, who hugged Agnes and gently patted Avia as she would a small child. Olivia was introduced and then retired, exhausted from the excitement. She thanked Agnes for her wonderful work and was gone, leaving the others to talk. Agnes was so shocked she too went pale. If Fabian and the others were all still alive, then they would still want her. Avia held her hand and wiped her own tears away. She had thought herself safe at Dyrham, but now she felt more vulnerable than before. She had now put her sister and father in danger and her sister's dear, sweet little baby Teddy, who she had only just met.

It was decided quickly and with sadness that they should go, and they would need to make a show of where they were going. They would go to her great-aunt's town house who had sadly passed away, the girls had been left the house in her Will for when they stayed in the city. She also left them with a handsome sum of money each, of which some they had used to make improvements to the house, and it was now a most comfortable and elegant stay, decorated in fashionable colours, mainly thanks to Cecilia and her wonderful taste.

They planned to set off at first light, then they would walk the fashionable routes and make a display of their presence, hoping the escaped prisoner still lingered on. Agnes they would hide with Avoca, he maybe had not recognised her, as she had worn a low bonnet and a very fancy cloak gifted to her from Belle and he would not expect a poor seamstress to acquire such an item; that was what they hoped. Avoca would stay with her and Jerome would parade with a childhood friend in Agnes's cloak and bonnet, much too Agnes's disapproval, especially when Jerome described her as neat and pretty. The next morning everything fell in like clockwork; the sun shone, and the sky was the bluest it could be - it was a dazzling winters day. Avia left a note for her father and Olivia, explaining little, other than there were going to Bath. They quickly boarded the carriage, smuggling Agnes and Avoca in, and ascended the steep-hilled park land towards the main entrance and huge gates that would take them on their way. Avia felt some excitement to be walking out with Jack despite the circumstances. They had still barely spoken of the ordeal and just enjoyed being together again. She had noticed that although he was very attentive to her, sometimes he would just drift off to faraway place.

As soon as they arrived, they took to the streets and had breakfast in the tea rooms of Sally Luns. Avia arranged for a delivery to be sent to the town house, knowing how Agnes loved the Bath bun. It was in the busy tearoom that they met Isabelle, Jerome's childhood friend. She was pretty; Jerome was quite right. She was also quiet and shy, perfect company for their day's work. She and Jerome talked about their mothers who were practically sisters from growing up together in the poor house. Lucky to survive, they now saw little of each other but would always keep in touch. Avia was glad Agnes was not here to see how well Isabella and Jerome fitted together. Their comfortable chat was filled with giggles and Avia noticed the odd touch here and there of affection and she feared that although Jerome and Agnes were very attracted to one another and had some spark, they were not well suited enough to last. Avia quietly held Jack's hand under the table. Her subconscious told her that nothing but witches and warlocks would come between them, ever. Jack responded by squeezing her hand as though he knew exactly what she thought and that he agreed.

The day was hard work and they walked far. Jack did not stop once looking for the jail breaker Fabian, but he feared he was now long gone and had either followed them or made his way to Stourton Hall. He began to regret his decisions and felt he put Avia and himself in danger. Jack was about to call off their strut-about when he spotted a commotion on the open park in front of the Royal Crescent. He urged the others to follow him and carefully they approached. Two men had hold of a man who tried to writhe free. The men called out to fetch the sheriff, and in their clasp they had the prisoner Fabian. For a chilling moment his dark gaze met Jack's eyes. Jack saw him look at Isabella; his disappointment showed in his expression. Their trick to hide Agnes had bought them a little time. The prisoner roared with anger and next he was gone in a smoky flash, leaving both of the huge men howling in pain as they looked at their badly burnt hands. By the time the sheriff came, the prisoner was gone leaving a flummoxed few and two men groaning with their hands in a horse trough to help ease the pain. Jack turned quickly. He gave orders that they must flee back to Stourton Hall to warn the others. As they left, a small army grew to search for the murderer and book thief with a sting in his tale. Jack knew they would never find him. He was gone now and would only resurface when the time had come.

The Chase

~~ * ~~

Solly and Carmenta returned from their chase the next morning and set about repairing the damage to the walls and balustrades. The morning was bright and crisp and the Hall seemed quiet. It was as though nothing was wrong; all felt peaceful and the beauty of the Hall shone. They knew from their nights work though that a lot was wrong and something bad was coming their way. After Solly had saved Ynes, he needed to see who could create such force, so they had tracked them quickly to their lair. They pursued the three nun-like witches who screeched through the woods, with no clue at all they were being followed. Solly and Carmenta were so close yet not once did their senses turn to see if anything had decided to check out the enemy. Their foolishness to attempt to take Ynes would backfire, as they led Solly and Carmenta straight to their lair that otherwise would not have been found. The cottage by the wild lake was just a smoke screen. A decoy deep in the woods was far from an ordinary stake out; it was like a castle. They had made a fortress using the natural caves and lay of the land with huge trunks of wood making walls, smoke smouldered from within, and the foolish threesome of witches shouted the password for the gate to open - rackety yet impressive, it was wound up.

Solly and Carmenta waited and watched; they saw many come and go. Gedahard was organising something big and Solly and Carmenta needed to know what it was. They held fast and watched the white warlock and many witches pour from the gates; they marched away from the Hall. Deciding to track them later, Solly took his chance to enter the castle calling with confidence the password, Ghupt Khula, and sure enough the gate wound up. Carmenta and Solly stood with their cloaked hoods firmly around them. The courtyard of rocks held the entrance to the cave that had been clearly worked on for years under the nose of the Hall; the plan had no doubt started after their first failure. This time, though, they seemed more organised and Solly suspected, by the site drawings that were laid out on a makeshift table at the mouth of the cave, that they knew of the sacred stone and that with the sacrifice of himself and Agnes, the coven would have all they needed for eternal life and domination. The stone was no doubt more important now than Agnes or himself he hoped. They both crept around and stole little nick-knacks that would not be missed, but would give them a connection to spy upon their enemy.

Carmenta looked at their potions and took samples of a few. She even snatched a whole jug of one strange golden liquid that they had many of. Solly could not help himself and took a book of interest called 'The Wickers' strangely with a library stamp, he knew it would draw suspicion; however, he hid his tracks so well they would never believe anyone from the outside had been in. Carmenta left a few unpleasant tricks that would make the coven suspect each other for missing things. Much to his surprise and sadness Solly found deep in the cave a wonderful snowy owl. He spoke quietly to the bird and gently untied the beautiful barn owl from his perch. The owl looked quizzically from his huge brown eyes and tilted his sweet white, heart-shaped face. Unsure at first, the owl stretched his pale brown feathered wings. Solly offered his arm to encourage the owl and the bird landed solidly on his arm and seemed happy to stay there; the poor thing had only ever known captivity, and it now choose to stick with Solly. Carmenta and Solly then eagerly started to leave. They left the coven's caves as quietly as they came. A group of cawing jackdaws hopped along the gates to the cave. Carmenta decided to capture them with a spell. She gave them snips of dried meat she had found in the cave and set them as spies to fly around and give a bird's eye view of their enemy. Satisfied they had done enough, they set off at speed and headed for the farm. They took the owl to Bertie's barn, fed him and promised to return. Solly felt sorry for the owl - he was too obedient and hopefully, in time, he could be set free. They travelled back out and picked up the stench of the travelling coven that was far too easy to track - Solly and Carmenta strangely enjoyed the hunt.

They soon found themselves on the ancient Hill with the fort and from there they could see a stone pattern much like the one on the plains and the circle of witches and warlocks with their candles and cloaks. Not wishing to be seen, they hid behind an ancient oak tree and took a poorer viewpoint, but it was enough to see what went on. The coven acted out some rituals, but thankfully there was no sacrifice. They studied from a far the witches that they knew of by Avoca's clear descriptions; the two warlocks, Fabian and Gedahard, clearly stood out. There was also a gathering of whom they presumed were other witches, warlocks, serfs and spies, all dressed in brown cloaks. Solly formed a plan in his mind that he would keep to himself for now. He turned and looked at Carmenta who stood watching in fascination. Solly asked her what she thought they planned and did. She tutted and muttered as always to start, and jabbered in her pidgin English that he could not easily understand. She then drew with her stick on the hard earth the hill that they stood on and the hill of the tomb. Carmenta thought there was a passage to the sacred stone that they sought and luckily had not yet been able to find it, at last they had some hope.

Carmenta and Solly decided to make their way home, as there was little else they could do that night and the dawn beckoned. On their way back Solly collected the owl from

Bertie's barn, who compliantly hopped onto his arm, and they rode back to Stourton Hall. Carmenta watched Solly. His freedom was changing him so much from when he had first escaped the temple. His head was held high and his strength was regaining, and he rode and did everything with such skill. She felt pride and safe with his presence, knowing he would figure out a way to keep them safe in that clever mind of his.

Jack's Warning

~~ * ~~

Avia and Jack returned to Stourton Hall alone. They left Agnes with Avoca hiding in the town house. Jerome had returned to the ale house in the wall; they thought it a good place to recover any other gossip. Agnes and Avia had shed tears when they parted company, unsure if they did the right thing; they were afraid of Fabian. Isabella, Jerome's friend, had tuned out be a little star and organised help for Agnes and Avoca so they did not have to go out for a little while. She found them a carriage and horses they could access at any time if needed and promised to visit them daily. Avia and she had struck up an instant friendship. Isabella was a shy, unassuming sort, who seemed to be thrilled by their adventures as she called them. Avia thought about her on the way back and looked forward to her visiting Stourton Hall, when the miserable mess was over.

Avia and Jack sat at the front of the carriage and Jack drove the horses, while Avia clung to his arm, enjoying the morning air and his company. The tracks were quiet and only a few workers with their water jugs and bread could be seen, glumly making their way to the mills; dowdy, pale and stick-like people, they walked with their sad eyes to the ground. Avia wished their lives were better and felt guilt for her extravagant life. Avia didn't know if it was something about those sad faces and solemn walks that set Jack off, but he suddenly started talking all about India and his captivity, the gardens and the walled pen that he lived in. He described the huge Bayan tree that gave him precious shade and how he had talked to that tree every day and treated it like a best friend. He spoke of the flowers he grew and exotic plants that Avia knew nothing of. In detail he described the foliage and flowers and the heat. He kept referring to the heat and dry dusty land within the walls of a castle that no one could leave, and then he spoke of the escape and how the girl had taken him. Shrouded in a long jama and headdress, he was pushed through the lanes of the fort bustling with people and animals laden with spice and grain. Jack talked of how he could barely breathe in the stifling heat. He stuttered and stopped, and he held onto Avia's hand. She did as always, not question or ask more, she just sat and understood and with each word he had spoken, she felt she had lived with him from her vivid past dreams.

The journey to Stourton Hall with the narrative of Jack's capture seemed to go with such speed. The horses smelt home and hastened to return to their fields and warm stalls and good care from their grooms. Jack turned off onto an old track that was hardly used. It led to an old disused barn, where they hid the carriage and led the horses quietly through the gardens and into the back of the stable yard. They then handed the horses over to the grooms and under the cover of the rhododendrons made their way to the Hall and the kitchen entrance. Avia fumbled with the key she had taken and finally they were back in, and they ran to see what news there was from everyone and Jack prepared to give his warning.

They had arrived just in time to hear Solly and Carmenta's account of their night and all that they had discovered. Avia listened, while she stared like she had seen a ghost, at the strange man who slept on her father's chaise lounge. As the words of covens, rituals, caves and cruxes filled the library's walls, each word to her echoed with more despair. She sat close to Jack who seemed so much stronger than herself, and when it was his turn to speak, she felt calmer and his words felt more normal as he described their encounter with Fabian. Miss Bonneville commended them on such quick thinking and such a good plan. She agreed Agnes should stay hidden, although maybe needed a little more protection, so she decided to send Harini, who could not be expected to fight against her own father, no matter how much she hated him now. Preeti was still weak, so she was also sent away to the town house with Harini. They were to make their way by traditional broom above the hills and woods, as the tracks were becoming too dangerous. Miss Bonneville sensed they had little time and she looked around at what she had left: Carmenta, Solly and Aethelbert and herself would be plenty. Poor Ynes was a wreck and Jack and Avia had no choice but to stay; they had done their job well though and led Fabian away from the town and back to Stourton Hall.

The Waking of Aethelbert

~~ * ~~

Miss Bonneville was beginning to feel impatient. She wanted her old life back she wanted to organise the house, help arrange dinner parties and prepare for the season ahead. In her head she screamed for normality, yet on the outside she as always appeared calm and in control, a trick she had learnt while in service for Fabian the Warlock. Miss Bonneville studied Aethelbert's sleeping face, ageless, yet some lines told stories of his loss and struggles. She wondered where he escaped to in his endless sleeps and wondered quite how his circadian rhythm worked; maybe he could sleep for a year or two. Despite feeling some strange comfort in his endless sleeping upon the master's chaise lounge, the time had most definitely come for his help and guidance - his knowledge would be the greatest and she prayed the most useful. She looked to Solly for his help in waking the infamous Aethelbert, as she knew he would be graceful and take on the task with kindness. Solly did not just shake his shoulders and call his name as some might to disturb a slumber, instead he called to the legendary man and talked of life and a different time and his brother the King Momolou and slowly Aethelbert came around.

At first he seemed embarrassed by his audience, then he sat up and growled he was hungry and thirsty. In an accusing way, he grumbled under his breath, 'Why wake a sleeping lion with no offering of meat'. Avia seeing his annoyance quickly summoned Bunty who rustled up a fine breakfast for them all, Stifled by the library, they all ate in the huge dining hall with Aethelbert at the head of the table - he was after all once the Lord of Stourton himself. Avia sat next to him with Jack, and Miss Bonneville, Carmenta and Solly all sitting on his end of the long table. Bunty served them as cook, footman and maid, and Avia thanked her openly in front of all. For a short time there was a comfortable silence as they ate and drank, all ravenous as many had had no time for food.

Miss Bonneville thought and thought how best to question Aethelbert without angering him in anyway. She could tell he was temperamental and liked things his way and as she formed a careful plan of questions in her mind, she heard a clearing cough and Aethelbert began to speak. He stood and paced the room.

His story was from the beginning in the valley long ago when the Cornovii arrived, from time to time he would look at Avia and smile with his eyes. He told them the story of the night alone on the stone and how he had prayed for his life not to end, not knowing he asked for eternal life. Aethelbert looked at his audience and hesitated a little, he then lowered his voice as though he was afraid someone else would hear his words, Aethelbert told them about how some of the tribe had discovered the stones powers and how they called themselves the Wickers and had eventually been banished by his brother the King for their revolt and witchery. Aelthebert then explained about his encounters he had had over the years with one particular wicker, who now called himself a warlock; a powerful man who meddled with gun powder. They were now enemies who fought for different outcomes: Aethelbert said that he wished to hide the sacred stone and its powers forever, fearing the damage it could do to man and the warlock wished to use the stones power for his treachery.

Aelthebert spoke of many characters over the years, and Miss Bonneville gasped when in his ramblings he mentioned the alchemist Eliphas and his brother Dastin, who had raised a witch hunt for Avoca all those years ago. Aethelbert knew the whole story and asked where the mother and daughter might be. Avia played her cards close to her chest for some reason; she could not be sure if she trusted her ancient great-great-grandpa. He sensed her hesitation and told her not to say, just so long as they were not in the Hall and were hidden somewhere safe - Fabian sought revenge and he blamed Avoca. Her daughter was born to be a sacrifice and would, Fabian thought, please the sacred stone, he hoped in return for a needed boast to his and the others dwindling powers.

Aethelbert had by chance heard from a reliable source of Fabian's plans to raise the stone from the earth's clutches and create a dynasty of his own around it, a place that would survive the ever-changing world. The site would cover a vast area, beginning at Stourton and stretching to Avebury and Stonehenge. Avia tutted he could do no such thing as the landowners would protest. Aethelbert dismissed her contribution in a kindly manner and proclaimed he was afraid that Fabian and his accomplices had the powers to rule. Fabian always had ideas way above his nobility - he thought of himself as a king of warlocks and of the occultist world. Fabian long ago felt he should have been king of Cornovii and not Aethelbert's brother, a power struggle of his own that he could never forget or forgive, the Cornovii knew though his heart was not pure.

The room went silent for a little while and Avia starred at this man she had looked at in ore, in his many portraits upon the wall, she know felt confused and scared of him, he to her was as bad as the witches and warlocks that wandered the woods.

Jack was the first to speak. He had taken in all the information and although some of it sounded absurd, he had to believe that Aethelbert told the truth, after all he had seen things and had things happen to him he never thought possible. He looked Aethelbert in the eye, unafraid of this legend he had heard of in a tale as a child. Jack was clear with his question and determined for the truth. Despite the plans of Fabian and his ruthlessness, he needed to know if Aethelbert had a plan to stop his old rival enemy from forming his invasion. Aethelbert paced some more, a little agitated by the young man's articulate arrogance, but he for once swallowed his short temper and grumbled to himself instead. He looked to Avia and asked her to bring her father's maps of the county and instructed Jack to help and to bring, candles, charcoal and paper weights.

While the maps were gathered along with other things, Aethelbert spoke quietly to Solly so no one could hear. He felt sure that Solly had a plan too, he had watched him carefully whilst in his supposed slumber and offered that a strong alliance between them could grow. Aethelbert ran his hands over the old maps and began to draw the underground world that Fabian had been creating for years. The cave entrance that Carmenta and Solly had found had natural tunnels and some unknown manmade entrances under the tomb of King Momolou and the fortress. They had reached inside the hill by tunnelling, yet they had still not reached the stone. All amazed by what had been going on under their feet for so long, they sat with their heads in their hands. Had they already been beaten? Aethelbert saw their dismay and reassured them. He admitted he wished he had realised sooner that Fabian and his sidekicks had been so busy. Jack found it hard to contain his anger. Aethelbert had it seemed wandered around aimlessly acquiring great fortunes and estates, turning his hand to whatever he wished, yet he had spent his many centuries on earth with a blind spot to someone he knew held a secret. He had been naive and purposefully had his head in the sand, like the huge ostriches that ran wild on the deserts of Rajasthan. Jack found him an irritating tyrant and he did not care that he was Avia's relative. What they needed now was action and all the hocus pocus was beginning to annoy him; he knew exactly what had to be done.

Jack stood and grabbed a stick from the fire bucket and pointed at the key entrances to the caves that he knew were once used for mining stone. He circled pressure points where the tunnels would easily collapse. He would hire Sparkie, aptly named for his talent in mining and explosions, and they would lure the coven and warlocks in and create explosives - they would be trapped for eternity. Solly immediately questioned his theory and plan as to how they would entice them all in and to everyone's surprise, Jack announced that they would offer Agnes as the sacrifice that they apparently needed. Avia cried out in protest at the thought of her dearest friend being used as bait. Jack took her hand and explained it was fine, Agnes would be able to escape. Miss Bonneville grumbled if Agnes could escape then they all could escape. Jack shook his head and disagreed, they all looked at him puzzled and he told them a story of his childhood adventures with Sparkie, his brother and himself.

Sparkie

Being poor in the winter was hard going for everyone, Jack was in his sixth year and it was a bad one; the firewood was damp and the crops were poor from a harsh summer of rain, the livestock were kept in the barn, and the fields sat full of barren mud that turned to ice as the nights drew in. There were still a few chores for the children, but with a desolate land there was little to do and with the little food and warmth, Jack's pa encouraged them to explore the woods by day and forage for any food or wood that they could find.

Sparkie, then Harry, had been sent to Jack's family for the winter. His ma had died from the fever and his pa worked down the mines; his shifts were long and his time on the ale was more needed than looking after a child. Glad of a small amount of coal and from the kindness of their hearts, Belle and Jeremiah took the lad on. He was no trouble, and was funny, and happy to muck in. Relieved he was not abandoned, Harry would do anything, so when they were told to go foraging in the woods, he was overjoyed and over the months the boys came to know the woods like the back of their hands. They played constant games of dragon sleighers and pretended often they were being chased and each time they had to find hiding places, so they knew every cave tunnel, tree to climb, woodcutter's shelter and hovel. One day they climbed up onto the tombed hill hat overlooked the rocky valley. They were busy collecting firewood from a fallen tree when a howl from what sounded like a wolf spooked them, so they bolted and that was when Harry fell. They heard his cries echoing away as they searched for him and eventually found a hole – they shouted down and heard Harry whimper a call for help. Afraid for their friend, Jack lit an old storm lamp and went down the narrow pothole and easily found foot holes like ladders on the sides. He found Harry bruised yet jolly at the bottom in the dark, glad to see Jack. They called back up for Bertie to come down and they started to explore the tunnels that led them in a maze and eventually bought them out into the grotto by the lake. For years they used the tunnels until the grotto was restored and the nymph statue was placed blocking the way out, the tunnel went nowhere else and they had hidden it with a rock afraid something would become trapped with no escape.

Then Jack went quiet and said he always went with Harry and Bertie and they had a pact never to go alone. Only one day, Harry and Bertie being a bit older, had gone to help at the manor with the sheep dipping.

Jack went looking for firewood and cold from the freezing rain he moved the rock and lowered himself alone into the cavern below. He dug from boredom while waiting for the rainstorm to pass, he fancied he might find some treasure and they would be rich forever more, instead he found a trap door that opened up to steps and a tunnel that he nervously and foolishly entered; he was lucky it was not a case of curiosity killed the cat, as the tunnel came to an end blocked by stone and by chance Jack slipped and saw a bolt. He brushed away the dirt and dust and found another trap door. Cautiously he opened it and climbed down into a purpose-built cavern with a tomb where a carved stone statue lay in wait; Jack studied the chamber for some time and found a strange pulley in the stone, he knew it was away out yet he had cleverly thought to jam his entrance back out and he nimbly left and never told a soul afraid his brother and Harry would want to go back.

Jack ended his story as an outburst of queries filled the room. Avia was still cross with Jack - for his suggestion and sulked, trying not to be impressed with his adventurous tale. Aethelbert knew he told the truth and was relieved that it was Jack who had found the tomb of his brother above the sacred stone and not someone else. Solly looked to Aethelbert and asked him to explain how Jack meant for Agnes to escape. Aethelbert explained the secret passage and its hidden pulley in the wall of the chamber. It was in the darkest corner, without knowing the correct stone, it was impossible to get out, it would take too long to solve if ever; the oxygen would be gone before a man could find the way out. Miss Bonneville injected that they were dealing with warlocks and witches not mere mortals, then Avia blurted that Agnes may be tied up and that anything could prevent her from escaping, Jack at least agreed with her and began to see his plan was useless. Avia was still furious though and would not calm easily, and even Miss Bonneville agreed there had to be a better way. The party then all sat again and scratched their heads for ideas to safely save the valley, hall and so much more. Solly stayed quiet and just looked to Aethelbert and Aethelbert knew it was his time. He asked Solly to walk with him around the lake - they had much to discuss that the others could not hear. Avia stomped off while Jack, Carmenta and Miss Bonneville studied maps and muttered ideas that were all dismissed.

They were shortly disturbed by Avia screaming and ran quickly to her aid. Bunty lay lifeless on the kitchen floor with a bloody mess on her head; they knew it was no accident, the attack had begun. Their only relief was that she was not dead. Miss Bonneville and Carmenta treated Bunty, and each took turns to sit with her; they both knew that they had come for the ring. With relief Carmenta still had it on a chain in her pocket and their own retaliation would start there and then.

The Spy

~~ * ~~

Avia was furious, sad, scared and in a foul mood. She had never ever felt cross with Jack and could not forgive him for his idea. She felt her necklace burn upon her neck - she touched the pretty pendent her talisman, but still she seethed inside and wished dearly she was with her father and sister away from this mess. Avia didn't even believe the stone was real and wondered why they all wanted to live forever when life was so hard to understand at times. She looked out of her window at the garden, grey and cold, and saw Solly and Aethelbert walking. She wondered what they spoke about and wished she could just listen to their words and so, for a distraction from her anger, she pulled on her hat and grabbed her cloak and muff and ran towards the garden despite the danger - she would pretend to warn them of Bunty's attack and maybe try a little eavesdropping.

Avia knew the gardens well and cut through the grotto quickly, staring at the nymph statue in disbelief that behind the wall a tunnel led to an ancient Kings tomb, her ancestor. She thought of Aethelbert and wondered if her father had any clue, or if any of his fore-bearers did; she doubted it very much. Avia found the path that would be directly above them and she crept down through the woody path where wood anemones, bluebells and snowdrops would carpet the floor in their chosen seasons. She stood behind a maple tree and listened hard. Their voices were quiet; she could, however, just make out a few words. It seemed that Aethelbert was to return to the tomb as his brother had wished him to all those centuries ago - he would guard the sacred stone for eternity in a slumbering state. Tired of walking the earth, he had nothing left to give. Avia shuddered at this thought and still did not understand how it would all work. She then clumsily tripped on a tree root and fell rolling down the slope. She was picked up by Solly who had run to her aid. Her pride was hurt but nothing else other than a little embarrassment, she thanked Solly while explaining why she came. Solly grinned, knowing full well she had been listening all along and Avia made it obvious by asking Aethelbert directly how staying in the tomb would work. Aethelbert explained, he planned to tell Fabian's a lie, that he knew he could not resist help it would entice the enemies in and they would never expect to be trapped.

Avia looked at Solly and again felt anger and uncertainty - did they trust this man? Avia began to walk away when she was called back by Solly, who convinced her it was safe to trust him and that she must not tell any one of their plan. Aethelbert looked at her and smiled and spoke kindly to her.

He talked of her grandmother and their family and how he had loved to watch them all from a far and see Stourton Hall grow in such splendour and charm. He had lived as the lord in Stourton castle hundreds of years ago and he remembered Avoca and Agnes and would not let harm come to his family or their friends. He tried to calm her saying that Jack was a good and decent boy who just wished to protect her and treat the situation in the only way he knew and that his explosive ideas may come to good use. Avia still felt cross, although allowed her strange encounter to carry on. She let him tell her stories of Stourton over the years and other lives he had lived, always moving on and coming back. Aethelbert then patted her gently on the hand and walked away. A huge grey dog walked with him that she had never seen before and waving his hand he faded into the distance.

Solly had gone and Avia stood alone on the stone bridge looking over the glass lake with the reflections of the trees; she felt tears roll down her cheeks and all she wanted was to see Jack and his smile. She turned and ran back towards the house colliding straight into Jack as she had once before. He had come to look for her to check she was safe and he quickly apologised for his foolish and hurtful idea. Avia gently pushed him, and they ran and played silly games as they used to. They found themselves at the temple looking over their dynasty holding hands and praying as they had done for Agnes on the market day that seemed so long ago. They both knew they had dabbled with fire that day and now the smoke swirled and engulfed them in a story they wished they could escape.

Matters of the Heart

~~ * ~~

Agnes and Avoca had loved their time, pushed together in hiding; it gave them both chance to understand one another and make up for a lot of lost time. They were similar in many ways, although Agnes was so much more refined. Agnes talked of her attraction to Jerome and asked her mother's advice as to how anything could work, being so different. Avoca before would have said that it could never work, a mortal man and a witch. She saw though that Agnes was different, but would have to learn that she would lose him one day and her pain could be great. She also saw another problem of more concern. She did not believe that Jerome was not already given to someone else. She had seen him with Isabella, their new sweet friend and watched how they were, so naturally close and meant to be. Agnes just grumbled that they were childhood friends, knowing deep down her mother was right. Her beau, as she liked to think, was not hers to take and although it pained her, she had to accept that their strange attraction was just that, a little spark of chemistry floating around in the air that could easily pop and fall flat to the floor. Avoca lightened the mood of her daughter's disappointment and discussed other amazing people that she knew and did a little meddling and matchmaking in her daughter's head. She had found the perfect combination for her little witch princess and when the time was right Agnes would see where her heart should really rest.

Avoca and Agnes were disturbed from their talk by a soft knock on the back door of the kitchen below. Thinking it was Isabella, Agnes keenly jumped up she was eager to see her friend and access her thoughts on Jerome; her matters of the heart had made her forget everything else. Agnes checked who knocked and to her surprise she found Harini and Preeti; she immediately let them in and called excitedly for Avoca to come see their new house guests.

The Coven in the Caves

~~ * ~~

The witches fought, scrapped and cackled - they reminded Fabian of hyaenas fighting over snips of meat. He sat with Wilma and Parnell, who distanced themselves from the uncouth and rude witches. Gedahard seemed blind to their ridiculous behaviour; so transfixed on his project, he was blind to everything. Lil, Mo, Prim and Grettle ran rings around each other with endless tricks and mischievous games to entertain themselves, bored by waiting and trapped by the warlocks, they regressed more and more, and it was only when a flying broom struck Gedahard upon the head, that he raised his voice and told them to go and torment somewhere else. The four witches left howling with laughter to the tunnels of the cave where their voices echoed as they chased each other - Fabian was sure the reverberation of their squawking was worse and he asked Gedahard if they were needed any more, could they not just pay them off? Gedahard growled that they owed him a debt. Fabian began to regret his collaboration; it was a shambles and Gedahard was annoying. He raged in his head that Gedahard had not brought the boy that Fabian wished more than anything to inspect; his only real reason for his long alliance with Gedahard was to meet the hidden golden child. While Gedahard had reassured him that he could see him in the temple of his castle when they got back to the Golden Fort, Fabian had snarled under his breath that the warlock was a fool not to bring him, he would have been the greatest sacrifice of all.

Parnell and Wilma did all they could to encourage Fabian to rid themselves of the white warlock and his creepy nuns and the wretched wench Grettle. She was worse than Lettice who hid away in the woods from them all. Grettle and Lettice were distant relatives and hated one another with a passion, due to a long family feud that had started hundreds of years ago over a fight between two brothers and a girl the brothers had both wished to marry. Parnell and Wilma had always tolerated Lettice and her crude ways; she was funny and cunning with a sweeter side. These vulgar creatures though, they could not bear. They both silenced themselves though for Fabian, as they owed him for saving them all from complete despair and without him they would be nothing more than wisps of witches, and although Josina had played a part in their return from there apparent death in Mora, they could not forgive her for escaping and just leaving them in the first place. Fabian seemed not to bear grudge and proclaimed it was Josina who had helped them survive she had found their spirits and bought them back to earth. The two sisters held a vengeful silence against their old friend though and secretly hid a burning desire to see her fail - they cared not for the capture of Avoca and Agnes - that was long forgotten. Josina, though, had nearly cost them their lives and now she had conveniently disappeared again, while they waited for the days to pass and the Eve of All Hallows. Fabian had said that the sacred stone would shine and give eternal life to all those in its path, so with their tunnels nearly finished and their plan in place, each waited for their life to be reinstated, instead of walking around in a weak and fragile state, in their forth coming centuries they would learn to pace themselves more carefully and return to the sacred stone.

Wilma groaned as the loathsome louts returned; they laughed like gurgling drains as they came out from the mouth of the cave. Grettle had been covered in pond slime and the despicable nuns were very amused by their antics, applauding themselves while howling at Grettle. Wilma turned her back and pulled her scarf around her ears; she was pertinacious in believing the hoodlums should be gone, and without word Parnell knew her sister's thoughts. The fellowship of the coven would not last long - there was no way on this earth that they were going to allow the gaggle of witches a chance of even a peak at the sacred stone; that was for them and Fabian alone. Fabian looked at the two sisters - he seemed to read their minds and maybe he thought they were right this time. With Josina gone and the others nothing but a nuisance, he looked to find a way to rid them of their burden. Gedahard had given him enough information and with all the Stourton witches running to hide in fear he had no need for extra help; he could handle Miss Bonneville and the other strangers well enough alone, especially with the deadly twins by his side. Fabian played with the fire as he thought how to obliterate the ineffectual merger. As he tossed more wood on his fire he heard a strange tapping noise. He hoped it was the owl that had returned. It was strange that Oka would escape after so many years of captivity. Fabian shrugged to himself in hope the owl was dead; he could not bear to think of anyone else owning his feathered pet. He called for the useless nuns to take a look around, but still the tapping noise continued. There was a commotion by the gate and Aethelbert was dragged into the cave fortress.

Fabian could not believe the turn of events and even Wilma and Parnell stood to take a look from their comfort by the fire. Fabian roared in anger as to how Aethelbert had found him and what did he want. Gedahard quickly put a dagger to his neck, insisting that he answered Fabian in haste. Aethelbert was in no mood for threats and swung around wounding Gedahard with one strike from his innocent-looking walking stick. Gedahard lay out cold on the rocks while the witches looked on and backed away hissing at Aethelbert. Fabian looked at this normally gentle and annoying man in disbelief. He was traditionally unlikely to retaliate in any way other than with words and clever tactics. It was, however, fortuitous and amusing that he had knocked out Gedahard the White. So Fabian stood back in hope that Aethelbert's foul mood would knock out the rest, but sadly they retreated, leaving Fabian no choice but to engage with their intruder. Aethelbert looked around at their cave fortress; he despised the whole place, it stunk of horror and deceit. He would not stay a moment longer and instead invited Fabian to walk with him in the woods; he proposed a trade. Interested by his offer, Fabian nodded and leaving all the coven uneasy, he followed Aethelbert through the opened gates.

From nowhere Argo appeared, Aethelbert's huge grey wolf hound; the enormous dog walked faithfully by his side. Fabian looked at Argo. He had seen this dog many times over the centuries, and he wondered how this was possible. If Aethelbert had in fact taken eternal life accidentally as he had always claimed, how did the dog also inherit its master's gift of life. As he pondered this he was interrupted as Aethelbert began to talk. He spoke directly, saying he wished for an end and how he would in secret like to pass his world over to someone he could trust, someone who understood the old ways of the Cornovii and the value of the land. He agreed that Fabian and he had not got on well in the past and asked Fabian if he could consider a quieter life, a more respectful way, a caretaker of his land, while he lay dormant in the fort with his brother. Fabian was no fool, and he first questioned his motive for backing down. Aethelbert was quick though to convince him that the beautiful land had to be saved and the stone could be accessed but not by force. Fabian then raised his dark eyebrows and was in, hook, line, and sinker - he could soon be the ruler. He then asked what of the others and the likes of Miss Bonneville. Aethelbert agreed this would stay the same until their natural passing and Miss Bonneville he felt had a calling to go elsewhere, as did Agnes and the other witches. Aethelbert also suggested that the stone would destroy those with an evil heart. Fabian was so self-obsessed - thinking he was perfect. He believed his heart was true and he had shown kindness and forgiveness to many, though he did not fancy the chances of others.

The afternoon grew chilly and the fog rolled in as Aethelbert and Fabian strolled back to the coven's cave. Aethelbert left him halfway and took a track he knew well. He said on the sacred night of the spirits, Samhain, he would show him the way to the stone in peace with his coven if he wished. Fabian followed the image of Aethelbert until it disappeared into the foliage and fog. He was elated, flummoxed and in total shock by the conversation and proposal. Fabian's arrogance did not allow him to believe that Aethelbert was not genuine; he saw no reason why he would not show him the way to stone. He rubbed his hands in glee. The stone would kill off Gedahard and his motley lot - their hearts were darker than a pike fish in the depths. Parnell and Wilma he would warn, he thought, perhaps their hearts were a little dark. Lettice he suspected would not come underground she was only happy under the skies, Josina he would ponder upon when she hopefully returned. Fabian began to like the idea of his new empire. He only had to wait a little while longer for the owners to pass on, and Stourton Hall would be his as he wished, with no trouble or attention. He cupped his hands in approval and for some reason praised himself for such good negotiations and smugly left for town to treat himself to a real super and a comfortable bed away from his coven and dreadful company.

Solly's Reflection

~~ * ~~

Solly wandered the huge Hall, fascinated by its beauty and grand portraits. He found Aethelbert in many as he thought. 'How similar to our ancestors', he imagined the family would proclaim and he wondered how many other dynasties Aethelbert had created on his endless wandering of the world. His brother King Momolou and the Jakhs were right, the sublunary man was not equipped to live for so long, they could not adjust to endless life wisely. Solly found his way back to the library where he loved to spend time and now it was less busy, he could partake in his favourite pastime, reading, researching and searching. He was busy up on one of the ladders at the top of a shelf in bliss when Ynes appeared in the library. She thought he did not really notice her, so engrossed in his findings, so she ignored him in the heights and took a chair next to the fire that miraculously burnt day and night. Hestia, Agnes's cat sat next to her feet preening herself by the heat. Ynes' head still thumped from her near abduction and she still shook with fear; she looked around nervously, thankful Solly was in the room. Ynes wished they were back in India in Carmenta's cottage by the village on the hill, there she felt safe and free. At Stourton she was feeling like she was within the castle walls of the fort and with her knowledge that the white warlock was close by, she was truly terrified, so she sat there quietly, not making a sound and listened to Solly as he turned pages and trundled along on the shelves rolling ladders.

Solly continued to read. He felt the small breeze as the girl he now considered to be his sister arrive with a slight whip of air, and without being obvious he watched her from under a book. She looked pale and thinner than ever and her poor little face looked so sad. He let her sit though and just ponder her afternoon away; she was still in shock and needed time to chase her demons away. He feared though that too much had happened to her and too many times. Her life was only stories of capture and mistreatment, mistakes and misery. Solly felt she should return to the cottage in India with Carmenta. He wanted them both safe and out of the way. He had just found a family - he did not want to lose them - and he had a bad feeling that was deep in his gut that wouldn't quite shift. He stayed on the top of his ladder holding the heavy green leather-bound book and he thought and reflected on all that had been said and done. He questioned and studied each piece of information he had in his mind and he carefully scrutinised it all, as though it was written in words on the pages that he blindly turned. Solly saw vivid pictures in his head, stories of the past jutted back and forth and always Fabian and Aethelbert were involved. Solly smelt a viper and he delved deeper. These two men, once of

humble birth were entwined so deeply. Solly began to disbe-
lieve that Aethelbert could be trusted; he saw a pattern
through the ages of conquering of castles and overthrowing
of kings. These two had been meddling for years; like a game
of chess they played a gambit, both dangerous components,
yet with real lives and fortunes they did not deserve. Aethelbert had convinced himself he had done good; Solly though
was not so sure. Solly slowly climbed down and threw a
blanket over the sleeping Ynes. He called for Carmenta who
came from nowhere and Solly made a speech that Jack, Avia
and Miss Bonneville all heard. They hung their heads listening - to his summary that was not for the faint hearted. The
truth though was accepted and Jack, relieved, shook Solly's
hand and offered his service to help in any way he could to
help Solly's inquest.

A Trip to Hanging Langford

~~ * ~~

Solly liked Jack from the moment they had met. Similar in stature, with a warm enticing grin and so like his brother Bertie, who he considered to be a good friend. Solly was thrilled to have found true friends, a joy he had never had before. They walked towards the manor stables with Avia grumbling behind that she again had missed her lunch and would be relieved when this mad goose hunt was over. The three mounted the ponies, taking the good sturdy Zani, Kari and Avia's childhood pony Mulberry, who she had neglected of late. Unshod, the ponies quietly left the yard and excitedly trotted while bobbing their heads up and down. Jack led the way and Solly took the rear with the shiny black Mulberry nestled in-between. They took straight to the woods and meadows and made their long trek to Old Sarum. In the ruins of the castle and cathedral, Solly hoped to find just one more clue to satisfy him that his theory was true. They reached the sight by dusk and lit candles to search. The night was lit well by the moonlight as it drifted in, and Solly found amongst the ruins his clue: two names that had been used more than once many years ago, and he found them with such ease. It was almost too simple: the Bishop Roger of Sarum and the Sheriff Edward of Sarum, both powerful men in the tenth century, creators of the cathedral and castle improvements and rulers of many more. The carved features on their weathered tombs gave likeness with no doubt to Fabian and Aethelbert. The two men from long ago were etched in stone. Avia and Jack ran their fingers over the graves and felt a cold twist within their hearts; these men had prompted and fought across the many storms of time, they conquered and took and when they were defeated into hiding, they would go and only resurface when safe in a new demise or country, both clever and deceitful. Satisfied with his findings Solly called for them to leave; they would make for the nearest coach inn before it grew too late - Old Sarum felt creepy, a place they would not like to stay over night.

They reached The White Hart at Ford where above its door, the carving of a white stag stood looking down upon his guests. The inn was adequate and warm and served a fine game pie. The locals stared at their smart and strange attire. They were left though to their own business, the three spoke little and just looked around each fascinated by the little portrait pictures that covered the wall. Each face gazed out from a time before with a little tale to give away, of wealth, poverty, love or adventure. Avia studied a picture of a man dressed in strange clothes with a scarf around his head next to a fine looking horse; his piercing black eyes looked beyond to something he saw with dread, as the horse nuzzled into his neck. Avia could not help wonder what their fate was. Solly broke her thoughts as he was astounded to have found a picture of Aethelbert and Fabian, interestingly side by side, both dressed in smart black cloaks with hats. They stood by a monument no one could make out.

The old coaching in had gone strangely quiet and a lady appeared, who they had not seen before her clothing looked thread bared and from another time, she seemed to float in a wisp across the room, Jack presumed that she was the lady of the house and timidly asked the frightfully pale lady who the men were in the picture ; pointing to Fabian and Aethelbert, she looked at Avia closely and laughed saying, 'she should recognise her own stock and blood'. Avia wriggled nervously, unsure how the pale lady knew who she was, while Jack pushed a little more as to where they were in the picture and who the other was. She snapped that they were up on Penn Hill at the old fort. The pale lady was suddenly sat with a jug of ale in her hand. She took three slurps and then began to tell them of the man she had met, in the very place they all sat. She said he was a foreign gentleman who called himself Frenchie. He came heavily armed and sold gun powder to the highest bidder and was a good acquaintance with the lord of Stourton Castle- she looked curiously at Avia, and carried on. She said strange people from other parts came in all of that week that the so called Frenchie stayed. She then grew serious and said a few terrible things happened around that time. She told them that two young lads were murdered and the hanging of a woman accused of causing their deaths by witchcraft; she said her old ma knew the story well and she went to find them something and disappointingly did not return. The three, full of pie, presumed she would not be back and took a room each knowing they needed to rise at first thing. Each one of them exhausted fell to sleep as soon as their head hit the pillow, bringing the morning quickly, with a dull and cold drizzle. They sat where they had the night before and ate a greasy cooked breakfast with hot jugs of milk. Satisfied, Jack handed over their payment to the bar lad. Before he left he looked at the portrait again and from nowhere the pale lady returned, she handed Jack an old rolled up scroll, she muttered he could keep it and hoped some good would come of their visit, then she was gone. Finding the others Jack was keen to leave, the pale lady gave him the creeps, while Avia and Solly reluctantly left the warm fires and shelter, soon saddled up, they rode through the greyness and by midday they had reached Hanging Langford and the thatched cottage belonging to Sparkie. Jack dismounted leaving the others in the saddle and waited for his heavy knock to be answered; a window flung open and a bright faired-haired woman carrying an infant called out to be quiet - she then blushed and laughed when she recognised Jack and disappeared, closing the shutters. She opened the door, greeting him warmly and asking him in. Jack gestured to his friends, and she called for them to leave the ponies in the barn and join her for tea. Solly helped Avia with the ponies, then they shook the damp off and went into the tiny cottage.

Low and cosy, it reminded Avia of Lottie's cottage, with washing by the stove and the kettle on ready for a bath or tea. They all introduced themselves, while Sparkie's charming wife Nora bustled around. She presented nettle tea and lardy cakes made to look as well as she could and apologised to Miss Avia, who accepted them with glee. Hungry and exhausted from the ride, she had feared another day would pass without any lunch. They sat huddled around the table with the baby gurgling happily on a rug by the stove. Nora had told Jack that Sparkie would be back within the hour; he had been in the mine that morning over at Powten Stone. Nora flicked her flame of golden hair and flashed her green smiling eyes, and her face lit up as she announced she could hear Sparkie and the cart.

Rolling down the dampened track came Sparkie with his cap worn backwards and his cart rattling along with lamps, spades and gun powder pots. He smoked a pipe as he walked with a limp that he had acquired from a little spilled powder that had set alight - he was lucky to be alive and still have a leg. He saw Nora waving and quickened his step. She greeted him as though they had been apart for a year and although his parlour was full of visitors, he went straight to the baby who they affectionally called Bish. After doting on his child, Sparkie turned to greet Jack and the others. He flung Bish into Avia's arms presuming she would wish for a cuddle with the tiny bairn, and Avia obliged quickly, passing the baby to Jack who she knew had some experience in holding infants - Avia was not sure at all and avoided the responsibility of a babe in her arms.

Jack was quick to finish the polite chat and banter and when Nora was just out of earshot, he asked Sparkie if he could do an explosive job for him. Sparkie was overjoyed to help, although a little mystified. The date and time was quickly arranged and Jack handed Sparkie a small, neat roll of tightly rolled notes. Hands were shaken and calling to Nora, they left as they had arrived. No one else saw them, so Jack was pleased and they rode hard back to Stourton Hall, in haste to be back in their protection zone.

The Paper Scroll

~~ * ~~

Jack, Avia and Solly arrived back tired from a hard day in the saddle and after a few chores and a clean up they met in the library. Jack carefully removed the old scroll from his satchel that the pale lady in the Inn had given him, he held it with paper weights on the huge leather desk. The hand-writing was messy and hard to read and many mistakes were made and crossed out. It was written as a narrative, most probably by another hand, so although hard to follow they understood the horror of the author's fears and sadness of the case that was named the hanging of Myrtle Pel Selwood.

The Hanging of Myrtle Pel Selwood

I remember the day as clearly as the white snow on the ground – the blood gurgling screams of Tabatha Brown. Her boys had both been missing for five days and their crumpled bodies had been found on the fortress that stood on Penn Hill. No one ever went there from stories of strange things happening. The boys named Arthur and Harold were no more than ten. Tabatha said they were too curious and explored to far from home; she had told them a hundred times that their curiosity would find them in a mess and I remember her saying they were often gone for far too long. They had their father's travelling gene and he had never come back. Poor Tabatha Brown didn't last long after their death. I visited her as a good neighbour should before she crumpled away, and she told me things that the boys had said. They were obsessed with spying on Penn Hill and said they had seen amazing lights, explosions and some scary folk that gathered like witches in fairy tales. The boys said they saw the Lord of Stourton a few times with his grey wolf hound and the French stranger who often stayed in the inn, Tabatha Brown held my hand as she went to her grave. She said, 'Those boys saw something that they never should have seen, I swear on my life, that's why they're both dead, something weird was happening with the Lord and the man called Frenchie who scares us all'. And then she was gone, and I said nothing, afraid if I did I would be next.

I saw before I left by her bed a peculiar old bottle she had been drinking from— I could smell the vile hemlock poison with just the smallest sniff, afraid for her soul and burial I threw the bottle away and only considered years later that maybe it was by another hand that she had died.

For poor Tabatha Brown was like her boys and her lost husband, always poking around into others business; she had been the biggest gossip for miles around, she knew everyones business better than her own; she was not a person to leave with a secret that was not to shared or have information that her boys may have been told her.
God rest her soul.

The days before and after the funerals of Tabatha and her two sons were hard for the locals. Everyone knew each other from the surrounding villages; people were scared and the crimes needed solving. There were tales of witchcraft on Penn Hill and it was not long before poor Myrtle was arrested. They found her in her hut deep in the woods; it was full of strange mixes the sherif and the law people did not understand. How could they understand, men who lived in towns. Myrtle was well respected for her healing powers — she knew the herbs for each ailment and had solved many fevers and more.

She didn't go easily though by all accounts, and bit and scratched like a wild cat; this did not help her cause. A sham trial was held in the tithe barn at White Cross, but she never stood a chance. I went along out of support for Myrtle. I tried to speak to save her, but my words like other were brushed away forgotten and misheard, under the influence of others of a more powerful status; they did not care, they had their victim. Prisoner or convict, guilty she was, for poor Myrtle the case was closed. We all knew the boys' murderers went free that day with their dirty secrets and evil ways. The locals stayed close from that day and the woods and hills of freedom were gone. All protected one another as best they could, knowing if another fell upon a secret they should not have, they would die by the same hand and another would take the death penalty. So a community was born of keeping oneself to oneself; they became quiet people who never challenged or looked beyond their own humble lives.

I visit the grave of Myrtle – its unmarked in a field by Penn Woods, just a simple stone with flowers and herbs that grow strangely in a circle, and some would say she still walks in the woods in the spring and summer months.

The boys and their ma got a gravestone that they share in the church yard of All Saints church in White Sheet parish, and people talk of the ghosts of the boys running up on Whitesheet Hill where they used to play, before they wandered further a field in search of more excitement, a dangerous game to play. 'God bless them all', Peggy Ford.

Peggy of Old Sarum

~~ * ~~

When the script was finished, Avia held her stomach as though she was going to be sick; she felt real pain that her ancestor had been involved in something nasty. He saw two young boys and a mother go to their grave and an innocent woman hanged. She believed the letter by the author. Peggy wanted them to be remembered always and no doubt paid someone she trusted to write it down. Peggy wanted this act of injustice to be found out one day and although it had taken nearly two hundred years to be read and understood, her daughter the pale lady she hoped could now rest in peace. Avia swore that those poor boys would be avenged. Jack took her hand and they walked together, as that was what they always did to think. Avia felt a tear escape as they walked towards the gardens. She questioned in her head - was all this built from her ancestors' wrongdoings in the past? She felt such anger and did not know how to manage how she felt. Jack as always calmed her and made her feel better, reminding her of the good that had come from the bad. He wished like Avia though, for Fabian and Aethelbert's time on earth to be over and wondered what game Aethelbert played. Did he really mean this time to finish it all? Which ever way, Jack was going to make doubly sure that from that tomb they would not stray.

Avia and Jack wandered back to the Hall deep in thought. Avia felt lost and out of sorts with this mysterious world she still grappled to understand. With Jack by her side though, she felt safe. They both walked with their heads down and when they looked up a strange sight greeted them. Stood on the terrace normally filled only with pots of neat topiary and grand statues, stood everyone; they looked over to Jack and Avia and smiled. Avia clapped for joy to see Agnes and everyone - it was a lovely surprise. Harini stood with her estranged mother Chandaria who clung to Bertie's hand, Preeti and Avoca stood with firm grins, Agnes and Miss Bonneville stood at the front with Hestia and chatter-pie, while Solly casually sat on the balustrades with Oka the owl on his arm and Carmenta and Ynes leaning in. Avia would have loved just then for a picture to be painted, as her beautiful friends stood proudly and strong. As they walked up the stone steps to greet them Jack shrugged, so much for a plan to keep everyone safe. They smiled and greeted one another; old and new friends, strangely bought together by a tricked witch who once left a daughter behind.

Explosive Ends

~~ * ~~

Solly no longer cared if he, Jack and Avia had got Aethelbert wrong; his meddling and mixing over the years had made too many wrongs and his associates were unsavoury. He had spoken to Carmenta, and they had agreed that the Jakhs were their only hope to help them sort the mess in a more civil way. They would that night lure them all to the tomb and with Sparkie's explosives, the coven and the help from the skies, Solly prayed it would all be over soon.

The day was spent preparing for the night ahead; every detail was thought of. Josina, still in her stone state, was taken to the fort on the hill; she could stay there forever hidden, with no help to ever turn back. Hestia yowled approval and hissed at the statue as it was taken on the back of a cart - the plot had started. The act of surprise was their main weapon; their enemy believed that most had runaway and even Aethelbert was now out of their new plot. He, though, would be true to his word in one part, Solly believed, if only to send them off the scent.

The Eve of All hallows, Samhain, was a still and moonlit night and the skies were filled with eerie clouds that shadowed and cloaked the travellers of the night. The silver moon lit up the mellow rocks and the bats circled the glade on the top of Penn Hill as they had for hundreds of years. The tomb and fort stood protected in the circle of oak trees that stood like soldiers in wait. The ancient oak trees would have seen the chronicles of Fabian and Aethelbert from the beginning, if only the great oak trees could talk. The Stourton protectors waited patiently and quietly, all nervous and in dread, and as they saw the procession with candles appear, each took a deep breath - the time had come. Solly whispered for everyone to hold their place and keep their senses under control. They watched Aethelbert lead his followers like the pied piper to the hidden entrance of the tomb. Miss Bonneville and Avoca watched Fabian closely, afraid he would smell the hidden explosives or sense their chicanery; ironically, his trade and passion for hundreds of destructive years would hopefully be the nail in his coffin. The planted combustibles below would congruously conclude with the Jakhs his timely end. His thunderous face looked to a new beginning of dominance; he had no suspicion in his once brilliant mind. Slowly each warlock and witch disappeared before their eyes. Solly, Chandaria and Harini held their breaths when they saw the white warlock Gedahard look up to the sky. Did he sense what Solly sent them? He paused for too long as he stared at the strange cloud formation that gathered above. Did he feel the distant warm wind pick up and taste the sand upon the air? At last

Gedahard turned his pale face to the ground and followed the others. Solly sighed with relief, knowing it had been a close one. Gedahard had met the Jakhs before and surely he remembered the signs before they appeared. They still feared he would recall that strangeness in the skies, but maybe it was too late for him now, for the eve had started and a trigger had been set. Solly and the others slowly walked from the trees and looked to the skies that turned a glorious golden colour; the breeze was warm and wrapped them all in the safety of the Jakhs. They appeared riding their lunar white horses high in the sky. The Stourton coven below waited ready to fight just in case. They felt the tremor as the explosives thundered under the earth and heard splitting noises from the fort collapsing into the ground. The Jakhs circled and gathered the spirit souls from the carnage and rumbling earth. The fort of Penn was gone, hidden forever deep within the hill and the sacred stone in dust returned to the skies to land with the Jakhs in the world that it had come from. Fabian and Gedahard's souls were captured with the others. Their eternity on earth was gone and powerless they would be trapped in another sphere. Around the strange movement of the ground, the oak trees stood fast, their roots entwined deeply into the earth and between their ancient web of shoots, chunks of sparkly, white stone clung, as the cavernous spring waters trickled endlessly on.

The Witches' Salute

~~ * ~~

Parnell, Wilma and Lettice walked slowly away from the cave fort. They wandered as though they just looked for berries and woodland herbs. They left behind the stormy arguments of the warlocks and screeches of the witches bickering amongst themselves. The morning was fair and they knew that The Eve of Samhain would bring an end to it all. Wilma had had one of her powerful dreams where she saw the future span out in front of her; the vividness blinded her and her fear was great. Although she did not understand a lot of it, she knew it was a huge warning of what was to come and within all the confusion she saw a statue of stone being buried by the fort on the hill. The three witches, once out of sight of the caves, flew at speed to the hill and found the cleverly disguised digging of a burial done only hours before; they toiled and pulled the statue from the soil and as suspected by Wilma, they pulled a lost Josina from the earth. Unable to move the heavy statue easily even with magic on their side, they tried to bring her around. Eventually they found an ancient spell that worked and slowly Josina returned to flesh and bones. She spat and cursed and was very floppy for a good while, and the three witches moved her out of sight and hid in the canopy of trees.

They settled in a huge archaic oak tree and waited for the night to fall, while Josina mumbled and struggled to come around. Her witch friends prodded her and gave her drops of water to keep her from fading. They all agreed Josina would be out of it for a good while and although it was tempting to get their revenge and leave her as stone, they each agreed she could be very useful to them though she would have to pay them in favours for years to come. Endurance and perseverance was an art form for the witches; they could not waste one of their own. Parnell had also found a wonderful discovery that had changed their plan; she had kept it secret from the warlocks. While she wandered the woods, she had found a special spring that spurted milky white water from the ground. She decided to drink it and within hours she was bouncing around like a spring rabbit. She shared her secret with Wilma and Lettice and now gave her miraculous tonic to Josina. The witches believed the water ran from the sacred stone and they bottled up as much as they could, hoarding it out of sight from all. The three witches had decided amongst themselves that they were bored of Fabian and his rules. They fancied a life away from the harsh cold winters and looked back to happier times in the warm winds of another place, so they would spectate the whole event with no intention of interfering or rescuing.

Wilma cringed when she heard the roaring dragon from beneath the hill. She knew its breath and fire would kill and the strange vision of the cloud-like horsemen captured any free spirits that broke free - she knew it was the end of Fabian the great warlock who had lived for so long, and Gedahard the white warlock of snakes and poison finally went to his makers. Wilma, Parnell and Lettice had to feel a tiny amount of sadness for the wretched Grettle; the fool and her son, both too greedy, like others had gone. The nasty nuns though were rotten to the core - they would not be missed by any sadly; it was a blessing that they found their end together. They felt pity for the others who had followed in hope, but they could not save them from their belief in eternity and wealth.

They looked over to the arch of oak trees knowing that their rival coven of Stourton all hid amongst the snarled and ancient oak and they applauded and respected that they had won the fight. The gentle valley they would leave and not return. Josina, when she came around fully, may not be so quiet; only time would tell how she would take the loss. She had loved Fabian for all of her life. Controlled and besotted she would be lost without his domineering character - she was his possession, and she was possessed. As they came out from the cover of the oak trees embrace, they stood plainly in the dazzling moonlight and they saluted a witches' salute of respect and surrender, taking the precaution to hide the weak Josina - a little untruthfulness was par to the course of a long witch's life; then they were gone in a silvery shining light.

Aethelbert's Farewell

~~ * ~~

When it came to the end, Aethelbert understood. He heard the explosions and sensed something far greater was coming their way. In a split-second decision he disappeared and in the confusion of gas, smoke and shrapnel, he just made it out by the skin of his teeth - one fraction longer and he would have been swept away into the vortex and gone forever. As he scrambled and scampered up and down the slippery tunnel he felt it pulling him back, and with every inch of his strength he pushed on and his many lives flashed vividly through his head - the times he had wronged others and engaged with Fabian - and as he emerged explosively from the tunnel through the entrance he had made long ago, and reopened only days before, now landing him into the cold water with the nymph statue, he immediately began to regret losing his chance to die. He felt guilt and sadness that his brother's tomb was now buried deeper, yet he still went on living.

Before he left the gentle valley, his once beloved home, he prayed that Avia would be a good caretaker and protect the beauty of the hall, gardens and valleys and he hoped she would realise that without his resolve it would not be as it was and sent her powerful thoughts of how all would be without his strength and resolv over the centuries. Whilst Aethelbert thought his thoughts of Avia he rubbed in his pocket a smooth shiny white stone, he tutted to himself that he had done no harm in keeping a small amount of the sacred stone. Aethelbert called for Argo his faithful dog who came and stood by his side. He asked him to stay in the valley and serve another from that day on; they must part company. Argo did not fuss and with his head down he walked away, obedient as always the huge dog sat dutifully like a statue by the grand entrance waiting for his new master to appear.

Aethelbert decided that night to take a different path. He walked on through the night alone; he would not stop and made for a place he had read was where the font of all knowledge had begun. His journey was far away and many centuries ago. Aethelbert knew he must travel far and never return - he headed for the monastery of St Anthony in the land of tombs and pyramids. He would serve there for the rest of his days, as a scholar and he hoped, a benefactor to all.

Aftermath

~~ * ~~

Avia woke early the next morning; her head hurt from lack of sleep. She prayed the plot had worked, although felt quite sick inside at the thought of what had happened in the night. Jack had gone but she had stayed in the Hall, afraid to see the end. She knew Jack was fine - he had left a little note as promised under her door on his return. She held the note with its simple words that meant so much to her, 'I'm back, Love Jack'. She put the note in her carved bureau and began to dress, hoping someone would be around to tell her everything was going to be fine; she hoped for little detail and just a positive summarise. Avia did not have the stomach for what they had done. No matter how bad things were, she wished there could have been another way. Avia wandered down to the library - it was empty to her horror, not one book or shelf was left, the fire lay lifeless, even the different looking clock had stopped with its hands stuck at twelve. In panic she began to walk through the other rooms, but each one was the same. They felt lifeless and dull, portraits were missing from the now grey, damp walls; the furniture was different and stale flowers dropped petals on the filthy floors. She looked to the garden and instead of manicured hedges, lawns and statues with roses waiting to bloom, there were thick thorny bushes. Avia began to run and with dread and each step she saw that more and more had changed; beautiful rooms were now dim and empty. The library was still the biggest shock - instead of walls of books and arte-facts, bare stone walls and cracked windows stood. She ran out of the Hall towards the stables and instead of a perfect yard with horses stamping and snorting over fine stable doors, stood a rackety pig pen and hut. The wind began to blow in a bitter driving rain as Avia ran towards the lake; all she found were trees and thick woodland, with endless thick mud. Sobbing, Avia called out for help, but everyone was gone. She ran back to the Hall and flung herself back through the strange door. Avia held her breath and ran to her reflection that stared back at her; a stranger looked from the mirror, a face she had never seen before. Avia screamed and ran and ran until she could no more. She slumped her-self outside by the once grand door, as the hail drove down upon her drab thin cloak that she had never worn before.

The Spectator

~~ * ~~

Jack had been up all night. He could not believe what he had seen and still sat on the oak tree branch; he did not move, transfixed to the spot. He was cold to the bone, yet still he stayed with the others. Some had gone to inspect the raise in the ground that still smoked slightly, others stayed close to him, and no one said a word. He remembered the huge explosion and rumblings and then the strange apparition of godly horsemen in the sky all golden and white; it was like some saintly painting in the vaults of an Abbey, the roaring had grown louder, as though a strange storm crashed all around and then it suddenly had all stopped and an eerie silence followed while a peculiar mist swirled about the hill. He had seen three witches stand and salute in a strange way and disappear. Avoca had told them who they were and how they meant to leave them in peace. Jack then thought of Avia alone in the Hall and he jumped from the branch and ran as hard as he could - she would be worried he feared. Although exhausted from his night, Jack could still run fast and he knew his way so well that he flew through the woods and valley to the gardens and the Hall and there on the step slumped against the door lay Avia; she was soaked from the icy rain and she held her head in her hands as though she was in great pain and by her side sat a huge wolf hound he had seen with Aethelbert, the dog nuzzled her and growled at his approach. Its huge bark woke Avia who screamed and shook; she ran to Jack and the wolf hound settled back down. Avia sobbed and sobbed into his arms. Jack tried to calm her while lifting her into the house, he lay her by the warm blazing fire and called for help. Lottie appeared in her neat maid's uniform and gasped at the state of her mistress. She quickly called for others for help. Shortly Avia was lying in her bed with Miss Bonneville and Agnes tending to her while Jack paced the halls. Avia's fever was bad, even though he knew Miss Bonneville would cure her if she could, he still sent for the physician. Knowing it would take an age for him to come, he cursed himself; he should have stayed with her instead of staying in the tree. Bertie and Chandaria came running in they had heard the news that Avia was poorly. Bertie had other news - he had had word from Belle that she would return home for Christmas. Jack hugged his brother. It was good news; he missed his ma and pa. Jack fought back tears after all the strangeness that had happened. He could not bear another step; he slumped in a chair and prayed.

The household ran around fetching things for Miss Avia and making sure everything was perfect; all gossiped when they could about the peculiar events. The Hall was gleaming and glistening with polished silver, flowers and fires, delicious smells rose from the kitchens as Bunty cooked wonders. All the staff bustled here and there as though nothing had ever happened. The people of the valley though were used to strange events and as they had for centuries, they would keep quiet and hold their tongues around others they did not trust.

The days passed and still Avia tossed and turned in her fever. Jack now sat by her bed - he read to her and told her his tales of India. As he wrote and drew them in his book, he felt like all of it was a dream from long ago. By his side sat the wolf hound Argo, who he fussed as he put his huge head on Jacks lap; occasionally he whimpered and nudged Avia. Jack was touched by the dog's sudden loyalty to his new master. Argo had no doubt saved her life with his warmth on that cold morning, when Avia had strangely wandered and collapsed.

Later that day carriages began to arrive. Jack watched them from the huge drawing room as Agnes took her vigil with Avia. He saw Lord Richard disembark and a lady he had never seen before, Olivia and her adorable baby, with many trunks being faffed around endlessly, and Cecilia and her husband and twins that he had never met - all marched into the Hall. Jack made himself scarce as they all settled in and went in turn to see Avia. He heard the concerned mumblings of her family. Unsure what to say himself and feeling like an intruder, he took the opportunity to sneak out. Jack wandered around the garden. He felt empty without Avia and thought how lonely and desperate she must have felt when he was captured in India. Without thinking, Jack walked to his old family home, the farm across the woods and fields, as he always had as a child. He felt his childhood had left him now and although still young, Jack knew he had changed. As he walked up to the farmhouse he saw Solly fooling around with Bertie. They looked up and ran to greet him with smiles and laughter; they then checked themselves and with the greatest concern asked after Avia. Jack shook his head - the grey rings under his eyes told a story of no sleep and worry. Bertie, with his arm around his brother, guided him to the farmhouse. The parlour was full; Bertie appeared to have a refuge for the unwanted clan of witches. Harini sat with her estranged mother Chandaria who seemed like a child herself, while Preeti, Avoca, Carmenta and Ynes sat around the table peeling potatoes and swedes while in deep conversation. When they saw Jack's sad face they went to his aid and asked how she was being treated. Jack explained the physician gave her leaches that Miss Bonneville discretely threw away and continued to treat her. For this they seemed relieved, leaches and endless blood draining were the worst possible action. They all asked many questions and with each answer Jack gave, another one came. Solly saved him and turned the questioning around to how they could help; he knew Carmenta could heal her. Carmenta was worried though. She sensed Avia chose to be in her state; she had held her hand the day she was found and she had seen something - Avia had to fight herself to survive. She went to Jack and told him that he was her only hope, she would do anything for him. Jack did not know how to get through to her though, she seemed to be unaware of anyone or anything. Preeti stood up suddenly. She muttered that Jack had to get her to Avia. She had to remove the bracelet, the bracelet was protecting her; however, in this case it could not define between the help of a witch and the hinderance of a witch. Carmenta eyed Preeti suspiciously and snapped that she should explain about her bracelet. Preeti impatiently told her of her stone charms and how she sealed the bracelet on with a spell that no witch could remove. Harini harshly asked then how they would ever get it off? As Jack pointed out, Avia's, sisters and father were there now; how were they to walk into the Hall and start performing spells while their precious daughter lay unconscious in her bed? The witches went silent. Preeti paced around the small room, then Avoca told her what she must do.

Preeti and Avoca left with Jack. Preeti was dressed in one of Belle's old uniforms from her time as a maid at the Hall. She was a little tall and the skirt rose higher than it should have, but Avoca just tutted and said it would have to do. Jack drove them in the pony and trap using Carmenta's ponies. Avoca gave her clear instructions and nervously Preeti listened. She was to find Miss Bonneville who would clear her path to Avia. Preeti had to act like a maid and speak little; her accent and features were a worry. Hopefully though, the Hall would be busy. Jack was to be a decoy and help keep the family briefly away. Preeti's biggest fear was her spell. She had never removed a charm bracelet and suddenly she was at the Hall with no preparation. Miss Bonneville was waiting for them by the door. She whisked Preeti in, while Jack went to the front door and was introduced properly.

Avoca headed for the woods - she looked for the spring water that she knew her old coven had found; they would never have given up without some bounty. She had kept it secret all those years, and she hoped the waters from the sacred stone still ran. Avoca could not believe that the stone was truly all gone. She felt it was more a smoke screen, a clever trick of Solly's, but whatever the case, there needed still to be enough spring water to save Avia, as it would take more than the removal of a bracelet; the girl she feared was delicate, like a butterfly on one of her beautiful flowers, a precious creature upon a swirling wind.

Jack Chit Chat

~~ * ~~

Jack took a deep breath and walked into the withdrawing room. The family sat huddled together. The children were in the nursery playing or asleep, while the adults were just praying for Avia. Jack was welcomed warmly and Lord Richard chatted to him honestly. He was clearly devastated by Avia's illness. Jack was introduced to his lady friend. Her name was Lady Alice Beaumont, her nickname was Lacey and she was smart and beautiful with an amazing American twang. She had travelled the world and knew more than Jack could imagine possible. Her chit chat was unbelievable and Jack was truly enthralled; he knew Avia would find her fascinating. Olivia and Cecilia had clearly met her before and they spoke to her with such fondness already. Jack felt so happy for them. So long they had lived with no mother, and although the Lady Alice was not in any way a mother type, she was someone they could share their lives with. Her warmth and kindness glowed from her and Lord Richard now had someone; he did not need to run away from everything anymore.

Jack fought back tears, he wanted Avia to be sat there by the fire with glowing cheeks, giggling and chit chatting back to Lady Alice and listening to her absurd and wonderful stories of her travels and discoveries, with not one tiny fraction of magic sewn into the words. Cecilia and Olivia at the same time felt the same and went to sit by Jack. Understanding his pain, the room fell silent and all the pleasant chit chat was gone. Their reality was that Avia maybe gone from their world. Her fever was so deep and had gone on for so long that the physician had warned them she did not have much time; he thought she was too weak to survive.

A Time to Forgive

~~ * ~~

Avoca found her spring; the trampled ground and discarded pots were a sure sign that her old friends had been there. She imagined how chuffed they would have been to find the spring of life, no longer her secret. With Fabian gone though, she felt no bitterness any more towards Wilma, Parnell and Lettice, she felt though that she could never forgive Josina and was glad she was gone for good, although she had nagging suspicion somewhere in her mind that she had had help from the others; she did not believe they would leave her in stone. Avoca pushed away all thoughts of the past from her head and filled her vessel with the thick, milky spring water, then she travelled at speed back to the Hall. Checking no one watched her she crept in through an open window and using the hidden passage she made her way to Avia's wing. She listened and made her way to the door where she could hear Preeti's gentle voice spinning her spells and prayed it was working. Avoca silently let herself in and stood by Preeti's side - the bracelet was off. Avoca felt such relief and Preeti gently rubbed on the scar it left. Avoca dabbed the spring water on Avia's lips and scar. Miss Bonneville could be heard talking loudly in the corridor, she was warning them that someone was coming their way. Preeti quickly put the bracelet in her pocket and hid Avia's wrist under the sheets and gently swept her hair off her face. Avoca and Preeti then disappeared through the window. They neatly tiptoed along the narrow ridge and moved onto a gully in the roof, narrowly escaping being seen by Tomsk the gardener, who trimmed the dead heads of a rose bush below. He looked up and shook his head, deciding he was seeing things in his old age. He began to mumble 'stocking feet and drainpipes, whatever next'. Tomsk continued with his pruning. Avoca and Preeti found their way down, away from any more near misses and made their way back to Bertie's farm. They ran through the meadows and suddenly felt a sense of real freedom. They did not have to care what anyone thought, they were free to roam with no fear of death or worse. They arrived at the farm feeling elated; they were positive Avia would now recover and they wanted to celebrate their success.

Harini Finds a Family

~~ * ~~

Harini enjoyed her mother's company. She was unlike a mother that she had read of in story books and as she had never been allowed to see her mother and her mother had never been allowed to see her, they had no memories and so it was extremely strange. Chandaria was lovely though and she spoke of her childhood often and how she had lived in a castle with many rooms and servants. She said the grounds went on for miles and she rode around them on her beloved horse Bali. Chandaria was more like a beautiful sister and without words the two seemed to agree to those terms. Harini just liked being with her and Bertie, she felt secure and happy and how she thought a young girl should feel. The house was small and shabby and unlike anything she had stayed in before - both Harini and Chandaria had always had enormous suites with their own bathing and dressing areas, instead of just a tin by the fire with a screen. Strangely though, both were happier than they had ever been. Harini knew that Chandaria and Bertie had fallen for one another and that she did not mind.

They all sat around the table and chatted about all sorts of things. Solly had become quite the entertainer and Bertie and him had become the best of friends, so their time together was fun and interesting and Harini felt she had a family for the first time in her life. She thought of Gedahard her father and felt no pain that he was taken or dead; he had never shown her kindness or compassion. She had been used for her powers and he had trained her well, Harini always suspected he kept her for something else and when she was told of the Schleswig curse everything made sense in the most disturbing way - Harini felt protected with her Stourton coven; she wished dearly though to leave that world far behind her. Like Agnes, she wanted to work and have her own life. Bertie had mentioned something about lessons and a teacher who lived in the village and sometimes held a room he called school. Harini was excited and had to wait for two weeks for lessons in other things than magic and spells.

Avoca and Preeti had moved with permission to the cottage by the wild lake. The place had been made to look smart and comfortable, and they were both thrilled as they decided what to do with their lives. Carmenta and Ynes had both left - they had returned to India with open invites for guests and promises of return visits. Carmenta had a few important ends to tie up, firstly she needed to find Ynes family and Yari her brother, in hope they could reunite, once Ynes was safe. Carmenta had to pay a visit to an angered Schleswig princes of the viking world to break she prayed an ancient curse.

Solly had chosen to stay at the farm. He felt he was needed for a little longer; with Avia still clinging to life and his need to protect Harini until the curse was broken. Solly also had a sense of something else, something he had not known before, he had fallen for someone very special and needed to work out how to let her know.

The strangest and strongest family was formed from loss, stealing and being stolen. They all only had one wish now and that was for Avia to get better. It had been a week now since Preeti had removed the bracelet and still she lay there as pale as a ghost; she did not move or speak and everyone thought deep down she was lost.

Belle's Return

~~ * ~~

Belle and Jeremiah walked into Stourton Hall like they had just walk off the Champs-Elysees in Paris as their clothes were so fine. Belle wore rouge on her cheeks and lips, her hair was put up in elaborate curls, her shoes were like porcelain with silk stockings covering what little of her ankle you could see - she was a picture of elegance. Jeremiah wore a pale suit with a cravat and a smart French bicorn hat on his head. The greetings from everyone was with great pleasure and they longed to hear their news. Belle was overwhelmed to have a full household greeting her and Jeremiah: Lord Richard and his wonderful new companion Lady Alice, who seemed to have quickly taken to be Lady of the Manor with no problems at all; she adored Miss Bonneville as Miss Bonneville did her; and she loved Cecilia's and Olivia's children. If only their dear mother Beatrice had been alive to see this day.

Belle was told, once she was sat down with a small brandy glass in her hand, of the fate of poor Avia and all the strange troubles that they had had and how Avia had been found out on the cold step, delirious and a breath away from death. Belle could not stop her tears from falling and held firmly to Jack's hand. She asked to see her and was taken along the huge hall and up the grand staircase by Jack. Jack filled her in quickly on how awful it had been and how the witches had tried to take the Hall and the night of the explosion and how Fabian, Aethelbert, Gedahard and the other witches were all gone, including they hoped Josina. Belle doubted that after hearing that Wilma, Parnell and Lettice had miraculously come back. As they walked into Avia's room, she asked her son to tell her more about Aethelbert and the legend that was real. Many things made sense to Belle now, stories over the years she believed to be true, sightings of him and things that had happened in the past and during his time as custodian of the Hall. Belle having barely digested all the information and horrors that they had faced, still had no clue of Jack's kidnap - he had decided to save that for another day. Jack hoped by not telling Belle all, she would find the clue to save Avia and understand why they could not steal her from the curse that she lay in for so long.

Belle sat holding Avia's small weak hand; she was too weak for a young lady who preferred to dig in the soil. She looked desperately at Jack as he paced the room, with his head in his hands. The reality of Avia's poor state felt more real with his mother there. Argo the dog began to pace with him, and Belle asked him kindly if he would walk the dog and open the window as it was stuffy in the room. Jack obliged and took the servants' stairs down to the workings of the house below. He grabbed Argo some food and then put on his heavy boots and coat. He walked with purpose to where he had no clue. He felt he walked the earth alone and he had to begin to accept the reality that his life could now be spent without Avia by his side - a lonely, sad road.

Belle fussed around Avia, straightening her sheets and brushing her hair, then dropped the brush and when she went to pick it up, she found a beautifully illustrated old book underneath Avia's bed. She opened the book and began to read. Something about the poems made her feel that they were real and as she spoke, she could see the illustrations so clearly, it was as though they sprung to life and danced around her in the room. Belle did not realise how long she stayed and she read until the light had faded. Lottie came in to light the candles and relight the fire that had begun to fade. She said that her husband Jeremiah had sent word he would return for her in the morning, knowing she would wish to stay with Miss Avia. Belle nodded and they hugged. Lottie told Belle how strange things had been and how they had all been sent away for weeks. She said the frost on the ground had even looked strange and the skies unlike a blue she had never seen. Belle patted her, with no answer, other than everything was more normal now. Belle left for her supper with the family. Leaving Agnes sitting with Avia, she handed her the book to read.

Agnes stroked the old book as though it were an old friend
and she began where Belle had left off. Agnes read the words
in both English and Sanskrit, her mother's native tongue.
For Agnes it was like reading music – the pictures were like
dreams and in a spell she could not stop reading the words.
While the others sat at the long oak table feasting on their
meats, Agnes stayed with her dearest friend and when she
could not read a moment more, she lay with a blanket over
her on Avia's bed and slept by her side as she had in secret
when Avia had trained her to be a lady, instead of an uncouth medieval stripling of a witch. Agnes was soon fast
asleep, and the book sat hidden under the blanket. When
Jack and Miss Bonneville came up later to check on Avia and
put Argo her protector back in her room, they decided to
just leave the two friends together; what harm could it do.
After Jack had reluctantly gone, Miss Bonneville stayed and
busied herself while the two girls slept. She stroked the dog
and asked him to give her a little yowl should anything
change. Argo she had found very receptive to her demands
and although Hestia hissed and spat and chatter-pie
squawked at the dog, the hound was an asset to the Hall.
Miss Bonneville thought of Belle's return and how wonderful
she was and deep down she now knew somehow that Avia
was going to be fine. Preeti had thankfully remembered the
bracelet protection could block the cure of a witch. As she

thought, she ran her fingers over the silver casement hidden deep in her pocket. She bought it out and unclipped the clasp and the dials turned and showed her the time and place she could go. With a smile of satisfaction, she placed it back in her pockets. Still thrilled, she had found it up on Penn Hill fallen from Fabian. She felt no guilt and thought it fair payment for all her years of service. Then she thought of something that until now had completely slipped her mind; she had to track down a mouse: poor Nanny Maud.

Banyan & Hawthorns

~~ * ~~

Agnes felt herself being drawn into a deep sleep. She remembered the poem she had read was a lullaby from long ago, and with her hand on the book holding Avia's cold hand, she floated away. Images flashed through her mind's hypnotic state and she fell deeper and deeper into the depths of another realm.

Agnes looked up from her sleep and saw Avia. She was stood shivering; the world around her was grey and dull. She was in an overgrown land with thick thorns and blackthorn growing everywhere. Agnes looked around Avia's landscape from her warm and colourful position in the Great Banyan tree. She could make out a lake and an old ruin; of the hall or castle, she could not tell. The stately house was grey and eerie, spikes spouted from its walls, a warning to any intruders. The windows were dark with shutters closed; no gardeners whistled around, no horses neighed and snorted from their stalls, no maids could be seen or fancy carriages pulled along the tree-lined drive – now just a rubble track barely passable by the hawthorn. Avia walked in her grey world with the dog Argo by her side and every so often she would slump down to the ground as she seemed to look for something. Each time Argo would nuzzle her just as he did in her room, and she would pull herself up on him and stand. And then Avia crumbled into the mud and poor Argo, however hard he tried, could not raise her again. Instead he sat close by her side, their fate the same, he would not leave her side. Agnes called out loud. She screamed Avia's name. Still though, Avia lay stranded in her frozen state, wet and cold on the sodden ground. Agnes sat and thought and as she thought she sang songs from the book. The tree swifts with their blue and orange feather tufts darted between the branches, while the malabar swung and hung gathering nuts and fruits. She saw below a tiger who crept low on the hunt and in the distance a royal elephant blew from its trunk. Agnes felt the warm breeze and she pushed the Banyan tree branches into Avia's cold grey world. She crawled along and swung down into the freezing landscape and ran to her dearest friend. Agnes petted Argo and lifted Avia's limp cold body and with Argo following, they climbed back into the welcoming warm branches of the Great Banyan tree. Argo took an almighty leap and landed on a huge branch that Agnes lay Avia on. The sun and balmy breeze warmed her frozen bones and Agnes mixed sapota and litchi fruits to a pulp and fed Avia with tiny amounts of the juicy flesh. She bathed her with the waters that collected in the huge leaves and then she sang the rhyme that Avia had once sang that had set her free and slowly Avia opened her eyes. Agnes hugged her with joy and felt that she had warmed. Avia sat and looked around in amazement at the sun-drenched colourful world. Agnes pointed to the frozen, thorny landscape from where she had come and promised her it was gone forever; now engulfed in colour and warmth. She could stay forever, and they ran in the scented valley of flowers and lay in the sea of fragranced petals. Agnes asked Avia to come back home, and she took her hand and led *the way and they walked into the garden with the lake and statues and beautiful trees. The magnolia flowers in delicate pink filled the branches and they wandered among the blossom and the seasons. As the garden changed they came to the cottage and the yew tree was adorned with the strangest flowers – where it had all begun. Avia grabbed a discarded trowel and dug a little earth and from her pockets she planted seeds from the flower valley and then patted the soil back over. She then sat with Agnes looking over the garden and to the grand Hall that glowed in its grandest way. Avia thanked Agnes and slowly hand in hand, the two girls walked along the pretty paths with Argo by their side, like ghosts they faded away and left the silver landscape and world of the Great Banyan tree and hawthorn far behind.*

Agnes slowly began to wake; she saw a glimmer of light and realised she slept on Avia's bed. Her dream was still real and she realised she held tight to Avia's hand. The book was open on the page with the poem they both knew and loved so much and she looked to Avia. Her face looked pink and not pale and she fluttered her eyes open and smiled. Agnes jumped up from the bed and ran around to her side and gradually Avia sat up as Agnes handed her the sweet milky water by the bedside. She then rang the bell for everyone to come. Agnes asked Avia if she had remembered the dream of the cold, dark place and the warmth and brightness of the Banyan tree. Avia did and shuddered; thanking Agnes for saving her from darkness, she then happily chatted about the seeds and the valley of flowers. One by one the family came, all tending and cooing, kindly they let her rest, each over joyed she had recovered, her father instructed that she should stay in her room and rest. Avia felt happy she had never known him so caring before and she briefly met Lady Alice, Lacey to her.

Later that day when Avia had managed to dress and sit by the window looking out, she turned to see Jack just standing and staring. Avia stood and fell into his arms and each of them stole their very first kiss. They sat on the chair together for hours as the darkness came, just talking and holding on tight, praying that they would never be apart from each other ever again. The gardens they would wander again in freely, with hope in their skips and slowly the memories would fade of the horrors that could have been.

Christmas Day

The family and friends gathered for the morning walk; a tradition for years, all dressed in fine new cloaks. Laughter and chatter filled the stunning lakeside promenade. Children ran with new wooden toys and others were giddy from a morning sip of boozy punch that glowed on rosy cheeks, arms were linked and the gardens admired. Agnes held her mother's arm with Preeti on the other, while Bertie and Solly fooled around. Chandaria and Harini walked close to each other as if in a dream. Solly would keep running past Agnes and gifting her pretty silver leaves or flowers he had made, and each time he tried to charm her with his smiles and funny tales. Agnes played it cool while inside she bubbled with joy. Solly to her was perfect, so well-read and interesting and like no one she had ever met before, he had the most amazing aura that she found truly mesmerising and she dearly hoped like Jack and Avia that they could be true.

Belle spoke with Lord Richard and Lady Alice, and admired Lady Alice's sparkling new diamond engagement ring while Jeremiah played with the giggling children, the sisters, Cecilia and Olivia, strolled elegantly with their husbands away from the group; they chatted of serious matters, while nanny Maud watched their children by the lake.

Jack and Avia hung back a little from the group. They watched their family and friends with such gladness, and holding hands they dived between the trees and stole as many secret kisses as they could, both elated by their love that they knew would never end. Avia ran back for a second or two on her own. She called Argo who growled angrily; he was vexed at something in the deep foliage. She held him by his thick leather collar and as she pulled him away, she glimpsed a piece of deep red silk float behind a tree with a swish. Avia shuddered and told herself to stop being silly. She called Argo to follow as she ran to grab Jack's warm and safe embrace; the moment she forced from her mind, it could wait for another day.

They both looked back at Stourton Hall that had seen many things come and go, castles and lords, warlocks and witches. Never had it looked so beautiful as it did on that Christmas Day. Miss Bonneville and Agnes had decorated it magnificently and as the short day faded to dark, the Hall came to life; it sparkled with twinkling lights. Stood like a doll's house, so perfect and inviting, with the gardens of temples and statues, wrapped by valleys of woodlands. A peaceful feeling fell. A time to enjoy its beauty, with no threats they hoped hiding in the woods, protected by the strongest coven that Stourton Hall had ever known, untouchable to any who might wish to try take it again.

The End

~~ * ~~

Other Books by Victoria J Hunt

Dolly Mouse & Friends

Tetonti & The Grand Quest

The Curate the Witch & The Casket, Amie's Ghost

The Little Yew Tree Witch (Book One 1st version)
The Stolen Winter (Book Two 1st version)

Sally in the Woods, A ghost story

The Revenge of Merga Bein, (The Orphan Of
Wiesenhule.)

www.ingramcontent.com/pod-product-compliance
Lightning Source LLC
Chambersburg PA
CBHW050840030726
47503CB00007BA/2251